The Accidental Siren

Other Books by Lexi Blake

ROMANTIC SUSPENSE

Masters and Mercenaries
The Dom Who Loved Me
The Men With The Golden Cuffs
A Dom is Forever
On Her Master's Secret Service
Sanctum: A Masters and Mercenaries Novella
Love and Let Die
Unconditional: A Masters and Mercenaries Novella
Dungeon Royale
Dungeon Games: A Masters and Mercenaries Novella
A View to a Thrill
Cherished: A Masters and Mercenaries Novella
You Only Love Twice
Luscious: Masters and Mercenaries~Topped
Adored: A Masters and Mercenaries Novella
Master No
Just One Taste: Masters and Mercenaries~Topped 2
From Sanctum with Love
Devoted: A Masters and Mercenaries Novella
Dominance Never Dies
Submission is Not Enough
Master Bits and Mercenary Bites~The Secret Recipes of Topped
Perfectly Paired: Masters and Mercenaries~Topped 3
For His Eyes Only
Arranged: A Masters and Mercenaries Novella
Love Another Day
At Your Service: Masters and Mercenaries~Topped 4
Master Bits and Mercenary Bites~Girls Night
Nobody Does It Better
Close Cover
Protected: A Masters and Mercenaries Novella
Enchanted: A Masters and Mercenaries Novella
Charmed: A Masters and Mercenaries Novella
Taggart Family Values
Treasured: A Masters and Mercenaries Novella

Delighted: A Masters and Mercenaries Novella
Tempted: A Masters and Mercenaries Novella
The Bodyguard and the Bombshell: A Masters and Mercenaries New Recruits Novella, Coming August 6, 2024

Masters and Mercenaries: The Forgotten
Lost Hearts (Memento Mori)
Lost and Found
Lost in You
Long Lost
No Love Lost

Masters and Mercenaries: Reloaded
Submission Impossible
The Dom Identity
The Man from Sanctum
No Time to Lie
The Dom Who Came in from the Cold

Masters and Mercenaries: New Recruits
Love the Way You Spy
Live, Love, Spy
Sweet Little Spies, Coming September 17, 2024

Butterfly Bayou
Butterfly Bayou
Bayou Baby
Bayou Dreaming
Bayou Beauty
Bayou Sweetheart
Bayou Beloved

Park Avenue Promise
Start Us Up
My Royal Showmance, Coming June 4, 2024

Lawless
Ruthless
Satisfaction
Revenge

Courting Justice
Order of Protection
Evidence of Desire

Masters Of Ménage (by Shayla Black and Lexi Blake)
Their Virgin Captive
Their Virgin's Secret
Their Virgin Concubine
Their Virgin Princess
Their Virgin Hostage
Their Virgin Secretary
Their Virgin Mistress

The Perfect Gentlemen (by Shayla Black and Lexi Blake)
Scandal Never Sleeps
Seduction in Session
Big Easy Temptation
Smoke and Sin
At the Pleasure of the President

URBAN FANTASY

Thieves
Steal the Light
Steal the Day
Steal the Moon
Steal the Sun
Steal the Night
Ripper
Addict
Sleeper
Outcast
Stealing Summer
The Rebel Queen
The Rebel Guardian
The Rebel Witch

LEXI BLAKE WRITING AS SOPHIE OAK

Texas Sirens
Small Town Siren
Siren in the City
Siren Enslaved
Siren Beloved
Siren in Waiting
Siren in Bloom
Siren Unleashed
Siren Reborn
The Accidental Siren

Nights in Bliss, Colorado
Three to Ride
Two to Love
One to Keep
Lost in Bliss
Found in Bliss
Pure Bliss
Chasing Bliss
Once Upon a Time in Bliss
Back in Bliss
Sirens in Bliss
Happily Ever After in Bliss
Far from Bliss
Unexpected Bliss

A Faery Story
Bound
Beast
Beauty

Standalone
Away From Me
Snowed In

The Accidental Siren

Texas Sirens: Legacy, Book 1

Lexi Blake
writing as
Sophie Oak

The Accidental Siren
Texas Sirens: Legacy, Book 1

Published by DLZ Entertainment LLC

Edited by Chloe Vale
ISBN: 978-1-963890-02-0

Sign up for Lexi Blake's newsletter
and be entered to win a $25 gift certificate
to the bookseller of your choice.

Join us for news, fun, and exclusive content
including free short stories.

There's a new contest every month!

Go to www.LexiBlake.net to subscribe.

Acknowledgments

I first published *Small Town Siren* in July of 2010. It was my first published novel, and I was so surprised at how it was received. There was a group of readers who welcomed me and who took these characters to their hearts. Here we are, old friends, fourteen years later, and Jack and Abby and Sam are going strong.

And so are we. We've been through some things in the last decade and a half, but we're still standing—some of us shakier than others—and we're still reading and writing and dreaming. Being back in Willow Fork after all these years was oddly easy. As with the Masters and Mercenaries kids, I thought I would struggle a little, but I'm enjoying watching the new generation thrive and seeing how the OGs have grown. But more than anything it gives me a chance to look back at these worlds I've created, to consider what I've learned in these fourteen years in the business.

I've learned to be brave. Taking that step to follow your dreams is scary. Failure is something we're told to fear, but I'm telling you this is not a baseball game. You don't get three shots and you're out. Keep trying.

I've learned to value myself and the work I do. Don't let anyone tell you that you aren't important. You are here for a reason. Discovering that reason is our purpose in life.

And most of all, I've learned there is no expiration date on talent and dreams. I was thirty-eight when I published my first book. I sometimes look around and every writer on social media seems to be twenty-five and a supermodel, and that can feel daunting. But they could be my daughters, and I'm so freaking happy there's a generation of young women seizing the day. I couldn't at that age. I wish them all the best, long and productive careers telling their stories.

This is for the older women out there who hold secret stories in their hearts. Who think those dreams have passed them by. It hasn't. Your stories matter. Your stories are needed.

I am fifty-three as I write this, and I'm trying new things, new avenues in storytelling. I've written a couple of screenplays. I'm learning and growing, and I will not allow the idea of my age to hold me back. Join me. Tell your stories. Take risks. Live this life we've been given as boldly as we want our children to live theirs.

That is our legacy.

Prologue

Willow Fork, TX

Jared Burch knew it was a stupid idea to hole up on the devil's land, but he didn't have anywhere else to go.

It was what they called Jack Barnes around town. The devil. His own mother claimed the man had been put on the earth to lead people astray. Jared had met the man, but it had been years before when he'd been a normal kid. Before his dad had died and his mom had married his stepfather. It was sometimes hard to believe there had been a time before Ezekiel Smith, that he'd had something of a childhood where he'd played with kids who lived close to him, and his whole world hadn't revolved around pleasing one man.

He hadn't managed to do it today.

He'd run, and the wrong way in his complete panic. He'd known his stepfather would follow him and use the shotgun on him if he didn't get out fast enough. After all. before he'd been kicked out, his stepdad had set his brother and stepbrothers on him. It had only been after they'd given him a walloping that Ezekiel Smith had delivered his judgment. Banishment.

Now he found himself on the outer range of Barnes's land. He seriously doubted the stories about Abigail Barnes being some man-eating siren, but he could believe Barnes could be ruthless. Not that he believed the crap his stepfather shoveled about Barnes. It was the twenty-first century, but sometimes he believed Willow Fork was stuck in 1892 or something.

He was absolutely certain his parents were since they'd chucked him out of the house for being a bad influence on his siblings. There were three of them. One older and his full brother. Two stepbrothers who were older. He was the baby of the "family" and yes, he put quotes around the word because they sure as hell hadn't felt like family today. Maybe not since the day he realized his older brother believed everything their stepdad taught them. Billy was one of them now, and he'd proven it mere hours before.

Jared shivered in the chill. Autumn in Texas meant hot days and chilly nights.

It wasn't fair. Anger warred with a deep sense of sorrow as he made his way across the flat plane that would hopefully lead him to the main road. He thought it would, but nothing had gone right today. All he'd done was dared to stand up to his stepfather. This time when his stepfather had punched, he'd punched back.

And then his stepfather told his brothers to defend him, and they'd given Jared a beating he was still recovering from. His brothers. His only friends.

It wasn't like he was allowed to play with other kids. Not that he was a kid. He was sixteen, and he barely had an education that would get him any kind of job. School wasn't important to his parents, and they'd made him drop out two years before. "Homeschool" had meant working on their ranch, reading the Bible, and learning not to talk back or have a single thought that went against their father.

And stay away from those heathen Barnes-Fleetwoods.

Well, he couldn't now unless he wanted to walk twenty miles, and damn it, it was starting to rain.

When his stepfather had tossed him out without a dime to his name, he hadn't exactly offered a ride. So Jared had started walking. He'd jumped the fence separating his stepfather's land from the devil's because there had been nothing else to do. He had to make it to town, and this was the fastest way.

Damn, it was getting cold.

He'd found one of the outer buildings the Barnes-Fleetwood ranch hands used when they got caught on the range after dark. Or when they were babysitting the herd.

His stepfather would have shoved a tent his way and told him to make do.

This place was kind of a palace compared to what he was used to.

He would get warm and be on his way.

The door opened easily. No lock, like what his stepfather put on every building and many of the rooms in their house. There was a lock on the pantry and the fridge, one on the room with the only television because his stepfather believed no one else could be trusted to watch and not to be tempted by the outside world.

Sometimes he blamed his real dad for everything. One day he'd been okay. Sure he was poor, but they'd gotten along. And then he'd died and his mother joined the most extreme church she could find, and now he was homeless because he didn't respect authority.

He wasn't sure there would be one, but he felt for the switch and breathed a sigh of relief when soft light illuminated the shack. Shack? It was a small house. Like one of those tiny ones he'd seen when he'd been in school. Sometimes he would see magazines or get time in the library on the Internet. He knew things, and he knew this was a nice place.

It wasn't his place, though, and he needed to get warm and get out before morning when Barnes would surely figure out someone was using his land. There would be a price to pay if he got caught. There always was.

Barnes was mean, according to the people around him. Barnes had more than once threatened his stepfather.

Sometimes Jared wished Barnes would have taken his stepfather out.

He shoved the thought away because he was too tired to be mad tonight. He ached. Every muscle felt weary after the trudge across the miles that separated his ranch from Barnes's.

Not his. It had never been his.

This ain't your home. Get out. If you call the cops, you'll get more of what you had tonight, boy.

And his mother had stood there, tears in her eyes, but she'd not said a word to defend him. His brothers had made sure he didn't take anything that didn't belong to him—and it had been made clear almost nothing belonged to him.

He found a bottle of water and sucked it down before shoving three more into his almost-empty backpack. He had a pair of worn jeans, two plain white T-shirts, and socks that had seen better days.

There was food in the cabinet. It was tinned stew, and he ate it cold because he didn't know how to cook it. Boys weren't supposed to do things like that. Women's work. When he'd tried to help his mom, he'd been smacked and told to be a man.

So he ate it cold and then stole the rest of that, too.

He should move on, but the cot looked so cozy. The cot looked like paradise. He wasn't even sure where he was going. He didn't have any friends. His brothers were the friends God had provided. There wasn't a homeless shelter in Willow Fork. He would have to make his way to a larger town. Godless Tyler probably had a place for people like him. Maybe.

He couldn't think about it tonight.

He turned off the light and lay down on the cot, pulling the blanket over him. He would rest his eyes for a moment. Maybe half an hour, though he wasn't sure how he would tell time since he didn't own a watch. His stepfather gave his brothers watches when they were deemed responsible enough. Until then, time, his stepfather said, didn't matter.

So it didn't matter. His sixteen years on earth didn't matter. Nothing mattered.

He yawned and his eyes closed.

Nothing mattered at all.

Jared stirred at the sound of hushed voices talking.

"Is that who I think it is?" a deep voice asked.

"Sure looks like Jared, though it's been years since I saw him up close," another voice said. "You know the kids call him Grim now."

He stayed as still as possible, panic threatening. He knew they all called him Grim. Because he didn't talk much, didn't join in on the laughter even with his own brothers. Laughter was paid for with pain in his household.

"I heard he dropped out," the voice continued, "and we haven't been in school together since his momma quit her job at the resort.

He moved over to the public school. You're a snooty rich pants who went and built a whole school so Livie and I weren't around the riffraff."

There was a snorting sound. "Sure. I did it to keep you in your societal class."

"I know why you did it, Dad." This voice was younger, somehow, and softer now. "You protected us. If he is who I think he is, you protected us from his asshole brothers. Don't. I'm working today. If I'm on the range punching cows, I get to cuss. And that is a family full of assholes. But Jared's a good kid, from what I can tell. I know I liked him when we were younger."

"He was your best friend in preschool and the cause of one of the weirdest parent-teacher meetings I ever had to sit through," the deeper voice continued.

"We don't run in the same circles now. I'm pretty sure his stepfather doesn't let him be friends with anyone outside that cult of his, but Sarah and Jess told me they broke down a couple of months ago and he stopped and fixed their car for them. Said he seemed kind, but his brothers aren't."

Jared kept still. Joshua Barnes-Fleetwood. The golden boy of Willow Fork, Texas. He was known for being a bit wild, and every teenaged girl in town wanted to be with him. Some of the adult women, too, if the rumors were true. Josh, who had been his friend until his momma lost her damn mind and sent them all to hell while she was desperately searching for heaven.

Hopefully the other voice was Sam Fleetwood. *Please don't be Jack Barnes. Please don't be Jack Barnes.*

He'd screwed up. He'd fallen asleep, and now he would likely go to jail or worse.

Or worse… Maybe that wouldn't be so bad. What the hell had life shown him that was good?

"He's awake," the deeper of the two voices said with a sigh. "Jared? Son, are you all right?"

Who could have thought the devil could sound so kind? But then he'd had a couple of encounters with the woman his stepfather called a Jezebel, Abby Barnes, and she was the single nicest person he'd ever met. He'd scraped his knee up real good once at a park, and she'd helped him. She'd explained how to take care of the wound and to tell his momma what had happened.

Then she'd bought him an ice cream cone, and he'd never told anyone how nice it had been. Even with his knee aching, he'd loved sitting in the park with that kind woman and her daughter and eating ice cream and feeling like he was normal for once.

The devil lied. Wasn't that what everyone in his church group believed? Hell, Barnes was right. There was church, and that was a normal thing. Church was often a good place to be. What his stepfather was involved in was a cult, and they preached the devil lied and misrepresented himself and cloaked himself like a righteous man at times.

Maybe his stepfather was the devil.

Or maybe his stepfather was simply a man with hate in his heart.

Jared could run. He could fight. He could believe the world was as nasty a place as Ezekiel preached and never open himself up to it.

Or he could ask for help, and if Jack Barnes wouldn't give him any, then at least he would have tried.

Slowly, he sat up, his face heating when he saw the backpack on the floor. It was raggedy, and one of the cans of stew had fallen out. There was a big man in jeans and a T-shirt, and a Stetson covering his dark hair. And a slightly smaller, younger version of the man beside him. Jack and Josh.

"I'm sorry for stealing, Mr. Barnes." There was a certain amount of resignation in his soul. Whatever happened next, he would take it. If Barnes called the sheriff, at least he would have a place to stay.

"The food is out here for anyone who gets stuck overnight," Barnes said.

Josh's lips curled slightly. "I think technically Grim here probably felt pretty stuck. Did you get lost?" Josh tilted his hat toward his father. "Don't be afraid of him. He's a big old teddy bear when it comes to strays. Did your stepdad finally kick you out? Everyone around town knows you're the only one with a lick of sense in your family, so it was inevitable. Is he the one who gave you the shiner?"

Grim. He'd hated the nickname, but it sounded right coming out of Josh's mouth. It didn't sound mean coming from him. And what had he meant by everyone in town thought he was the sensible one? His stepfather and brothers always told him how dumb he was. He touched his left cheek and winced. "I told him I wanted to go back to school. He disagreed with me. I tried to tell him I could make my own decision. He took exception to that."

"It looks like he beat the shit out of you," Josh said, and his father winced but let it go.

"Do I need to get the sheriff involved?" Jack asked, looking a whole lot like Jared's nickname.

The thought had Jared getting to his feet. "No, sir. I'll be on my way."

"Grim, he wasn't going to call them on you," Josh said, his expression serious. "He was going to report your stepdad, but if he did protective services would be notified and then we have to worry about you going into the system because I don't think your momma is going to stand against her husband."

"No, she won't." Maybe it wouldn't be so bad. If he had a roof over his head and food in his belly, it might not be terrible. But he doubted his stepfather would accept the outcome. "He would find a way to get me back and… I don't know if I'd survive the next beating."

Barnes was quiet for a moment, then looked to his son. "You got any problem with what I'm thinking?"

Josh smiled and seemed to light up the small space. "You and Pops have been worried about him for a long time. He seems like he could use some help. And you know Mom and Livie will have a ton of fun buying him clothes." He grimaced. "Sorry, buddy, that will be a nonnegotiable fact of life."

"The truth is your mother has also been worried about what went on in that house. She tried to tell Margie she could come to us if she needed help, but I think she's too scared."

Mrs. Barnes had worried about his mom? "She is, but it's more than being afraid of my stepdad. She's sure if she doesn't do what he says, she'll go to hell."

A long sigh came from Barnes's chest, and kind green eyes pinned Jared. "I'm sure your stepfather's said a lot about my lifestyle. I need to know if you're afraid of me, son. I'm going to ask if you would like to stay here for a while, but I don't want you to be afraid to say no. I'll still help you, but I'll find someone you feel more comfortable with."

Now that he was standing in front of the man, he wasn't afraid at all. He remembered how Jack Barnes would come to the little school room out at the resort his mom had worked at and play with the kids. He would take them all out to the stables and let them see the horses. "You've been kinder to me in five minutes than my stepfather was my whole life, Mr. Barnes. But taking me in could cause some trouble for you. If he knows you're helping me, he'll likely try to force me to come home."

"Let me worry about that and you worry about the two women who are going to make you over." Barnes shook his head. "They'll probably try to force you into dress shoes."

"Yeah, you should think this through, Grim," Josh joked with a grin.

But he was tearing up. All of his life he'd looked over the fence separating his stepfather's land from the Barnes-Fleetwood Ranch, and while his stepfather preached heavily against the family, the well-kept fence seemed like a barrier to a better life.

Suddenly he didn't mind the nickname. Grim was what he was most of the time, what he felt when he'd looked over that fence and saw Jack Barnes and Sam Fleetwood riding across their land, laughing and joking with their ranch hands. What he felt when he saw Abigail hugging her kids like they were her whole world and he knew no one would hug him because affection spoiled a child.

His stepfather had always told him this world didn't matter. This world was only a way to get to the next.

But everything good seemed to be across that fence, and now he'd been invited in.

"I could work." He didn't want the man to think he would be a layabout. "I've worked my stepfather's ranch since I was a kid. I know what to do. I could be one of your hands."

Barnes stepped up, clasping Grim's shoulder. "You will, but only the way Josh works. Part time, and no cussing if you're not working. At least not around Mrs. Barnes. You'll go back to school with Josh and Olivia. I know this will be hard to believe, but I have been worried about you, son. Sam, too. We've talked more than once about what we would do if you came to us and needed help."

"Why?" Such a simple question, but it was the whole world to him.

"Because we've needed help before," Jack replied. "I've been in your shoes. I've had nowhere to go and no one to depend on. I've been hungry and scared, and I'll be damned if I let another kid go through that alone. Like I said, you are welcome to stay here. Not as a worker. Not as a guest. If you want, this can be your home, or I'll find you a place somewhere else if you want out of this town. If you want a fresh start, I'll find a good place for you in Dallas or Austin."

"I don't think I ever got started here, Mr. Barnes." Or rather he had and then he'd gotten off track. He'd been young, but he still remembered how it felt to be Josh's best friend.

Was it wrong to want to see if they could be friends again? Would he be a burden to all of them?

Josh held out a hand. "I know this is going to sound weird to you, but I always knew somehow we would be friends again. Come on up to the house and we'll get some real food into you." He shook his head his father's way. "What is wrong with you, old man? Tinned beef stew? No wonder you can't keep ranch hands."

Grim braced for Barnes to erupt. If he'd talked to his stepfather like that, it would have meant an immediate beating.

Instead, a grin broke over the man's normally placid face. "Sure, son. You know I can't get rid of them. We're all old men now. I need some youth. I want to live up to my reputation and start running this place like *Yellowstone*."

He didn't know why Mr. Barnes would run his ranch like a national park, but as they joked, he felt himself relax.

Maybe, just maybe, it would be okay.

* * * *

Childswood, Oregon
Eight years later

Nora Holloway stared at the body, the vision not quite reaching her brain. It wasn't real. Because if it was real, then her husband was dead on the floor.

The idea of his death didn't spark sorrow because he was an

abusive asshole she planned to divorce.

Don't think you can leave, Nora. You have nothing. I'll ruin you.

He'd already ruined her.

He'd ruined her the day he'd married her and brought her into his hell.

"Micah?" His name came quietly out of her mouth as though she didn't want to wake him. She didn't. He was sleeping. Or maybe she was and this was a dream.

Micah's body didn't move. He was face down on the living room floor, a pool of blood forming around his body.

How was this a shock? She'd always known he would come to a bad end, but somehow she'd thought she wouldn't be here to witness it. She would either have found a way out or he would have killed her.

"Damn, but you are a lovely woman," a deep voice said. "Even standing there over my brother's dead body, you still manage to look hot."

She turned, fear coursing through her. If there was one person she feared more than Micah Holloway, it was his older brother, Ted. Ted stood in the hallway leading to the magnificent foyer of the McMansion Micah had first brought her to three years before. He'd carried her over the threshold, and a few weeks later he'd smacked her for the first time. This beautiful house had become a cage. Ted was taller than Micah, his features darker. He was the head of the family, though his father was still alive. He'd taken over the family company and ruthlessly pursued money and power. His wife was a shell of a woman who knew how to smile without a light in her eyes, when to nod and agree.

Nora had known that was exactly who she would become if she stayed, but now she feared she'd waited too long.

Or maybe he would be reasonable. "I don't know what happened. I walked in and he was here. I was out having dinner with friends."

A brow rose over Ted's dark eyes, and he looked far too calm for a man who had found out his only brother was dead. "Were you? See, I don't think you were. If you were out with friends, then you would have an alibi for this mess we find ourselves in. But if, say, you were out at the lake house practicing with the .22 you bought illegally, then no one would know because you didn't want anyone to know."

Her heart threatened to seize. She'd been quietly taking self-defense classes, and she kept the gun in a locker at the gym. She'd run it by before coming home because she didn't trust Micah not to go through her things. "How do you know that?"

One big shoulder shrugged. "Because I had someone follow you. That was how I knew the timing was right. You see, my brother has been a liability for a long time, and now he's run up debts with some nasty people, and I'm fairly certain the feds are about to come after him."

Her breath caught as she realized he was holding a gun in his gloved hands. A familiar-looking gun. "You killed him."

"I did what I had to in order to protect us all," Ted said, coming into the light for the first time. He looked neat and tidy in his three-piece suit. Like a man who'd merely stopped by after a long day at work. "And by us, I do not mean you."

The implications twisted through her brain. "You're going to tell everyone I did it? How did you get my gun? I just left it."

"Yes, there will be footage of you walking into the ladies' gym roughly twenty minutes after Micah was killed by a .22 caliber pistol." He held the gun up. "This one, but the cops will find yours exactly where you left it, and they'll discover you've fired a pistol in the last twenty-four hours."

Her hands started to shake. "Why are you doing this?"

"What—killing Micah? Because he's a dumbass. Or setting you up? Because cops like a neat and well-explained crime. You've been talking about leaving. You've whined about Micah hurting you to whoever will listen. So here's what I'm thinking. You could try to tell the cops I'm the one who spent months setting you up. I have an ironclad alibi, by the way. Good luck since you'll be dealing with a public defender. No more money for you, honey. Or you could decide to plead self-defense and again, good luck with that. Either choice you make, no one's looking my way and the feds no longer have a target."

"I'm not letting you do this to me." Outrage sparked through her, but she had to also remember he was a dangerous man. How easy would it be for him to say he walked in on her and she attacked him like she had his brother? He had to take her down.

"Or, you could take the bag sitting on the bar, get into your car, and run."

"So you can hunt me down?"

Ted shook his head. "Why would I do that? If the police find you, there's some small chance one of them will believe you. It's better if you're simply not here. If you're on the run, the focus remains on you. See, that's what I call a win-win. I mean except for Micah, but then this is what happens to dumbasses who don't listen to solid advice and embezzle a shit ton of cash so he can try to pay off his mob connections. I'm afraid my brother likes to gamble."

How was this happening? Surely this was some nightmare. "Are you insane?"

"No, I'm quite of my right mind, Nora. And I think I'm being rather kind giving you this shot. That bag has everything you need. I know you have access to another car. You were planning on running anyway. I assure you Micah wouldn't have handed you a bag with ten thousand dollars cash and a couple of burner phones and a credit card and false ID you should change as soon as possible. I want to give you a day or two to get as far as you can. Unless you want to come to a different arrangement." He was too close now, and the hand not holding the gun came out as though he wanted to touch her.

She stepped away.

His hand flattened out, and he gave her some space. "No? It might not be so bad. You could be my dirty little secret. I'm not as violent as baby brother here. The current situation notwithstanding. I don't feel the need to smack my woman around. Too much effort. It's better to find a damaged one and bring the bitch to heel. But since you won't have to be out in public…"

God, he was really doing this. He had her in a neat trap, and she couldn't think of a way out. She only knew one thing. She wasn't giving in to him. "I assure you if you try to lock me away, I'll make what you did to Micah look like a restful evening."

"There's the spark I knew you had. I know you won't believe me, but I always knew you were too good for my brother. Let's see how long you can last. You should run."

So she did.

Chapter One

Willow Fork, TX
Two years later

Joshua Barnes-Fleetwood was only half listening to the argument currently going on between his sister and Dad. He was far too busy watching the brunette. She moved across the dining room floor with the grace of a woman who had never once before carried a tray of drinks in the midst of a rural diner where people let their kids run a bit wild.

She barely managed to stop when Austin Parker chased his brother across the room, nearly cutting her off and sending all of those drinks right to the floor.

Her jaw clenched, and she seemed to take a long breath before making the decision to continue her dangerous journey.

Damn, but she was pretty.

She'd started working at Christa's Café a few weeks before, and Josh barely knew her name. Nicole. He only knew because a name tag was part of the uniform. His Aunt Christa called the fairly short pink dresses with a white apron retro chic, but Josh thought it was sexy as hell.

On Nicole. His aunt did not wear one, thank god.

"Dad, don't be ridiculous." His sister was using their weekly family outing to protest their father's schedule.

His sister butted heads with their father from time to time. Dad, not Pops. Pops pretty much gave Livie anything she wanted. And him. And Grim and Mom. Sam Fleetwood was a sunny man who didn't try to hide the fact he was a marshmallow on the inside.

Jack Barnes made up for it with loving authority and long discussions of discipline. His dad was big on discipline.

Josh was wondering if that pretty lady liked a little discipline.

He glanced over and noticed he wasn't the only one looking. Grim's eyes were on the brunette, and Josh knew that look. His best friend was hungry, and not for the chicken fried steak he'd ordered.

"Josh went out last quarter. He spent two weeks in Broken Bend at the Rockin' R. One would think it's my turn. It's almost like you don't want me to be the face of your company," his sister complained.

"Baby, you know that's not what the problem is." His mother took a sip of her tea and shook her head. She sat where she always did. In between Dad and Pops. They had been together, living openly as a threesome, for his whole lifetime and people still stared.

The good news was, he didn't give a shit what random people thought. He cared what his friends thought, what his family thought. But he couldn't care about anyone who would judge his parents for loving each other. He'd learned that lesson at a young age, or perhaps he'd simply been born without the component for shame when it came to sex.

The brunette barely avoided tripping over a chair in her way. It made her twist slightly, giving him a nice view of her backside. She was slender but curvy in all the right places.

That fine ass was begging for a spanking.

Yeah, he might not have been born with a big capacity for shame, but he had come into the world with certain needs. He'd come by them honestly, and his father hadn't made him feel bad about it. Nope. When he and Grim had gotten caught with their first woman—a college freshman when they were still in high school—her father had threatened to kill them both while Jack Barnes had sat them down and had the "talk." And then when they'd turned eighteen sent them to Dallas for a summer where they'd trained at a place called The Club.

Him and Grim, not him and Ashley Hill. Her father had caught her in bed in between Josh and his best friend. It had been Grim who'd jumped out of the window with him and who'd had the foresight to grab Josh's pants as he'd jumped so he wasn't running across a pasture with his dick swinging.

"Josh doesn't want to go to Colorado so he can chase after two boys." Dad pointed out the problem he had. "You can take the California trip next month."

His pops chuckled. "I never would have thought our baby girl would fall in love with a couple of nerds."

Grim's head turned, frowning Pop's way. "That is not a good way to refer to people anymore, Mr. Fleetwood. I'm a nerd."

His pops shook his head. "Now, see, maybe I no longer understand the definition of the word. In my day it was smart kids who studied too much and didn't get laid. I don't think that describes you, son. Now you're real good at the studying part, but you've pretty much run through most of the women in East Texas, and a whole bunch of Dallas and Austin."

Josh laughed as Grim turned a shade of pink. Grim had shame poured into his system at a young age, but they were working on the problem. And his pops's description was wholly accurate. They might have had some trouble getting started, but they had the ménage thing down. He and Grim were practically a rite of passage for the women of East Texas.

"I'm only saying Livie has the right to pant after anyone she wants, even if they are kind of weird and scare me," Grim admitted.

"I am not panting after Will and Bobby." His sister was pretty much the spitting image of their mom, and when he looked at it from an outside eye, he could admit they were both gorgeous women. But she totally panted after the Farley brothers. She had ever since they were kids. She would see them once every couple of years and moon for months.

And his dad was right. They were kind of nerds. But Grim was wrong. Nerds were cool these days. The Farley brothers would be worth millions one day, or they would cause the end of the world. Or maybe get locked up because they became supervillains.

Josh wasn't sure, but he was interested in the outcome. Of course if they ever gave in and allowed Livie to become their queen, they would definitely veer into supervillain territory. His sis could come up with an evil plan like no one else.

The trouble was, he kind of thought Livie might not be their type. But his sister didn't listen to his instincts.

He breathed a sigh of relief as the brunette made it to the table and managed to get the heavy tray down.

Grim was back to watching her, too. Then he turned, and a brow rose over brown eyes.

Josh grinned and slowly nodded.

And that was that. Nicole was on their radar, but then he'd known she would be the minute he'd caught sight of her weeks before. Grim had been in Dallas attending a conference. This was the first time he'd had a chance to see the woman Josh had been thinking about. He wouldn't approach her without Grim.

Begin as you mean to go, but it looked like he was going to get his shot.

"Besides," his sister was saying, "the last I heard Bobby and Will are working on their doctorates at MIT. I'm not offering to go to Massachusetts to explain our new accounting software to the physics department. I'm offering to go to Bliss and spend way too much time teaching an ex-football player how to use a spreadsheet. I say that because I know James Glen will run the minute he sees me and I'll end up hanging out with Trev and the girls the whole time."

Because his sister could be a bit much. The Circle G was run by the Glen brothers and Trev McNamara and his partner Bo O'Malley. The G was a partner ranch in his fathers' organic cattle collective. They'd started out just the two of them—Jack Barnes and Sam Fleetwood—and now they represented the interests of over twenty independent ranches across the country. Josh split his time between actually working the ranch, running the day-to-day business of the company and traveling around to train their partners on everything from new accounting software to all the legal crap Uncle Lucas could come up with.

"That's because you scare the crap out of Mr. Glen, Livie." Grim might still call their parents Mr and Mrs, but he did not have the same issue with their sister.

Grim treated Olivia like the sister he'd always wanted after being raised the youngest of a brood of asshole brothers. Years later and Grim still went quiet when one of them walked into a room.

"I do not." Olivia's green eyes rolled, and she sipped on her Dr Pepper. "I'm perfectly nice."

She was. Olivia could make a room light up with her smile, but she could also tear a strip off anyone who got in her way. She had a zest for life that drew people to her. He liked to say she was all the best parts of their parents. She had their mom's kindness, their pops's joy, but knew when to bring out Dad's ruthless will.

Josh himself was all about ruthless will, and if he got sent off to Colorado, he wouldn't be able to solve the mystery Nicole presented. She had a certain look about her.

A bit haunted. A lot innocent.

If he left, he worried she might move on, and any chance to peel back her layers would be gone because he was also almost certain Nicole was in trouble, and he intended to see if he could help.

And also if she needed an orgasm. He'd found sex was excellent at clearing a person's head and helping them think straight again.

"Livie should do the Bliss run," he said, sitting back and picking up his burger. It had been his turn to choose their Saturday night dinner spot. It was something they'd done since they were kids, not that there was much to choose from. Willow Fork, Texas, was a town of roughly three thousand people, though it served a larger rural community. There was a honky-tonk with some great bar food, a nice Italian place, two fast food joints, and Christa's. Sometimes they splurged and went into Tyler.

He remembered the first time Grim had come with them. He'd sat in the booth at the honky-tonk staring down at his burger. He'd eaten it like he was starving, and Josh had realized his friend was.

Starving. For food, for attention, for affection and friendship.

Grim had come a long way under his parents' loving care. He no longer shrank back when the old biddies of the town sent them all the stink eye or turned their noses up. And by old biddies, he didn't mean merely old or female. There were plenty of middle-aged male biddies in this town.

"And why is that?" Dad's brow had risen in that "you better have an excellent explanation since it's actually your turn to do training and you doing your job might save my precious baby girl from those ravenous nerds who likely want to eat her up" way.

Yeah, he spoke Jack Barnes well, and he had an excellent excuse. "Grim and I have a trip planned for next week. We're going to Austin."

They were going to spend the weekend at a club there. A BDSM club. They'd started regularly attending a club called Subversion. It was further away than Dallas, but at least there weren't people there who had once changed his diaper. It was a real mood killer as a topic of conversation, and it came up way too much at the decadent palace known as The Club.

His dad sighed and sat back because he knew those weekends were sacred. "All right, then, but Olivia, I better not get a call from the sheriff about you swimming naked in ponds you do not own."

Like he'd said, his sister could be a little wild.

She grinned. "It was hot, and the pond looked nice and cool. How was I supposed to know that Max guy would freak out?"

Because that Max guy freaked out about everything, and his daughter, Paige, was one of Olivia's favorite people to plot with. Maybe sending his sister to Bliss was a bad idea.

"Oh, no," a feminine voice said, and he looked up. Nicole slid across a massive pile of ketchup some kid had dropped on the floor.

Josh was up and out of his chair in a second, reaching out and letting her fall into his waiting arms.

Big brown eyes stared up at him as she slowly realized she hadn't hit the floor and likely come out of the whole escapade ruining her not-so-pristine uniform. "Sorry."

She was even prettier up close. She had big eyes and brown and gold hair that looked wavy despite the fact she had it scooped up in a bun on top of her head. She looked at him for a long moment as though seeing him for the first time.

And then she was scrambling up. Grim had gotten out of his chair and picked up the notepad she'd dropped. He helped her find her balance, and she stared up at him, too. This was right where Josh wanted her. Small and soft and in between them.

"No need to apologize," Josh said with his most charming smile. "We're happy to help."

Grim said nothing, simply handed her back her pad and watched her with hungry eyes.

Her breath hitched, and she smoothed down her skirt. “Thanks, again. I’ll go clean that up.”

She hustled away, and they both watched her.

“Yes, we need to worry about Olivia,” his mom said with a sardonic twist of her lips.

“Well, I’m not worried about her,” his pops countered. “Now Josh and Grim looking at the new girl like they could eat her up when she’s obviously a woman on the run, that’s something to worry about.”

If Pops had heard gossip, he wanted to know. He sat back down.

“Why would you say that?” Grim got to the point first. His plate was already empty. Sometimes Grim still ate like someone would take it away from him if he didn’t hurry.

Dad sighed. “Because we’ve seen it a time or two, and there are already some rumors about her. She talked Christa into giving her the job with only one reference, and convinced her to pay her wages in cash. She’s staying at the motel that rents by the week, and she pays cash for that, too.”

“Not everyone has a bank account. There are any number of reasons she doesn’t.” Josh didn’t judge a person. Hard times hit a lot of people and in different ways. He’d been lucky enough to not need money, but he had friends who did.

Grim nodded, obviously taking the cue. “Yeah, she could be down on her luck. It could be anything.”

“Or she’s on the run from something,” Pops said, putting an arm around Mom’s shoulders and leaning in. “Speaking of, darlin’, I think you’re in some trouble.”

Olivia made a gagging sound, but Josh liked that his parents were still all over each other.

Dad grinned and whispered something in Mom’s ear.

He wanted a similar situation for himself someday. For him and Grim. Oh, he likely wouldn’t get it from Nicole, but they could have a nice time.

And if he could help her out, he would do that, too. He glanced to his left, where she was walking into the kitchen.

She didn’t know it yet, but they were coming after her.

* * * *

Nora Holloway liked being Nicole Mason for the most part. Mostly because no one wanted to put Nicole in jail or in a grave to hide their secrets. Of course, Nora hadn't spent her days and nights wearing a uniform that made her look like she was on a seventies sitcom and carrying trays of sloshing liquids through a moving obstacle course.

She'd started to think of herself as Nicole. There were times when Nora and her problems seemed so far away.

And then there were times when she was absolutely certain law enforcement was standing right behind her, ready to take her in for a crime she hadn't committed.

"You okay, honey?" Christa Wade looked up from the deep fryer. They were light on staff this evening, so she was helping out in the back. Her current employer was an older woman with what seemed like endless energy and enthusiasm. And kindness. "I sent Lance out to clean up. I'll have a talk with Sharla Simmons. Her son cannot use my condiments for impromptu art projects."

It was so different from the cities she'd lived in. "The kids are feral here. They scare me."

That got her boss smiling. "Oh, a lot of our children live a bit of a free-range experience."

"Are they like wild animals? More afraid of me than I am of them."

Christa's head shook. "Nope. Country kids fear nothing except their momma's wrath. You'll get used to them. The good news is when they're misbehaving, their parents will take care of it if you point it out. Now you didn't answer my question. Are you okay? Milly said you slipped."

Oh, yes, and she'd seen a broken bone in her future. Or at least a lot of humiliation.

And then all she'd seen were deep green eyes and a jaw made from granite. It wasn't like she hadn't noticed the gorgeous cowboy. He'd been in a couple of times, and it took a lot to not drool over him.

But she was smarter than the average girl because she'd been way stupider in the past. She knew exactly what a man could do to a woman.

But they weren't all alike, and you're not going to be here a month from now. What would it hurt to blow off some steam? It's not like you've been to bed with a man in...years. God, it had been years. Her life was getting away from her, and she wasn't enjoying even the smallest part of it.

Her heart ached because it wasn't like she could go out there and flirt with him.

Or his incredibly intense and hot brother. He hadn't said a damn thing, but the look he'd given her had told her all she needed to know. Or maybe they were cousins. She wasn't sure. It was the first time she'd seen the mystery cowboy with his family. The dark-haired older man was definitely his father, and she thought the red-haired woman was probably his mom, making her younger version his sister. But she wasn't sure where the gloriously gorgeous blond man fit in. He was older, too, but those two men were timeless.

"I'm fine. I didn't fall or anything. And I know I'm clumsy, but I'll get better." She had to. She couldn't afford to lose this job because her car was in desperate need of repair. She'd had to dump her original car and pay too much for a piece of crap since she'd had to find someone who would take cash and not request the normal paperwork.

Now the car needed work or it would break down entirely, and she was stuck in Willow Fork. That was sort of good and kind of bad. In the weeks she'd been here she'd discovered the town was split in two. One side was friendly and welcoming, and the other looked at all strangers as potential...she wasn't sure. Enemies. Criminals. Women who might lead the men astray. It was weird.

Christa was definitely part of the good side of town. She put a hand on her shoulder. "I know you will. You're already better. You handled the dinner rush this evening with ease."

She wouldn't say ease, but she was going to get through it. Of all the jobs she'd had over the last two years, this was the one she felt safest at. She'd bartended at a couple of places in LA where they were willing to pay her under the table. She'd done a lot of housekeeping work, but she'd been surprised to find exactly how many people thought the women who scrubbed their floors were less than human.

All in all, Christa's Café was a good place despite the feral children. It had nothing to do with that freaking gorgeous cowboy because that was going nowhere.

She looked out over the counter to where the cowboy was pushing back his chair. The auburn beauty—the younger one since the older one was stunning, too—rolled her eyes at something he'd said. Definitely a sibling.

"That's Josh," Christa said quietly. "He's a good kid. Though I guess he's not a kid anymore. I love Josh. He calls me Aunt Christa, but you should know he's a little on the wild side."

"He's mean?" Her brain went there. Immediately. Every single time she thought of a man, her first question was would he turn into a freaking monster. She knew that wasn't what wild meant, but the words were an impulse.

Christa frowned her way, though it wasn't an irritated expression. It was more curious, and that felt dangerous. "No, honey. Josh is the least mean kid I know. However he has been known to go through women. And he has some…nope. I'm not talking about that. You should know that he and Grim are both lovely men, but they have bad reputations when it comes to the amount of women they can run through, though I've also heard no one's complaining. And that is my lecture since you are obviously a whole-ass adult woman who likely can spot a charming player from a mile away, no matter how good intentioned he might be. You seem a little fragile."

She was beyond fragile. She'd been broken and put back together so many times she wasn't even sure where her original parts were. It didn't matter because she couldn't exactly start a relationship with anyone. Not when there was a warrant out for her arrest. For murder.

Once her car was fixed up, she was going to finally make her way to Mexico and then further south. She would lose herself in a big city and try to find some kind of a life.

The cowboy named Josh looked her way as he held the door open. Their eyes met, and he tipped his hat toward her. He was big and broad and now she understood the phrase sex on two legs.

What would it hurt to be the next in line to try this Josh guy out? It wasn't like she was going to be here in another two weeks. Three, tops.

Then the other guy looked her way, his dark eyes finding hers, and she swore she could feel the man's hunger. It didn't scare her the way it should have because she was apparently extremely horny and incapable of behaving like the walking *Dateline* episode she was.

Nicole forced herself to turn, picking up her notepad. The last thing she needed to do was get in between two relatives and potentially start a fight that would bring a whole lot of attention her way. It was one thing when she'd thought she could hop in and out of Josh's bed, but another when his brother/cousin/relative to be discerned later also made her heart pound and looked at her like he could eat her up. Still… "Why do they call him Grim?"

Christa waved at the woman who was likely Josh's mom, and then leaned over as the door closed behind them. "His real name is Jared, but I'm afraid he got that nickname in school and it stuck. His stepfather is a bit of a fire-and-brimstone type, if you know what I mean. He's happier where he is now. But he's still got some family around I would tell you to stay away from."

She felt her eyes widen. "Like the ones who stand in front of the library at the community college and call all the girls who walk by whores? I took that catering order out the other day and they were obnoxious."

Christa's eyes rolled and her head shook. "That sounds like them. Look, hon, this place is full of church folk, and like all folk there's good and bad. Most of the churches here are loving and kind. One is a little snooty, but the one Jared was raised in is dangerous, in my opinion. He got out, but they're still around. Be careful around Ezekiel Smith and his boys and anyone in his church."

Nicole huffed and looked to her boss. "Ezekiel? Did his mother want him to become a weird cult leader?"

Christa shrugged. "It's fitting and honestly, Grim is, too. I love Jared. My best friend took him in years ago, but there's still a darkness about him I don't know will ever go away." She sighed as one of the line cooks announced an order was up. "That's all the maternal warning I'm going to give you today. I think that's Jimmy's chicken fried steak. I wish he would eat a salad every now and then."

"I'll take it." Salads weren't big at the café. She grabbed the plate and started for the dining room floor.

Just a few weeks more and she would start a new life.

Chapter Two

Grim brought the big truck to a stop. Even from the parking lot he could hear raucous music coming from The Barn. At one point in time it had been run by the Sandbergs, but they'd retired a few years back and now their daughter owned the place. Tally Sandberg was roughly his age, and she'd brought a youthful flair to the only honky-tonk in a twenty-mile radius.

Olivia leaned forward from her place in the back, reaching around to plant a kiss on his cheek. "Thanks for the ride. I'm meeting some friends, so don't worry about me getting home." She shifted and gave Josh the same easy affection. "You two behave. And Josh, thanks for being such a big old perv. I really do want to go to Bliss."

Josh sent his sister a frown. "They're there, aren't they?"

Olivia slid from the back seat and shrugged. "I don't know, but it might be fall break at MIT. We'll see. I'll be out at the *G* helping the olds figure out accounting software and watching the McNamara girls make their dads crazy. The last time I was out there Miranda was circling around Logan Talbot like a shark looking for supper. Everyone is afraid of her. It's good drama."

She waved and practically skipped into the honky-tonk.

"Well, my sister would know good drama." Josh's head shook. "We are not telling Dad about the fall break thing. I don't want to miss going to Austin."

"Are you sure?" Their trips to Austin were a vital part of their lives and had been for years. The BDSM club was one of the only places in the world Grim felt like he could be his true self. The club. The ranch. The shelter he'd taken over and modernized. He felt like himself when he was working.

He'd felt like himself earlier when he'd caught sight of that waitress. That beautiful, sexy woman who practically called out to his real self. The part of him that needed to dominate.

Beyond feeding him and giving him a place to call home, Jack Barnes had seen a need inside him, one that could have gone unfulfilled or could have exploded at some point and wrecked his life. Instead, Jack had sent him and Josh to be trained, to learn to control their impulses, so they could give the women they shared as much pleasure as possible.

A brow rose over Josh's eyes. "You don't want to go to Subversion?"

"I do, but I saw how you looked at her." He didn't have to indicate who he was talking about. They both knew.

"Nicole." Josh sat back. "I'll admit I've been watching her. And Pops is wrong. She's fine. I haven't figured out her last name yet or I would look her up on social media. I would ask Aunt Christa but the minute I do she'll talk to Mom, who will start making wedding plans."

Abby was hungry for more grandbabies since the ones Josh's older sister had given them lived hours and hours away. And were teenagers. Abby wanted a baby to cuddle, but that wasn't happening any time soon.

"I don't know. Mr. Fleetwood has good instincts."

Josh shrugged. "If she has a problem, then we can help her solve it."

So Josh thought she was in trouble, too, but he didn't want to bring it up until after they'd slept with her. The man might not share DNA with him, but Josh knew Grim as well as any brother. Grim would want to solve the problem first, and that had cost them sex on more than one occasion. Sometimes when a woman's problems were solved, she went back to her fiancé.

Josh groaned. "Fine. Yes, I think she's probably got some

trouble. Maybe financial or something."

"I'm sorry about Kerry Thompson, but she really was in love with her fiancé." She'd also been too submissive for them. He needed a sub in the bedroom, but he wanted a woman he could count on.

He often wished he didn't need Josh as his second half. It would have been easy to fall in love with Olivia Barnes-Fleetwood. She was the right mix of crazy bitch, loving woman, and submissive, but she'd become his sister so long ago.

And he did need Josh. They fit, somehow, and he'd given up the thought of dating without Josh. Though mostly he slid into bed for sex while Josh escorted the woman around since not a lot of ladies wanted to be treated the way Abigail Barnes-Fleetwood had all her life.

Josh waved that off. "I have a feeling about this one."

"Have you even talked to her yet?"

A shrug gave Grim his answer. "Don't need to. You know I don't have this feeling often. I'm sure I'm right. Knew it the minute I saw her, and so did you."

He didn't trust his instincts the way Josh did. "Then why do you want to go to Austin?"

"I kind of thought we might invite her with us," Josh replied. "If it works out. And if it doesn't, then we can drown our sorrows in all those pretty, sweet subs."

The submissives at Subversion were gorgeous, and some of them were sweet. Some of them had claws and wanted to sink them into the obvious heir to the Barnes-Fleetwood empire. As plans went, Josh had kind of covered all the bases. "So how do you want to approach her? Are we sure she's single?"

"I do know that much." Josh turned in his seat. "Aunt Christa hired her two weeks ago. Her car is at Al's shop, and he's waiting for her to be able to pay for parts. I would bet she's got a couple of weeks until she's able to make that payment, and then it depends on when he can get the parts for that old clunker. She's probably stuck for a month at least. We've got some time to work on her, to see if she's interested in the lifestyle."

Which lifestyle? Naturally they didn't fit into one neat category. They practiced BDSM and required a ménage relationship to be happy.

He wanted a relationship where he wasn't in the shadows.

You've let them corrupt you. You're going to Hell. That whole family is, and I'm going to be the one to send you there someday.

Grim shook off his stepfather's nasty words. Ezekiel was still alive, still trying to suck any joy from the world around him. He started sermonizing every time they crossed paths. Well, if he was alone. If Jack or Sam was with him, his stepdad made himself scarce.

But that was neither here nor there. It could be hard to find a woman who needed two Masters.

Abigail Barnes-Fleetwood didn't come along every day.

"All right." It wasn't like he hadn't taken one look at that gorgeous girl and had all the same thoughts Josh had. "Where do you want to start? Did you want to ask her out? Do you think she's already heard the rumors about us?"

Josh sighed and fiddled with the brim of his hat, a habit that let him know his brother was thinking about how to handle him. "I don't know if she's heard the rumors, but I can tell you she doesn't put up with the gossip nonsense. I saw her disdain when she served Lisa Brice and her friends. They were making fun of everyone, being real loud and nasty, and Nicole did not like that."

How closely had Josh been watching her? "Have you been eating every meal in town while I was gone?"

"Not every meal," Josh admitted. "She's gorgeous and I feel some… I don't know. I feel a pull."

And Josh always followed his instincts. "All right. Do you know where she lives?"

"She's staying in the rattrap on the outskirts of town."

It was a motel with a certain reputation. One it had earned, and the thought of any woman staying there on her own scared him. "You let her stay there?"

"Well, I haven't exactly introduced myself yet, so telling her she's moving felt like a stretch," Josh replied. "Nah, but I might have someone watching out for her. I asked the sheriff to up his nightly patrols and call me if anything bad goes down. I paid the owner to put an extra lock on her door. She thinks it was just maintence."

"Tell me you didn't keep a key." And they called him the intense one. Josh Barnes had a bit of a god complex, but he'd come by it honestly. Jack was pretty much the be-all, end-all of authority in their lives, and Josh was following in his father's footsteps.

Of course it was a loving authority. An authority that truly wanted what was best for everyone he watched over. But until you knew a person, it could come off sketchy.

"Of course I didn't. I haven't even run a trace on her." Josh's hands were up like he was completely innocent. "I'm giving her privacy. I know what happens at that motel, and I don't want her getting caught in the crossfire. Let's get to know her and then if it seems to be working, we can gently start showing her apartments that don't have a ton of drug dealers in them."

He still thought Josh was running too hot, but he also wasn't opposed to starting something as long as it was real. Nothing seemed real. It was like he could live in the Barnes-Fleetwood house, but he'd always be Ezekiel's stepson. He could go to college and get a degree in veterinary medicine, but he was still just Josh's friend, the one he shared women with but mostly for sex.

"Hey, I know that look. You want to go to Dallas this weekend? I know you like that Daisy girl we met at the restaurant. This doesn't have to be all about me."

She'd been the hostess at a place called Top and she was a stunner, but he was pretty sure her father was some kind of Irish mobster. Oh, he'd been told the man was a security executive, but that felt like a good front. Her father was kind of crazy and had explained in no uncertain terms that his precious saint of a daughter wasn't getting involved in some godforsaken threesome. There had been other names mentioned and a lot of cussing he didn't fully understand, and all he'd done was ask the young woman out.

Though he had fully planned to get her in between him and Josh.

"I can handle Li O'Donnell if that's what the problem is. She seemed to like you. I could be the one who slips in and out this time," Josh offered.

He believed in Josh, but he thought he was overestimating what a mad Irish dad could do. And the truth was he didn't want Josh slipping in and out. He wanted what Jack and Abby and Sam had. "I think I'm kind of sick of that."

Josh got quiet. "Yeah, me, too. So we're looking to get serious?"

Josh could be single minded at times. Grim knew he was considered the broody one, but Josh covered his weird quirks with a sunny smile. One of those quirks was an utterly ruthless will when he decided to turn it on. When Josh decided it was time for them to get married, Grim knew he would find himself with a ring on his finger and a wife between them in short order. The problem was, they needed to find the right one.

"I would like to find a woman who doesn't mind dating us both. At the same time. In public. Everyone knows." That was the problem he truly had. "There's no one in this town who didn't know I was sleeping with Alyssa Gates while you were technically dating her."

"You told me you didn't mind."

"I didn't with her because I kind of hated her."

Josh shrugged. "That's fair. So did my momma. I got a whole lecture on how I should be smarter than this."

He'd avoided that lecture, though he had been put through Abby and Olivia sitting him down and gently trying to figure out if he was emotionally traumatized by the relationship. In some ways, it was the best he could have gotten because he hadn't been the one who had to sit around while Andrea's friends bitched about everything from the food at the café to how their boyfriends spent too much time fishing.

He'd been fishing and happy, but lately the idea of never having an acknowledged girlfriend bugged him.

He wasn't that sad-sack kid who simply wanted to get through a day without a beating. He'd conquered a lot of his insecurities and fears. He'd conquered college and veterinary school and had a damn fine job he was proud to do.

That should count for something.

Josh was staring at him. "I'm so curious what's going through your head right now."

"I'm tired of being the dirty secret."

A big smile lit Josh's face. So often people viewed him as a younger version of Jack without ever considering how much influence Sam Fleetwood had on him. There was a joy in Josh.

Sometimes Grim thought he was more like Jack in that way. Cautious. Willing to feel happiness but always on the lookout for something crappy to happen.

Josh slapped his arm. "That's what I wanted to hear. Good. We're farther along than I thought we were. So let's get out there and let Willow Fork know we're not playing anymore. Josh and Grim are serious about taking a sub."

Yeah, they would have to explain that, too. *Hello, gorgeous girl. Would you like to date two guys and also submit to them sexually in the bedroom? The good news is we both know how to do laundry.*

Sam and Jack had insisted he know despite the fact that the big house had a housekeeper. They'd explained when he and Josh were on their own, they wouldn't have a person hanging out who wanted to clean up after them.

The first time Abigail had walked into the apartment he and Josh shared during college, she'd taken the whole weekend to teach them how to clean. And how to get what she'd called "that smell" out.

Now he and Josh had a cleaning schedule for the small house they lived in on the ranch's land. Olivia had a suite in the main house but spent a lot of her time either on the road or in the apartment they all shared when they were in Dallas.

When they were in Austin they stayed at Subversion. Their memberships included a nice suite of rooms.

He'd paid for his own membership. To an elite sex club.

Yeah, he'd come a long way.

Could he go all the way? Could he get the life he wanted?

The only question was how did they get started? They needed to game plan. A long, slow seduction was called for. They could go into the café tomorrow morning and start up a casual conversation with her. Flirt a little. He could manage some charm. Maybe they could ask her out to lunch. That could be a nice way to ease her into starting to think about having a relationship with them. They would take their time and get to know each other before they got into a situation that could get serious.

Josh slid out of the cab of the truck.

Which was odd since they were planning on heading back to the ranch. "Uh, did you feel the sudden need to line dance?"

Josh settled his hat on his head. "There's no time like the present, and our potential sub is walking into a honky-tonk all by herself."

He looked over and sure enough Nicole was standing in front of a station wagon that had seen way better days since Grim was pretty sure they didn't make those anymore. "Is that Trista's grandma's car?"

Josh's lips quirked up. "Didn't you hear? She's started her own taxi service. All the ride shares turned her down since she's nine hundred years old and probably shouldn't be driving, but she swears she's saving up for a sportscar."

So Nicole had already made one poor choice this evening. "You think she's meeting someone here?"

Josh shrugged. "I know she's not serious about anyone, so even if she is I think we should give her choices. Come on, brother. I suddenly feel the need for a beer."

Grim followed his brother.

Their slow seduction had just gotten a whole lot faster.

* * * *

Nicole stepped out of the station wagon.

"You sure you want to go in there, hon?" the elderly woman who'd introduced herself as Gwen asked. She had a helmet of blue-gray hair and a sweet smile.

She also had a lead foot. "I'm not going in to party, Miss Gwen. Sometimes they let me work a shift. Or at least help clean up. I'm saving to get my car fixed."

She fished out the seven dollars the ride cost. Yup. She needed her car. Still, she added a couple of bucks because tipping was karma, and she could use some.

What she didn't tell the nice lady who'd driven her out to The Barn was that she didn't want to sit in her musty motel room where she was fairly certain her "neighbors" were cooking meth and those two creepy guys came around at least twice a week to ask her if she'd found Jesus. In that motel? No. But as they were ones who called women whores for wearing pants, she was pretty certain neither of them had met the Lord's son either.

"I'm looking at a mustang," Gwen said with a big smile that showed she was only wearing her top teeth. "I can't wait to put those youngsters to shame. And forget about what I said. You're young. You get in there and have a blast. Find a couple of cowboys and get them to fight, and whoever wins goes home with you. Oh, I loved those days. Make sure they aren't armed. That was the mistake I made. Good-bye, dear. Give me a call if you need a ride home."

She peeled out, proving that station wagon still had some life in it.

So did Gwen.

Sometimes Nicole wondered if she did.

There was a whole bar right there with bright lights and loud, rocking music and vibrant people having the time of their lives, and she hoped someone would slip her forty bucks to clean the bathrooms and wipe down the tables.

And if she couldn't find a ride back she'd be out another ten, so she would actually have netted a whole twenty bucks.

How long had it been since she'd danced and enjoyed herself?

Not since the minute she'd married a monster.

With a long sigh, she turned and started for the door and ran right into another woman.

"I'm so sorry." She managed to catch herself.

A gorgeous redhead stood her ground. She was wearing well-worn jeans and a Western shirt that hugged her every curve, the pearl snaps undone to show off a bit of impressive cleavage. She recognized the stunning woman from the diner. She was the cowboy's sister or cousin or whatever. Shit. Was he here? Of course he was. Where else would he be on a Saturday night?

"I'm not." Redhead gave her a brilliant smile. "Hey, we haven't met. I'm Olivia. You're new. I saw you at the café earlier tonight."

Nicole nodded. "Yeah. I started working there a couple of weeks ago. I'm Nicole."

She was glad they didn't seem to be exchanging last names. Sometimes she forgot that one. In her defense, she'd had four over the last two years. It could confuse a girl.

Olivia's eyes widened as she looked at something in the parking lot behind Nicole and then suddenly she was beside her, hooking her arm around Nicole's and leaning in conspiratorially. "Well, Nicole, why don't you let me show you around? Come on in, and the first round's on me."

"Oh, I wasn't planning on drinking. I'm here to ask the manager if I can help clean up after hours."

"Then you have hours and hours before you need to work," Olivia said. "Besides, you already worked a whole dinner shift. Let me buy you a Coke if you don't want something stronger."

"I was going to hang out upstairs." Nicole found herself swept along by her new friend. "They have this room, you see, and it's pretty quiet."

"Oh, I know all about that room. I wish I didn't know about that room, but my parents are open about things they should shove way deep down," Olivia said as they entered the lobby. The music was louder here but not too bad since the honky-tonk had a dining area, though from here she could see the neon lights from the dance hall. "You know everyone complains about their parents being repressed and stuff, but do they ever consider the opposite?"

"Uh, I don't know. I guess I never thought about it." She wasn't sure what was happening. Maybe she was being kidnapped.

Olivia waved to some friends but hustled Nicole over to a quieter section. There were a couple of bar areas here in the large complex known as The Barn. The one off the lobby was where people waited for a table. At this time of night, the dining room was only half full, so the forward bar was fairly empty.

"Well, it's terrible. My mom and dads got it into their heads that if they were open about sex, I wouldn't get a complex." Olivia sat down at a table for four, patting the chair beside her. "The complex is real. I'm afraid to walk into any door of my house. I learned to knock at a young age. How about you? Your parents uptight?"

"Oh, my parents are kind of… I don't know what they are. My mom left when I was seven and Dad remarried and started a new family, and I was kind of like the unpaid babysitter. Let's just say I find *Cinderella* triggering." Why had she said that? She'd learned to say as little as possible about herself over the last couple of years. She'd learned to blend into the background so as few people as possible noticed her.

Maybe that was way easier in the big cities she'd been in or the tiny farm towns where no one looked at her at all because she'd been picking tomatoes or helping bring in the citrus crop. She'd melted into groups that no one wanted to acknowledge existed because they were paid mostly under the table.

"How many siblings?" Olivia held a hand up, gesturing to the waitstaff.

How did she get out of this? She'd kind of planned on talking to Tally and then sneaking up to the room Olivia seemed to think was terrible so she could take a nap. It could be hard to sleep at the motel. Between the drug deals and the sex workers, nighttime could get loud.

"I have a couple of half sisters," she murmured. "I should go and find Tally to see if she needs me tonight."

A tall guy with a *The Barn* T-shirt on walked up, placing a couple of napkins in front of them. "Hey, Livie. New Girl. Tally's not in tonight. Are you Nicole?"

She nodded.

He winced. "I'm sorry. I was supposed to call to let you know everyone came in tonight."

Damn it. She'd come all the way for nothing. Now she would actually be in the hole.

"Sorry. I got caught up in the rush. She told me not to expect you until around midnight and you're early," he said. "How about some fries? On the house."

Olivia groaned. "We can do better than that. Nicole here is my brothers' latest crush, so I thought I would get to know her. We're going to need a pitcher of margaritas and some nachos."

Wait. What? "Your brother?"

"Brothers," Olivia corrected. "There are two of them, though you should know one is more of a found-family brother meaning my dad found him hiding out in one of the dorms because he got kicked out of his house."

The waiter huffed. "Best fucking day of Grim's life. I think about it a lot. That boy went from a nasty cult movie set to the nicest family in the county. And he got to have Abigail Barnes as his new momma. She could be my momma any day."

"Eww," Olivia protested with a frown. "She's my actual momma, you know, Ed."

Ed winked her way. "And you look it, Liv. I'll get those nachos in."

"I'm sorry. I'm confused. I haven't met your brothers."

Olivia shrugged. "Yeah, sometimes you don't need to. But they're great guys, and I think they would like to get to know you. And the nachos and margs are totally on me. Unless you want to head back to the rattrap and spend the evening counting the meth deals. That could be fun, too. Or you could let me ply you with liquor and we could dance, and at some point my brothers will show up because they totally saw you walking in here. It's why I hustled you away. If they got to you first, I wouldn't have the opportunity to get to know you. So, half siblings. Were they evil?"

Nicole sat there for a moment. The smart move would be to walk away because this woman confused her, and she wasn't sure she could trust the whole big sis/best friend vibe she was giving off.

Would it hurt to sit here and have a margarita and talk to someone interesting? She wasn't even considering the whole gorgeous cowboys had a crush on her thing. Again, she wasn't about to come between two brothers. But it might be fun to dance and pretend like she wasn't in a Lifetime movie for a night. She could pretend she was in another movie. A comedy.

"We don't have to talk about your family, if you don't want to." Olivia's voice had gone softer, like she was trying to coax a scared puppy. "We could talk about something else. I have a lot of crazy stories about my brothers."

"They were kind of evil." No one had asked about her in forever. She'd become invisible, and it felt good for a moment to be seen. And she didn't want to count the meth deals. "Like from birth, I think. You know most babies are sweet and cute, but my stepsisters were crazy demanding, and that did not stop as they grew up. They can throw a fit, if you know what I mean, and I'm talking about as teens. I was in college by then. I had to work full time, too. My dad used my college fund as a down payment on an SUV. Because he knew I wouldn't mind. I minded."

"That's awful. I have to admit, despite the fact that I complain about the amount of my parents' public displays of affection, they are awesome," Olivia said as Ed placed a pitcher of margaritas in front of them.

"Jack and Sam and Abby are all kinds of awesome. Don't let the pearl clutchers of the town tell you otherwise," Ed said with a nod as he started pouring a drink for Nicole. "I have no idea where this town would be without the Barnes-Fleetwood family."

So they probably did a ton of charity work. It already sounded like they'd taken in a kid who needed a home. But she was confused. "Your dad's name is Jackson Sam? That's unusual."

Olivia's lips curled up, and Ed laughed as he finished pouring her drink.

He stepped back, holding his hands up. "And I will leave you to the explanations. The nachos will be right up, ladies."

Olivia shook her head. "Nope. Jack and Sam. As in Jack Barnes and Sam Fleetwood."

Her parents were two guys. That was totally cool with her. "That's nice. It's probably hard in a small town. Is Abigail your birth mom?"

"She is," Olivia agreed. "She's also married to my dads. I'm going to lay this out to you so there's no tiptoeing around it. Everyone in town knows, but I rather thought you might not. You seem to keep to yourself. My parents are a threesome and have been since before I was born. They're married and committed to each other."

Nicole felt a smile cross her face. Like a kinky romance novel. "That's cool. Like, good for your mom."

Olivia laughed. "That is the reaction I was hoping for."

"I don't judge. Never. Love is love, and if it doesn't hurt anyone else, I say go for it. Besides, if your parents have been together for that long, they sure as hell beat my mom and dad's traditional marriage and equally traditional divorce."

"Our parents are anything but traditional," a deep voice said, and she found herself turning and looking up into green eyes that she could get lost in. Josh gave her a smile and frowned his sister's way. "I thought you were here to meet friends."

Olivia's eyes lit with mischief. "I found a new friend."

"Liv," Josh began.

"Why don't you introduce us, Olivia," the brother from another mother said.

Nicole knew that was supposed to be a question. But that wasn't a question coming out of his mouth. That was a command, and it kind of made her heart race.

She wasn't coming in between brothers. If she started a bunch of gossip, people would look at her. She'd done a good job of flying under the radar.

"I would be happy to, Grim," Olivia said before turning Nicole's way and wrinkling her nose. "His real name is Jared, which is a lovely name, but he's pissed at his father for dying and leaving him with a prick of a stepdad, so everyone calls him Grim. He broods a lot."

"Olivia." Josh was the perfect picture of outrage.

Grim simply smiled and held out a hand. "That was a pretty fair assessment. Our Olivia never prevaricates."

He did not talk like some ranch hand off the range. He was a lot like his nickname except when his lips curled up, there was the sweetest dimple in his cheeks. She was suddenly slightly afraid of taking his hand. Like if she touched him this thing, this pull she felt, would be real, and that would be the stupidest thing she could do.

Still, it was rude to ignore him. She put her hand in his, and she was wrapped in warm strength as he placed his other hand over hers.

"And I'm Joshua." He took her other hand, and she was between them.

Holy hell. Were they…

Just because their mom and dads were a threesome…

Really upped the odds that they wouldn't mind. Except they were brothers. Except they weren't blood siblings.

Except… She was deeply confused, and it would be smart to run right this second.

But it seemed like so much more fun to sit here and talk and pretend she was normal.

"I'm Nicole," she said and wished she didn't sound so breathless.

They both let go at the same time, as though they were coordinated movements. They sat in the two unoccupied chairs.

"I thought you two were calling it an early night." There was no small amount of teasing in Olivia's tone.

"There's a lot of plans changing," Josh acknowledged and then turned slightly to the bar. "Ed, bring two beers and double whatever my sister ordered." He turned back to her, giving her a smile that damn near melted her panties. "So, Nicole, where are you from?"

Ah, there it was. She could see reason through the fine mist of lust. "Chicago."

It was a well-crafted story and one she didn't have to use often. She'd discovered most people wanted no more than the minimum facts before they felt comfortable talking about themselves and then she could nod along and give up nothing else.

Olivia looked like the cat who'd gotten all the cream as she started talking to Grim and Josh. Like a woman who'd set her brothers up to succeed.

Would it be so bad? Why couldn't she have a single night of pleasure? She would be out of this town in a week. She would have the money, and the mechanic had told her the car would only take a few days to fix.

What if she could see them for those days? On the sly. Or not. It wouldn't matter if she was leaving. They could talk about the mysterious young woman who worked at the café, dated two men, and then disappeared.

Or they wouldn't because something new would come along and they would forget her. Like these two men would forget her.

But she didn't have to forget them. She would be in another country by this time next year, trying to make a life for herself.

Couldn't she go a little wild now?

"You are a long way from home," Josh said. "How did you come to be in our town?"

She sat back and decided to go with the flow for once.

Chapter Three

Josh stopped as they reached the truck, and he realized Nicole wasn't as close as she'd been before.

It was almost one in the morning, but The Barn was still rocking behind them. Neon lights split the darkness, and the thump of music formed a soundtrack.

They'd danced and talked and had a couple of drinks, but not so much he couldn't try to seduce the gorgeous woman. She'd had two margaritas and then switched to water. He and Grim had done the same but with beers. He didn't want a drunken hookup with her.

But he did want her. Like crazy want her. Like he hadn't felt in a long time. He knew damn well it was too soon, but he would make it work.

Except she looked worried now.

"Hey, you okay?" He stopped, giving her some space.

"She's worried, and probably rightfully so." Grim leaned against the truck with a sigh. "Nicole, nothing has to happen. We can take you home and drop you off. All I ask is you let me see you safely home. We probably should have sent you with Olivia."

Their sister had left half an hour before with her friends. She'd offered Nicole a ride, but the gorgeous dark-haired woman had wanted to stay.

Had she changed her mind?

It could be damn hard to be a woman in the world. "Do you have a friend you can call?"

She grimaced. "I have the number to a cab."

Josh snorted. "No, you have the number to Gwen Stapleton, who is surely asleep by this point. And honestly, she shouldn't be driving, much less pretending to be an Uber." He needed to make her comfortable. The night had been even more amazing than he'd thought it could be. Nicole hadn't preferred one over the other. She'd spent time dancing with both of them, and when she'd gotten looks, she'd simply ignored them all. When she'd been slow dancing with Grim and Josh had moved in behind her, she hadn't seemed surprised. She'd matched her movements to theirs, and he'd known this could work.

But not if she was afraid of them. Hanging out in a public place was one thing. Being alone with them was another.

"Darlin', if you're worried, we can walk right back in there and find someone to drive you home that you feel more comfortable with," Grim offered.

She bit her bottom lip, and then her head was shaking. "Who would that be? The only people I know in this town are Christa and the other waitresses, but I don't know them well enough to ask them to pick me up."

"I know Christa," Josh assured her. "She's my momma's best friend, and she will come get you. I would be all right with Christa taking you home."

"Our concern is that you get there safely. That's all," Grim assured her.

One hand went to her hip, and her sass was back. "Oh, really? So you two weren't going to try anything?"

Josh held his hands up as though to show he was harmless. "Nothing at all, if you tell me no."

Her lips formed a straight line. "And if I'm not capable of telling you no tonight?"

His cock kind of jumped in his jeans. That was what he'd been looking for. "You know what we want, right?"

She nodded slowly. "You both want me. You want to take turns."

"Not at all. There won't be any turn taking. Both of us will be with you the whole way," he vowed.

"Except we won't, because if she's not capable of saying no, it's my responsibility to do it for her," Grim reminded him.

Sometimes Josh thought Grim had been around Dad too much. He took the Dom role seriously, while Josh had spent his life being raised by subs and watching how they all interacted. He didn't like to think of his parents that way, but it was true, and sometimes a sub liked to play with words. "Nicole, he's worried you mean you think you've had too much to drink. He often takes things literally. Or he's worried you're scared of us."

Her expression softened, and suddenly she moved closer to Grim, getting in his space. Her hands came up to cup his cheeks. "I didn't mean it that way."

Oh, she was perfect for them. He'd known there was a deeply submissive streak in this woman. She hid it well. She'd likely learned not to let that part of herself out or someone would take advantage of her. Josh intended to show her how safe she was with them. Safe to be herself. Safe to submit and indulge and find the pleasure and joy that could come from serving her Masters.

Grim practically melted. "I don't want you to be afraid of me. I know I'm a big guy, but I wouldn't hurt you. I take consent seriously. This is not something where you say yes once and then we do whatever we want to you."

She bit her bottom lip. "And if that doesn't sound so bad?"

"It's too early." Josh needed to make things plain. "We don't know you well enough to play those games. Grim's right. If you want to spend the night with us, you need to understand that it only goes as far as you want. Any no from you will be honored by the two of us. All we want is the chance to spend some time with you."

It was a little lie. He already wanted more. She was sweet and smart and made him laugh. She was good with Grim.

Her head turned slightly, though she didn't move away from Grim. "It's just sex for me."

Now she was the one who was lying. She clearly wasn't a woman who seduced men on the regular.

"Is it because there are two of us?" Grim asked quietly.

"No," she whispered as though the thought hurt her.

"Because you wouldn't be the first woman who wanted nothing

more than sex from us. Mostly they want to date Josh and they let me sneak into bed," Grim admitted.

"I would never do that to you," Nicole declared. "No, that's not the problem. I have to leave pretty soon. I have a job waiting for me. As soon as my car is fixed, I need to head on out."

Ah, there it was. Yep. Pops was right, and she was probably in trouble. But it was way too early to push her. He needed to get a feel for the situation. If she was in money trouble, he could easily fix that. If she had some asshole stalking her, well, that would be fun to fix. He was the right mix of his dads. He could ruin an asshole both mentally and physically. "How long do you think you're staying here in Willow Fork?"

"A week," she murmured. "Two, tops."

He let his hands find her hips. "How about you spend that time with us? When we're not working, of course. I work my dads' ranch, and Grim here is a vet because there was zero way I was going to that many classes."

"Yeah, so says the business major." Grim seemed to have calmed, and his hands were stroking over her hair. "But he's right. When we're not working, I would love to spend some time with you. It doesn't have to mean we're getting engaged or anything. It's nothing more than spending time with a beautiful woman."

One of her hands came back, and her fingertips brushed over Josh's jawline. "It's been a long time for me and the idea of…spending time with you…I think I would regret not doing it, but I am going to leave."

He was sure she thought she was going to. But if he had a couple of weeks to build some trust with her, she might come around to his way of thinking. "Then let me kiss you."

Grim turned her so she was facing Josh, his big hands holding her against his body. "Kiss Josh. You're going to find we're bossy when it comes to this, but I do not want you to forget you're in control."

Her breath hitched, and he could see the creamy swell of her breasts against the V-neck of her shirt. "You have more than one kink, don't you?"

Josh felt his lips curl. "Oh, my darlin', you have no idea."

He had zero shame when it came to his sexuality. His sister

might complain about their parents' deep belief in sex positivity, but Josh reveled in it. It was freedom to be who he was, and that was a Dom.

He moved in, his hand cupping her cheek as he looked down at her. "Bossy doesn't begin to cover it, but Grim's right. All you need to say tonight is no and everything stops."

He didn't want her to say no. He wasn't going to give her a single reason to stop this train now that he'd gotten it rolling. He could be fairly vanilla, and then introduce her to more interesting play later.

It wasn't like they hadn't been quietly topping her all night, and she'd reacted beautifully. When some cowboy Josh didn't know had asked her to dance, she'd shaken her head and stepped back between them as though they were protection. They were. She needed to learn to trust that instinct.

It started with pleasure and continued with proving to her that when they said something, she could count on them.

But mostly pleasure.

"I'm not saying no now," she said, her chin coming up.

Oh, he liked the fact that she could challenge him. "I'm glad, but the choice is yours. I don't intend to make it hard for you. I intend to make this the easiest choice you'll ever make."

He lowered his mouth to hers and let their lips brush.

"This is where I've wanted to be since the minute I laid eyes on you, girl," he whispered.

Her breath hitched again, and he could feel her breasts against his chest, though she was held in place by Grim. It seemed to do something for her.

He kissed her again. Soft and sweet, and then he let his tongue run over her lower lip. His body started to sing, every muscle and inch of skin coming alive.

He'd been right about her. So fucking right.

Her tongue came out tentatively, and he let himself feast on her mouth. She tasted like sunshine and sin, a heady mix that made his brain fritz and got him so hard he couldn't breathe.

He broke off the kiss because as much as he never wanted to stop, he also wanted to watch her with his best friend.

Begin as you mean to go.

"Now kiss Grim, and then we're getting in the truck. You want to go to your place or ours?"

She frowned. "Mine is a dump, but I think I would feel better there."

So they would be spending the night in the sleaziest motel in the county when they had a perfectly lovely house all to themselves.

He would work on the problem. "Your place, it is."

Grim released her. It was Josh's turn to get his hands on her. He caught her wrists and drew her back against his chest. The motion made her breasts swell and pushed her toward Grim.

"Kiss the hell out of him, sweetheart, because I'm taking you in the back with me and getting warmed up," Josh promised.

Grim growled. "I knew we should have taken your truck."

"That's what you get for being way too much of a control freak." He was perfectly fine with that right now since it gave him the opportunity to spend some time with their sub.

Grim's head shook, but then he leaned over and kissed Nicole.

She didn't know it yet but that was exactly what she was—their sweet submissive.

* * * *

Nicole couldn't think straight as Josh climbed into the cab behind her.

What the hell was she doing? It was stupid. They were out of her league and she was in so much trouble, but she hadn't been thinking about the fact that there were police after her and her husband's whole family wanted her dead when she'd been kissing them.

Them. She'd kissed both Josh and Grim. She'd spent the nicest couple of hours with them, and that was all. She didn't want the good time to end, though she knew in the morning it would.

And she would have some memories to sustain her.

"Come here," Josh ordered.

He was right about the bossy part. The trouble was she kind of liked it.

It had been so odd to feel comfortable around two men she'd met only hours before. Maybe it had been the buffer of having

Olivia with them most of the night. Nicole shied away from men. She certainly didn't jump into bed with them. A man had accosted her earlier in the night, asking her to dance. He'd asked politely, but she'd felt a leer in his eyes and she'd instinctively stepped back between Grim and Josh, and the fear that had flared melted away.

She's only dancing with us tonight, buddy.

Josh had said the words and Grim seemed to get taller, and the man had quickly walked away.

She found herself on Josh's lap in the comfy cab. It was a nice truck. She would bet Grim had spent everything he had on it since he was a rural veterinarian. Despite the advanced degree, he wouldn't make a ton of money in a place like this.

And Josh helped around his father's ranch.

They weren't some rich boys out for a good time. They were like her. Their families didn't have money and power that could crush her.

"You're worried again." Josh whispered the accusation in her ear.

She wasn't worrying any more tonight. She was taking her two hot cowboys back to her room and letting go of everything else. All that mattered was these two men tonight.

And if she spent more time with them, then that was all right, too. She'd meant what she said. She didn't give a flying fuck what the people of the town thought of her as long as she could keep her job. Since it appeared her employer was well acquainted with threesomes, she thought she was pretty safe.

A week. She could keep them for a week. Maybe two. Not long enough to fall for them. She'd been honest about leaving, and as long as they were getting the sex they wanted, they wouldn't ask for more.

"I don't worry when you kiss me," she offered.

"Then let's get you relaxed again." Josh's mouth covered hers and heat flared.

The minute these men got their hands on her, she went up in flames. She felt her nipples tighten as his tongue delved deep, mastering her own.

She wasn't naïve. These men were into some kinky things, but hadn't she always wanted to explore more? Her sex life seemed dull and dreary, and then any sex she'd had was merely to keep her husband placated while she planned to get away.

This wasn't part of a plan. This was something new and different. Something for her. Something that made her feel free even as they'd restrained her.

They'd held her, offering her up to each other, and she'd gotten hot and wet at the thought.

Her damn pussy was making the decisions for now, and she couldn't help it. They weren't hearing a no from her tonight.

She could feel the hard line of his erection under her ass. Damn but he felt big. What would it feel like when that hard cock was stroking inside her? It wasn't like she'd never had sex. She'd had plenty, but she'd done it for the wrong reasons. She'd done it to keep her boyfriend or to hide her plans.

She was having sex for one reason tonight. She wanted it. She wanted them.

"You're going to kill me, darlin'," Josh said with a sigh.

"What's she doing? I'm going to need a play by play. It's a good twenty minutes back into town," Grim groused.

"She's wriggling on my lap, making my dick so hard I can't breathe," Josh explained.

"I didn't mean to." She wasn't sure why she said the words so quickly.

His arms tightened around her, and she felt the most delicious nip to her earlobe. "Now that is a lie, and you need to understand there's no place for lying here. Lying will prove to me you're a bad, bad girl."

His fingers were slipping under the waistband of her jeans. She was the one who couldn't breathe. "I'm sorry."

Another nip. "Don't be sorry. Be honest. Were you trying to get my dick hard?"

"Yes," she admitted with a gasp as those callused fingers made their way down. Was he going to touch her right here in the truck as they moved down the highway? She'd expected a kiss, but she found her legs spreading, making it easier for him. "I like the way you feel, Joshua."

He growled against her ear. "That's what I want to hear. There is no need for you to hide here, girl. There's zero place for shame between us. You want something, I'll consider it. You should understand I don't have a lot of boundaries when it comes to sex."

"He was raised by the happiest perverts ever," Grim said with a chuckle. "So he means that."

She wondered what it would have been like to be raised in a family like Josh's. They would have been hard working and likely not had a ton of money, but they would have had each other. Ranching was hard work, and having two husbands to count on had probably been wonderful for Abigail Barnes, though she would have worked hard, too.

Would hard work be okay if you loved the people you worked with? Worked for?

Micah hadn't worked a day in his life. She was done with rich boys, and Josh and Grim seemed to be from a completely different world. Her husband certainly wouldn't have taken time to ensure her pleasure.

"Stop it," Josh whispered. "Whatever you're thinking about, stop. You stay here in the moment with me. There's nothing outside the cab of this truck. There's nothing to worry about because all that matters is here and now."

Here and now seemed pretty nice. She let the thoughts fly away and concentrated on the feel of Josh's hand skimming over her skin, the way his breath felt against her ear, the low, deep tone of his voice.

"Spread your legs for me."

Up ahead Grim groaned but kept his eyes resolutely on the road.

She did as Josh commanded because there was no way that had been a question. But it was okay because she believed him when he told her all he needed was a no to stop everything. She was in control. She was never in control. Her life felt like a runaway roller coaster that kept plunging downward. There had been no choices to be made that didn't send her deeper and deeper into despair.

But this, oh this felt like joy.

"Hold still," Josh whispered. "Do you want me to touch you?"

He was touching her, but she did want it to continue. "Yes."

"Yes, Josh or yes, Sir."

Now she knew exactly what his kink was, and her heart rate ticked up. She'd never once had a lover who wanted to… What did they call it? Play. She'd never played. She'd had two whole lovers in her life, and one had been okay and one had been utterly thoughtless. "Yes, Josh. I want you to touch me."

"Do you want me to rub your little clit and get that sweet pussy all hot and wet?"

She feared she was already there, and he was about to find out. Still, there was only one answer because she rather thought he wouldn't be turned off by how wet she could get.

She shivered as she felt his tongue caress the shell of her ear, and he gave her another nip. Damn, that felt good. What the hell was this man doing to her that she would throw all good sense overboard? She'd always considered herself a woman who couldn't be manipulated with sex, but Josh was proving her wrong. "Yes. I do, Josh. I want you to touch my clit."

She wanted it more than she could have imagined. Her brain was fuzz, and her body was fully in control now.

She gasped as one big finger slid over her clitoris, and her vision went hazy.

"Tell me, Josh. I'm the one driving and not getting my hands on her. You owe me a detailed description," Grim groused.

"Don't let him fool you, baby." Josh's words rumbled over her skin. "He loves this part."

"Not as much as I'm going to love getting my hands on you," Grim vowed.

But he wasn't watching them through the rearview and he wasn't driving like mad because he wanted his turn.

Grim was controlled. Grim was cautious. He wouldn't put them at risk.

Would he be as controlled and focused when he was inside her?

The idea sent a shudder through her even as Josh stroked over her clit, and she could feel him press two fingers against her, opening her labia.

"She's soaking wet, brother," Josh said in a low tone. "I could fuck her right now, she's so ready. Not that I'm going to. I'm going to get her panting for us."

She kind of already was, but Josh proved he could take her higher. The pad of one finger circled her clit while she felt another delve inside her.

"She's trying to move against me," Josh said. "This pretty lady wants to steal an orgasm. Should we let her?"

"Nicole, you be still," Grim commanded. "You're going to take what Josh gives you and not make a move or a sound until I let you know it's okay. Do you understand me?"

"And if I don't?" Nicole asked.

"Brat," Josh said, but it was with a chuckle.

"Well, for starters he'll stop doing what he's doing and we'll start talking about the concept of discipline," Grim offered.

That got her attention. "Discipline?"

Grim's eyes stayed on the road. "Yes, Nicole. Discipline."

"He means he wants to spank your pretty ass, baby." Josh seemed to understand she needed a translator.

Spanking? "I don't know how I feel about that."

"Then you should mind," Josh replied.

She went still. "You like to spank women?"

Grim hesitated for a moment, letting Josh start to work his magic again. She shouldn't be having this conversation while her brain seemed to have relocated to her pussy.

"Only if it works for you," Grim admitted. "For some women…some people…it's not just women...they find a certain amount of pleasure in spanking. If it's done right, it can be a good experience. Some people need it as a release emotionally. Some for sexual pleasure."

It took everything she had to concentrate on the conversation. "But you don't."

"No," Grim agreed. "I get something from a woman like you trusting me enough to let me take her there. *There* being what we would call sub space."

"The professor is in the house," Josh whispered. "Grim, can we save the lectures for another time? Baby, stay still until Grim tells you to move and then you can go wild. This is a way to bring him in, to have all three of us involved. No one is spanking your pretty butt without permission, but I think you'll find we're both good at it. Now stay still. Be a sweet girl and listen to Grim's orders."

What would it feel like to be placed over Grim's lap, her ass exposed? It didn't scare her the way it should because she'd watched how disciplined these men were. They hadn't drank too much.

They'd protected her all night, ensuring she always had what she needed. When she'd wanted a water, Josh had gone to get it. When she'd wanted to dance, Grim had done it, though she could tell it wasn't something he did naturally. Him swaying awkwardly with her had been the sweetest thing.

Josh's thumb pressed down, and it took everything she had not to rub against it. She wanted to. The orgasm was right there.

But she stayed still, the frustration oddly satisfying because she didn't think for a second Josh would deny her as long as she played the game.

It was a game where they all could win.

"She's trying so hard," Josh said. "I can feel her practically vibrating with need."

She wanted to cry out because she was on the edge, but she kind of believed him when he said Grim would give her a lecture on the spanking stuff, and she wanted the orgasm.

But a good cry would be a release, too. How long had it been since she'd been able to cry? Every day was about survival, about making it to the next. Somewhere along the way she'd lost the ability to sit down and wring all of the negative emotions out of her.

Probably because the negative emotions—fear and shame and anxiety—were the only ones she'd felt in forever.

"Take it, Nic. Have all you want," Grim offered.

And she was off the leash. She pumped against Josh's hand, rubbing with abandon. The orgasm was almost immediate. The wild sensation ran through her like a flash fire, burning away all the bad crap that had been in her brain and leaving only pleasure, only the feeling of warmth and satisfaction. She cried out, riding the wave for everything it was worth.

All the while, Josh held her. His strong arms kept her close, and he kissed her neck as he worked to give her everything she needed.

She finally went still, slumping back in his arms, her body pulsing with afterglow.

And all the man had done was put his hand down her panties.

"That was perfect," Grim said from the front seat.

They weren't moving any more, and Nicole vaguely realized they'd made it to her craptastic motel. Why had she decided to take them here? At the time it seemed better, safer, but now she was pretty sure she would have gone wherever they wanted her to go.

It would be okay. It wasn't like they were pampered rich boys. They wouldn't judge.

And the ride had been perfect.

Grim shut off the engine and opened the back door, reaching in for her.

He picked her up like she weighed nothing, and she realized she was ready for even more perfection.

Chapter Four

Grim had been pretty sure he'd ruined the whole night bringing up spanking way too soon, but as he looked at Nicole laid out in his best friend's arms, he realized Josh had absolutely saved it for them.

"Thanks," he said as he peeled Nicole off Josh's lap and hoisted her against his chest. "You okay or do you need to clean up?"

The way she'd sounded, she'd probably wriggled and thrashed, and he could imagine what that had done to Josh's cock. He knew simply listening to her had him standing at attention.

"I barely managed to keep myself in check," Josh admitted, climbing out of the cab. "Let's get her inside. Don't forget to lock it up. You know where we are."

"We could go to your place." Nicole wrapped an arm around his neck. "I feel better about it now. I was trying to be careful, but I don't have to be tonight, do I?"

His heart twisted in his chest. She was so vulnerable, and he wanted to be the one who made sure no one took advantage of that. "You don't, baby, but I think we're bedding down here for the night. It's another twenty minutes back to the ranch, and I will die if I don't get my hands on you soon."

"It would be faster if you didn't drive like my grandma," Josh groused. "Come to think of it, Granny drives way faster."

"Grandma Diane doesn't have my deep sense of responsibility

to keep everyone alive," he shot back. He was careful for a reason. He'd been given so much by Josh and his family he would never risk any of them. And he wouldn't risk Nicole, either.

He was already in deep with this woman, hence the uncool almost-lecture on spanking. He could practically hear Josh telling him to chill the fuck out and take things slow on the "we want to tie you up and do nasty things to you" front.

Thankfully, she didn't look worried now. She had a dreamy smile on her lips, and her eyes were soft.

"Where's your key, darlin'?" He wanted her out of this parking lot as soon as possible. It looked like someone was checking in next door. He got a vague glance at a blonde before she rolled her suitcase inside. She seemed oddly normal for a motel guest. More suburban mom than the usual criminal element.

"In my purse, the front pocket," she murmured as though she couldn't care less if they looked through it.

Maybe she wasn't in the kind of trouble he was worried about. It didn't matter because he and Josh would handle it no matter what.

"Got it." Josh had her purse in hand, closing the truck up and moving to her room. "You would think we were back in the stone ages. Who still has actual keys?"

No key cards for the Willow Fork Sleep Easy Motel. He was sure the owner would laugh if anyone asked if they could check in on their phone. He wasn't sure Jerry Nevins had joined the cell phone revolution. As far as he could tell the man still used a rotary phone on a landline.

He wanted to take her to the magnificent hotel attached to Subversion. Half this rattrap would fit into the suite he and Josh always stayed in. She deserved the best, and he wanted to give it to her. She could be their pampered princess of a sub. A little bratty. A whole lot sweet.

Josh got the door open, and Grim carried her in.

Josh turned on the lights, and the room was neat, if a bit shabby. It didn't matter. Nothing mattered except the woman in his arms.

He sat down on the king-sized bed, grateful that at least it seemed sturdy. He leaned over and kissed her. Her mouth flowered open under his. He could hear Josh moving around. He would be making sure everything was locked down and they had what they needed. Sure enough, when he looked over there was a line of condoms on the nightstand.

His whole body felt alert and alive. This was happening. They were starting something with her, and it would be important.

He let it slide away. He didn't need to put pressure on any of them this evening. Tonight was about pleasure. Tomorrow they could start talking. Slowly. They would ease her into the relationship they wanted.

"You are so gorgeous, girl." Josh proved he was already a step ahead of Grim.

"So fucking beautiful," he agreed.

"I don't usually feel that way," she said quietly. "But I feel real good tonight. I'll feel even better if you kiss me again."

He lowered his head and let his mouth find hers. Kissing Nicole felt natural to him.

He'd loved the whole night. Even dancing. Not once had he found himself wondering when he could slink away and find a quiet place to read or get some work done the way he normally did when surrounded by people.

It wasn't so bad when she was there.

"Tell me what you want." He was going slow. He was tamping down all his instincts to tie her up and haul her back to their place. Those, he'd been told, were his inner-caveman instincts, and he was supposed to…not suppress them exactly, but to try to round out the hard edges.

It was funny how he almost never heard his stepfather in his head anymore, but Jack Barnes was always there.

"I don't know." She was staring at him like he was something special. "I guess I want to explore. Maybe not the spanking thing tonight, but it doesn't scare me the way I thought it would. I thought this would be something that went fast, and then you would be gone."

He shook his head. "Not happening, girl. We're spending the night if you let us."

"Then I want you to show me," she whispered. "Show me what it means to be with two men."

That he could do. Starting right now.

He kissed her again even as Josh moved in. His best friend had already gotten his shirt off and was taking his place on the other side of Nicole. "Kiss Josh."

Her head moved, tilting so Josh could take her lips.

This was what he needed. He'd been restless lately, his work not fulfilling him the way it used to. The club worked for a while, but what he needed was an actual relationship, a woman they could truly care about and share.

The fact that he was almost certain she was lying to them about any number of things didn't matter. She was lying about this great job she was going to get to in a couple of weeks, lying about having friends in other cities.

She was alone. She needed them. She just didn't know it yet.

Sex, it seemed, might be an excellent way to prove to this cautious woman they could be trusted.

"I'm going to take off your shirt," he whispered. They would get to a point where he could do what he liked and trust her to stop him if she wasn't on the same page, but they weren't there yet. He worried she might stay silent, and he wanted her to have every opportunity to make her wishes known.

She turned on his lap, facing Josh and holding her arms up, giving him permission.

He eased the T-shirt over her head, letting his hands skim her waist and then the sides of her breasts. Her skin was warm and soft, like the woman herself.

Her bra came next. He twisted the clasps with the ease of a man who'd done it many times. He liked to undress their women, to present them to Josh. To make them feel like the gorgeous gifts they were.

He tossed the bra to the side.

"Damn, you're beautiful, Nicole," Josh said, his eyes on her chest.

Grim couldn't see her, but he could feel her. He let his hands run up her sides again but this time he stopped at her breasts, cupping them and testing their weight in his hands. He ran his thumbs across her nipples and bit back a groan. They were hard nubs, and the fact that he could smell her arousal made his dick jump.

Josh had primed her, and now they could spend all night

showing her exactly how it felt to be worshipped by two men.

Josh put a hand in her hair, smoothing it back even as Grim stroked her nipples. "Nicole, how do you feel about getting Grim in your mouth? I know it's something I'd like to see."

Bastard. He shot his partner a what-the-fuck look because he knew exactly what he was doing. If he got the first blow job, then Josh would get inside her first.

Josh gave him a "well, buddy, I'm quicker than you" look.

Nicole's chest swelled in his hands. "I feel good about it. I should warn you, though, I've been told I'm not great at oral."

It was obvious she'd had some assholes in her past. Possibly the one she was running from. He couldn't tell if she was running from a person or trying to get away from her problems, but it didn't matter tonight. Nor did it matter who had her first. What mattered was how she felt on the other side of this. "Only because you didn't have the right lover, darlin'. I'm going to teach you what I like, and I expect you to do the same for me. Good sex doesn't simply happen. We have to make it happen."

"You believe that?" Nicole asked, her head laying back on his shoulder as he stroked her breasts.

"Yes, we do," Josh replied, his hand coming up to tilt her head so she had to look him in the eyes. "We're not going to be selfish and we're not going to be quick. We want hours and hours to learn your body, to figure out what gets you hot and what makes you come so hard you scream out our names."

Her only response was to groan and wriggle her ass over his dick. Yeah, he had no idea how Josh had managed not to spill in his jeans.

Suddenly the idea of having her mouth on his cock wasn't a bad one. Not that it had been in the first place. This was how they tended to work. They negotiated. The first blow job would be okay since he knew Josh wouldn't watch for long.

"Get on your knees, baby, but take those jeans off first," he ordered, giving her breasts one last gentle stroke. "I want to feel your mouth on me. You tell me if it's too much. You only take what you can."

"He says that because his dick is so big," Josh offered.

Nicole slid off his lap and got to her feet. There was a tremble to her hands as she started to undress, but he didn't think she was afraid. He worked the buttons of his shirt, not wanting to leave her alone. Not this first time. There would be plenty of times later when they would have her naked while they were clothed, but they had to build trust first. Besides, he didn't want anything between them. He wanted her hands on him, craved it.

He wasn't sure why he was drawn to Nicole, but he'd learned long ago some things were meant to be. Sometimes if a man was open to it, the universe gave him a bounty. It was up to him to take care of those gifts, to never take them for granted.

Josh moved in behind her, letting his fingers brush over her shoulders. They looked beautiful together. They would make a gorgeous couple.

Could she handle what the town would throw their way? How harshly society would judge them?

"Don't," Josh said, even as he lowered his head to her neck and started kissing her. "Not tonight."

His best friend knew him well.

"Is something wrong?" Nicole asked, hesitating at the fly of her jeans.

"He's always worried about hurting someone else, and he's thinking about the fact that this town can be hell on anyone different. He's thinking about my parents and what they went through, but we're going to concentrate on tonight and nothing else," Josh vowed.

"I wouldn't care." Nicole's eyes found his, and he saw the will there. "If we were together, I wouldn't care what anyone else thought. I've tried to fit in and all I got for it was pieces of myself taken away. I won't give up on good things to please people who don't matter."

His heart clenched because she likely didn't know how bad it could get, but damn, he'd needed to hear those words. "Then take off your clothes. You already know we think you're gorgeous. Show us."

She took a long breath and then shoved her jeans to the floor along with her cotton undies, kicking them to the side. Her eyes went to his chest. "I think you should show me, too."

He pulled his boots and socks off and stood, wearing only his jeans and boxers. When his hands went to the fly, she moved in, covering his hands with hers and brushing them back so she could twist the button loose. Her eyes were down, watching as she slowly lowered the zipper.

He gritted his teeth because she was going to do him in. Every cell in his body felt awake and alive and a little desperate as she cautiously undressed him.

Josh stepped back, watching Nicole the entire time.

Grim's cock bounced free, the hard length jumping the minute she touched him. Heat flashed through his system, and he forced himself to breathe. He wanted to toss her on the bed and pound himself inside her, but it wasn't happening.

She was getting what she needed tonight even if it killed him.

He managed to get the jeans off along with the boxers, kicking them to the side. He watched as she palmed his cock.

"I think you're beautiful, too, Grim." Every word came out breathless. "Why do they call you Grim? Olivia's answer seemed a little sarcastic."

Livie was entirely sarcastic. "I wasn't raised like Josh. My parents…my stepfather…he didn't believe in joy. He always told me any happiness should be found in heaven, and it mocked God to laugh or have fun when it came to what he called earthly delights."

"Earthly delights meant anything at all," Josh explained. "So Grim didn't learn to smile a lot until he came to live with me. He was serious all the time, and someone took to calling him Grim. It stuck. My momma and Olivia tried for a long time to get everyone to call him Jared, but Grim likes the name."

He wouldn't say he liked the name. It simply felt more real than Jared. "The people who gave me the name no longer matter. The people who called me Grim are still in my life."

"Jared is a beautiful name, but I understand the necessity of transformation every now and then." She went on her toes. "You should know I like you no matter what you call yourself."

A kiss brushed over his lips and then she was moving again, dropping down to her knees.

He was too big, too tall. He settled back on the bed, spreading his knees wide and allowing her to move between them. "Touch me."

Her eyes were soft and filled with desire as she cupped his balls.

It took everything he had to not come then and there. She moved up, wrapping her hand around his cock as she leaned forward and swiped a tongue across it.

Grim's eyes damn near rolled to the back of his head.

"Spread your knees wide, sweetheart," Josh said.

Yes, he knew the game plan. Josh wouldn't simply sit back and watch when he could be involved. This would teach her what they wanted. Her in between them always.

"Do what he says." It was time to get bossy with her. She seemed to respond so well when he took control. "But don't stop taking care of me. If you do, he'll stop."

"What's he…" She gasped, and suddenly her hands were on his thighs, holding on. "Oh, my god."

What he was doing was eating her pussy like a starving man.

Grim reached out, sliding his fingers into her hair and twisting lightly. "I meant what I said. You don't want him to stop, do you?"

She shook her head slightly and then leaned back in, sucking lightly at his cockhead. She moaned, the sound reverberating across his flesh.

Her tongue whirled around him, tentatively at first, and then she seemed to settle in.

He glanced to his right and caught sight of the three of them in the mirrored closet door. It was the kind that folded out to open, but Nicole had it closed so he could see everything. Josh was under her, his head between her legs, hands holding on to her thighs so she was balanced as he devoured her pussy.

She looked sexy as fuck leaning over and working his cock. Her hips wriggled, acknowledging the pleasure she received, and she gave it all back. To him.

Nicole was gorgeous in between them, fitting there with a perfection he couldn't have imagined.

She sucked him deep and then Josh must have hit some perfect spot because just as he could feel the back of her throat she moaned, and he couldn't hold back any longer.

He fisted her hair as he came, wild pleasure flowing through him. Nicole took everything he gave her, drinking him down even as she rode out her own wave.

Nicole sank down, her head across his lap, and it was obvious she was spent.

But they weren't done with her.

Not even close.

* * * *

Every inch of her skin felt alive as Nicole took a deep breath and felt Josh slide from between her legs.

Had that really happened? Had she given Grim a blow job while Josh blew her freaking mind with his tongue? He'd tongue fucked her, eaten her pussy like no one had before.

It had to be a dream, except she could taste Grim on her tongue, the salty sweetness of him coating her mouth, his masculine scent filling her senses. She wasn't this girl. Woman. She wasn't the woman who had crazy sex.

Of course she also hadn't thought she would be the woman on the run from the cops for killing her husband, but here she was. Maybe it was time to throw out all expectations and take what joy she could find.

She felt big hands cup her ass, and she remembered she was naked. With two hot men, and they seemed to like what they saw.

You're too fat, Nora.

Why did you lose all that weight? You look like a scarecrow.

Sometimes Micah's voice haunted her, an echo of a nightmare that was constantly chasing her. She couldn't do anything right. Now she realized it was all about control. It hadn't mattered what she'd done. She couldn't please him. No matter what way she went, he would find something to criticize because criticism was the point.

"You taste so sweet, sunshine," Josh whispered into her ear. He covered her back, his arms wrapping around her waist even as she clung to Grim.

She'd decided to believe them. At least for the night. "Grim tastes perfect, too."

A low chuckle had her tilting her head up so she could look into amused dark eyes. Grim's big hands came out, stroking her hair. "I will take your word on it, baby. Now come up here. Are you too tired? Because I think Josh would like to get inside you."

She'd expected Josh to start fucking her from behind while she blew his best friend, but he'd surprised her. Josh Barnes was a ridiculously giving lover, and there was no way she would deny him. He'd given her two earthshaking orgasms without taking anything for himself. But she didn't want it to be only Josh. "Will you hold me?"

Grim's gaze went soft. "Always."

It was a bittersweet word because their *always* wouldn't last long. Tonight would last forever in her memory, and that would have to be the *always* she got.

Josh moved from behind, and before she knew it she was being settled back on the bed, her body lain out against Grim's. He was behind her, his legs opening hers. It was a vulnerable position. Wanton and blatantly sexual, and she felt weirdly precious.

Had she ever felt this wanted? Was this the feeling she'd been chasing her whole life? The one she'd missed out on in childhood, the one that led her to a terrible marriage?

Grim kissed her temple, his hands restless on her body as she watched Josh kick off his jeans.

"I know I've said it, but I won't stop until you know how I feel," Josh said, pulling off a condom from the roll he'd lain out earlier. "But you are gorgeous, girl. You are sexy and beautiful, and I can't wait to get to know you better."

He wouldn't. He couldn't know the real her, but she wasn't going to turn him down. He was a gorgeous god of a man, and he would forget this time, or rather it could be a fond memory years down the line when he and Grim had found their perfect woman and settled down, someone who would appreciate them and work hard for their future.

It wouldn't be her, but she had tonight.

Josh was utterly masculine, standing at the end of the bed, his cock jutting from between powerful legs. He was a stunning man with dark hair that curled around his ears and piercing emerald eyes. His shoulders were broad, and every inch of the man was cut and muscular. He was so beautiful it almost took her breath away.

And he made her feel beautiful in a way she never had before. She was the girl no one noticed, the one who sat in the back and did her work without a lot of fanfare. And then she'd been the girl who hid. She didn't feel hidden with these men.

Grim's hands cupped her breasts, reminding her he was there. Everywhere their skin touched felt alive and warm. How long had she been numb? Years it felt, long before Micah died and she'd been a pawn in his brother's game.

Something was waking inside her, something she'd never felt before.

Josh climbed on the bed, covering her body with his. He leaned over, taking her mouth in a hungry kiss. She could taste herself on his lips and tongue, a tangy cream. Could he taste Grim on her? There was something wickedly exciting about the idea that even now they were all together. She and Josh were kissing, but Grim was on her tongue. Josh kissed her until she was breathless, and she could feel the arousal he'd satisfied flaring back. She'd had the most powerful orgasm of her life, and she already felt the need again.

What were these men doing to her?

It didn't matter. All her questions fled as she felt Josh's cock at her pussy. He'd joked about how big Grim was, but Josh was huge, too. She whimpered as he started to breach her.

"You okay, baby?" Josh held himself still.

She didn't want him to stop. She tilted her pelvis up, forcing him deeper inside.

Josh groaned, and his head fell forward. "Oh, baby, later on we're going to have such a talk about who's in charge of this. But I can't stop for discipline tonight. I have to have you."

His hips flexed, and she groaned as his cock filled her up. She was deliciously stretched. Nicole wriggled, trying to get used to the feel of him. Then she felt something hard against her back.

"Baby, you're going to make me come all over again. I hope that shower is functional because you're getting dirty tonight," Grim vowed.

They wanted to cover her with them, with evidence of their desire for her. She welcomed it. She wrapped her legs around Josh as he started to thrust inside her.

It felt so fucking good to be between them. It made her wonder what it would be like if Grim was in her… Had she thought about having Grim in her ass? She'd never considered anal sex, but it might be worth it to have them both inside her.

Then she wasn't thinking about anything but Josh's big cock

sliding inside her over and over again, about Grim's hands on her breasts, his mouth next to her ear as he told her how sexy she was, how much he wanted her.

How he couldn't wait for his turn.

They weren't words she'd ever thought she would hear. She certainly wouldn't have told anyone they would be so sexy her pussy would clench at the thought. Those words Grim whispered shot straight to her soul in a way she hadn't realized she needed. They made her feel wanted, protected, precious.

Beloved.

This had never been her fantasy. She'd never thought beyond finding a nice guy to settle down with, to build a life with. The sex would be more for him, the affection for her.

But this sex was affectionate. This sex was centered around her in a profound way.

Josh kissed her again before he twisted his hips, and her breath caught in her chest.

His lips kicked up in the sweetest, sexiest smirk. "There it is. That's your sweet spot, baby."

She hadn't known she had one of those, but Josh Barnes was proving she did. Her clitoris had gotten a workout, but this spot deep inside her threatened to overpower everything.

Josh settled in and worked over her, his gorgeous face a mask of desire. For her. For what she could give him. Them.

"Don't hold back," Grim commanded. "You give us everything. I don't care who hears."

After all she'd had to listen to, she didn't care either. She'd been a quiet church mouse all her life, and now she wanted to shout to the heavens. When the orgasm enveloped her, she called out their names over and over again, called them out until Josh's body went stiff, his rhythm losing its precision as he obviously careened over the edge. His jaw tightened and he pumped into her, grinding against her and giving her a glorious aftershock of pleasure.

She lay back, spent in Grim's arms. Josh's head fell to her breast.

A deep sense of peace overtook her as she laid her hands on Josh's silky hair.

They were hers. Even if only for a little while.

Chapter Five

Josh yawned as he rolled over in bed and reached for Nicole.

Damn, but there was nothing he loved more than waking up with a soft, sweet woman in between him and Grim. It was even better this time because something real had happened between the three of them the night before. Every gut instinct he had told him last night was a turning point for him. Like the day he'd found Grim hiding in the dorm in the back field. He'd known something had changed and his life wouldn't be the same again. This morning was another of those moments. Things had changed.

The curtains were closed, but there was a thin stream of light that let him know it was long past sunrise.

Which didn't matter because it was Sunday, and he didn't have to be at work this Sunday. He was absolutely certain his sister had already given their parents the news he and Grim had found someone new and likely wouldn't be around for Sunday dinner.

Nicole sighed in her sleep and settled her head against his chest.

In the low light he could see the way her chest moved slowly, gracefully, in her sleep, how her long lashes laid against her cheeks. She was soft in sleep, the wariness he'd sensed the night before gone.

What was she hiding?

It didn't matter. He would figure it out and then he and Grim would fix the problem and they would all discover if this thing between them could work.

He already knew the answer, but he needed to pretend to be unsure. He'd found sometimes his utter confidence could be a bit off-putting. So he would smile and tell her they were feeling things out, and in a couple of months he'd slip a collar around her neck and a ring on her finger and voila, future secured.

There was a buzzing sound to his right. His cell. With a sigh, he reached over and grabbed it. It was a text. From his sister.

Momma says you should bring Nicole to Sunday dinner.

He bit back a growl. His parents could be intrusive at times. It was all the love and healthy attachment and crap that most of his other friends didn't have to deal with. Most parents wouldn't want to meet the woman their son had shared with his best friend the night before, but not Abigail Barnes-Fleetwood. Nope. She would want to welcome that woman and likely tell her too many stories about how deeply focused he'd been as a child.

It wasn't his fault he knew who he was and what he wanted. At the age of four.

He quickly typed back.

No. We're not scaring this one off.

His sister sent back a rolling eyes emoji.

Fine but you tell Momma yourself. And don't be surprised if Grim gets an emergency call. Pops and Dad have been down in the barn since daybreak. Something's happening with one of the bred heifers, and they're trying to take care of it themselves.

Josh groaned and let his head fall back.

His fathers were a menace. Why the hell had they sent Grim through college to become a vet if they didn't want him to do his job?

He didn't want to go home right now. They needed time to cuddle her, to take her to breakfast and spend the day with her. He got the feeling she was going to view the night before as some crazy one off despite what he and Grim had told her. The last thing he wanted was for her to retreat after all the progress they'd made.

But he also didn't want his dads to throw out some piece of their aged anatomy because they were too stubborn to call.

We'll be there in twenty. Don't let them hurt themselves.

He rolled out of bed after gently disentangling himself from Nicole. Maybe they could take care of the situation and still spend the afternoon with her. He could go with Grim and if he wasn't needed, come back and pick her up. He could take her out to the house and show her around.

And fuck her again. Definitely fuck her again. If there was a way to gently ease her into staying with them, he would find it. He wanted her out of this rathole as soon as possible, but she was a skittish thing.

"Grim, we have to go. Pops and Dad are playing vet," he said quietly, not wanting to disturb her.

Grim's eyes came open, and he groaned. "Damn it. I was worried about one of the bred heifers. She's been off her feed for a couple of days."

Josh dressed quickly and then leaned over. Nicole was in the center of the bed, blankets tucked around her and looking so soft and sweet his heart actually clenched.

Damn, but she might be the one. The real one. They might be ready to really start their lives.

"Hey, baby, I'm taking Grim back to the ranch," he whispered.

Her lips curled up, but her eyes stayed closed. "Okay."

"I'm coming back as soon as I can. I'll take you to breakfast and then we'll head out to our place." He smoothed her hair back.

She yawned and turned over. "Sleep."

"Yeah, baby, you sleep. I'll be back before you know it." He leaned over and kissed her forehead before pushing off the bed.

"I don't want to leave her, but if we've got some kind of virus about to go through the herd…" Grim began.

"Then you have work to do, brother." Josh pulled his boots on. "I'll stay as long as you need me, but I'd like to come back."

Grim nodded. "Yeah. I think we should stay close to her for the next couple of days."

He finished dressing and moved for the door, his voice low. "I do, too. Did you notice she seemed to be having a bad dream earlier?"

Grim closed the door behind them and made sure it locked. "Yeah, she was saying a name. I didn't catch it."

"Michael, maybe. She was scared of him." Josh looked back at the door. "Maybe we should take her with us."

"Let her sleep. I get the feeling she doesn't do a lot of it," Grim said, keys to the truck in hand. "Hopefully we're panicking for nothing and I won't need your help. You can come right back and bring her out for Sunday dinner."

"And let my momma scare the crap out of her?" What was Grim thinking?

"Abby is the best," Grim countered. "She doesn't scare anyone."

"My momma will start planning a wedding by dessert, and she'll start talking baby names shortly after."

Grim shrugged as he hauled himself into the driver's seat. "I don't have a problem with it."

Josh sighed and got in. "I don't think it's going to be easy. I think we're going to have to slow play this with her."

Grim put the truck in reverse as a tall blonde stepped out of the door next to Nicole's. She glanced up and down the street and then started for the office. "Don't you want to get her out of here? Although the new guest looks like she doesn't belong here either."

Maybe the clientele was changing. Or the blonde hadn't realized what a dump the place was when she booked it online. If this motel even had a website. "Damn straight. I'm planning on getting her out of here as soon as possible, but we have to be tricky about it. We need a game plan, brother."

"Well, we're pretty good at coming up with one of those." Grim started down the highway that would take them to the ranch. "You'll come back and hang with her while I deal with the problem. And I'll talk to Abby and ask her to curb her enthusiasm. But I don't think feeding Nicole is going to scare her off."

No. She'd eaten everything they'd put in front of her the night before, and she'd done it with relish. Like food had been nothing but a necessity for a while now. Like she hadn't indulged in a long time.

They talked about how to gently ease her into the relationship as they drove to the ranch. When they pulled in, the first thing Josh saw was his pops stepping out of the big barn, a concerned look on his face. Sam Fleetwood was a sunny man who smiled most of the time, so his expression had Josh sitting up.

"Damn it." Grim parked the truck, obviously getting the same vibes he was.

Josh followed him, slamming the door behind him. Olivia was walking out from the main house, carrying two bottles of water. Grim jogged across the lawn toward the barn, but Josh caught his sister.

"What's going on?"

Olivia kept walking. "I don't know. Dad's been cussing up a storm, and Pops is worried. They were going to call Grim in, but I told them you were already on the way. They didn't want to disturb you."

"I'm supposed to be disturbed," Grim called out. "I'm a damn doctor. I did not go to seven years of school for fun."

Grim took that shit seriously, as his father was about to be reminded.

Pops nodded as Grim ran inside then turned to Josh. "It's not good. She won't stop vomiting. I have no idea what the hell is going on. I'm heading out to the pasture she's been in to see if she could have gotten into something she shouldn't have."

"I'll go with you. I'll grab the ATV," Olivia offered. "Mom told me to make sure you're hydrated." She pressed one bottle into Pop's hand and gave the other to Josh. "Make sure Dad gets this, and I've got my cell if you need me. Mom's inside. She could not handle the smell."

Josh stepped inside the barn and could understand his mother's hesitation. The acrid smell of vomit reached his nose, and he had zero idea how his father and Grim were standing there like it didn't affect them.

"I need to take some samples, but she's been ingesting something toxic," Grim said, dropping to one knee. The heifer was lying on her side, her swollen belly obvious. "I don't know if we're going to lose the calf or not. It depends on what she's been eating."

"Sam's going out to investigate," his father said. He looked up as Josh walked in. "Hey. I'm sorry to call you. I know you were on a date."

"It's fine." He wondered how long his father had been up. Likely since dawn. His fathers still rose early, the cowboy in them so deeply ingrained it was hard for them to take time off. "I'm going to help out here and then go back and pick her up. I thought she could come to Sunday dinner, if Mom can refrain from embroidering her name on the family quilt."

The words brought a smile to his father's eyes. "You know she only wants you to be happy."

"I think sometimes she's pointing out I'm not getting any younger and she already had Lexi by my age. Well, Lexi was already in grade school by my age." He put a hand over his nose. "She does not understand how hard it is for two men to find a wife. She had it easy."

His father put a hand on his shoulder and led him back out. "Don't you say that around her. You know she's had it hard, and it's never stopped. And you need to think about your momma's experience when it comes to dating this young lady. What do we know about her?"

"I know I care about her," Josh admitted. "I know I felt an instant connection to her."

A brow rose over his dad's eyes. "And after a single night you want to bring her to meet your family?"

"Yeah."

His father shook his head, a chuckle coming from his mouth. "Well, sometimes this old world pays us back in ways we didn't dream of. I can't talk you out of this, can I?"

Josh shrugged. "If you don't want to meet her, it's okay. You give me a date when my feelings will be valid to you, and I'll mark it on my calendar."

His father sighed. "See, that is karma biting me in the ass because I can't exactly give you a lecture on how stubborn you're being. I knew your momma was the one for me and Sam after our first date. Sam knew before I did. But you need to be sure before you start parading her around town."

"She said she doesn't care. She knows what we want." Josh had told her, but he wasn't so sure she'd taken them seriously. If he had to guess, she hadn't been treated well in relationships before, and it wouldn't be the first time a man had lied to a woman to get into her bed.

Which was why she should have woken up next to him.

"Knowing what you want and dealing with being in a nontraditional relationship are two different things," his father said. "I think it's safe to say it hasn't bothered me or Sam, and your momma has made a happy life for herself here, but she was older and more settled into who she is. She'd seen a lot, and those experiences built her confidence. I know it was hard on her when she was younger."

Because his mother had been born in Willow Fork, and she'd had a relationship with the richest boy in town as a teen. She'd been pregnant with Lexi when he'd died, and Abigail Moore had been driven out of Willow Fork. She'd found a way to put herself through school and build a life for herself and her daughter. She'd only come back to Willow Fork when her mom needed help, and then she'd met his dads.

The thought of Nicole being put through the same treatment made his heart clench. "You don't think it was worth it to Momma?"

"I know it was." His father gave him a sympathetic look. "But like I said, she was older and more settled. It's hard for you to understand because you came out of the womb knowing exactly who you are and making not one damn apology for it. I'm afraid you got that from me, and coupled with the stable childhood we managed to give you, it's made you far more centered and grounded than I was at your age. For a long time Sam was my focus and this ranch was ours. We didn't even think about marrying a woman until we were well into our thirties and we loved one who could handle everything we needed."

"Dad, say what you need to say and say it plainly." He wanted to get to the heart of whatever was bothering his father. "You don't think she can handle the pressure that will come with being in a nonconventional relationship. You don't even know her."

"No, but I know people, and I know if you've never had a ménage relationship in your life, it can be hard to wrap your head around," his father said.

The whole conversation was making Josh antsy. "So you think we shouldn't ever get married."

"I think you know a lot of women who have been around these types of relationships, who won't think twice about loving two men. Whose families won't blink at the relationship."

He knew exactly who his father was talking about. Most of his father's closest friends were in similar relationships. They understood both ménage and BDSM because their parents lived the lifestyle. He knew damn well his fathers and their friend Julian Lodge would have been thrilled if he and Grim had hit it off with Chloe Lodge-Taylor, but they were just friends. The same had been true with Greer and Harlow Dawson, the daughters of Ben and Natalie and Chase Dawson. They felt more like his sisters.

"But Nicole's the one I feel for."

"All right, then you need to pursue it," his father said with a nod. "But be careful with her and be patient with her. Watch her because sometimes our women try to spare us by not telling us they've been hurt. She will get looked at differently."

He didn't understand. "There are women my age who go through guys like they're sampling chocolate, but if they're from the right family, no one questions them. If they're from the wrong family, they're whores. I can sleep with anyone I want and I'm just a guy sowing his oats. Nicole should be able to do anything she likes and as long as she's not hurting someone, the world shouldn't have a damn opinion."

"I agree with you, son, but that's not how this town works, and it likely never will. I think most of the younger generation is better, but even there you've got mean girls and assholes who will find it fun to ruin her."

His heart ached at the thought. "I don't want to ruin her."

"You won't ruin her," a familiar voice said. Pops was leaning against the barn door. "Your dad is forgetting so much of our courtship. I know Abby was older and more settled, but she also had been through all of this before, and I know damn well it scared her. Not once did your dad think of backing down. Do you know why? Because he knew we were good for her. I would have moved her out of here if she couldn't handle it because she was the center of our lives. Don't let worry get in your head. Grim will do enough of that for the both of you. Remember one thing. You are a king in this town, and if they don't respect your queen, they can accept the consequences."

Willow Fork, for all it liked to look down on the Barnes-Fleetwood family's unconventional relationship, was also dependent on them. The two biggest employers in the town were the Barnes-Fleetwood Collective and The Willow Fork Tranquility Spa and Resort. For the most part his parents were completely reasonable.

But there was a time to be ruthless. He would never threaten someone's job for not liking him. But if someone tried to cut Nic down to size, he would show them what he could do. "I understand. I'll get the word out. No one messes with her or they get to deal with me."

"They get to deal with your family," Pops said. "All of us."

His father nodded. "All of us. I'm sorry, son. I guess the truth is I'm older and feel like I have more to lose. Your sister already spends most of her time either in Bliss or Dallas, and I don't like the idea of you and Grim leaving, too."

"We live here, Dad. I mean at some point we're going to want to add on to the house, but neither one of us has any intention to move," he pointed out.

"You might have to if Nicole can't get what she needs here," his father countered.

"What else could she need? She won't need money." This was a ridiculous argument. "It's early. Can we not borrow trouble?"

"There won't be any trouble you can't handle," Pops said. "Between you and Grim, you'll take care of anything that goes down. Now, I found the problem, and it could be bigger than we think."

"You already went out to the back field?" He knew Pops was spry, but that was fast.

"No, I didn't have to. I got a call from Jim Hazelton. He sells us alfalfa, and it looks like somehow our last shipment was contaminated," Pops explained.

Grim walked out, pulling off a pair of latex gloves. "Let me guess. Blister beetles?"

"And that is why you're the smart one, son," Dad replied. "How fucked are we?"

"I think we caught it early enough." Grim started for the barn door. "But I'm going to need some hands to help me check the rest of the herd. Josh, we need to set up for exams and then you take a shower and get out of here. You made a promise to our girl. Go and get her. Maybe spending the day examining cattle will be fun for her."

It wouldn't, but it would tell him a lot about Nicole and if she could handle what they needed.

"I'll go get Momma." Olivia joined Grim. "It's going to be a fun family day."

They would earn Sunday supper, but then they always did.

Josh joined his fathers and got to work, his mind on Nicole the entire time.

* * * *

Nicole looked around the motel room and wondered why it seemed so lonely now. They'd only been here for the night. It shouldn't feel like she was missing a piece of something important.

She glanced over at the pillows on either side of her. They'd slept next to her. At least she'd thought they had. Now she wondered how much of the night before had been a dream. Not the sex, of course. She was damn sore. The sex had been real, but all the emotions had to have been one sided since they hadn't even stayed around for breakfast. For some reason, she'd thought they would stay.

Tears clouded her vision as she realized no one had left a note. She checked her crappy phone. It barely had text messaging. She'd dutifully put in their numbers the night before at the bar, and she'd given them hers. Maybe there was a message there.

Nothing.

They were gone.

Why was that such a kick in the gut? She'd known she couldn't have them for long, but now she realized how much she'd counted on having a couple of days with them, a few wild and wicked nights. Sweet nights when they made her feel like she was normal, like she was worthy.

She sat in bed for the longest time, listening to the sounds of people moving in the room next to her.

Why on earth had she believed them? She had nothing. Not a damn thing to her name. She'd given them the only thing of worth she owned—her body and her caring and affection. Why should they stay around? They were gorgeous, and she was a normal woman. Not even normal. God, she was a woman who was wanted for the murder of her husband. She should thank her lucky stars they hadn't stuck around because she was almost certain those men would be damn nosy. Their sister, too.

Had Olivia known all they wanted from her was a good time?

She was an excellent wingman. She knew exactly how to push someone into her brothers' arms. If Olivia hadn't been there, making her wait, she would have gone up to the second floor and read a book and hoped there was a job for her at the end of the night. But no, Olivia had tempted her with margaritas and nachos and friendship.

She wondered if Olivia was laughing her ass off this morning at the young woman who so obviously didn't belong anywhere at all.

Nicole pushed off the bed, dragging the sheet around her. Even alone it felt weird to be naked. It hadn't the night before, but she'd been fooling herself.

She took a shower, forcing herself to move. It didn't matter two men she barely knew were done with her. Nope. She'd had what she wanted, too.

That was how she needed to look at things. She'd gotten what she wanted and hadn't even had to deal with two needy guys.

It was perfect.

Except how was she going to feel the next time Josh came into the café? He was a regular. How was she going to feel when he came in with the kind of woman he could care about? The kind he didn't leave far before morning came.

Was their whole sharing thing a big joke? They'd made it out like they were wounded souls looking for someone who could handle their needs, but had it been a way to slip in and out of her bed?

As far as seduction techniques went, it was a good one. It had absolutely worked on her.

Now she had a whole day to waste since she wasn't scheduled

for a shift.

Her stomach growled. Why couldn't she be one of those women who wasted away when she was heartsick? Nope. When her heart hurt, she wanted pancakes. And she'd expended a ton of energy the night before.

So now she had to drag her sorry ass to the café since she didn't have any groceries here. She'd eaten her last protein bar and hadn't worked up the will to walk two miles to the store and two miles back.

She sniffled and forced herself to put on some makeup, to dry her hair and put it in a neat ponytail. Forced herself to put on clean clothes. She would go to the café and order what she could afford, and maybe if she was lucky Christa would need some help with the after-church rush. Sometimes it got overwhelming and she stepped in for an hour or two. The tips from the church crowd weren't the best, but it would pass some time. Tomorrow she would work her shift and go to the mechanic and give him the go-ahead to fix her car. By the end of the week, she would be able to pay it off and she'd be gone by the weekend.

Another few days and she would be on the road to Mexico, Josh and Grim in her rearview mirror.

Hopefully she would have learned her damn lesson.

She wished she hadn't slept so well the night before. She'd had one dream, and Grim had been there to wrap her up and ease her back to sleep. After that she'd slept like a baby, and she hadn't in so very long.

Maybe the nightmare had been the reason they hadn't hung around. Her dreams could be…upsetting.

She closed the mirrored door to the closet.

Just the night before she'd looked at herself in that mirror and watched as she'd been between Josh and Grim. She'd thought about how sexy they looked together.

Now she looked weary.

Last night she'd been ready to explore some insane new world with them, and today she was right back to the world she actually lived in, the one filled with anxiety and pain. The one where she never stopped looking over her shoulder.

She'd been fooling herself when she'd thought about taking this time and leaving. She stared at the woman in the mirror.

You thought maybe they could save you. You thought if they could love you, you might be able to tell them, and then you wouldn't be so fucking alone. Then you wouldn't have to fight this fight forever.

A deep sense of sorrow wrapped around her. If she loved them, would she want to drag them into her hell? They could get hurt or charged with aiding and abetting. No. All she was ever going to get out of those glorious men was a couple of nights.

It was better this way.

Deep breath. She was going to hold her head high. It wasn't like she cared what anyone thought.

Of course when she'd said that, she'd thought they would be together for a little while, like she would be in a relationship with them. Then she wouldn't have cared. It felt different being their latest one-night stand.

The one thing she wasn't going to do was stay hidden inside this motel room. She shoved the book she was reading in her bag. She'd picked it up at the Willow Fork Library's recent fund-raiser sale for a buck fifty. It was a fantasy romance by one of her favorite authors. Books, she'd come to realize, were a thing she couldn't give up.

She would have whatever was on special and order a lot of coffee and read her book and then she would forget about them.

She walked out into the morning light, making sure the door was locked behind her.

"Hey, neighbor," a feminine voice said. "I don't suppose you know where I could get a cheap breakfast around here?"

She glanced over and there was a lovely blonde woman wearing jeans and a T-shirt that showed off her every curve. She was definitely older than Nicole, but she had a timeless beauty that made it hard to peg her age. At least late thirties, but she could be fifty with excellent skin care and genetics. She had deep blue eyes and a friendly smile.

Nicole hadn't seen her before, so she must have gotten in yesterday. Her room had previously been rented by three men who claimed they'd come for the hunting. She wasn't sure what they'd been hunting except for beer and a fun place to sexually harass women. Having a chick next door would be a welcome change. "Christa's Café. I might be biased but my boss makes an excellent breakfast, and it's not expensive. Nothing around here is, really. Except car repairs."

"Don't I know it," the woman commiserated. "Car repairs are hell anywhere. I'm Heather, by the way. I'm here for a couple of weeks. My mom lives close by, but my sister's already staying there, and I am not about to sleep with her and five dogs. This was the only motel in town."

The last was said with a sad sigh.

"Yeah, like I said most things around here are cheap, and you should be careful." The woman looked out of place here. Probably like she herself did.

She'd felt like her place had been in between Josh and Grim. She'd been so perfect in between them, their hard bodies sheltering hers.

And now they were gone and Cinderella was right back to work. Hopefully.

"Oh, because of the…" Heather gestured around. "Clientele? Yeah, I think someone was working last night on the other side of me. Hard, if you know what I mean."

She felt her whole body flush. "I'm so sorry. The walls are thin."

A grin lit the woman's face. "Not you, honey. No. I'm talking about the other side."

Nicole felt a wave of relief. "Oh, you're talking about Claudine. Yeah, she's a sex worker, and a diligent one, too. Nice lady, though." She frowned. "I don't know why I said *though*. Like a sex worker can't be nice."

"It's shitty what society drills into us, isn't it?" Heather asked, her expression turning thoughtful. "Personally, I want to thank her for her service because I saw some of the men she met with last night, and she is helping the world."

"It's definitely work." Work she hadn't had to find. Yet. It was funny how much more she understood Claudine. Before, she likely would have viewed her as a person to avoid. Claudine was funny and nice. When Nicole had first gotten into Willow Fork, Claudine had been the one to tell her to go to Christa's if she wanted a job. Of course she'd first asked her if she wanted to tag team some of her clientele, but after a gentle if shocked rejection, she'd come up with a more reasonable plan. "I'm walking to Christa's if you want to come along. It's not far. About four blocks."

It would be good to have someone to talk to. If she didn't, she would likely think about them the whole time. She wasn't cut out for casual sex.

It hadn't felt casual.

"I could use a good walk," Heather said with a brilliant smile. She opened the door to her room and reached in, coming back with a purse in her hand. It was a designer thing that was completely out of place here in this dilapidated motel.

It was a Chanel. The classic quilted shopper. She'd had one once. Her mother-in-law had told her it might help people forget she wasn't one of them. Rich and well bred, she'd explained. Wearing the right clothes and carrying the right bag could help her fit in. And also, she should have some plastic surgery to fix that nose of hers.

There was nothing wrong with her nose. If there had been or she'd been insecure about it, she wouldn't have had a problem with surgery. Whatever got a person through a day and all, but she'd never felt bad about her nose until her mother-in-law made the comment.

Nicole stared at that bag as Heather locked up. "You know there's a bed and breakfast across town. And a resort about ten miles outside of town. I've heard it's real nice there."

Heather frowned and then seemed to realize what the problem was. She gave the bag a shake. "This is straight off Canal Street. Well, the Denver equivalent. Don't tell on me, please. I like to think of it as faking it 'til I make it, if you know what I mean. And I looked into the spa. It looks amazing and also super expensive. I'm afraid this is what I can afford." Her smile was back. "I've got a car if you want a ride."

She glanced over to where Heather gestured. The car was obviously a rental, and it was small and compact. It didn't go with the handbag either. That handbag should be attached to a Benz at the very least. Maybe Heather was telling the truth, but Nic was still wary. "I like the fresh air. Thanks. But you should try Christa's."

"I will." She moved in beside Nicole. "And honestly, I could use the fresh air, too. I have to be out at the hospital in a couple of hours, and it always makes me feel like I'm in a tomb."

She softened at the other woman's words. It had to be hard to take care of someone you loved. She started down the street, the commute familiar and soothing. "Sure. You can join me."

This place wasn't scary in the light of day. She was fairly certain most of the bad elements were sleeping now, but it was nice to have someone to walk with.

"So why are you hanging around the motel? Do you have family here?" Heather asked.

"No," Nicole replied as they started down Main Street. "I don't have any family. I was married and when my husband died, I decided to take off for a while. See some of the world. My car broke down and I was pretty much out of cash, so I got a job and here I am."

"You must have loved him a lot." Heather said the words with a hint of longing. As though she knew what it meant to miss someone.

"I didn't. He was an abusive bastard, and I was lucky to get out alive." Somehow she couldn't lie today. Last night had stripped her bare. "I'm sorry. That's a lot for a new friend. I'm a little raw today. My husband wasn't a nice man. He was kind of a bait and switch. He love bombed the hell out of me, swept me off my feet, and once there was a ring on my finger, he started tearing me down inch by inch."

It should have been a lesson to her. Men were willing to say and do a lot to get the sex they wanted. The truth was she was lucky Josh and Grim hadn't wanted to play nastier games with her. They'd talked about spanking her and tying her up, and in the heat of the moment, it had seemed like a good idea, but hadn't she learned?

"I'm sorry to hear that," Heather said. "I'm married, too. My husband had some anger issues in the beginning, but he worked through them."

"Well, mine didn't get the chance." She couldn't tell this woman she'd just met her life story. She'd been honest enough for the day. "He had a heart attack."

Heather sighed, a sympathetic sound. "I don't know what I would do without my husband. He's a rock. When Mom got sick he put me on a plane and told me to do whatever I needed to do. He's back home with our kids. We have two. A son and a daughter. My son is twenty-two so he doesn't need much, but my baby girl is fourteen going on forty-four. She's going to kill me."

Heather seemed pleasant enough. Nicole fell into an easy walk beside her, trying to focus on what she was saying. She was from Colorado where she worked as a nature guide. They turned down the street that would lead them to Christa's, and Nicole noticed the church was letting out. She'd slept way too long.

She hated this particular church crowd. There were several churches in Willow Fork. This one tipped the least and complained the most.

Heather was talking about her mom, but Nicole got distracted by the young woman staring at her from the churchyard like she was some bug she wanted to step on.

What was her name? She'd come into the café several times and was always giving off mean-girl vibes. Usually she ignored Nicole because she didn't seem to see "staff" as worthy of attention until someone screwed up her order.

She wore her Sunday best—a dress that showed off her blonde hair and fit body, and heels that looked like they would be hard to walk in. Alyssa. That was her name.

Alyssa proved she was used to those heels as she strode across the lawn, making a beeline for…damn it. Nicole. That woman was coming her way, and it looked like there was a hell of a bee in her bonnet.

"Hey, waitress," she called out.

"Do you know her?" Heather asked.

"Not really." What was happening? Everyone seemed to be staring at her, talking behind their hands, whispering to one another.

"You whore," Alyssa said, her pretty face flushed with anger. She pointed a perfectly manicured finger Nicole's way.

"Try again." Heather suddenly sounded like a woman who could force someone to change their mind.

Alyssa ignored her. "Everyone knows you took Josh and that freak Grim back to your motel last night. I don't give a damn about Grim. Please take him, but Josh is mine."

Did this woman think she cared about what a bunch of uptight assholes thought of her? She'd meant what she'd said the night before. If she'd been with them, she wouldn't hide. She'd gone through so much worse. "I did not see your name tattooed on him. Did you write it in pen or something? Because he seems to shower on a regular basis, and pen will wash off. You should get that tatted up."

"Oh, we're going this way?" Heather's brows had risen, and there was a smile on her face. "I thought I was going to have to defend you."

"I'm not as mousy as I look." She wasn't mousy at all, but she didn't normally like to draw attention to herself. However if Alyssa wanted to throw down, she could do it. After all, she'd be gone soon, and it didn't look like anyone else was going to challenge her. "Alyssa, does Josh know he's yours? Because he did not act like he knew last night, and I don't think you're going to get far with him if you don't take on Grim. He's not a freak, by the way. He's a lovely man."

Who hadn't wanted her the way she'd hoped, but she wasn't going to let this woman disparage him.

"You're not even ashamed," Alyssa said like it was the most shocking thing in the world.

"That I am an adult single woman who had blindingly spectacular sex with two incredibly hot men? No. I'm fine with that. Now if you don't mind, I'm trying to get to the café."

"You think you'll still have a job after what you've done?" Alyssa asked, crossing her arms over her chest. "I don't think the good people of this town will want you serving them when they hear how you spend your nights in bars picking up men and taking them from women who would be good wives. I think I'll have a talk with your boss."

"You mean the woman who is basically my mother's sister?" a deep voice asked. Josh was standing there. He'd parked a big SUV right in front of the church and he'd changed clothes. He wore a fresh white T-shirt that showed off muscular arms and jeans that clung to him. His dark hair was slightly mussed as though he'd gotten out of a shower and not dried it completely, and he had the sexiest scruff along his jaw. "You're going to walk into Christa's and threaten my girlfriend's job?"

What?

"She called her a whore, too," Heather added.

Josh's eyes went positively arctic.

"I don't care, although sex worker would be more polite," Nicole replied.

"See, that's what I always say," Heather agreed, and then gave Josh a once-over. "Girl, he's hot. Is the other one…"

Nicole nodded. "Every bit matches him."

"Josh." Alyssa squared her shoulders. "I've been meaning to reach out to you. I know I hurt you when I said the things I said, but this is getting ridiculous."

"What is getting ridiculous?" Josh shook his head. "We broke up six months ago, and it isn't like we've spent a lot of time together since…let me see if I remember…I'm a massive pervert who can't expect a woman to choose him."

"So you're not tattooed with this woman's name." She wasn't sure why Josh was here, but he was. "I told her marking you with pen was a bad plan. She seemed to think I should have known you belonged to her."

"Nicole's been handling her nicely," Heather added. "I'm her new neighbor. We were going to breakfast, and then we were playing out some weird *Scarlet Letter* thing."

Josh stared out over the lawn where a good portion of the town was staring right back at him. "Just so we're clear, I know how this town treated my momma when she came back and married my dads. She's been happily married for over twenty years, not that it means anything to you people. What you need to understand is if you're going to have a problem with Nicole, you're going to have a problem with me. Understand I will hear every name you call her, write down every single one of you who makes her feel bad, and there will be a reckoning. You think my daddy could be ruthless, you haven't met me yet. I'm Jack Barnes with a deep sense of privilege. I'm Sam Fleetwood, who knows no one's sending me to jail. And while we're at it, stop talking about Grim like he's some kind of freak. He's one of the smartest men in this town, and we're lucky to have him. The next time your poodle can't crap, don't bug Grim. Do I make myself clear?"

The crowd broke up and quietly started moving away, not a one of them looking Josh in the eyes.

"Well, everyone told me you were bad news and not much of a gentleman," Alyssa pouted.

"I might not be much of a gentleman, but I know what's mine, and I take care of it. You are not mine so I don't care." Josh started walking Nicole's way. "But this one is, and she is not where I left her. Miss Heather, thanks for helping her out, but she's got a date she seems to have forgotten."

"I didn't forget any…" She gasped as Josh hefted her over his shoulder like a sack of flour. Her ass was suddenly in the air, and his hand came down in a resounding arc.

"That was for not calling to tell me you were leaving," Josh announced.

"Oww," she said, though it hadn't truly hurt. It had sparked against her flesh. "I'm going to breakfast with my new friend. I was walking her to Christa's when that nasty woman accosted me."

Josh turned and started for the SUV. "Christa's is that way, ma'am. Sorry to take your breakfast friend, but she's coming with me. And now I know to tattoo my name across her ass so she'll remember who she belongs to."

Nicole held her head up and saw Heather waving, a grin on her face like she'd enjoyed the show.

Well, it was obvious they'd had a breakdown in communication, and Josh was a little overstimulated.

And he had the nicest ass.

She enjoyed the view while she could.

Chapter Six

Josh settled her into the seat, his gut in knots.

What the hell had gone wrong? It was a nice Sunday outside. He'd looked forward to spending more time with his brand-spanking-new girlfriend, and this time maybe they would get to the actual spanking. In his head he'd seen a nice breakfast, showing her around the ranch, watching Sunday football, sneaking off to fuck her again, and then Sunday dinner and more fucking. Very wholesome, with a side of perversion. Sure it had gone off track, but damn, he hadn't expected to see the entire congregation of the Willow Fork Baptist Church standing on the lawn, basically pointing and calling his girl a whore.

And what the hell had gotten into Alyssa's head?

"Are you okay?" This was everything his father had warned him about.

Nicole frowned up at him. "Well, I'm intimidated by you now."

Damn it. He'd been careful with her. He'd been polite and a gentleman. Sure he'd eaten her pussy and shared her with his best friend, but she hadn't seen his ruthless side. "I scared you."

Those gorgeous eyes of hers rolled. "I'm not scared, Josh. I'm annoyed. You and Grim left me and then you roll in like you own me or something. I was getting breakfast with my new friend. You're the one who chose to leave, so we didn't have plans. I'm not going to let you walk in and out whenever you want. So I would appreciate it if you would move out of my way and let me get back to my friend."

He felt his jaw clench. Damn it. He did not need her attitude this minute. She was obviously under some misconceptions. He'd been surprised when he'd gotten to the motel and found her gone. Lucky for him, he knew she'd be on foot, and it wasn't like downtown Willow Fork was hard to search. Of course there was one thing he hadn't been able to do. "Why didn't you answer your phone? I tried to call you."

Her eyes widened slightly. So she thought she had the upper hand in this minor argument. "It was almost out of battery. I forgot to charge it last night, but I checked before I left. You hadn't called me as of twenty minutes ago."

"You didn't charge your phone?" She was a woman living alone in a dangerous part of town. She needed her phone.

Now those gorgeous brown orbs narrowed in irritation. "Well, I had my mind on other things last night. I was too busy following other orders. Orders like *sit on my dick, Nicole*. *Ride me hard, Nicole*. Not once did either of the bossy men pause the sex to tell me to charge my phone, and if you say it should be unspoken or something, you're going to get the same sass I gave your evil ex. You are the one who left without a call when my phone still had a baby bit of charge, and you decided not to leave a note."

This was where he was confused. "I told you we had an emergency when we left."

Her head shook. "No, you didn't."

"Yes, I woke you up. At least I thought I did. My sister called because we have a sick bred heifer, and Grim is the vet. My dads are good at what they do, but they don't have Grim's skill." It had been a shitty morning. They'd figured out the problem and now had another twenty head to worry about. "I didn't want to leave you."

Her expression had softened. "I'm sorry. I thought you left. I thought…"

"You thought we were done." He could guess what had gone through her head. He leaned over and brushed his mouth against hers. "I'm not done, baby. Not even close. I told you I would come back out after I dropped Grim off. I intended to, but they needed me."

"Well, now I seem all full of myself and selfish since I did kind of curse your name a little."

He felt his lips tug up. "Just a little?"

She flushed a pretty pink. "Okay. I was hurt when I woke up and you weren't there. I told myself it wasn't like you promised me anything."

That was where she was wrong. He slid a hand along her jawline, tilting her head up so she had to look him in the eyes. "I promised you a lot last night, and I intend to fulfill every single one."

This time when he kissed her, he didn't hold back. He let his tongue run along her lips until she opened them and let him in. He was well aware that they were in public, but he wasn't about to hold back. She needed to know how it was going to be. His father was wrong. He understood what his dad had been trying to tell him, but Nicole could handle it. She'd handled Alyssa with ease from what he could tell.

Of course her bravado might be exactly that.

He pulled back, staring down at her. Damn, but he loved her face. He searched it to see if she was holding anything back on him. "Baby, are you okay?"

"Well, I am now," she replied, her fingers coming up to brush over his cheek. "I was way more upset when I thought you used me. But now I'm upset because I realized you have terrible taste in women."

Someone moved behind him. People were walking all up and down the street, and there was no way they were missing this scene. He'd made his point, but now he needed to get her away from here. "I'm going to be honest. Alyssa was my mistake. She was a nice girl when we were in high school, though we didn't go to the same one. If we had, I might have picked up on her mean-girl vibes. My parents kept a pretty protective circle around my sister and I, and later Grim. We went to a private school, and most of our friends had parents who were active in my parents' lifestyle. So I didn't spend a ton of time with her. Mostly at parties. I remembered her being real sweet. She came back from living in Austin for a couple of years, and I asked her out. It obviously did not work. I'd like credit for having better taste now. And, baby, I can make sure she never says a bad word around you ever again."

"I'm not sure I want to know how you would do that, Joshua Barnes." She reached over and grabbed the seatbelt, clicking herself in. "I hope you have breakfast where we're going. And that Grim's there."

There was the difference. What he hadn't told her was that Alyssa was sweet as pie to him. She'd been a little spoiled, but affectionate, and seemed so proud to be dating him, and she changed when Grim came around.

Oh, she'd slept with him. Enthusiastically, but she'd made herself plain she didn't want anyone to know about it. Grim could be their dirty secret, but he would get pushed out when the time came to settle down.

"He's there. And I will be sure to feed you." He closed the door. If he could sneak her past his momma. He planned on sneaking her into his place and introducing her later in the afternoon. After he'd explained how his parents could be…a lot.

He could handle Alyssa fine since she worked as an accountant at the meat packing plant. The one his fathers owned, along with their business partners.

What Nicole didn't know was how much this town was reliant on his family for jobs, for economic development. If his father had wanted to, he could have burned this town to the ground when they'd tried to reject Abigail Moore. Instead she'd become Abby Barnes-Fleetwood, and over the years she'd made a place for herself here. There were some people—most of them had been standing on the church lawn a few minutes ago—that still referred to her as "that woman," but his mother sometimes seemed to revel in it.

Like Nic had a few moments before. She hadn't seemed angry or embarrassed. She'd seemed annoyed.

He shut the truck door and started around the back, ignoring the looks he received.

"Shameless," someone muttered under his breath.

Yes. He was utterly shameless since he didn't think he'd done anything to be ashamed of. They could all bite his ass, and it looked like Nic was on the same page.

Of course she thought they had a time limit. She'd told him the night before she was planning on leaving. It was why he had to rush this courtship thing along.

He had no intentions of her heading off to some other job. She didn't need a job at all. He and Grim could take care of her. He slid in beside her, something still roiling through him.

He started up the truck.

"I don't remember you waking me. I sometimes sleep pretty hard," she murmured as he started down the street. "Most of the time I don't sleep. I have trouble with it so when I finally do, I tend to be out of it."

"Yeah, you seemed to be having a nasty dream last night."

There was no way to miss the fine flush crossing her face. "Did I say anything?"

She'd said a man's name. Michael, maybe. But it wasn't said like she was missing the bastard. No. She'd begged him to stop. In the dream she'd been trying to get away from him.

It was his first real clue, but he didn't want to push her about it. Not now. "You tossed and turned and seemed scared. Once Grim got his arms around you, you settled right down."

She stared out the front windshield. "That's good to know. And it explains why I slept so hard."

"Your eyes came open and everything." She'd looked soft and sweet. "We had a brief conversation. I'm sorry. I thought you would remember. I wouldn't have left you at all if we'd had another car."

"No, it was good you went with him," she said with a nod. "I'm sure he could use another set of hands. I've never been on a ranch before. You said you lived in one of the outer buildings? But Olivia lives with your parents?"

"Yeah, Grim and I moved into the guest house when we came home from college," he explained. "It's small, but it's pretty nice."

"I'm sure it is. So your dads work on this ranch, too?"

She really didn't know. She had no idea how wealthy his family was. Olivia had mentioned it the night before. His sister had approved of Nicole and said something about finding one who wasn't either impressed or turned off by their family. Impressed by the wealth they'd accumulated or turned off by their lifestyle. Nic hadn't seemed to know anything about he and Grim. "Yeah. They've worked there for most of their adult lives. Dad and Pops did. Mom didn't come around for a little while."

How much should he tell her and how much should he let her discover?

"Ranching is hard work," she said, watching the café go by as he headed toward the highway.

"As we were reminded this morning. Every day, really," he replied. "I don't remember a time when I didn't ride fences with my dads. I was born and put straight into a saddle."

Josh couldn't remember a time when he hadn't ridden. He'd followed his dads around as a kid, waking early to get to spend time with them before his mom would drive he and Olivia to school out at the resort.

It had been a great childhood. One he wanted for his own children someday.

Yeah, that was probably a good way to scare her off, so he wouldn't mention he was already long-term life planning around her.

He could be intense, or so he'd been told.

"Do you like horses? We could take a ride this afternoon."

"I've never ridden before," Nicole admitted.

"Then I'll have to teach you." He would enjoy the lessons.

She turned in her seat, a serious expression on her face. "You know I have to leave soon. Is this even worth it? I want to spend time with you and Grim, but I have to be honest. I have to leave as soon as my car is fixed."

"Okay, if you're being honest, tell me why and where you have to go," he replied.

"I told you. I have a job waiting for me."

"A job that will wait for you while your car is being fixed but won't, say, send a car to pick you up? Or make arrangements to accommodate you?" The way Josh saw it, this story of hers made no sense. If it was an important job with a big company and they wanted her there, they would make accommodations. If it was a regular job, they likely wouldn't wait for a couple of weeks. They would fill the position and move on.

She turned, staring out the window. "It's with a friend of mine. I'll be working with her. I wasn't scheduled to start until next month. I wanted to get down there early so I can find a place to live."

She did not like him asking questions. He was pushing, and he could lose her. He needed to go about this a different way. He might have to figure out her problem on his own.

He gave her a breezy smile. "Well, I'll take any time you can give me, darlin'. I know Grim feels the same way. If we don't have a lot of time, we should make the most of it, shouldn't we?"

She seemed to study him for a moment. "I guess so. I wouldn't mind seeing the two of you while I'm here. When I'm not working, of course. I usually take extra shifts if someone wants to go home. It's not like I have anything better to do, but I have all of today off. I don't have to be in until lunch tomorrow."

"I'll make sure you get back in plenty of time. But maybe you can spend the night with us."

She turned his way, a little grin on her face. "Is your place cleaner than the motel?"

That got him smiling because it had been bad. He'd taken a hot shower after lying on that floor. "You'll find Grim and I are very orderly men."

They also had a housekeeper who thoroughly cleaned twice a week, but he didn't have to mention that. He just had to get her into their place and show her how nice it could be.

"How far do you live from your parents?"

"Not far at all." Sometimes it was too close for comfort. His dates had often gotten a wave from his family as they started for home. His parents liked to have breakfast on the patio by the pool on those days. Nosy. "Did I mention my parents can be a lot?"

"I think they sound charming." Nicole's tone had gone soft. "And they've been married for a long time. I think it says something about them. They worked hard and stayed together. It's nice you get to see them often."

Every time he opened the door or looked out the window.

"Do you live in one of those dorm things?" Nicole asked. "I read about them in a book once. The workers on the ranch all lived in a big house together. The single ones. On a big ranch there can be multiple houses for the workers. I imagine your parents live in one of those."

Did she think he was a hand? "Sweetheart, you do know my

parents own the ranch, right? When I say they work on the ranch, they're the owners. I work for my dad both in the field, and my sister and I handle a lot of the day-to-day operations of the business."

A wary look had come over her face. "I thought most ranches were corporate owned these days."

"Yes, my parents own the corporation. See. That's our name right there." He pointed out the big sign over the gates leading to the main house. Barnes-Fleetwood Ranch. It was done in a beautiful wrought iron and adorned with roses weaving in and out of the letters. The gates were open at this time of day but the security system would close them after dark, and then whoever wanted in would either need a code or to call through the intercom.

Nicole sat up straighter, her eyes widening in a way that did not seem like wonder. "Corporation?"

This was usually the time when a woman got super interested in what he did. He didn't get that feeling from her. She seemed almost wary. "Yes. We are the largest independent organic ranching collective in the country. We have partner ranches all over the States, and we collectively bargain with vendors. It's how we compete with the big guys."

She seemed to breathe a sigh of relief. "Oh, so you're a small ranch but you work together with other small ranches."

"I wouldn't say small." He moved the SUV down the long road that led to what he liked to call the commune. His parents might have started out either poor or solidly middle class, but they'd made up for lost time. He and Olivia hadn't known a home that didn't have a host of beautifully done buildings to service the vast amounts of land making up the Barnes-Fleetwood Ranch. "My dads bought this land a long time ago. They were smart enough to keep their mineral rights."

"Mineral rights?"

In the distance he could see the main house. It was a sprawling two-story home. "Yes, they bought the land with pretty much everything they had. From what I understand, they had just enough cash to buy some cattle to start. They grew from there."

"That's nice. I bet it was hard work."

"It was and is, but I think my parents would safely say it got easier when they found millions' worth of natural gas reserves."

She sat up in her seat, her eyes taking in the compound ahead of her. There was the main house with its elegant circular drive and four-car garage. Off to the side was the pretty guest house he and Grim had taken over when they'd first returned from college. The barn was barely visible, and she wouldn't be able to see the dorms because they were hidden by the house. "You're rich."

"My parents are rich," he corrected, though all of this would be his someday. His and Olivia's. His half sister, Lexi, had laughed when they'd tried to give her a third. She'd said the ranch her husband owned was more than she could handle and to leave it to her siblings.

Grim didn't know he and Olivia already planned to cut him in.

But that was a long, long way away. His parents were super healthy and would hopefully live to see a hundred and likely be the orneriest old folks ever.

"Hopefully Grim is done, though he'll likely have to check in on his patients, but otherwise, we'd like to spend the afternoon with you," he said, rounding the big house and moving to his.

"That would be nice." She said the right words, but something was going through that girl's head, and he wasn't sure he would like it.

He parked beside Grim's truck and turned her way. "Is everything okay?"

Something was different. Her breezy bratiness was gone, and there was wariness back in her eyes again.

Still, she smiled and reached to unbuckle her seatbelt. "No. I'm fine. I wasn't expecting all of this."

Then Grim was coming out of the house, opening her door and helping her out of the car.

She was lying. It was about more than expectations. His family wealth bothered her, and he wanted to know why.

Josh got out, his mind working the problem.

* * * *

Nicole let Grim practically drag her out of the cab.

"Hey, I missed you." He wrapped his big arms around her,

lifting her off her feet.

He smelled like soap and shampoo. He'd obviously recently come out of a shower since his hair was slightly wet.

She breathed him in, loving how he wrapped himself around her. How safe he made her feel. It was way too fast, but she'd missed him, too. She'd played down the hurt she'd felt, but there had been such relief when Josh had driven up and explained what had happened.

Was it all an illusion? Like the idea these were hard-working, hard-scrabble guys looking for a good time.

What had changed? She was still only here for a week or so. She still had gotten more pleasure from these men than she could have imagined. It didn't make a difference if they were rich.

Except she knew how rich people were when they didn't get what they wanted.

She was giving them what they wanted. Sex.

So nothing had changed. They had zero reason to look into her or ask a bunch of questions because she was doing exactly what they wanted. What she wanted. She was enjoying them for the time they had. So it was fine. She could be here and not worry about the fact their living situation was different than she'd thought. Honestly, if she walked away from them before she could get out of town, there would be way more questions, so she should stay.

How freaking fast her pussy could rationalize something that should send her screaming the other way.

"She thought we left her," Josh said. "She was heading out to breakfast all on her own because she is an independent woman. Also, we should watch out. She believes in tattoos as a form of proving ownership."

Grim set her down, his dark eyes looking over at Josh. "What?"

Josh had a way with words. And she couldn't forget how talented his tongue was. "I got into a verbal altercation with one of Josh's former girlfriends, who took exception to me spending the night with her intended."

Grim frowned. "Intended?"

A low groan came from Josh. "It was Alyssa. Apparently she thinks at some point I'm going to come around, and I shouldn't like have a life until I'm ready for the vanilla picket fence wedding she's planning."

"But we haven't seen Alyssa in months," Grim argued. "Why would she think that?"

"She's obviously delusional." And would probably cause trouble if Nicole was staying around long term. Of course, all of this would be a problem in the long term. She was sure Josh's parents would want to know about any woman who was with their son for more than a few weeks. People like this could hire private investigators because they wanted to keep their kids safe from people like her.

But it wasn't like she was meeting their folks. She was here for breakfast and sex, and there would likely be a football game in there somewhere since it was Sunday in Texas. She glanced over to the big house. It was probably a five-minute walk away. They would hole up in this house and likely no one would even know she was here.

So she should relax.

"Do I need to talk to her?" Grim asked.

She wasn't sure she wanted to know what Grim would have to say to Alyssa. "No. I handled it. Everything's fine, and the entire church downtown knows I don't care what they think of me."

"What exactly happened?" Grim's brow furrowed in obvious consternation.

She didn't want to go over it. Now that she was here, she wanted their time together to be peaceful. "It doesn't matter. I'm sorry I thought you guys had left me high and dry. I slept really hard and don't remember Josh telling me you had to leave. So I woke up and decided to head over to the café to see if Christa needed any help with the church crowd. I was walking with the lady in the room next to me when the Alyssa person decided she could scare me. She can't. I've been around way bigger bullies than her."

She'd been around truly dangerous people. She'd seen real evil. Alyssa was a selfish princess who thought the world revolved around her. She was young. The world would grind her down and she would either figure it out and grow or become bitter and take it out on everyone around her. Likely the latter.

"You said she called her out in front of everyone." Grim looked Josh's way, but his arm went around her shoulders.

He was such a warm man. She found herself leaning into him, but she didn't think this was as big a deal as Josh seemed to. "It was some church people. And Heather. She's the new girl. She was surprisingly cool about it. She seems real solid."

Heather hadn't looked embarrassed at all. She'd stayed at Nicole's side rather than trying to get out of the line of fire.

"It was the entire congregation," Josh explained. "There's going to be gossip."

Grim cursed under his breath. "Then my father's going to know."

"It's not like we were going to hide her," Josh replied.

She wasn't sure she completely understood, but she needed to calm her guys down. "I'm sure everyone has forgotten about it by now."

"Nicole." Olivia was jogging across the gorgeously green lawn, waving a hand. She was in jeans and a T-shirt, her auburn hair shoved into a baseball cap. "Holy crap. I got off the phone with Emmy. Did you pull out Alyssa's hair? I knew it was fake. No one's hair grows a foot in a month. Wait. That sounds like I'm shaming but I'm not. Like girl, do you, but she lies about it and makes other women feel like shit, so I can be happy you pulled her extensions out."

"What?" Nicole stepped away from Grim, surprised to see Olivia. Way more surprised to hear what she was saying.

Olivia was out of breath when she finally made it to the small house. "I just got off the phone, and it's all anyone is talking about. How Alyssa tried to pull her mean-girl act but Nicole punched her in the face and pulled her hair out. Did you keep it? Like a trophy? Because I would."

"I didn't punch anyone." What had happened? How did Olivia know? "I talked to her about twenty minutes ago."

"And then I heard Josh told everyone he would wreck their lives if they said another word about you." Olivia was grinning like this was the best thing that had ever happened. "And the preacher at the First Baptist Church held a session to pray for Josh's soul. Now I heard that, but I also heard one where he's actually trying to find a way to exorcise you. I don't think he knows what that really means."

"It means he thinks I'm the devil, and he's right when it comes to this," Josh said.

"Josh didn't threaten anyone." Mostly. He'd been intimidating, but she wouldn't call it threatening, exactly.

"Oh, I'm sure he did," Grim countered. "You remind them who runs this town, brother?"

"I did, and I believe my point was made," Josh affirmed.

Who runs this town….

Who do you think runs this town, Nicole? It's certainly not you, so you can try to go to the police or a judge, but my family owns them all. So get back in the house and keep your mouth shut.

A chill went through her.

"It wasn't made very well if they still talked about her," Grim pointed out.

Josh shook his head. "I can't stop gossip and you know it. All I can do is make it clear that she's protected."

"He's right about the gossip. This town runs on it," Olivia added. "Hey, it's not a big thing. Believe me. As the focus of so much gossip, I happen to know that something else will happen and they'll…well, I wouldn't say forget, but they will move on. I heard Andrew Kohl is coming back from LA with his tail between his legs and a potential venereal disease, though I'm pretty sure his momma thinks you get that from crossing the border into California. She's not very cosmopolitan, if you know what I mean."

"Everyone's talking about me?" Nicole heard the quaver in her voice.

"They're talking about me, darlin'. It's what they do. They talk about my family." Josh pulled her into a hug. "I'm sorry. This is my fault."

It wasn't, but it was her problem. If people talked, then they asked questions. If they asked the right questions, then they could blow up her existence.

"Hey, you're shaking," Josh said, concern in his voice. "What's going on, baby?"

She tried to ignore the anxiety sparking through her. Normal. She had to pretend to be a normal woman who didn't lose it at the thought of a little gossip. She was trapped. If she'd known how wealthy they were, she would have avoided them, but she hadn't, and now there were feelings involved. Dumping them would bring up more questions.

And she didn't want to. She wanted these days. She could go into the shop tomorrow and give them the down payment and be out of town by the end of the week. She'd thought to build up some more cash, but that wasn't possible now. A couple of days wouldn't hurt, especially if she kept a low profile.

Yes, she could still make this work, and she should since walking away would cause them to get curious. She was fairly certain she didn't want to deal with a curious Josh.

"I'm fine though I'm not good with confrontations." She actually didn't mind them anymore. She'd been a mouse, but a couple of years as a fugitive had taught her where to spend the few fucks she had left.

She'd liked standing up to Alyssa. It made her feel seen, and she so often felt like a shadow clinging to the corner of wherever she happened to be. She'd felt like she had backup from Heather, and then Josh had charged in.

Josh stared down at her like he was trying to ensure she wasn't keeping anything from him. "All right, but I expect you to come to me if anything happens. If Alyssa comes near you, I want you to call me."

She nodded. He'd put his number into her phone the night before, and so had Grim.

Something changed in Josh's eyes, his gaze going from concerned to hot in an instant. As though the minute he decided she was all right, his intentions turned. "Olivia, Grim and I are going to fix some breakfast for our…for Nicole."

The way he was looking at her she felt more like she was about to be breakfast. And just like that all her serious thoughts fled and her pussy took over. Grim was at the door, opening it and offering to take her inside.

"Oh, you don't have to do that. Momma has some…" Olivia blushed. "Okay, ewww. I'm going back to see if the dads need any help. I'll let them know you are unavailable."

Josh simply flashed his sister a grin. "For many hours."

Olivia was walking away. "Eww. That's not for you, Nic. They're my brothers. I think they're gross. You have fun because they aren't your brothers."

She sort of heard Olivia, but it didn't matter because she was stuck on the look in Josh's eyes. This was what passion felt like, what real sexual chemistry meant. All these men had to do was look at her and she felt ready. Her body softened, brain going fuzzy.

"Go on inside. I need a minute. We're going to start your training, and I need to be in control," Josh said. "Go with Grim."

Something about the way he said the words had her obeying without her usual questions. Maybe it was the word *need* coming from him. He'd given her all the things she'd needed over the course of the last night and this morning. She wanted to do the same for him.

Grim's hand covering hers helped make walking away from Josh easier.

He led her inside their house. They'd made it sound like some small bachelor pad, but the place was huge and light and airy. It was beautiful, and she couldn't help but look around.

Her trepidation was back. These people had serious cash.

"Hey, look at me." Grim got into her space. "I fucking missed you. I've spent the morning dealing with vomiting cows, and I told myself if I got through it I would clean myself up and be ready for you. You are a sight, gorgeous."

He made her feel that way. Grim was so big and masculine. He'd taken a shower but he hadn't shaved, and she loved the dark, bristly hair that clung to his jawline. She reached up and brushed her fingers over his light scruff. This was what she'd missed the night before, being able to explore these men she'd taken as her temporary lovers.

When Grim lowered his mouth to hers, she wrapped her arms around him. His tongue was in her mouth, and she felt deliciously invaded. Grim's kiss was overwhelming, making her blood start to pump, her nipples tighten. His hands found the cheeks of her ass, hauling her up against him so she could feel how fast and thoroughly she affected him. His cock was hard against her belly.

"Take off your clothes and get ready for Josh." He whispered the command against her lips before setting her on her feet.

She knew she should think about the implications of Josh talking about beginning her training, but she'd made her decision. She was taking this time with them, and that meant being in the moment, staying mentally with them. It meant shoving aside her fear. She locked it away along with her husband's awful words and actions.

In this place, he never existed. This place was for her and Grim and Josh.

She shed her anxieties as she shed her clothes. They would be there when she put them back on, but for now she felt free.

"Damn, you're even more gorgeous in the light of day, sweetheart." Grim had taken off his T-shirt, revealing his muscular chest.

She couldn't take her eyes off him. He had some scars, but those did nothing to take away from his overall beauty. He was a gorgeous man, and for now he was all hers. She laid her palms flat on his pecs, heat seeming to flow from him to her.

One hand came out to cover hers, holding it against his chest. "You need to let me know if we get too intense for you. There's nothing we do together that's not negotiable. You can stop us at any time, but I hope you trust us."

She did. That was the problem. "Are you going to tie me up?"

She'd spent some time thinking about what they'd meant when they talked about kinks. She'd read a romance novel or two. Or a thousand. After the night before, she suspected that bondage and dominance were the tip of their sexy iceberg.

"Yes, I am," he admitted, his eyes on her breasts.

Her nipples were hard pebbles, tightening at the thought of him putting his hands on them. "I think I can handle that."

"You're going to be helpless."

"Yes," she whispered, not saying the reason why the words came so easily. She could say yes to them because she trusted them, because she wouldn't be helpless. They would always help her. This was a way to play out fantasies.

And she'd just realized one of her fantasies was to trust someone so much they could take away all of her abilities to protect herself and she would still know that it would be all right. Because they would never betray her.

"I'm going to play with your little asshole, sweetheart." Grim's thumb rubbed a circle around her right nipple. "I'm going to push a plug in to open you up because we're going to want to fuck that sweet hole of yours."

She knew what he meant and the why behind it, and she couldn't summon up the sense to be anxious about it. If she didn't like it, she would tell them and they would stop, but she was going to give it a shot.

"Okay." She couldn't take her eyes off his lips. They were so lush and soft looking, in contrast to his ruggedly masculine jawline. But she was starting to think that was simply who Grim was. At first glance he looked rough and intimidating but his gruff exterior protected a soft heart.

A brow rose over his dark eyes, and one half of those gorgeous lips tugged up in a grin. "Just like that?"

He shouldn't be so surprised. They'd shown her a lot about how good it could feel between them the night before. She'd felt safe and secure with these men—something she never thought she would feel again.

She might never have felt as safe as she had last night. Certainly not in the last few years.

"Just like that," she said with a sigh because he was so pretty. Such a pretty man.

"She knows we won't hurt her." Josh's deep voice came from behind, and she felt his fingers skim over the curves of her hips as he moved in. Then his breath was on her neck, and she could sense the change in him. "Nicole trusts us, and that's why we can push her a little. Baby, I want you to get to your knees, sitting back on your heels. You have palms up or down on your thighs. You choose. Then I want your head bowed in a submissive position. This is how you greet us before we play."

There were rules? She shouldn't be surprised. She'd read books about BDSM, but hearing the words from Josh's mouth sent a shiver down her spine.

She could follow rules. If they didn't change all the time. If they weren't merely there as an excuse to torment and torture her. If the rules were out there and they would follow them, too, she would always know where she stood.

"How do you two greet me?"

She gasped as Grim twisted her nipple, pain shooting through her, but it was oddly exciting.

"Brat," he said, but he was grinning like this was exactly what he wanted from her. "And we greet you like this."

His mouth covered hers, tongue sweeping in as his hands moved and he held her flat against his body. Skin to skin, she felt electric, pure anticipation flowing through her now. All the rest of it could wait. It was easy to shove aside her trepidation at how wealthy they were. Nothing mattered in the moment except how they could make her feel.

"And this," Josh said as Grim turned her to him. His hands came up to cup the back of her neck, and he practically inhaled her. He took her mouth in a ravenous kiss, like he needed her to breathe. Nicole softened, letting him control her movements, following him in this dance he seemed to need. When he released her, his gaze was hard. "Now do as I told you. Greet us so we can start your training."

Nicole stepped back and sank down to her knees, her skin against the soft rug. She took a deep breath and spread her knees, placing her palms up on her thighs, and let her head fall forward.

She was ready.

Chapter Seven

Grim felt like his cock was going to freaking explode and he hadn't even gotten undressed yet. The night before had felt hot and intimate, but seeing her with her head bowed in the light of day did something to his heart.

She was here with them. She wasn't trying to hide it, and she'd apparently announced to the entire town—the Baptist portion at least—she was their girl. Theirs. Not simply Josh's.

Josh moved around her naked body, his inner top already in firm control. He studied her carefully. "I need your spine straight."

"Unless she's uncomfortable," Grim said.

Josh's eyes narrowed as though saying *what the fuck*.

Nicole sat up, leveling her torso straight over her gorgeous hips. "I'm perfectly comfortable, Grim. Should I call you Sir?"

"Sir will work for now." He was normally as in top space as his best friend at this point, but all he was thinking about was her comfort. He needed to get his head in the game.

Except that was the problem. This didn't feel like a game.

He didn't want to be her Sir. He wanted to be her Master when they were playing.

He wanted to be hers all the time.

"Grim is right. Sir works for now. If we get more time together, we would like to take you to a club in Austin we enjoy," Josh explained. "Perhaps we can earn a different title from you, but for now we're your Sirs and you're our sweet little pet. Nicole, you are the single sexiest woman I've ever seen, and watching you like this is a revelation. This is everything I need."

"Am I allowed to ask questions, Sir?" Nicole's head remained bowed.

"Of course," Grim said quickly.

Josh sighed and gave him a "we're going to have to work on this" look. "Today you can. When we're in a more formal setting, I'll ask for you to stay in the scene if possible. What do you want to know?"

"Why?" she asked.

Grim's heart twisted because he wasn't sure he was ready for how deep he was in with this woman, but he wasn't about to back away.

"It's a formal way to greet your Doms." Josh had switched to what Grim liked to think of as his academic mode. He might joke about not being as good at school as Grim, but Josh excelled at any subject he enjoyed, and D/s was something he'd studied like it was his damn job. "It helps us all get into the right frame of mind to enjoy this time together."

His best friend was smart, but he'd misread her. "She's asking why we need this."

Josh frowned. "Is that what you're asking?"

"Yes, Sir. Thank you for translating, Grim," she said, and he could hear the smile in her tone.

It was the sweet way she said the words that made his heart ease. She was curious. She wasn't judging. "For one thing, you've given us one of the most important things about this lifestyle. Dominance and submission can help facilitate communication between partners. It can seem weird to talk about sex, but it's important. As to your question, I think we have two different answers. Josh was born this way, and I was made."

"Well, if we're having this discussion, you can look up." Josh got to one knee in front of her, and it was obvious while he was slightly irritated—because he was horny as hell—he was going to take the time to explain. "I don't know why I'm like this. Maybe because I was raised in a D/s household. My father is the Dom and my pops and Mom are his subs. This is how they live. I assure you neither Pops or Mom would tell you they feel like they're under Dad's thumb. He's what we call an indulgent top. It's a lifestyle to other people, but to me it's my life. It makes sense to me. So when Grim and I first started having sex, our dad took us to a club and we spent time training. We learned about sex and pleasure and more importantly, consent and how to protect and take care of the women who bottom for us."

"My stepmom told me if I got pregnant, I was on my own. She said the only way to stay safe was to keep my legs shut," Nicole said with a wry twist of her lips. "The Internet was my best sex ed teacher. I think your parents did a better job. Until last night, I would have told you sex is just a way to get close to a man."

Josh nodded. "Your sexuality is a part of you, and a part you shouldn't feel ashamed of or deny. It's a gift, and there's nothing wrong with indulging your needs. You don't seem to mind being naked right now."

"I'm as surprised as you are," she admitted. "It feels nice because I'm not worried you're going to use it against me."

"How would we use it against you?" Grim asked, not liking the fact that it felt like she knew people who would.

"You could tell me how fat I am," she explained quietly. "Or I'm too skinny. I…was married once. We're divorced now. To say he was mean to me would be an understatement. I was young, and I didn't look for red flags. I didn't even love him. I liked him, and I wanted to start my life. He was good at love bombing me, and I hadn't had enough affection from my parents. I fall for a love bomb every time."

Grim had heard the term and hated how she was having to use it. "No love bombs from us. How we treat you won't change. We'll put you first."

She turned her head slightly. "I believe you. I know I shouldn't. It's too soon, but I'm following my instincts this time. The truth of the matter is I knew there was something wrong with my ex, but I loved the attention and I wanted to be wrong. So I'm trusting myself this time. As much as I'm trusting you. It feels good to, if that makes sense."

"It does," Josh replied. "And that's what I do. My instincts tell me to take control during sex. During a lot of things, to be honest, but I don't need as much control as my dad has. Grim doesn't need to submit the way my pops does. Pops is even more submissive than my mom. Grim needs something different."

"I need the control because for most of my life I had none," Grim explained. "My mother married a man who can only be described as abusive and manipulative when I was very young. He pulled me out of a school I loved, and for a long time I was stuck in what seemed like prison to me. There were times he beat me so badly I didn't think I was going to make it, and he convinced me for a while that I deserved it. I cling to discipline because I think it fights the chaos of my youth in a way. The lifestyle also taught me how to have a healthy relationship with sex. But, I can play this another way if you need me to."

Her nose wrinkled. "I'm enjoying this. I just wanted to know. Maybe if I know why it works for you two, I can understand myself better. I do tend to fall for attention, and I haven't had any in a long time. But I don't think you're trying to maneuver me into a position where you can abuse me. You should know I don't take that crap anymore. I'm not the same person I was at nineteen."

"Understood," Grim agreed. "No abusing assholes allowed."

"Are we through with the psychological portion of the session?" Josh asked impatiently.

"I'm absolutely certain we're not because you love a good mind fuck, brother, but I think she has the answers she needs." Grim reached for the rope he'd set out earlier, knowing there was zero shot that they didn't play with her this afternoon.

In his head he'd planned a long afternoon of toying with their new sub. She didn't have to work today so that meant she needed to relax, and what better way to relax than tied safely in his ropes. She would be utterly helpless and at his mercy.

Since he was planning on keeping her tied up for a while, he'd decided on some simple bondage to introduce her to the experience and to make it easy for him to manhandle her. "Arms up, love."

Her eyes widened at the rope in his hands. "What are you doing?"

"See, this is why letting her ask questions is a bad idea," Josh pointed out.

"Well, she's new." He turned back to her. "Baby, I'm going to tie you up and we're going to play with you. You won't be gagged so you'll be able to talk and tell us if anything's uncomfortable."

"Did you trade your dick in for a marshmallow?" Josh asked.

He couldn't help it. "I'm not going to scare her away."

"Guys, don't fight." Her arms were up, her breasts outthrust. "I'm curious. Not afraid. Let's get this going. Although we need to talk about the gag thing."

"We wouldn't need to talk at all if you had one," Josh pointed out.

"I think I should be able to pick between the gag and the plug thing I've already been told to expect today," she said as primly as a naked woman could.

Josh's eyes narrowed. "You think you have choices, girl?"

Her lips curved into the sexiest smile. "I know I do, boy, and I think you're probably going to spank me for some of them, but I find myself strangely intrigued. See. I blow right through all the red flags."

"Ain't no red flags here, but you're right about one thing," Josh promised. "I am going to spank that sweet ass at some point in time today. But it's not about punishment. It's about play. It's about bringing you as much pleasure as we can. Nic, I want you to let go. For the next couple of hours, be here in the moment with us."

Grim started to wrap the rope around her, a sense of peace flowing over him. He loved the act of tying up a sub, loved how his mind could forget about everything but the next tie, the way the rope wound around her gorgeous flesh. It was an art. He spent his days far from the creative fields. This was where that part of his personality could come out.

"Forget about anything but pleasing your Doms and letting them please you." Josh's voice had gone deep, and he obviously thought they were back on track because he sounded patient again. His focus was wholly on Nicole as Grim worked the ropes around her breasts, making them thrust up, her nipples hard points already. "You don't have to think about anything at all because we're here to take care of you."

"I can do that," she replied. "I want to learn about this. I want to know if it works for me."

"It works for you." Grim ran a hand across her shoulders. "You relaxed when I started tying you up. I think you're going to find you're a bit of both me and Josh. You are naturally submissive, but you went through something that made you need it even more."

"Like Grim," Josh said with a shake of his head. "He seems to think he wasn't a take-charge guy before, but I remember him as a headstrong kid. You know we went to preschool together, and Kindergarten through third grade before his momma lost her damn mind. We asked our second-grade teacher if she would wait for us to grow up so we could marry her. Now that was a parent-teacher conference."

Grim started weaving a pattern around her hips after he helped her to her feet. He kissed the small of her back as he worked, all the while inhaling her scent. Arousal. He'd been right about her being naturally submissive. Her body craved this.

Could he make her crave him?

"You've known each other that long?" She remained still, allowing him to move her this way or that.

"Yes, since we were kids." Josh stood back, watching as Grim tied her securely. "He was my best friend. Then his father died and his mom remarried and to say that his stepfather didn't approve of my family would be an understatement."

He didn't want to think about this right now. He wanted to concentrate on her. "You can have all the stories later. For now, I think you should put your mouth to better use."

"I thought you were going to drag this out forever," Josh groaned, his hands going to the back of his T-shirt. He dragged it overhead and tossed it aside, kicking out of his boots.

Josh could get out of his clothes with the speed of an Olympic sprinter when he wanted to. And he obviously wanted to. He stood in front of Nicole, who had her hands tied together. It was time to show her how fun bondage could be.

"Can you feel the rope along your spine?" Grim asked, sliding his fingers under the specialized knots he'd placed there.

She nodded. "It's heavier against my spine. I don't actually think I can do what you want me to in this position. I need my hands, Sir."

"No, you don't," Josh assured her, running a hand over her hair.

His cock was thick and long, practically brushing against her cheek.

"Open your mouth, baby." Grim was fairly certain his dick was going to explode, but he had a job to do and it was one he'd been looking forward to. "I'll handle the rest."

She gasped, and he took control of her body, using the rope to steady her. She was a sweet weight as she leaned forward. Josh took control of her mouth, thrusting his dick inside as Grim started a gentle rhythm.

Josh kept his eyes on Nic even as he spoke. "You give her a fun knot? Never mind. I think she feels it."

The "dress" he'd made for her had a knot that rubbed against her clitoris when he maneuvered it properly. He wasn't as soft as Josh thought, though. He'd made sure she couldn't manipulate it herself. He had to give it to her or she got nothing at all.

Nicole groaned as he tightened his hold and the knot moved into place again. Her pleasure would hum against his skin.

And he controlled all of it. She didn't fight him, merely allowed him to move her along Josh's cock. She was at his mercy, and it did something for him. Something? It did everything for him. He moved with her, carefully constructing the dance that would bring her pleasure. She sucked Josh, obviously not caring about anything except the task he'd set for her.

What had she said? She craved attention. He could give her all of his attention, but he suspected she needed something else. Good attention. Praise. "Such a good girl. How does her mouth feel?"

"Like fucking heaven, brother," Josh managed. "She's so gorgeous like this. Do you like your dress, sweetheart?"

She hummed, her hands tied at the wrists and limp in front of her. The way he'd tied her, they formed a *V* around her breasts, pointing down to what he suspected was a soaking wet pussy.

"That's right. I'm glad you like it because I think you need to wear it for the rest of the day," Grim promised as he gave her more slack and she took Josh's cock to the root. "You don't have to worry about anything because I'll carry you around."

"Your feet won't touch the ground, sweetheart. Take it all, baby." Josh threaded his hands in her hair and held tight.

The slight gagging sound she made as Josh forced his cock to the back of her throat made Grim's dick tighten. It was time. He twisted the rope and felt her come.

Then it was Josh's turn. He fucked her mouth with ruthless precision, giving her everything he had. When she fell back, Grim caught her.

"Kiss me." She licked her lips. It was a challenge.

She had no idea how kinky he could be. He kissed her, plunging his tongue in and tasting the saltiness of Josh's release. It didn't bother him at all. He didn't want to be with Josh sexually, but Josh was an important part of his sexuality, and he didn't hold back or prevaricate.

When he released her she looked drugged with pleasure.

Exactly how he wanted her.

And now the real fun could begin.

* * * *

Nicole gasped as Grim stood and made good on his promise by picking her up and carrying her.

Except she'd thought it would be more romantic. He was carrying her like luggage. Whatever he'd woven at her back was sturdy enough to hold her weight.

She was completely at their mercy, the ropes holding her so tight. She liked the feeling, but this part was weird. "Uhm, Grim…"

She couldn't exactly see where they were going. She could see the floor, and it was a nice light wood. Probably super expensive, like the rug she'd been on earlier. It had been soft and perfect under her. She'd thought about how they could lay her out on that rug and she would be comfy and cozy.

She could also see Grim's booted feet. He was the only one who wasn't naked yet, and there was a certain impatience in the way his left foot tapped as he stopped.

"Yes?"

"Well, I thought the carrying part would be different," she admitted.

The air around her seemed to still, and she heard a chuckle from behind her. Josh seemed amused, but that was not the vibe she was getting from Grim. Even though all she could see were his well-worn boots. "You don't like the dress I made for you? It comes with a carrying handle. Are you uncomfortable, Nicole?"

Ooo, his voice was deliciously dark and deep. She took stock of where she was. Her body hummed with satisfaction, and while she felt a little heavy against the ropes, it wasn't an uncomfortable position. He'd properly distributed her weight.

She'd loved when he'd controlled her movements. It had felt…freeing in a way she'd never known before.

"Not really. It's just weird," she admitted.

"All right. I'm going to explain this to you because we haven't gone over all the rules," Grim began. "When we're playing, unless you want something to stop, let it be. I put you in those ties, and that's where I want you to be."

"Where we want you to be," Josh added. "When we're playing, don't question us unless you're afraid or uncomfortable."

Which she was neither.

Josh knelt down, and she could see his handsome face if she twisted her head. She was wrapped up like a mummy. Well, if the mummy was held together with rope and had her boobs hanging out, and also had recently been given a mind-blowing orgasm via knot.

"Shift her," Josh said.

Grim moved, and she could suddenly see Josh easily.

"Hey."

"So let's talk about discomfort and what it means because I think you're about to get a baby plug worked into that tight asshole of yours, and I don't want you to think you can get out of it by crying and pleading," Josh was saying. "The plug won't hurt you."

"It might if I use the ginger lube," Grim admitted.

"I'm so comfortable. This is my favorite dress." She didn't want to find out about the ginger lube any more than she wanted to play around with a ball gag. The men were apparently serious about their toys, and there were a couple she wanted to avoid. "And I know I need the plug because I want to be in between you two. I'm very sorry, Sirs, and I promise I'm going to go with the flow for the rest of the day."

A little growl came out of Grim's mouth, and she was suddenly moving again.

They would have to work on his communication skills. He spent a lot of time around animals.

"An excellent apology." Josh walked next to her down the hallway, and then she was in a lush bedroom. The wood floor gave way to carpet, which would likely feel good on her skin.

Someone turned on the lights, and a golden glow illuminated the room.

Nicole gasped as she was lifted high and landed on a soft bed. A big bed. A really big bed.

Oh, it was nice. So much nicer than anything she'd been on in the last few years. Definitely nicer than where she'd been sleeping the last few weeks. And she could rest in this luxury, perfectly certain bullets wouldn't fly in from the drug dealers next door.

She was rolled over, and Josh stared down at her.

He circled a nipple with his forefinger. "You look good in this. Grim did an excellent job." His finger trailed down her body, skimming over the ropes until he found the juncture of her thighs. "And this seems to have worked well. Did you enjoy the knot?"

She bit her bottom lip, staring up at him. He was one of the most beautiful men she'd ever seen, and he seemed to want her. "Yes."

She could still taste his arousal on her lips, and she couldn't forget how she'd still had Josh's taste in her mouth when Grim had kissed her like he would die without her. Without them.

Josh and Grim loved each other, were committed to each other, but their sexuality demanded a woman between them, a woman who could connect them to each other. A woman they could lavish with affection and share their common caring through.

She so wanted to be that woman. In another life…

Nicole let go of the thought. There wasn't a place for regret or worry here. Here she was their sweet plaything who only had to worry about pleasing them. It was okay because all they wanted to do was please her, too.

She kept her eyes on Josh, who stared down at her with such open affection. His hand cupped her cheek, thumb running across her bottom lip.

"Your mouth felt like heaven, baby," he said. "I loved how you sucked my cock. No one's ever felt as good as you."

He seemed to be taking the attention thing seriously, and she had to admit it did something for her. She probably shouldn't enjoy being praised for her fellatio skills, but hey, if one was going to perform a sexual act on her brand-new guy, one should probably want to do it right. "Thank you, Sir. I enjoyed it. I never did before. I liked how Grim controlled me. It felt like I was really with both of you."

"You are with both of us. Make no doubt about it, and now we're going to start to show you what that means," Josh promised. His body was muscled from years of working on a ranch. He wasn't a gym guy. He'd earned that body with daily manual labor, something that set him apart from the rich people she'd known before.

In her head she knew rich people were like everyone else. There were good and bad. It just took her soul a minute to catch up. Still, it was easy to shove it aside while looking at those notches on Josh's hips. His hand sat on her belly, playing with the ropes that held her tight.

"Turn her over for me," Grim commanded as he walked back into the room. He'd ditched his shirt and jeans, getting down to his boxers, though his cock was starting to poke out of them. He held a plastic thing in his hand.

Yep, he was about to shove that up her backside.

She felt like Alice in a kinky Wonderland.

Josh easily lifted her up, and she found herself on her belly, cheek against the soft comforter. He gripped her hips with both hands. "Bend your knees. We're going to bring you up to the edge of the bed so Grim can get you ready. The rope will help you keep the plug in. An hour or so today, and then we'll work you up to a bigger plug."

Because she was going to take a cock in her ass. Cocks. Their cocks. She wrapped her brain around the idea as Josh maneuvered her into position, the ropes tightening as he folded her in half. She was on her knees, her arms in front of her, ass in the air.

She was so vulnerable. So open to them. In this position she could feel the rope against her asshole, slightly scraping against the tender flesh.

She flushed as Josh moved in behind her and pushed the rope aside, revealing her tight hole.

She was tied up and men were touching her in a place she never would have imagined, and Nic realized she was relaxed. Aroused, but no warning bells were going off. There was nothing in her brain that even told her she should be on the lookout. She was either completely mad and naïve or they were perfect.

When she felt the warm lube at her hole, she forced herself to breathe.

"Just a little pressure, sweetheart," Grim was saying. "If it's too much, let me know."

Josh climbed on the bed with her, lying down beside her so she could see his handsome face. "It's not going to be too much. She likes this more than she thought she would. You're what we call a natural submissive. Very rare to find one out in the wild."

He was distracting her from the pressure—which was not all that little. As Grim pressed something hard against her, sensation sparked through her, and she wasn't sure she loved it. It wasn't pain, but it also wasn't pleasure. Still, looking at Josh's gorgeous face made that jangly sensation a distant thing. "Are you calling me feral?"

He grinned, and his hand came out to push back her hair. Then he was simply staring at her like she was a miracle he got to witness. Like she was precious, and he didn't want to waste a minute of his time with her. "Maybe a little, baby, but you should know I'm good at taking care of strays. I tend to make them mine."

Grim started to circle her with what felt like the tip of the plug. He gently pressed in and rotated, gaining ground with each pass. "He's talking about me. You should know he's kind of a possessive bastard."

"I take what's mine," Josh insisted, his eyes still on her.

"You do, brother," Grim replied quietly. "I think I might get possessive of this one, too."

They were talking about her like she wasn't lying there with her ass in the air listening to them. Except all of their physical attention was on her, of course. This was what it would be like to be with these men. She would be at the center. They would work together to bring her pleasure and comfort. These weren't men who would expect her to take care of them. She would. She would do it because she wanted to, not because that was what they demanded of her.

You can't even cook. What the hell good are you? If my brother hadn't...

The episode flashed through her. It had been a night not too long after they'd been married. He'd been drunk and he'd railed at her, stopping himself only when he'd mentioned his brother. Then he'd walked out, and she hadn't seen him for days.

"Hey, wherever you are, come back to me, Nic. Come back to us," Josh whispered.

His words coupled with the hard slide of the plug settling deep inside her brought her back to reality. This was real. This thing between the three of them, and she didn't want to give Micah another second in her head.

"I'm here," she promised. "And the plug isn't so bad. I thought it would feel tighter."

Josh's lips curled up in the sexiest "I know something you don't know" grin. "Just wait."

She heard the sound of a condom tearing open and realized what Grim was about to do.

She braced herself as she felt his hands grip her hips and his cock begin to penetrate.

"There you go." Josh kissed her cheek. "Now you feel it. How tight is she, Grim?"

So tight. There was no space. She wasn't sure how he was going to…and then he flexed up and stroked against her sweet spot, nearly making her sob with pleasure. They'd gotten her so hot, so ready, that what should be uncomfortable felt like heaven.

"We'll have to give her two or three before we get inside her because there's zero chance we're going to last." The words came out of Grim's mouth on a harsh grind. Like it was taking everything he had to get them out. He held himself against her, and she could hear him breathe.

"Speak for yourself," Josh taunted. "When I get in there, I intend to stay for a long time."

She wanted forever. She wouldn't get it, but this felt like bliss. Being between them would be something she would never forget. When she was an old woman still hiding away, she would remember the time two cowboys had adored her with their bodies.

Grim pulled something, and the knot on her clit tightened as he stroked inside her again and again.

Josh kissed her, sweet affection that did nothing to take away from the raw sexual pleasure. Those kisses reminded her this wasn't mere sex. This was something more.

They were something more.

Grim rode her hard while Josh gave her his softest self. He kissed her even as the orgasm overtook her and she moaned into his mouth. Then she felt Grim lose that magnificent control of his, and he fucked her hard. Over and over, he thrust in and dragged out until he finally gave her everything he had, calling out her name and completing the act.

He fell on the bed beside her, and she could feel his warmth.

"That was… Oh, baby, that was fucking incredible," Grim said, a chuckle in his tone. "We're going to have to do that more often. But for now, let's get you cleaned up. There's a football game on."

Josh kissed her one more time. "Yeah, I'll go get beer from the big house. We're out. I'll have to sneak in because you know my momma will have something to say."

"Get some chips, too." Grim moved beside her and then she was up in the air again, the rope between the cheeks of her ass holding the plug in. "I'm hungry, and we need to feed our sub."

Okay, so there was more to being theirs than mind-blowing sex and a growing affection.

She was luggage.

"Grim, shouldn't you let me out of the ropes?" Nic feared she already knew the answer to that question as they approached the doors to what she supposed was the bathroom.

"Why would we do that?" Grim managed to get the shower on.

Why indeed?

Nic didn't know, so she was going with the flow.

Chapter Eight

Josh half watched the game playing out on the TV. This was how they spent most Sundays, though normally they would be at the big house watching with the dads on the massive TV in the media room.

But he definitely wouldn't be doing that when they had Nicole so beautifully trussed up. There were limits to his parents' openness. Josh was pretty sure his momma was naked a lot but he'd never had to see it, and for that he was eternally grateful.

There was a reason they never played at a club where he knew his parents would be.

"You want a drink, sweetheart?" Grim was staring at the woman on his lap like she was the most precious thing in the world.

She grinned at him, taking to the whole bondage kink with the enthusiasm of a champion. "Yes, please."

Grim held the glass with the straw to her mouth, and Nic took a long sip of the iced tea she'd asked for. Grim had washed her up and settled her onto his lap and had been serving her treats for two hours.

All the while Josh watched them and wondered if this was how his father felt when he looked at Pops and Mom. Like they were his whole world. Like it was his job in life to take care of them.

"Is something wrong, Josh?"

It was the first time he'd heard anything from Nic except perky acceptance or sighs of pleasure since Grim had played around with the knot he'd made several times. He wouldn't even look away from the TV, just tug on the right rope and let friction do its job, and then Nic would sigh and wriggle and the corners of Grim's lips would curl up in a way Josh had never seen before.

"He's brooding. It's a thing he does," Grim said.

"Really? You know I'm not the one called Grim, buddy," Josh pointed out.

Grim shrugged and set Nic's glass back on the side table. "And yet you are a broody bastard. I'm not the one everyone's afraid of."

"Afraid?" Nicole started to bring her head up.

Grim eased it back down. He'd changed into sweatpants and a T-shirt. They were his "I can get out of these very easily" clothes. "Not like he'll beat them up afraid. Josh can be sunny and happy-go-lucky seeming."

"But then he threatened a whole bunch of people who were leaving church," she said almost sagely.

She was forgetting a few salient facts. "They were being mean to you. I won't let anyone be mean to you."

Her eyes closed as though she was perfectly content. "You can't stop everyone."

"Now that, my sweet pet, feels like a challenge." He liked a challenge. He still wasn't sure if he was going to kick Alyssa's overly privileged ass out of his company come Monday morning. She could find another job. Maybe the church would hire her. He might kick her momma out, too. On principle. If she'd wanted to keep her job, she should have taught her daughter to not be so awful.

Nicole's eyes opened again, and she looked properly wary. "Josh, don't do anything. It doesn't matter. I don't care what a bunch of people I don't know think of me. I spent a whole lot of my life with people thinking I'm some kind of doormat. Being a Jezebel is a lot more fun than a doormat."

He was so interested in her past. Which she rarely talked about. She was good at trying to divert his attention. He'd played her game up until now, but it was time to start being ruthless. Up until now he'd been willing to go along with the whole "this is only for a couple of weeks" thing.

He didn't want a couple of weeks with her. He wanted

everything. And there was zero chance Grim wasn't falling for her. Falling? Hell, that boy was already gone. He was staring down at her like she was the sun in his sky. Grim relaxed around her.

Grim was going to get his fucking heart broken if she did what she said she was going to do and left.

"Who would think you're a doormat?" Grim asked, his fingers running through her hair. She was still in her rope dress, but he'd released her hands and they were under her cheek. She looked sweet and sleepy and a bit angelic to him. Though most angels wouldn't lie around naked, their body spread out over two men.

She yawned, and her eyes closed. "All of Childswood."

Grim's eyes met his. A freaking clue. "I thought you were from Chicago."

Her eyes opened, and it was easy to see she was awake now. "Oh, it's my high school. Childswood High. I wasn't popular."

He needed to ease her back down. If she thought they were probing, she would come up with an excuse to leave. He wanted her here and happy. Napping would be excellent since then she wouldn't notice when he slipped away.

It was time to start solving the mystery of Nicole Mason. He knew it was quick, but he was sure. She was the right one for him, and it didn't matter what she was running from. He would handle it.

But he had to make sure he didn't become the thing she was running from.

"I was incredibly popular." He winked at her, giving her a slightly arrogant smirk sure to make her believe he was thinking about himself again. "I was the star of the baseball team."

Grim snorted. "He was terrible at baseball. He couldn't catch to save his life. Now he was excellent at throwing his body in front of running backs. And his golf game is adequate. I was obviously the baseball hero. Or I would have been if my stepfather hadn't decide it was Satan's game. Pretty much any game was Satan's game. Strangely except Jenga. He was totally into Jenga."

She rolled so she could fully look up at Grim. "You know this is why you're a pervert. You had an unhealthy relationship with sex…well, from what I can tell, with everything, and now you feel like you have to make up for it."

"Okay, then how do you explain Mr. Good Sex over there,"

Grim argued with a wink. He was so flirty with her. She brought out a light side in Grim that Josh had worried was gone forever. "I assure you his parents never used the word *shame* around him."

"Untrue. There was plenty of shame heaped on me during the brief time I rebelled," Josh reminded him.

Grim nodded. "Yes. It was a terrible time. I thought your dad might disown you."

Nicole's eyes went wide, and she lifted her head to look at Josh. "What did you do?"

She whispered the question like it was a secret.

He wasn't the one keeping secrets. He took her feet in his hands, squeezing lightly until she sighed and bit her bottom lip. She was the most sensual thing. "I rebelled against my father in the most heinous way I could. I thought about going to Texas A&M for college."

It had been a brief thing, and mostly to see if his father would lose his mind. He had.

"You see we're a Longhorn family," Grim explained. "And Longhorns and Aggies are a little like the Hatfields and McCoys. We take our college football seriously. During the season, I make it a point to never wear maroon because it makes my dad…makes Jack's eye twitch."

He'd been right the first time, but the fact that Grim had actually gotten the words out proved how fucking good Nicole was for him. He rubbed her feet and her eyes closed again.

"Football. It's always football," she said quietly.

"It used to be our favorite pastime," Grim said. "Now it's torturing you."

He tweaked her nipple, and she yelped before giggling and settling back in.

She was asleep in minutes, and Josh was able to ease from beneath her feet.

"I think I'm going to make a beer run," he said. "I steal anymore of the dads' and Momma will start talking about rehab. Livie will say I'm getting a beer belly."

A brow rose over Grim's eyes. The one that said he didn't buy what Josh was selling. "You think we need more? Maybe we should take it easy."

Oh, his partner knew exactly what he was planning on doing. "It's nice to have extra. You never know when we'll have guests."

Nicole wrapped an arm around Grim's leg, using his lap as her pillow. She shifted, getting more comfortable, but it was obvious she was down for a nap.

Be careful, Grim mouthed.

Josh nodded and stared at them for a moment. Everything he wanted was sitting right there. His best friend and their sweet sub. He couldn't lose them.

And that meant figuring out why she thought she had to leave.

An hour later Josh walked out of the garage and into the parking lot where Al Holt allowed people to park the cars he was going to work on. Al ran a small auto repair business. He did mostly engine work. Any body work would have to go to one of the larger towns to the north, but if someone needed a new alternator or a tune-up, Al and Sons were the way to go here in Willow Fork.

"She's the sedan in the second row." Al was in his sixties, with white hair mostly located around his ears and the back of his head. Normally he wore coveralls, but today he was in jeans and a Cowboys sweatshirt. In the background Josh could hear the sounds of the halftime show.

Al lived over the garage with his son, Greg. Once he'd asked Al why he called the place Al and Sons since Greg was his only son, and Al had given him a grin and told him a man could still dream.

"She seems like a real nice young lady," Al said, not leaving the steps that led down to the parking lot.

"She is a nice lady." He looked up at Al, who'd worked on his family's cars for as long as anyone could remember. He wasn't exactly a friend, but he seemed to respect his fathers and was always polite to his mom. He also spent a lot of time at the local rec center playing checkers with the group of old dudes who practically lived there. Men might not like to admit that they gossiped. They would say they were simply discussing current events. "What's being said about her, Al?"

Al frowned and raised his hat slightly so he could scratch behind his ear. "Well, not a lot until today. I've talked to her a bit about her car, but she seems to keep to herself. Says she was on her way to a new job, but her car broke down. That felt fishy to me, but I stay out of other people's business."

He did, but he often heard things. Al was one of those people who didn't talk much so people often forgot he might be listening in. "Anyone else questioning why she's here?"

"I don't think she's here to cause trouble, if that's what you're asking. I know the sheriff can be nosy, but she hasn't been on his radar up until now. Though if what I heard happened at the church really happened, you might have your dad do that thing where he reminds everyone who he is. I think a lot of people around here think Jack Barnes has gotten cuddly in his advanced years. I'm pretty sure the old scary as hell Jack can show up at any time."

"There's nothing cuddly about my father when his family is being threatened." Josh wasn't sure his father would consider the sheriff trying to move Nic along a threat to his family. After the conversation they'd had this morning, his dad might be okay with it. Which was precisely why he had to figure out what was going on with her. If someone was after her, there was no way his father's protective instincts didn't take over. If he spent time with Nic, his father would see how sweet she was, how perfect she was for him and Grim. "Why would the sheriff suddenly be interested in her? She's been here for a couple of weeks."

A brow rose over Al's eyes like he thought Josh was being naïve. "You've spent too much time traveling lately. The sheriff's dating Alyssa's cousin. They seem to be real close."

"And I employ most of Alyssa's family. You might point that out to the sheriff if he mentions Nicole's name. Unless he wants to take care of a bunch of unemployed relatives, he'll leave her alone."

"You know as long as she's at that motel, he's got easy reasons to check up on her. He has deputies out there at least twice a day. I've worried about her. Now I hear there's another single lady staying there for a while."

Her new friend. What had her name been? Hannah? Heather? He thought he remembered Nic saying something about her mother being sick, but he'd never seen the woman before. It was possible she lived outside of town and he'd never met her. He needed a last name.

But Nic becoming friends with someone temporarily staying at a motel wasn't what concerned him now. "She'll be staying with us soon, so don't worry about that."

A brow rose over Al's eyes. "You're moving fast, Josh."

"I always knew I would when I found the right one." He'd merely been marking time, waiting for Nicole. He needed to go easier on his sister because he rather thought that was what she was doing, too, but she didn't have a Grim to remind her she wasn't alone. She didn't have a partner to help her.

He still didn't think it would be the Farley brothers.

"Well, the first thing you should do is get her a new car. That one is on its last legs," Al admitted. "She thinks the alternator is all she needs, but nothing is in real working shape on the vehicle. It's old and hasn't been taken care of. That thing has over two hundred thousand miles on it. And I'm pretty sure she was living out of it at some point. I don't like to be nosy…"

He did. "What did you find?"

"She keeps blankets and a pillow in the trunk. I only got in there to inspect the car," Al said.

"Did you find anything else?"

"No, but I didn't look real close," Al admitted. "Look, Josh, if you asked me I would say she's on the run from someone, likely an ex. She has that look about her, and she damn near panicked when I told her how much it would cost. I don't think it was entirely about money. I think she wanted to keep going. I'm sorry, Josh. That part is old, and I can't order it until I have the cash in hand."

Josh waved that concern away. "I'm not upset with you for that. I understand you have a business to run."

"So you want me to arrange to sell that junker for parts?" Al asked. "Like I said, it's old and there are some parts that could make her a couple of hundred. Otherwise, I would have it cubed like your daddy did."

He rather thought Nic would have him cubed. He'd heard the stories about his dad's predilection for smushing vehicles that offended him into small cubes. He'd been told the cube his pops kept in his office used to be a motorcycle. "I don't think we're in a place yet where she would take a car from us, but I'm pretty sure I can get her to stay with us while her car is being fixed. It's an old part, right?"

Al grimaced. "Yeah, and I'm afraid it could take a while even after I order it."

"Oh, I think it should take a couple of weeks. Maybe a month," Josh said. "Maybe it's stuck on a container ship that's trapped in the bottleneck at the Panama Canal. I read something about that."

Al nodded. "It's not that much of a stretch. I did tell her I would have to order the part and I couldn't until she made a down payment. You trying to keep her around?"

"I think that women on the run keep running until they find a place that feels safe enough to take a risk." Josh had been thinking about it all day. He wanted to respect her privacy. No. That was a lie. He knew he should respect her privacy. What he wanted was to know absolutely everything about her, to track her every movement in case she needed him for some reason, to be a couple of steps behind so he could ensure she was safe and no one hurt her either emotionally or physically. That was what he wanted, but he would be content with knowing what she was running from. Then he could plot and plan and get her out of whatever situation had put the lost look in her eyes.

Though when he'd left her, those eyes had been closed, and there had been a peaceful look on her face as Grim petted her.

"Well, I'll be happy to delay the situation for a couple of weeks," Al agreed. "Honestly, I don't feel right fixing the alternator when I know damn well it's going to fall apart again. The whole car is held together with duct tape and baling wire. It would be a miracle if she made it to Austin in one piece."

"Hey, Dad, game's back on," Greg said from the upstairs window. "Hey, Josh. How's it going? Grim doing okay? I heard there's an outbreak. Kind of expected you to be knee deep in cows beside him."

An outbreak? "We had a couple of bred heifers get some tainted feed. We're working with the feed store to figure out what's going on. Where did you hear that?"

Greg leaned over the balcony railing. "Uh, I might have heard something about it from his brothers."

They weren't Grim's brothers. Josh was. Josh and his parents and Livie were his family. "What exactly did they say? And which ones are we talking about?"

"Oh, they were doing the thing where they scream at people going into the park or walking down Main Street." Greg seemed to wave it off. "It was John and Peter. You know how they are. They wave the Bible around and pretend like they're the dress code enforcers. I think the ladies look perfectly nice in their leggings. They're taking an exercise class so I don't see the problem. But those boys take exception. I don't think they read the part about plucking thine own eyes out."

"I could do it for them if they have trouble," Josh promised.

"The women ignore them. But today they were talking about evilness killing the town, and how all the cows are going to die because we put up with wickedness," Greg explained. "I didn't think much of it until I heard from one of the hands what went on this morning. Sorry if he wasn't supposed to talk."

That wasn't the problem. "Nah, it's fine. Grim's handling it. They're being assholes or it's a coincidence. I don't see how they could know, but it's not like it matters. You let me know if they keep talking about it. Al, thanks for helping me out."

He shook Al's hand before the older man disappeared back into the shop. Greg gave him a wave as he returned to watching the game. Josh glanced over at the car and then his watch. He couldn't be gone too long. He pulled his cell phone out and dialed a familiar number as he approached the piece of crap Nicole called a car.

And apparently home every now and then.

The thought made his gut turn. Anything could happen to her out there with nothing but the windows and easily broken locks keeping her from the world. He'd thought the motel was the worst place for her, but sleeping in her car on the streets was definitely worse.

"Hey, Josh. What's going on. Haven't heard from you in a while," a feminine voice said.

Harlow Dawson. She was one of the kids he'd grown up with, the ones who formed his family. Harlow, her sister, Greer, and their parents lived in Dallas, though over the years they'd done a lot of work for the company. Her fathers, Ben and Chase Dawson, were private investigators while her mother, Natalie, was a painter and ran a gallery.

Greer worked with their mom, while Harlow had taken after their dads.

"I've been working. You know how it is." Josh took in the car, holding the key he'd stolen in his palm. Borrowed. He would put it back, but he wanted to take a look first.

"Our parents don't want to travel for work anymore, so they send us. Yes. I certainly do. Be glad you spend your time in sales meetings. You only had to go to college. I had to go to college and then pass Big Tag's kill-the-girl training school. It was terrible. I was in it with some people who I think are training to be assassins, but my dads insisted I go if I was going to do anything dangerous."

Actually, he was happy his training had been in how to handle a ranch and run a business. He'd heard the man they called Big Tag was kind of intimidating, and that was coming from kids who'd grown up around Julian Lodge. Josh had met Mr. Taggart a number of times. He'd made the mistake of hitting on his daughter once.

Oddly, the man hadn't threatened to kill him. He'd gone over a long list of things Kenzie Taggart had mastered—including her black belt in tae kwon do. And then he'd given him a lengthy document he called a release of all liability.

Josh had known when to back off. "Yeah, I try to steer clear of certain parts of Dallas." Not that there wasn't a Taggart who'd been an excellent mentor to him, but the man didn't live in Dallas. "I got a favor to ask, Harlow."

"Of course. Is it work related? Someone stealing from the company store?" The question was asked with a teasing tone. She liked to tease him about his wealth.

Like she should talk. Her fathers were ridiculously wealthy. They worked because they got bored if they didn't. "No, it's personal."

"What's going on?" All the teasing gone, her voice had softened. It was easy to talk to Harlow Dawson because she genuinely cared about her friends. She had a soft heart and hands trained to bash in a man's head. If they hadn't been practically family… Well, she still wouldn't have been perfect for him since Nicole was the one. But she was one of the coolest women he knew.

"Grim and I have a new girlfriend," he explained, looking over the lines of the sedan. It needed a paint job. And a new bumper. The rear had multiple dings, one of which was starting to rust. There was nothing in the back seat, and the front was every bit as neat. She'd cleaned it out before dropping it off. "I'm worried about her."

"Worried about her how?" Harlow asked.

"I think she's in trouble, but she won't talk. She's afraid of something, and I can't push her to tell me at this point."

"How long have you been together? You didn't mention her when I saw you a couple of weeks ago."

He sighed. "I've met her since then. Look, I know it sounds quick, but she's…she's perfect for us."

"Say no more." Harlow stopped him. "I hear about how my mom knew she would marry my dads within a week of meeting them, and then Dad says he knew the minute he met her and it only took a week because Papa screwed things up by taking his sugar, and I'm pretty sure that's something gross I shouldn't have to hear about. So I accept this is serious and you need to figure out what her problems are. I need a name and any information you can give me. Where's she from?"

"Chicago," he replied, taking the key and pressing it into the trunk's keyhole. "Though I'm almost certain it's a lie. Nicole Mason. Might not be her real name. I took a picture of her driver's license. I'll text it to you."

"Okay. I'll start with a skip trace and go from there," Harlow explained.

"She says she's got a job waiting for her in Austin." The trunk flipped open, revealing a neat space. There was a folded blanket, two small pillows, a set of sheets. She had a set of light-blocking shades she likely used when she wanted the illusion of privacy. Something else had been bugging him. "And look for a Childswood High School. If you can't find it, take a look around to see if there's a town named Childswood."

She'd been half asleep when she'd whispered the words. And then totally awake. She hadn't meant to mention the place. She'd covered or maybe she'd told him the truth, but he wasn't sure.

"Got it," Harlow said over the line and then paused. "Josh, maybe you should slow things down if you think she's lying."

"If she's lying, she's got good reason." Under the blanket there was a stack of books. All romance, from what he could tell. She'd hidden those books like they were her treasures. Now that he thought about it, she'd had a couple of books on her nightstand.

"You think someone's after her, but sometimes that person is actually a whole police department. Maybe the FBI," Harlow pointed out.

"Who hurt you?" Josh said sarcastically, and then fucking remembered. "Har, I'm sorry. I shouldn't have said that. It was a dumb joke."

Someone had hurt her and quite brutally. She had a reason to be suspicious. "It's fine. It was a long time ago." Her voice was unnaturally cheery. "But I do know what I'm talking about. If you don't know this woman's history, then you could be playing a dangerous game, and you don't know the rules."

He gently put back the blankets, covering her books. It looked like she'd taken as much as she could out of the vehicle and into her temporary home.

He was probably going to look through her other belongings, too, and it would be far easier to do when she was staying with them. "The rules don't matter. Not with her. And that's why I'm calling you instead of Uncle Ben. I think you'll keep things quiet until I have everything in place and I'm ready to bring my parents into it."

Uncle Ben was the infinitely more reasonable of her dads. Ben and Chase Dawson were twins with weird connections that sometimes seemed a little on the psychic side. But where Ben had gotten all the normal, all-American Ken doll energy, Chase was definitely Mr. Hyde. He was a great guy, but he sometimes decided he was judge, jury, and executioner. A fact Harlow's ex-boyfriend should have thought about.

"I'll check into this for you, Josh, and you know I'll keep the dads out of it," Harlow replied, her tone softer. "I'm happy for you, you know."

She was still heartbroken, but Harlow was tough, and she knew how to love her friends. "I know. Thank you, cousin."

There wasn't blood between them, but they'd grown up together in a way that felt as close as family.

"I'll get back to you when I know something, and Josh, be careful," she said and the line went dead.

His heart ached for Harlow, but he couldn't even consider the idea the woman who'd curled up on Grim's lap had ever done something seriously criminal. She wasn't on the run from the cops. It was something else. Something traumatic.

He closed the trunk and moved around to the passenger side of the car. There was one place he hadn't checked. The glove compartment. It was normally where car guides went to die, but sometimes a person shoved things there they didn't want others to find.

He flipped it down and sure enough, there was an old driver's manual along with a couple of parking tickets. Not from Willow Fork. There was one from Denver dated two years before, and another from a place called Papillon a few months ago.

So she wasn't the best parker in the world. He could work on that.

But hadn't she said she lived in Chicago until a few weeks ago?

He closed the glove box and pocketed the key, which he would slip into her purse when he got back to the house.

He slid his cell in his pocket and considered the fact that Nic was going to be pissed if she ever found out. He was willing to risk it. What he wasn't willing to risk was losing her. He couldn't protect her if he didn't know what she was involved in, and he didn't trust her not to run if he pressed her too hard.

The crap with Grim's brothers was another story altogether. It was annoyance, but it would bug Grim.

It might be nice to take some of this tension out on John and Peter. But it would have to wait.

All he knew was no one was going to fuck with his family, and Grim and Nic were at the center of the family he wanted to create.

He would protect them from everything. Even themselves.

Chapter Nine

Grim stood over Nicole, brushing back her hair. "It's just a meal. They aren't scary. I promise."

"I don't know that it's appropriate for me to meet your parents. And I'm not dressed for it. I'm dressed like I'm going out to breakfast with hopes of being asked to stay to work for the lunch rush." She looked adorable in her jeans and shirt, her hair now pulled back in a ponytail. She looked young and sweet, and now that he knew how well her ass took an anal plug, she was even more beautiful than she'd been before.

He was in a romantic mood. Though he was afraid Josh was going to fuck everything up. He'd understood Josh wasn't merely running into town to grab some beer. They'd talked briefly today about visiting the auto shop to see what was up with her car. They'd discussed trying to fix the car themselves and hoping they could still convince her to hang around with them or at least let them come with her to Austin for a while.

And they'd talked about quietly sabotaging her efforts to get her car fixed. Not a fair thing to do, but he didn't believe she really had a job.

He'd been thinking about it all afternoon. Nic was her own person and had every right to make her own decisions, and he and Josh were being what Livie liked to call alpha holes.

But damn it, he wasn't going to let her go when he genuinely believed he was good for her. She'd fallen asleep wrapped in his ropes and clung to him. She'd kissed him like he was everything she wanted.

"I think you look beautiful," he said, lowering his head to hers and breathing her in. She smelled like his soap, and it did something for him.

Her hands came up to run along his neck. "Thank you but I'm still not sure I should walk into your parents' house looking like this. Rich people have expectations."

Now they were getting somewhere. Josh had mentioned she'd gone stiff when she'd realized how wealthy his family was. "They're not like that. I assure you Sam will be in jeans and a T-shirt, and Jack will either be in the same or a Western shirt. They don't dress for dinner. We always have Sunday dinner all together, and Josh and I want you to get to know our family."

"But I won't be here for long. I have to go to Austin."

"Austin's only a couple of hours away," Grim replied. "I don't understand why you moving means this has to end."

"Somehow I don't think you'll want to spend all your time driving," she said. "Besides, I'll be working so I won't be able to drop everything to see you."

"I would respect your work. And I don't mind a drive," he insisted. "What I do mind is the thought of not seeing you again. I know it's fast, but I feel something with you I've never felt with a woman."

Her arms tightened around him. "I feel the same about you and Josh. But I have to go to Austin. I can't back out of my job. It's important to me."

"Which is why I'll drive to Austin," he promised. "It's not far away. Didn't you say you were off this weekend?"

She nodded. "Yes, but I sometimes hang around in case Christa needs me, or I'll try to work out at The Barn."

"Come to the club with me and Josh." He knew he should talk it over with Josh, but they were going to Subversion, and he couldn't see them playing with anyone except Nicole. If she wasn't there, he didn't see a point in going. "If you don't want to go, we'll stay here with you."

"I don't want to ruin your plans."

"Baby, we made plans to go to the club a long time before we met you. It's a lifestyle club, so we go there to let off some steam." He was trying to be delicate, but he wanted to make one thing plain to her. "I'm not interested in letting off steam with anyone but you. So if you can't come, there's no reason for us to go. It's two days, Nicole. Two days out of time. Two days where we get to lock out the world and be who we are. I want those two days with you."

She reached up to run her hand over his cheek. "I want it, too. Yes, I can go. But it's probably the only time. I have to concentrate on work soon."

He stared at her, taking in how her eyes had flecks of gold and her hair had deep tones of brown. He wanted her to trust him. "Is there something you want to tell me?"

She took a long breath, and when she brought her head up, there was a smile on her face. One he didn't trust. "Not at all, and you're right. I'm being inflexible. There's no real reason this has to be completely over, though I don't know how well I'll do long distance."

Was she placating him? "If there's something you need to tell me, I'll listen, and you should understand I won't judge you."

Her face flushed but she shook her head and stepped back. "I'm an open book. I'm not interesting, as your parents are apparently about to discover. I'm afraid I mostly can talk about the café and cleaning things. I've gotten good at cleaning things."

He hated that she put some space between them, hated how she was smiling at him but he could see he'd upset her calm.

She seemed to shake it off, and she glanced in the mirror. "I wish I had some lip gloss. Where did I leave my purse?"

Shit. She might figure out something was missing. He'd seen Josh steal her keys. He wasn't sure if he was going to look through her car or her motel room, but he knew she would notice if those keys weren't in her bag.

Where the hell was Josh?

"Like I said, you look beautiful." He turned her around and lowered his head to hers as he heard the back door open.

Relief flooded through his system. Josh was back and in the nick of time. He kissed Nic, holding her tight and giving Josh time to cover his tracks.

She couldn't know what he'd done. She would run, and Grim would get his stupid heart crushed because she was the one. He knew it deep in his bones.

"Hey, sorry I'm late. I had to go to two different stores to get beer. The gas station was out, so I went to the grocer. You two find something to do?" There was a smirk on his face as he leaned against the doorjamb. His best friend looked completely innocent. Well, innocent when it came to stealing and putting his nose where she didn't want it. Not so innocent when it came to his eyes going over every inch of Nicole's body. "Though I'll admit I liked your rope dress better. But I suppose you can't wear it to dinner. If you do it, then the dads are going to want to do the same with Mom, and we need boundaries. So many boundaries."

Nic's jaw dropped. "You knew they would invite me to dinner?"

Josh shrugged. "You're here at six p.m. on a Sunday, and there's a seat at the table for you. So many of my friends have had Sunday dinner with my family. It's no big deal. They'll barely notice you're there. They'll ask a few polite questions and then my dads will discuss how the Cowboys played and what their playoff chances are, and Mom and Liv will talk about the latest book they've read. You might want to listen in. Those conversations can get wild."

"Josh, do they think I'm a friend or do they think I'm the chick you both slept with last night?" Nic asked, her lips in a frown. "From what I can tell, everyone in town likely knows by now. You carried me away."

"Did you?" Grim wished he'd been there. "See, that seems gallant of you."

He would have picked her up and cradled her to his chest and been her knight in shining armor. Everyone would have known Nicole was protected by him.

"He threw me over his shoulder like a sack of potatoes," she corrected, and seemed to include Grim in her general displeasure. "Sort of like you carried me around like luggage."

Grim frowned Josh's way. "You're supposed to treat her like a lady. When you need to abduct her because she's being stubborn, you pick her up gently and cradle her against your chest. So everyone sees her pretty face."

Josh shrugged him off. "Well, at the time her face was more angry, and I was worried about her use of language. They got to see her pretty ass. You're the one who carted her around this afternoon, so maybe don't judge."

"There is a time and place, brother. When she's in my ropes, I get to do whatever I like. When she's on the street and we're in the vanilla world, we should kidnap her like gentlemen."

Nicole's head dropped, her hands covering her face as she laughed. "You're both crazy." She swung her head up, the frown replaced with a joyous smile. "And you can't kidnap me. Also, Grim is right. There is a time and a place, and I liked the rope thing way more than I thought I would. It was a nice way to spend the day."

Josh had come in the back door, so he would have walked by Nic's purse. He would have put back whatever he'd taken. Grim kissed Nic's forehead. He'd pushed her enough for the day. "Go get your lip gloss. We need to head up to the big house."

Josh looked down at his watch. "Damn. It's later than I thought."

"Yeah, I should probably get home." Nic kept looking for a way out.

He didn't intend to give her one. "They're lovely people, and I'm pretty sure tonight is enchilada night. You do not want to miss Benita's enchiladas. They're delicious."

She turned to Josh, a pleading look on her face. "You really want me to meet your parents?"

He moved in and cupped her chin, staring down at her in that overly serious way of his. "Now more than ever."

She sighed. "Fine. I'll be ready in a minute."

Grim waited until he heard her walking down the hall toward the bathroom. "What did you find?"

Josh kept his voice low. "She's been living in her car, and I think she slipped up earlier."

He knew exactly what Josh was talking about. "Childswood. It's not a high school. I would bet it's the name of the town she's from."

"I called Harlow."

Grim nodded, approving of the decision. If he'd called in her dads, they would loop in Jack and Sam. This was his and Josh's problem. "Good. I got Nicole to agree to come to Austin with us later this week, but it was a close thing. I think she plans on leaving us when her car is fixed. But she doesn't want to. She feels like she has to. It's almost like she thinks she's protecting us."

"Well, she'll find out it's a two-way street." Josh glanced down the hallway. "I have no intention of allowing her to leave. Something's going on, and when we figure it out, we solve the problem for her and then she won't have a need to leave. Her car is going to be harder to fix than she thinks. Al hasn't even ordered the part yet. It's an old car, so he might have trouble finding one."

"You have to be careful tonight. She's skittish," Grim warned him. "We need more time with her."

"Yeah, I've got a plan for that, too," Josh said.

He shouldn't be surprised. He'd been thinking about the problem. "We bring her back here after dinner and fuck her until she falls asleep, and then one of us drives her to work in the morning and picks her up and brings her right back here."

Josh nodded. "Great minds do think alike, brother.

"She's nervous about meeting the parents."

Josh waved the worry off. "I happen to know they're going to find a lot to talk about. Now before she gets back you should know your brothers spent the afternoon preaching something about wickedness causing the apocalypse, and the apocalypse is the bred heifers dying."

"They're not going to die. I got to them fast enough." The last thing he needed was his bio brothers causing trouble right now.

"Do they think it's the eighteen hundreds and Grim's a witch?" Nic was smiling again, a grin lighting up her whole face. "Oh, or is it me? Am I the wickedness killing the cattle off?"

Josh moved into her space, his hands going to her hips. "Hey, if there is wickedness here, it's almost surely me."

"Yeah, but you're the rich kid. Your wickedness will be overlooked. Grim and me are the ones in danger," she replied, but it was easy to see this conversation wasn't bothering her.

She'd said she was an open book, and she was when it came to her emotional state. He could tell when she was nervous, when she was happy, when she felt safe.

"Then I'm going to have to protect you both," Josh said.

He held her close and looked back at Grim, his gaze a vow.

They would both protect her. From everything.

* * * *

"So, Nicole, what is it you do for a living?"

Abigail Barnes-Fleetwood looked damn good for her age. She had auburn hair and green eyes and looked like an older version of her daughter, who was sitting across the table from Nicole.

The elegant table in the stunningly luxurious house. It might be a ranch house, but these weren't hard-scrabble ranchers. This was a wealthy family, and their home showed it.

It was almost like she was back in Childswood, sitting in the dining room of her mother-in-law's house. She'd been forced to sit there every holiday and listen to all the reasons why she wasn't good enough to be one of them. She wasn't well educated. She wasn't amusing or charming or any of the other -ings that would make her suitable.

She'd given them time to get used to her and then she'd told Micah she would never step foot into his parents' house again.

She'd spent two days in the hospital and was there at the next mandatory dinner party.

She'd been asked a question. It was best to answer and not anger anyone. "I'm waitressing right now, but I start a job in Austin in a couple of weeks. I'm going to work in the marketing department of a small corporation."

Nice. Neat. Easily malleable for most situations. She'd sat up late at night constructing the reply. It was general enough to not tempt someone to ask more questions. It sounded boring and normal, and most people let it go.

"Which corporation? I know a lot of the Austin business world." Jack Barnes sat at the head of the table. There was zero doubt the man was the authority figure of the family.

She felt herself flush and her stomach churn. "It's a start-up. I'm one of their first employees."

"What does the company make? Or are they a service

provider?" Jack asked.

She forced herself to take a drink of the sweet tea she'd requested. It had tasted delicious only moments before. "They sell restaurant equipment."

It was all she could think of. She'd heard Christa complaining about the company that provided her refrigerators.

She knew absolutely nothing about buying or selling restaurant equipment.

Sam nodded as he scooped up some refried beans. "So you're going into sales."

Nic felt like there was a spotlight on her, like she was a one-woman show and the audience would decide if she got another booking or closed down all in one night. Of course they wouldn't simply close her down if they figured out who she was. They would call the police and have her arrested.

"I think Nicole would be great at sales." Olivia had been playing the role of cheerleader.

"Is sales what you did in Chicago?" Abigail asked politely.

The parents seemed nice, but it was obvious they were feeling her out. She'd hoped they would view her as a passing fancy, but she was definitely getting vet-the-new-girlfriend vibes off them. "No. I waitressed in Chicago. And I'm not in sales. I'm in marketing. That's what my degree is in."

Well, it would be if she'd been allowed to finish her last year of college. She'd been dumb and gotten married.

She'd put her last year of college off because he'd said he wanted to spend more time with her. She could go back later, he'd promised.

He'd lied. It was what Micah did best.

"Do you have a place to stay in Austin?" Jack was one of the most intimidating men she'd ever seen. And she'd been in the room with a murderer.

Somehow Nicole thought Jack Barnes would have handled the situation better than she had. "I'll stay with a friend until I can find an apartment."

"Why didn't your friend come get you when your car broke down?" Sam asked.

"Because she's incredibly stubborn and doesn't like taking

handouts." Josh seemed to take charge. He was an awful lot like the man who had to be his biological dad, but maybe he seemed less scary to her because she knew how cuddly he was. "Kind of like some other people I know."

"I didn't take handouts, son," Jack said with a slightly shady grin.

"No, you took blackmail payments," Sam shot back.

"Sam," Abigail chided. "New friends."

Olivia leaned over, whispering Nic's way. "Dad's sperm donor was a married politician. When he tracked him down, he got the money to buy this ranch in exchange for him staying quiet about the circumstances of his birth."

"Years later, his father got caught doing all kinds of shady shit. He died in jail, but we did get a real nice uncle out of it," Josh said like it was a normal thing to confide.

"Yeah, Lucas is awesome," Grim acknowledged. "But I'm still trying to figure out how Abby's daughter married Jack's brother and it's okay. It still feels weird to me. Like how does that tree work?"

"It's also weird because Lucas is Dad's half brother," Olivia added. "So he's our uncle but also our brother-in-law."

"The branches get real twisty," Josh agreed.

"It's perfectly legal," Abigail said, eyeing her kids. "And you know it. There's not a bit of blood between them."

"No, but Uncle Aidan sure is," Josh quipped. "And why do we call him uncle? Because he is really just our brother-in-law. You want to take that one, Dad?"

Jack laughed, the sound booming through the room. "Fine. I'll quit asking questions." He smiled Nicole's way, and the man was so beautiful when he smiled. It made her understand how gorgeous Josh would still be thirty years from now. "Nicole, my children are pointing out that maybe we should ease into getting to know each other. They think I'm being too nosy. I don't mean anything by my questions beyond sheer curiosity."

She could almost believe him. Almost. "It's all right."

"I thought they were doing that thing where they hit a new friend with all the weirdness of our family in one go to see if she or he can handle it," Sam said. "More than one newbie has fled in terror."

She had to smile at the thought. Though she was still trying to wrap her mind around the stepdaughter marrying half brother thing, and apparently someone else had been thrown in, too. This was a complex family. "I'm made of stronger stuff, sir."

"Just Sam is fine," Sam Fleetwood said with a sunny smile. "The Sir thing does not work with me."

"Sam," Jack said, his name a warning.

"Yes, Jack." Sam had the sweetest smirk on his face as he looked to Jack like he had a secret. "I'll behave."

It hit Nic what he'd meant. "Oh, because I meant polite sir because you're a guy and you meant capital S sir because you're a…" What the hell was she saying? "I mean. Of course, I'll call you Sam. It's a nice name."

"She blushes frequently, Josh. She's never going to be able to play poker," Jack pointed out with a chuckle. "But she's also correct." Jack looked to Josh and Grim. "Am I going to get in trouble for going down this road?"

What road? She didn't want to be on a road.

She wanted to enjoy this excellent food. She wanted to be excited about meeting her boyfriends' parents. She wanted to be able to believe she had some kind of future with Josh and Grim.

"She's okay with the lifestyle, Dad. She's taking to it well, and that's all I will say about the subject," Josh explained.

"We're taking her to Austin this weekend." Grim seemed decidedly ungrim. He was practically cheery.

They'd told his parents they were taking her to a sex club. Not in so many words, but it was obviously a code.

She felt a warm hand on her wrist. Abby gave her a soft smile. "Sweetie, parents always know. If you were vanilla and Josh had told me you were going away on a trip, I would expect you would be intimate. It's a part of life, and a good part of it. No one's going to ask invasive questions about it, but know we support you as you explore this lifestyle, and there's no judgment at all here. I've been in your position. It can feel odd to be so open, but I think you'll find it's freeing once you embrace the idea there's no shame in loving someone the way they need to be loved, in allowing yourself to be loved the way you need to be."

She was not going to cry. She was absolutely not going to cry.

In mere moments Abigail Barnes had been more of a mother than she'd ever had. Nic was certain she hadn't meant to be, but a deep well of longing opened inside her. Had she ever truly been loved?

It felt like it when Josh tossed her over his shoulder or when Grim grinned down at her and offered her a chocolate because he'd tied her hands together. The sex was phenomenal, but it was the sweetness of those in-between moments that were getting to her.

It was the genuine intimacy of being with them that made her long for something more.

But she couldn't cry here at the table. There would be questions, and she couldn't answer them.

I'm crying because I'm falling in love with your sons, and I can't be with them because I'm wanted for murder and someday they're going to do a true crime show about it and you'll see my face and be so shocked.

You'll be ashamed to even know me.

But I didn't do it. I didn't.

She couldn't say any of those things so she choked the emotion down, shoving it as deep as she could. "Thanks. I'm looking forward to going to Austin, though I hope Christa doesn't need me."

"You deserve time off," Grim insisted.

"When was the last time you didn't work?" Josh asked. "You get off work and go looking for more work."

"Well, today counts. I wasn't allowed to work today," she pointed out.

Abby smiled as though she understood what it meant to deal with bossy men. "I think Christa can do without you for a few days. If she needs someone to fill in, I still have my old uniform."

Sam winked her way. "Damn straight you do, baby, and you still look good in it."

Olivia groaned. "Pops, no. Don't. I'm trying to eat."

Sam simply upped the wattage on that smile of his. "Daughter, how do you think you got here?"

"Oh, we are not going there." Josh's head was shaking. "Momma, what have you been reading lately? I noticed Nic likes to read."

It was news to her. "You did?"

He nodded her way. "You had a couple of paperbacks in your room. Momma and Livie are big readers, though you should understand they pretty much only read one thing."

"Not true," Liv said, a hand on her chest as though to say what me? "I read a lot of things. I read suspense."

"Where the detective solves a murder as he's railing the heroine," Grim explained.

"I read fantasy." Abby seemed to pick up on her daughter's vibe.

"Where a bunch of fairies rail the heroine," Josh added.

"Oh, I recently read a science fiction where the heroine's spaceship lands in a prison colony," Liv said with a grin. "And she totally gets railed hard. But I mean they were unjustly imprisoned."

"So what we're saying is we read a lot of super spicy romance," Abby explained. "And the boys make fun of us, but we don't care."

"That's what I read, and I'm pretty sure I read the prison colony one." Nic felt infinitely more relaxed talking about books. "Have you ever read the Texas Temptress series?"

Both women got very excited.

"Every single one," Abby declared.

"Which is weird because they're written by my sister," Josh said with a grimace. "And those are some hardcore books. From what I've heard."

Nicole ignored him, looking to Abby because this was world-shaking information. "Your daughter is an author? Your daughter wrote *Dallas Delights*?"

"And that is how our sister became more interesting to our girlfriend than we are." Grim sighed.

"Hush, son," Abby said. "The women are speaking now."

But she said it with a grin on her face.

And for the first time in forever, Nic felt like she belonged.

Chapter Ten

"Are you sure you don't need another set of hands?" Nic asked as Josh pulled the truck up in front of the motel.

"I have no idea how long it's going to take, baby." Grim slid out of the back seat.

He'd insisted she take the front when they'd gotten called out on another bovine emergency. This time Grim had to drive about forty minutes out of town to deal with more of whatever bug seemed to be hitting the cattle population of Willow Fork and its surrounding area.

"But I wish you would stay at our place." Josh had made his preferences clear.

Nic was sure if he'd had time he would have argued further, but Grim insisted on getting out to the Settleman's ranch as soon as possible. Apparently time was of the essence. "All my stuff is here, and I have to go to the mechanic's shop tomorrow morning anyway. I've been fine at this motel for weeks."

"You could be more fine at our place," Josh insisted. "You can grab your things and we'll drive Grim out and then I'll take you home."

She wasn't going to argue with him. It would be hours and hours on the road when he should be helping his brother. "I have to work tomorrow if I'm going to go to Austin with you this weekend. Leaving Christa down a server for the weekend isn't a great look for me. So I better not be late to the shifts I'm actually working. Or do we want to cancel the Austin trip?"

Josh frowned her way, his eyes narrowing. "Oh, we're going to Austin."

That sounded like a threat, but it was one she didn't take too seriously. Josh didn't like having his seemed-reasonable-to-him advice rejected. He would get over it.

Or not. Sometimes it was hard to remember that they had an end date and it was rapidly approaching. The idea of staying with them at their place until she needed to leave had been tempting, but she still had to work. For the week or so it would take to fix her car now that she had the cash, she would have to earn some more. Every dime she had was being spent on the car. She would need money to get out of Willow Fork.

"Hey, maybe you should come with us." Grim opened her car door and held a hand out to help her down.

"Or maybe I should stay with her," Josh offered.

Nic shook her head. "Absolutely not. Grim needs you. I'll be fine. I'll see you tomorrow. I work the lunch shift, so I get off at 5:30." Wow, she was being presumptive. The night seemed to have gone well with their parents. She'd spent hours talking to Abby and Olivia about books. They'd sat out on the patio and had a couple of glasses of wine while the men watched the evening football game. She'd been ready to explain all the reasons she needed to go back here when they'd rushed in and hustled her out. "I mean if you want to see me. You might not have time tomorrow, which is fine."

"I'll pick you up at 5:30. We'll go to dinner and talk about what we're going to do in Austin," Josh said.

Grim's eyes rolled as he pulled her close. "He'll have us at the diner for lunch. We'll see you soon, baby. And keep your cell charged this time. I want you to call us if anything happens here. I know you've been okay so far, but this is not a safe area. I hate leaving you."

If she didn't move this along, she might find herself tied up in the back of the truck, Grim carrying her around like luggage at his house call. Nope. She wasn't ready for that yet.

She went on her toes and kissed him. "Good night. I had a great time with the family."

"You fit right in," Grim whispered. "I knew you would."

She moved back, though she didn't want to. She wanted to stay wrapped in those strong arms. Grim was a big old teddy bear. Under his brooding exterior there was the sweetest, kindest man. "Have a good night."

"Nic," Josh called out. Josh was opposite his brother. Josh looked like the all-American, happy-go-lucky cowboy. But there was a darkness to him. She couldn't explain it any other way. In this case she didn't view the darkness as dangerous. There wasn't any evil in Josh. There was a deep willingness to take on the bad things of the world, an eagerness, almost. He would slay the dragons and enjoy the process. "You lock the door. I'm not going anywhere until I'm sure you're locked in, and if anything happens and you don't call us…"

"Yeah. My ass will be red. Promises, promises." No, he didn't scare her, and that was the scariest thing of all.

She strode to the door as she heard Grim climb into the seat she'd vacated. She waved as she used her key and let herself in, locking the door firmly behind her.

It was more than a minute before the truck pulled out of the parking lot.

Likely because they'd argued about whether they should go at all. The woman who ended up with those two men would likely be driven crazy by their overprotectiveness.

She would also be loved and coddled and tied up and spanked and given so many orgasms, life made sense for once.

Nic took a long breath. It wouldn't be her, and there was no use in wallowing in that knowledge tonight. She had a spectacular weekend to look forward to.

And she had a new book. Abby had given her a copy of the latest Alexis Ann O'Malley novel. It was something called an ARC. She wasn't sure. All she knew was that this sucker wasn't even supposed to be out for three months, and then she'd have to find a library that had a copy and get on their waiting list.

But no. She got to read it now. Tonight.

She turned and stopped because something wasn't right. She'd closed the bathroom door. She was sure of it. She remembered doing it.

Housekeeping was once a week. This wasn't some fancy hotel.

Most people stayed either by the hour or the week. If she wanted towels, she went to the office and someone gave them to her.

So if the bathroom door was open it was because someone had been in here.

Someone had been in her room.

Had she closed the door?

Yes. She'd turned off the lights and closed the door because she wanted to deal with as little space as she needed to. She didn't want to walk in and worry about someone rushing out of the bathroom. At least with the door closed, she might hear it opening. It was why she ensured all the closet doors were closed as well. Why she checked the windows to make sure they were locked and placed a chair under the door handle every night except the previous one.

When Josh and Grim had been here she'd felt perfectly safe.

She didn't feel that way now.

A cold streak of anxiety rushed across her spine. Was someone in the bathroom? Were they waiting in there for her to investigate so they could catch her?

It had been years, and she'd almost decided that the Holloway family had forgotten about her. She hadn't searched for them online or tried to keep up with what was happening in Childswood. It felt like if she did that, she was opening herself to trouble.

The cops wouldn't be hiding in a bathroom.

But the men her husband had owed money to might.

Or she was being paranoid and she'd only thought she'd left the bathroom door closed.

A knock caused her to jump, barely stifling a scream by clasping her hand over her mouth.

"Nicole? You in there?" a feminine voice asked.

Relief flooded through her. She wasn't alone. She threw open the door and Heather stood there looking solid and secure. There was something about the woman that screamed competence. "Hey."

Heather's blue eyes widened. "Honey, are you okay? You look like you've seen a ghost. Please tell me this place isn't haunted because I could believe that."

Nic glanced back. "I thought I closed the bathroom door. I guess I'm being paranoid."

"I'll go check it for you." Heather walked in and strode to the bathroom door.

"You don't have to," Nic began.

"It's okay. I check my room every time I walk in," Heather assured her. "It's not paranoia. It's smart when you're staying in a place like this. Anywhere, really. It's not like women at the Hilton are immune to attackers."

Heather disappeared behind the door, the light coming on. It was only a few seconds before she reappeared. "Nothing. No one lurking behind the shower curtain. I always check there. Always. Too many horror movies."

"I'm sorry. I was sure I'd closed it."

"I saw maintenance walking around earlier," Heather offered. "Well, I saw a dude in overalls with a toolkit. And I overheard the manager complaining about the fire marshal coming out next week to check that they're up to code. It could have been that. They have the right to come into the room for maintenance."

She didn't like the thought, but it explained the situation. "That makes sense."

"You okay? You were gone all day. I wanted to make sure that cowboy didn't break you."

"Break me?"

"In the best of ways," she replied with a grin. "He reminds me of a lot of the guys I know. I hang out with a lot of cowboys and ex-military men. They can be awfully possessive, if you know what I mean."

"Well, he did toss me over his shoulder when I didn't come with him."

"I got the feeling you didn't mind that. Should I have protested?"

"No. That's kind of Josh's love language." And Grim's was tying her up and feeding her treats. "I'm sorry for freaking out. I've been in bad positions before."

"It's okay." Heather put a hand on her shoulder. "Do you want to talk about it? Sometimes that helps. When I was younger, I had this guy who decided he owned me. I thought we were friends. He wanted something more and wouldn't take no for an answer."

"Yeah, I know the type. He ever hit you?"

Heather nodded. "Yep. He shot me once."

Nic felt her jaw drop. "He shot you?"

Heather dropped the left shoulder of the robe she wore, revealing a tank top and the beginnings of an old scar right above her breast. "Well, he didn't do it himself, but I totally blamed him for it. When he was stalking me, I assure you I checked every bathroom. All I'm saying is I know what a bad relationship looks like, and I would say you've had one in the past."

Nic sniffled, the events of the day coming down on her. Would it be so terrible to talk to someone? Heather seemed nice, and it wasn't like she would see her after she left Willow Fork. "I was married to a man who enjoyed hurting me. Now I'm dating a couple of guys who are into spanking and I like it. Is that perverse? Shouldn't I be afraid of them?"

Abby wouldn't be able to give her an outsider's opinion. Neither would Olivia. They were both too invested in the lifestyle. She definitely wouldn't talk about this with her boss. It would be too weird. But maybe she could open up to Heather.

"What you are describing is two completely different things." Heather sat down on the edge of the bed.

"I don't know. I've heard the word *control* used a lot. That's what Micah was trying to do," Nic said quietly, admitting her fears. That Josh and Grim's sweetness was a front, and they would turn into something else. Something hard, something that would drain her until she was a husk of her former self.

Like her sister-in-law had been.

Heather seemed to think about the situation for a moment. "Control is the object of the abuser. Your husband used pain and terror to control you. In the case of that cowboy, I would bet control is a tool for him. Control is a way to enhance… Are we talking about sex?"

Nic felt herself flush. "We don't have to."

Heather seemed to breathe a sigh of relief. "I'm more than happy to. I only wanted to make sure we're on the same page. So they like to play games?"

Nic nodded. "But what if the games are to set me up for something else?"

"What if they're just there to enhance your pleasure? To explore the relationship in a way a lot of couples never do?"

"Micah was sweet in the beginning," Nic admitted. "He didn't hit me until after we got married. I didn't have anyone to talk to back then. I was scared, and I believed him the first time when he said he was sorry and wouldn't do it again."

Heather patted the place beside her. "How old were you when you got married?"

"Twenty-one," Nic replied, sitting down. Heather was easy to talk to, and she wasn't as worried about screwing up like she had earlier when she'd mentioned Childswood. Heather was just the woman next door. She wouldn't think about delving into Nic's history. "My parents weren't around, so I suppose I was desperate for a family. They had money, so it felt like security. I still don't know why he picked me."

"Picked you? To marry?"

"Yeah. There were so many other women, and if he didn't love me, I don't know why he would pick me." It was something she thought about a lot. Why out of all the women he'd known had he picked her?

"Maybe it was because he knew you didn't have anyone else," Heather pointed out. "Did you have any friends at the time?"

She thought about her friends from time to time. Not that there had been many. "Yes, but I kind of lost touch with them after we started dating."

Heather nodded as though she knew what came next. "Because he wanted you in his world. He was a predator, and he was looking for the perfect prey. So he did what he needed to do to separate you from your support systems."

"Not that I had much of one, but yes, I had a few friends. And I didn't call them when things went bad because it had been too long. And I was ashamed." She hadn't been able to pick up the phone and admit how wrong she'd been, how she'd let Micah take over her entire life. "He did a great job of isolating me."

"Watch the new guys," Heather advised. "I would bet they won't do anything to keep you away from friends. I would bet they would be as protective of your friends as they are of you. At least that's what I heard. I might have asked around about them."

They were great guys, but the truth was she'd screwed up so long ago. "It doesn't matter. I'm not staying."

"You going to explore more of the world?" Heather asked.

"Something like that." She should stick to what she'd told the rest of Willow Fork. "I have a job coming up. I won't have much time for socializing. That's why I shouldn't worry about falling into some trap they're laying. I think I'm going to get all the good stuff and escape before anything bad can happen."

She said the words with a jaunty smile, but it was easy to see Heather wasn't buying it.

"Or you could understand that the past isn't a road map of the future. You could give it a shot. Like I said, I asked around about Josh after this morning. He seems like a good man to know. His family is influential."

She'd been down that road. "So was Micah's."

"All right, Josh's family seems beloved," Heather corrected. "I heard a lot of crap about their lifestyle, but almost everyone had something nice to say about them. They have helped this community a lot. I heard something about one of the kids in town getting into legal trouble and Josh bailing them out and helping his family find the resources he needed. And apparently his brother is some kind of grumpy saint who heals all animals. They don't sound like bad guys."

"They're not. His family is great." She'd started the evening intimidated by Jack Barnes, but he was nothing more than an older version of Josh. Calm. In control. Ready to protect his family.

Would he protect his family from her?

"All I'm saying is it seems like a relationship you might want to pursue," Heather said.

Nic shook her head. "No. I'm having fun. Nothing more." She wasn't, but she had to start wrapping her head around this fact. She was leaving. She wasn't the magical one for them. "I don't think I could handle two men long term. How can any woman?"

"Happens more often than you would think," Heather murmured. "There are whole towns of trios. Or so I've heard. Anyway, I wanted to check on you. I don't suppose you want some company. I know it's late, but…"

"I would love some." She didn't want to be alone. It didn't matter that there was a decent explanation for why the door had been open. She was still anxious. She still felt like someone was watching her.

"Cool, because something is going on in the room next to mine and while I have decided that it's consensual, I don't need to hear it." Heather made herself comfortable.

Nic went and locked the door. It was nice to have some company.

* * * *

Grim glanced down at the clock and was happy he hadn't done what he'd wanted to and tied up Nic and brought her along. Maybe not tied her up but made her stay close. It was three in the morning, and he was exhausted. And covered in stuff she would not find sexy. Nope. Maybe he needed to keep some parts of his job hidden from her. To maintain a certain mystique. Let her think he sat around giving puppies vaccinations rather than spending most of his time with his hand in some part of a cow it shouldn't have to go in. Doctors wore delicate gloves that covered their hands. Vets ended up with a full-on sleeve to protect them because they were almost always more than elbow deep.

"She seems stable," Josh said, yawning behind his hand.

"Yes, she does." Gail Settleman wore jeans and a sweater, her hair piled high on her head. "She looks like she's been seen by a proper vet who knows what he's doing and not some weird psycho who wants to pray over her." That bit was said toward her father. She turned back to Josh and Grim. "Not that I don't believe the Lord can work miracles. But I think he also expects us to be sensible enough to use the tools we've been given."

It had taken him some time to piece together the fact that he wasn't entirely welcome here. Which was odd. When he and Josh had finally made it out to the ranch, Gail had been waiting with her father, Tom, hanging around in the background, watching him like a hawk. One of their hands had been there waiting to help out along with Gail, but Tom hung back. Usually he was a hands-on kind of guy and they seemed to get along.

"She does seem better," Tom allowed.

"Is there something wrong?" Josh crossed his arms over his chest, frowning Tom's way. "You know you can always find another vet if you don't like how he works."

Grim closed the big leather medical bag his par…Jack and Sam and Abby had given him during his last year in school. It was expensive and well crafted. Made to last. He would be hauling this thing around when he was eighty. Of course if Josh did too much of the protective big-brother routine, he might not have a job at all. "It's fine. It's late and we're all tired."

Gail paled, ignoring him completely and making her plea to Josh. "No. I adore Grim. He's the best. Don't mind my father. There's not another large animal vet for miles. We're so grateful to have Grim." She finally turned his way, a pleading look in her eyes. "We wouldn't know what to do without you."

"And I'm grateful to have the work." He still wasn't sure what was going on.

There was a subtext he was missing. Maybe it was because he was so damn tired.

Maybe it was because now that he'd gotten through the crisis, all he cared about was Nicole. If it wasn't so late, he would stop back by her room and make her pack up for the night. But he suspected he would definitely be the asshole if he woke her up and made her drive twenty minutes to get to their place, and then she would have to get up early to work her shift and he would have to drive her twenty minutes back.

She should move in and they could find her a job with the company. Then he didn't have to worry about her being in that rattrap motel. If he could get her a good enough job, he might not have to worry about her leaving Willow Fork at all.

And he'd proven his point because he'd meant to try to figure out why Tom seemed so distant with him.

Josh's eyes narrowed, proving he was still working on the problem. "Tom, you been listening to rumors? I thought you left that church of Ezekiel's."

Damn it. He should have known. His stepfather was busy at work trying to undermine him in any way he could.

Sometimes he wondered what the hell he'd done to the man beyond wanting to have his own life, besides thinking for himself. "What's he saying about me now?"

Gail looked toward her father, her mouth a flat line. "You want to tell him what all you old men are talking about down at the senior center? Want to admit the nasty rumors you told me? Go on, Dad. You always told me I should never say something about a person if I wasn't willing to say it to their face."

Tom's whole body went tight.

"Yeah, I'd like to hear it." Josh's tone was glacial.

Someone needed to dial the tension back. He knew how his stepfather worked, and Tom was of a mind-set that certain rumors could worry him. His daughter, while religious, wasn't superstitious and didn't believe Satan was around every corner. But there was a harder, more old-school bedrock to Tom's faith that hadn't been instilled in him by the Willow Fork Presbyterian Church. "Tom, what did he tell you? Did he say that the cattle getting sick is God's judgment on us? Particularly you, for being too tolerant of sin?"

Gail's head fell back and she groaned as she looked her father's way. "Your prejudice is going to cost us the best big animal vet we've ever had. Grim, I…"

"Gail, it's okay. Let me talk to him." He gentled his voice, the same way he would around an anxious animal. "I know you don't agree with my lifestyle or the way the Barnes-Fleetwood family chooses to live, but do you honestly think God is punishing you for not… What exactly do you think he's punishing you for?"

Tom's expression went mulish. "Your stepdaddy was pointing out that God has rules and when we don't follow them, he punishes us. Like in the Bible."

"He sent his only begotten son to earth so he wouldn't have to punish us anymore." If there was one book Grim knew backward and forward it was the Bible. It had been the only book he'd been allowed to read from the ages of twelve to sixteen. "Our sins are forgiven through him. No need for the Almighty to hurt some cows to make a point. This was a problem with the alfalfa. We all get ours from the same place, and that's why we're all having this problem. It was contaminated with blister beetles."

Tom's eyes went wide with understanding. "Oh, no. I'm glad I didn't give that to the horses."

Because the toxins associated with the beetles was almost always deadly to horses, but cattle and sheep handled it better. "We're going to help you dispose of any leftover alfalfa, and I'll file all the forms so the feed store will replace the feed, and they'll handle my bills since this was their responsibility. But I don't want you to worry about anything but taking care of your herd. I'll work with Gail to make sure everything gets done."

Tom sighed, and his hands found his pockets. "I'm sorry, Grim. Your stepdaddy is a powerful preacher."

"Of hate," Gail said under her breath.

"I didn't know about the beetles," Tom admitted. "And one of your brothers mentioned that you might…well…you might be trying to wrangle up some business."

Josh cursed but Grim stayed calm. Of course they had. If he wondered what he'd done to his stepfather, he definitely wasn't sure what he'd done to his brothers.

Josh was his brother now. Olivia was his sister. He'd love to see someone try to tell Olivia they were kicking one of her brothers out of their home.

But then Olivia had been raised in love. Maybe that was the difference. His brothers hadn't been strong enough to withstand the constant wear down their stepfather had given them. They'd been torn down to their basic forms and rebuilt into something Ezekiel Smith wanted them to be. Grim hadn't. He'd been stronger—and it was strength, he realized now. It wasn't stubbornness or stupidity. It was strength. It was the will his biological dad had wanted him to have, had gifted to him.

"Tom," Josh began.

But this battle wouldn't be won with intimidation. This was a battle that could only be won with kindness. He gestured for Josh to let him handle it. "Tom, I promise on the soul of my father—my real father—that I would never harm an animal or put one in danger for any amount of money. I believe in what I do. I'm sorry if they said those things about me, but they are not true. All I can ask you to do is look back at my actions and watch what I do going forward."

"Like you'll come back around," Tom said with a defeated shake of his head.

"I'll be back by tomorrow to check on your herd," Grim promised. "And if you need anything at all, I'm a phone call away. If you're worried I'm harming your herd in any way, I'll find another vet to come out here for you."

"Why would you do that?" Tom asked.

"Because he's a freaking saint," Josh grumbled.

Poor Josh. He wanted to kick some ass in defense of his family, and no one let him do it. "Because I'm a vet and I won't let my clients down. No matter what Ezekiel says. What I've figured out recently is that my time with that man was an aberration. I had a great dad. He taught me a lot, but he died. And then I found two other dads who loved me for no other reason than the fact that I needed love. They taught me I'm capable of anything, including caring about people who don't care about me."

Tom's eyes came up, and there was a sheen to them. "Damn, Grim. I'm sorry. You should know they're talking about you."

"No one else believes them," Gail said, her eyes rolling.

But there would be others. At least he seemed to have fixed things with Tom. He would have done that for Gail's sake alone. Gail had always supported him, had helped him ease into the community after he graduated and finished his internship. "It doesn't matter. I'm going to clean up, and I'll get that paperwork done in the morning, if you don't mind."

"We appreciate everything you've done," Gail said quietly. "You come clean up in the big house when you're ready. I've got a batch of cookies and a bottle of rum I brought back from my cruise last week for such an occasion. I'll make a basket for you boys. And I'll throw in a sampler of that hand lotion I was telling your momma about on Sunday."

Gail started up the long walk to the big house.

"Sorry, Grim." Tom tipped his hat. "We do thank you."

He followed his daughter.

Josh stared after them. "Your stepfather is heading for trouble."

Grim started to pack up. "It's nothing he hasn't tried before and nothing I can't handle. You do not have to bring the dads into this."

Josh turned slightly his way. "You're no fun. You know Dad hasn't recently eviscerated anyone in a metaphorical fashion. He's getting antsy."

"He can stay antsy." He wasn't putting Jack Barnes in the line of fire. "Ignore them and they'll find someone else to hate on."

Not for long, but he'd had respites when Ezekiel decided Taylor Swift was in league with Satan and needed to be brought down with a carefully thought-out social media post. Or a completely unhinged one that should get him on a couple of watch lists.

"At some point the man's going to push this too far, and you need to understand I won't let you get hurt," Josh vowed.

But it wasn't tonight. "If he ever gets dangerous again, I'll let you and the dads handle him. For now, let's get cleaned up. I've got a mountain of paperwork to do, and I have to get it all ready because I'm not working while we're in Austin with our sub."

In a few days, he wouldn't have to think about anything except her.

He was looking forward to some peace.

Chapter Eleven

Nicole couldn't escape the feeling that she was being watched. Maybe it was nothing more than all the gossip that had spread after Sunday's showdown with Josh's evil ex. Maybe she'd simply made a misstep that put her on the town's radar, and in a couple of days they would move on to something else, but Nic wasn't sure and the knot in her gut made her think it was past time to move on.

She adjusted her purse over her shoulder as she looked up at the auto mechanic's shop. She had the money in her bag and with tips over the next two days, maybe she could head out before she was supposed to go to Austin with the guys.

Or maybe going to Austin would throw off anyone who was watching her. Maybe going to Austin was actually a way to solve her problems.

She was getting good at justification.

"Hey, sorry. I had to take that," Heather said as she joined her on the steps leading up to the office. She'd decided to tag along since her mom was being tended to by a home health nurse today. She'd declared it was her day off and joined Nicole.

It was nice to have a friend, but she kind of wondered what Olivia was doing today. Heather was nice but she was probably almost old enough to be her mom. She talked about her kids and husband a lot. And the town she was from.

If Olivia was here, Nic could get her to talk about Josh and Grim. She could hear all their childhood stories.

It was good she was with Heather because Heather reminded her of everything she had to lose. She'd already lost her chance to have a normal life. If she wasn't careful, she wouldn't have any life at all. She wasn't going to get to have kids with her husband, wouldn't enjoy living in a quirky town. She wouldn't have a solid job like Heather's.

She would be alone, and at some point the law would catch up to her and she would either die or go to jail for a crime she didn't commit.

All in all, it was a pretty shitty future, so why was she fighting the glorious present she found herself in?

A man walked by, his big dog on a leash. His eyes trailed her way and a frown crossed his face before he suddenly needed to be on the other side of the street.

Oh, yeah, that was why. She was rapidly becoming the town pariah.

"He seems fun." Heather wrinkled her nose. "Do I smell or something?"

Heather wasn't the reason that man had crossed the road. "I think that's more about me becoming the town whore. I'm sure that Alyssa chick has been running my name into the mud." She shook her head. "It doesn't matter. Let's get this done so we can go to the store."

Not that she would buy anything, but she would help Heather. And then she would work her shift and possibly see Josh and Grim for the last time if she could get her car back tomorrow or the next day.

The thought of leaving them sent her into a tailspin, but what else could she do?

"They're not open yet." Heather pointed to the sign on the door. "They don't open for another fifteen minutes. Do you want me to knock?"

It was only fifteen minutes. She could wait. She sank down on the top step. "It's fine. I thought I would get out here early. I guess small towns run on a different clock than the city."

Heather sank down beside her, setting her gorgeous bag at her side. "Where I come from, time definitely runs slower."

"I thought you came from here."

She shook her blonde hair. "No. My mom moved here after I was long grown. We actually lived up in New York most of my life, but then I traveled a lot and ended up in this little town for a job." Her lips had quirked up like she was remembering something lovely. "I fell for that town. It was a while before I could live there, though. After my husband and I finally got our shit together we moved there, and we've been building a business ever since. You should come sometime. It's mountains and weirdness and surprisingly good coffee."

She would love to be able to visit. But she didn't want to get her new friend's hopes up. "I'm afraid I'll be working a lot soon."

Heather turned to her. "I know. Your dream job. I'm excited for you."

"I wouldn't call it a dream job." More like her never-ending nightmare. She wasn't handling this conversation the way she should, but she found she couldn't work up the will to fake it around this woman.

"Oh. I guess I thought because you moved your whole life for it that it was something you'd always wanted." Heather seemed to think about it for a moment. "Okay, then I have to ask. Why? Does it pay that much better than Christa's?"

She should never have opened this up. Nicole scrambled. "Yes. It's a good bit more money and lots of room to get promoted."

"Is it more important than the guys you're seeing?" Heather asked. "Sorry. I know that's intrusive, but I feel like I've gotten to know you and it's so obvious to me you're crazy about those men. And from what I've heard from my mom, they're good men. I mentioned I have a new friend who's in an odd dating situation and she knew exactly what I was talking about. She said she's been hoping Josh and Grim could find someone nice to settle down with. She said we haven't had a good wedding here in a long time and when those boys settle down, she expects fireworks. I think she meant that literally, like their dads have promised a ceremony the town won't ever forget."

It was good to know they had at least one fan rooting for them, but she could also see why Jack and Sam might have said that. "I bet their own wedding wasn't a big affair. I heard this town was hard on Jack and Abby and Sam."

Heather sobered. "Yeah, I got that story, too. Mom didn't move here until after they'd been married for a while. She said things settled down, but people still talked. Is that why you want to leave? Are you afraid of all the gossip?"

Nic snorted at the thought. "I don't care what anyone thinks except the people I love. I care very much what they think, but I tend to make up my own mind. I spent too many years not able to make my own decisions."

"Because of your ex-husband."

Nic nodded. It felt good to vent. She wouldn't talk about this with Josh and Grim because there was a possibility that the guys would go all alpha-male, protect-our-woman on her and try to find her ex. Who was dead and buried. And that could open a whole line of questioning she was trying to avoid. So Heather was her go-to girl when it came to venting about her previous life. She'd decided it was safe enough. After all, she wouldn't see the woman again in a few days no matter how much she wanted to. Heather felt like family already, like the mom she'd wished she had. And she only said that because Heather had a son who was a mere three years younger than she was. Big sister. That was probably a better way to go. "Micah didn't like it when I disagreed with him. He was a my-way-or-the-highway kind of guy. Except when I tried to take the highway, he punched me in the gut. Never the face. That would have invited questions. But he learned where he could hurt me."

"Honey, I'm so sorry about that," Heather said, putting a hand on her.

It was easy to be with this woman. Willow Fork, for all its problems, was making her soft. She leaned against her friend, reveling in all the affection she could get because the world would be cold again soon. "I got out. Eventually."

"I can't imagine how much that cost you." Heather was quiet for a moment. "How did he take the divorce?"

Normally she would feel like she was on a sheet of ice that had cracked under her feet, but she was sure Heather was merely being kind. It was right there, the impulse to talk to someone about what she was going through. How many times had she longed for someone who could help her work through the problem? Maybe if she was careful she could get some advice. "Not well. He's the reason I had to move."

"I was wondering about that. Does he know where you are?"

Nic shook her head. "I'd like to keep it that way."

"Are you worried he'll try to hurt you again?"

"I'm worried he'll try to kill me." Now she wasn't talking about Micah. She also wasn't lying. She definitely worried that Ted would kill her if only to keep his own culpability in his brother's murder under wraps. "I'm afraid the whole family took exception to me leaving."

"In a kill you way?" Heather sounded horrified.

"Well, they were an intense family. What I didn't know at the time was that they have ties to some nasty people. Like criminals. They look like the perfect American family from the outside, but when you scratch the surface, there's so much corruption."

"Seriously? Like what kind of crimes?"

"I don't know if the business was used for crimes, but I know my husband had mafia ties that had to do with his gambling," Nic said with a sigh. "Ted told me he took a lot of money from the company. Enough to get the attention of the feds. He did it to try to pay off the people he owed. Not that I could prove it. If I could have, I would have gone to the cops. Instead my choice was to get a divorce. It was scary, but I'm on the other side now."

She would never be on the other side.

"It doesn't sound like you are," Heather said quietly—almost cautiously. "You're still making decisions based on what could happen. Do you think they're looking for you?"

"I hope not, but if they are, I'm ready to defend myself." Nic lowered her voice. "That's why I freaked out last night. I thought…I don't know what I thought. There's no way they know where I am."

Heather was quiet for a moment as though processing the information. "Okay, I'm going to ask a couple of questions, and I don't want you to get scared. I'm asking because I can help you. I've helped women get out of bad situations before."

Despite the words, Nicole felt her anxiety tic up. "I thought you said you had a business with your husband. What do you do?"

"We have a business guiding nature hikes and river rafting and pretty much anything else you can do in the mountains," Heather replied. "But one of my coworkers is also a paramedic, and where I'm from they take training classes that help them identify at-risk people. Women, kids, old folks. It would not be the first time I helped a woman who needed a way out. Do you have secure ID?"

She knew this was the moment she should walk away, but she didn't fucking want to. Nic was tired of being so alone. If Heather knew how to do things, why shouldn't she reach out for help? Could she get through the rest of her life never talking to another person about what was really wrong? "I started out with a couple of IDs, but I'm down to my last one. The one I have right now was very expensive. It's got some tech on it that makes it harder to use for facial identification if someone takes it. I have to find someone in Austin who can help me if I need to change names again."

"I'll find a name for you. Of who can help you. Not a new name. You should pick that." Heather was taking this news like a freaking champ. "There's a network of people who help women leave bad relationships. I can put you in contact with them, but Nicole, you should think about talking to your men."

She shook her head. That was one piece of advice she couldn't take. "I don't need that kind of drama. I assure you if they knew the truth they would run as fast as they can. No. It's better to keep things light between us."

"That young man didn't look like he was keeping things light when he hauled you away. He looked serious about you."

"Josh can be intense. So can Grim, but we've all agreed to the parameters of the relationship." Except she'd lied to them because if she could leave before this weekend, she might. Or might not.

She was trapped between doing the expedient thing and what her body and heart wanted more than anything—more time with them.

"If you're certain," Heather allowed. "But I meant what I said. You don't have to go through this alone. I can help you. Why don't you tell me what happened?"

She couldn't tell her that story or Heather would be calling the police. Luckily she was saved by the door to the shop coming open, and a man who looked to be in his late thirties/early forties stuck his head out.

"Hey there, Miss Nicole," Greg greeted. "Sorry. We were out back working on Leah Raine's old Jeep. Didn't know you were here. Come on inside."

Nic stood, taking a deep breath and thanking the universe for the save. She needed a halfway decent story to tell Heather if she wanted the woman's help. "No problem. We were just enjoying the nice weather."

Greg held the door open for her and Heather.

"Hi, I'm Heather Turner. I'm staying in town for a couple of weeks and find myself right next to Nic here." She walked in, and Nic followed her. "I thought I'd come down with her. It's a nice morning, and I could use the steps."

Nic was fairly certain Josh and Grim would be irritated she hadn't waited for them, but they should get used to the idea that she was independent.

Or not. They should sadly get used to the idea that she would be gone soon. And she was about to find out how soon. "I have the cash for my car. Your dad gave me an estimate of twelve hundred dollars. Which seems high. Couldn't I buy a whole car for that?"

Greg frowned. "What century are we talking about buying from? Do you have a time machine because if we went back to the fifties, we might be able to find a car for that much. Do you want to look on Craigslist? I bet we could find some scam artists who are willing to sell you a car that works long enough for them to disappear."

She did not appreciate his humor. "I get your point. Here's the cash. How long do you expect the work to take?"

Greg accepted the payment, opening the register and making a couple of notes as he logged the payment. "Oh, it's a pretty easy fix. I suspect we'll be done in a day, two tops, once we get the parts in."

Nicole's stomach threatened to clench. Two days. She would have to make a major decision in two days. Somehow she'd thought she might have more time with them. If she was stuck here, then it wouldn't hurt to see them. But if she had the chance to run, she had to take it, right? "So I'll have the car back before the weekend?"

Greg looked up. "Well, if by the weekend you mean two or three weekends from now, then yes. You'll have it before *a* weekend. I guarantee."

Nic was confused. "What? I thought you said two days tops."

"Two days after I get the part," Greg explained. "I'll order it tonight, but it's taking a couple of weeks to get anything in these days. Everything is backed up in some canal. Wouldn't have this trouble if we made anything in this country anymore."

She did not have time for his political opinions. "Three weeks? Are you kidding me? I've already been here for three weeks. You knew I was going to fix my car but you didn't order the part you knew would take three weeks to come in?"

"Well, you hadn't paid for the part," Greg said, altogether too reasonably. "You can't expect us to front you the money."

"People do it all the time." She felt her teeth clench. "If I were in a city…"

"She's good." Heather stepped in. "Order the part and let us know when the car is ready. We'll be going now."

"I don't…" Nic began but Heather hauled her out. "He has my money and my car, and I'm stuck here for weeks."

"There's nothing to be done by arguing with that man," Heather said sensibly. "You're in a small town where the next nearest shop is over an hour away, and you would have to start this process all over again. If you need a ride to your new job… Oh, there's no job, is there?"

Slowly she nodded, frustration forming tears in her eyes. "I never stay in any one place this long. Never."

Heather reached for her hand. "I'm going to help you. I have to go home for a couple of days, but I'll be back on Saturday, and I'll have thought through a plan by then. I think I might know a place where you can go, but I have to make some arrangements first."

She felt like her damn life was ending and Heather was throwing her a life raft. "Why would you help me like this?"

"Because once I needed a place to go, too." Heather squeezed her hand. "Also, the town I live in is kind of known for being welcoming to anyone who needs to find some bliss. Let's do this. Let's move you into my motel room and check you out of yours so even if someone found out your name, it will look like you've left. You can stay there or with Josh and Grim."

"I'm supposed to go to Austin with them this weekend. There's a club there," she said, her mind whirling. Should she believe this woman? Or was she making a terrible mistake? She'd handed over almost all of her cash. She would get tips from her shift this afternoon, but it wouldn't be enough to get her out of Willow Fork.

Panic threatened to overtake her, but Heather was right there, telling her to breathe.

"Go with them. Let me work some things from my side," Heather said.

They started to walk toward the town square with its shops and restaurants, where people were out walking dogs and kids played on the swings in the park. It was all so normal. Normal people living normal lives. They wouldn't be happy every moment. They would suffer tragedies, get sick from time to time, but they had the potential to be content.

She would never find that if she didn't take a risk.

"I didn't divorce him."

Heather stopped. "I know. You ran for your life, and whatever you had to do to get away is fine with me, but we're going to have to talk about it someday. Not now. When you're ready to tell me the whole story, I'll be ready to listen."

Nic felt tears caress her cheeks.

A buzzing sound broke up the quiet moment, and Heather sighed as she pulled her cell out. "I'm sorry. I have to take this. It's my son."

Nic nodded. "Go on. I'll wait here and then we can go to the store if you like. Although you might find they're friendlier if I'm not with you."

Heather's nose wrinkled. "Hush with that. I'll be right back." She slid her finger across the screen. "Hey, sweetie. What's going on?"

She began to talk to her son and Nic found a bench. She sat down and watched the world flow around her, wondering if there was a place for her in it.

* * * *

Josh looked out over the office space on the second floor of the building where the Barnes-Fleetwood Collective's administrative work was done. His fathers had purchased the building on Main

Street years before and changed the former mixed-use office center into an ultramodern space. Not that one could tell from the outside. His mother had taken over the Willow Fork Historical Society when he was a kid in what the town liked to call the Coup of the Century. It wasn't really a coup. It was a case of the society needed money and his mother had it.

Sometimes he wondered if his dad thought they'd made the wrong play. He'd been unwilling to give the society a dime if his wife wasn't the chairman of the board. His mom had turned right around and denied all the changes his dad wanted to make to the façade of the building.

That had probably been one hell of a spanking.

He groaned. He shouldn't have even thought that.

"Hey, Josh. I set the reports on your desk, confirmed your reservations for the club this weekend, and pulled the employment files you asked for. Are we finally firing Alyssa?" His assistant stood in the doorway, a mug of coffee in her hand. Sandy was more of an office manager, and she never let him forget the fact that she'd changed his diapers when he was a baby.

He wondered what it was like for people who lived in cities where not every citizen remembered how you used to accidently pee on them as a small infant.

And the coffee was for her, not him. He'd been told in the beginning that he should get his own.

Now his parents were another story. Sandy would trip over her own feet to make sure Abigail Barnes-Fleetwood had her coffee exactly how she wanted it and made sure there was always Coke in the fridge because that's what the dads preferred.

"I'm reviewing a couple of things," he replied, turning from the window and moving back to the big desk that his father had occupied until he'd decided Josh was up to the task of running the business portion of Barnes-Fleetwood.

The day he and Olivia had taken over, Jack Barnes had saluted his kids and run out of the office after declaring himself a free man.

Sandy's brow rose, and she adjusted her comfortable cardigan. She'd been with the company for over twenty years, and sometimes Josh thought the only reason his dad didn't watch them like a hawk was he knew Sandy would step in if anything went wrong. "Josh, everyone knows what she did to your new girlfriend."

"That doesn't mean I have a business reason to fire her, and my uncle will have my hide if I put the business in legal jeopardy." He sank down into the big chair. Olivia hadn't wanted the larger office, claiming it was too cold in here and the view from hers was better.

Sometimes he thought it was because she'd known how much responsibility came from sitting in their father's chair.

"I'll ask around," Sandy offered. "Her mother's been an excellent employee over the years, but I think Alyssa causes too much drama. If you want her gone, we'll find a way. Now, you've got a call on two, and I've been told to make Olivia's flight plans to Bliss. When is someone going to tell her those boys can't love her the way she needs?"

Josh groaned. "My sister is stubborn. You try telling her the boys she's dreamed about since she was six aren't going to give in. I keep thinking one of them is going to find a partner and get married and dash that dream of hers, but then I think about how few good prospects there are here."

"She'll go to Dallas and drown her sorrows there," Sandy said with a shrug. Sandy liked to keep up with the younger generation's antics.

That was kind of what he was terrified of. "I'll make sure she goes to Austin. Those are the only Taggarts that don't scare the crap out of me. Who's on the phone?" He needed to get ready to go to the very club they were talking about. There were scenes to prepare and romantic gestures to plot. He had a couple of weeks to convince their sub to stay with them. Grim would simply tie her up and fuck her, but he kind of thought they needed a soft touch with her, too. He'd already called his contact at Subversion about ensuring their suite was perfectly stocked. "Is Liv in? Can she deal with it?"

"It's Harlow Dawson, and she asked for you. I can send her to your sister…"

Josh stopped her. "No. I'll take it. Thank you, Sandy."

She gave him a nod and closed the door as she left. Josh picked up his phone. "Hey, Harlow. What's going on?"

"Josh, I've got some news, but you aren't going to like it."

His stomach threatened to turn. He glanced over at the clock. It was only an hour or so until he was supposed to meet Grim and pick up Nic at the café. "Tell me."

What was he going to do if this was bad? How would Grim handle it if there were real problems to face?

"The driver's license is a fake and a pretty good one," Harlow said in that matter-of-fact manner that let him know she was in detective mode. It was the same tone she used when she told a spouse their partner was cheating on them.

"All right." He could handle this. He'd known there was something in her past. "So she's running from something. Likely a bad relationship."

"Maybe," Harlow allowed. "Or she's running from the law. I don't know yet. What I know is the only Nicole Mason in the Chicago area is a ninety-year-old grandmother of ten. Also, I didn't find a Childswood High School or any towns named that in the state of Illinois."

Not so surprising. "All right. So we're working from the theory that Chicago is all bullshit and she's from somewhere else. If someone's trying to hurt her, she would hide her past. And don't say or if she's running from law enforcement."

"As long as you know the she-could-be-a-mass-murderer part is implied," Harlow quipped. "Now what I have found is there are twenty Childswoods across the States. It's going to take me a while to search them. I don't suppose you want to send me a good picture of her so I can run it through facial recognition. One of the things whoever created her license did well is use a laminator that fucks with the picture. It's fairly new technology, so I was impressed. She had to have laid out some cash for this sucker."

Which explained why she needed to work to fix her car. His heart kind of clenched when he thought of how little she had, how vulnerable she was. Would she even think about letting him help her? Or would she run from him? "I'll see what I can do, but now that I think about it, she's camera shy. Olivia tried to take a selfie with her the other night but she said she couldn't stand pictures of herself."

"Or she understands that pictures of herself could lead to IDing her."

It was obvious Harlow had suspicions. He wasn't going to listen to them. "I'd like some other explanation than she's a criminal on the run."

"Cool. She's a vampire and she doesn't want anyone to know she doesn't age."

He did not need her sarcasm. "Your parents didn't spank you enough."

"My parents didn't spank me at all, and neither did yours. I won't go into why because we already have to deal with that crap on a daily basis," she said with a chuckle before she got serious again. "I could use a picture, Josh. I know that feels like you're betraying her, but it's common sense to know who's actually in your bed."

And she should know. "I'll do what I can. We'll be at Subversion this weekend."

"You didn't want to take her to The Hideout?" Harlow asked, and he could hear the grin in her tone. "Gabriel will be devastated."

"No, I like my clubs luxurious." Gabriel Lodge had teamed up with some of the Taggart kids to form their own club, but he was also doing the whole got-to-make-it-on-my-own thing and refusing to use his hefty trust fund. So The Hideout was…rustic. That was a good word for it. "Also, they're better behaved at Subversion. I don't want to have to kill Lucas Taggart because he flirts with my sub, and watching Chloe and Seth is painful at times."

"I know. I wish they would fuck already," Harlow admitted. "I'm waiting for the moment when Uncle Julian finds out his daughter is sleeping with Big Tag's son."

"Big Tag's fuck-boy musician son." Josh chuckled but then remembered he had some problems of his own. "I think my father's worried about what kind of trouble Nic could be in. I wouldn't put it past him to call your dads for help. I know I said not to involve them…"

"But if I let them know I'm looking into it, they'll trust me," she concluded. "I've got my own spies. I'll check it out. If I think I need to intervene, I will, but Josh, you have to know what I find will come out eventually. I can hold my dads off for a couple of days, but if Uncle Jack asks them for information, they'll give it to him."

Sometimes it was hard having the Godfather of Ranchers and Doms as a dad. "I only need a week or two."

He would find a way to get her to open up to him. He and Grim would wrap her in love and affection and as many orgasms as her gorgeous body could handle this weekend. They would prove how devoted they were to her, and she would open up to them. She'd already started. When she was sleepy or satisfied, sometimes she said things he knew she wouldn't when she was focused.

"I can give you a week or two if your dad hasn't talked to mine. If he has, well, I'll give you a heads-up before the shit hits the fan. Which is why you should send me a picture," she replied. "Do you think it's smart to invest this much time with a woman your father is suspicious of? I'm going to take it this is all coming from Jack and Sam thinks she's lovely."

Pops was an optimist. Always. Which was probably why his dad was such a careful man. He had to take care of both of his subs. His loves. He might not love Grim in the same way his father loved his pops, but Grim was one of his soul mates. They didn't have to get physical to be necessary to each other. He had to protect Nicole and Grim, and that meant he needed information. "Yeah, that's pretty much how the conversation went, though it's not like Dad doesn't like Nic. He's afraid she's in trouble, and he doesn't want to get blindsided. I'll get you what you need."

His dad was right. They had to know the truth so they could face it.

"I'll drive down to Austin on Saturday. I'd like to meet her and see if I can make any observations," Harlow explained. "Until then, get me that picture and watch your back. Talk to you soon."

She hung up and Josh sighed, his mind working on the problem.

Chapter Twelve

Nicole looked at the big man sitting on the couch in front of her and couldn't help but stare. And hope she wasn't drooling. He was a delicious-looking man. If one went for glorious Vikings in their prime. Which she didn't.

"Do you have any questions, Nicole?" Case Taggart looked perfectly comfortable in the luxurious room that served as Club Subversion's conference room.

"She usually talks more than this," Grim said with a frown. "I guess she's distracted."

Oh, that sounded like a warning.

"You know if she doesn't want to talk, ball gags can be fun." Josh frowned her way, too.

Definitely a warning. So they knew she was staring at the pretty man. She couldn't help it. She wasn't truly attracted to Case Taggart, but he was like a painting by a master. She couldn't help but stare at it.

"I understand the contract and I'm happy to sign," she replied.

They'd been at the club for a few hours, taking a nice tour.

Everything about the last few days had been nice, and she wasn't sure she was going to be able to work up the will to leave them.

Could she trust them with her secrets?

She was practically living with them. Oh, the majority of her things were in Heather's motel room. She'd taken her friend up on her offer, and now she wasn't losing thirty-nine ninety-nine a day. But she'd spent every night back at their place. Josh had taken to coming into the café right as her shift ended, and then Grim picked them both up in his truck. Sometimes they grabbed dinner before heading back to the ranch. Sometimes they went up to the big house and spent an hour sitting around the table, laughing and talking and enjoying each other's company.

She was sinking into the joy of being a member of a real family, and it was amazing and frightening all at the same time. The scariest thing was how calm she'd been. She believed Heather. When she got back from Colorado, Nic was going to talk to her. Heather knew about domestic violence survivors. Heather would listen to her.

And then she would be ready to talk to Josh and Grim.

It was almost time to make her stand.

"I would normally ask for you to have someone negotiate on your behalf," Case explained.

Ah, when he opened his mouth, she could see there was a real man under all his blond, god-like beauty. "But we live in the twenty-first century, and I'm an adult woman who can make her own decisions."

"Yeah, she's deciding right now how hard the spanking is going to go." But Josh was chuckling, and he winked at her.

"She didn't mean any disrespect, Master Case." Grim was definitely the rules follower of their family. Josh made the rules. Nicole didn't care about the rules, so that left Grim.

When she thought about it, they meshed together quite well. Without Grim, Josh could become a possessive tyrant. Without Josh, Grim might never ask for what he wanted.

Without them, she would be so fucking sad.

Case Taggart had a wide grin on his face. "Oh, I think that's a perfect response. Don't you, baby? Come here. I'd like you to meet my wife, Mia."

The woman who walked in the room was this man's natural mate. She was tall and blonde and stunning. She grinned as she sank down on the couch next to her husband. She leaned over, brushing her lips across his, and it was obvious these were two people deeply in love.

"I thought you were in New York settling Heath in," he said.

"He's happily in his new condo, and I caught a ride back with Riley." The gorgeous Mia—who reminded her a lot of her new friend Heather—turned their way. "Our son is taking over the marketing department for a division of our family company."

"Yes, and as a Taggart," Case grumbled. "Damn brother-in-law offered my only child a million and his own private jet if he would legally change his name to Lawless."

"He was joking about that." Mia's nose wrinkled. "My brother can be obnoxious at times. I'm the lone girl, so Heath is the only one of the nieces and nephews without the Lawless name. Just wait until one of Drew's daughters gets married. He's going to lose his mind."

Now Nic was staring for another reason. "Lawless?"

"Did I not mention that?" Josh asked like forgetting your family was close friends with one of the greatest technological minds of the last century was no big deal. "Yeah, Mia's family runs a company called 4L. Case is the head of their security division."

"And Mia stays far, far away," Mia said with a smile. "Our main offices are here in Austin, but there's a big 4L office in New York, and guess where my son decided to be?"

"He needs some freedom, baby," Case said. "Honestly, he needs to be somewhere where neither of our last names mean anything. That's what your brother doesn't understand. As a Taggart as long as he stays out of the security business he's a regular guy. There is no outrunning the Lawless name. Josh knows all about that. Is that why you never changed your name, Grim?"

Grim seemed taken aback by the question. "What do you mean?"

"I thought they adopted you. Jack did, right?" Case asked.

From what she could tell, the Barnes-Fleetwood family treated Grim exactly the same way they treated Josh and Olivia. If she hadn't been told they'd taken Grim in, she would have assumed he was their biological child.

"He did that so he could protect me from my stepfather, and I'll always be grateful, but I loved my dad." Grim reached out, his fingers tangling with hers as though he needed support to talk about the subject. "My biological father was a good man, and changing my name felt like I was erasing him. Especially since my brother did change his last name. Not legally, but he refers to himself as Smith not Burch. I guess I didn't want to erase him."

"It does," Case said with a nod. "Though if you and Josh follow the whole double up name thing, your wife is going to be a Barnes-Fleetwood-Burch. Or Burch-Barnes-Fleetwood."

"Fleetwood-Barnes-Burch sounds like a band," Mia added.

"I think we'll deal with that when the time comes," Josh said with a shake of his head. "Mia, do you mind showing our sub to the women's locker room? The club is about to open up, and I don't want to miss our scheduled play time."

Play time. She was going to play with two gorgeous men in an opulent club. Anxiety flashed through her. Did she belong here?

Mia stood. "Of course. Come with me."

She gave Grim's hand a squeeze and stood to follow her out because there was nothing else to do. "See you soon."

Grim stood and brushed his lips over hers. She was about to step back when he cupped her cheeks and stared into her eyes. "I'm so glad you're here with us. It finally feels right." He kissed her again, lingering this time. "I know it's intimidating, but it won't always be."

He always seemed to know how she was feeling. Grim's quiet words sent her anxiety fleeing. How had he felt walking into this building for the first time? He didn't have the Barnes-Fleetwood name. He hadn't grown up around wealth and privilege. He'd probably felt exactly the way she had.

"Hey, what about me?" Josh asked, moving in. He kissed her and whispered into her ear. "I hope you enjoy the fet wear, but know I'll have you naked before the end of the night."

A bolt of heat shot through her as she stepped back. This was why it was perfect to be with both of them. Grim knew how to ground her and Josh how to make her fly. "I'm sure you will."

She would have them naked, too. Naked and surrounding her. Tonight they planned to take her together after days of prepping her for anal sex. Tonight she would know what it meant to be their woman.

She stepped away and followed the ridiculously wealthy Mia Taggart out into the hallway. "I'm Nicole, by the way. They forgot to introduce me."

"Yes, they were obviously preoccupied." Mia started down the elegant hall. "I've known Josh and Grim for a while now. Since they joined the club at the tender age of eighteen, and they've never once brought a woman here much less someone they refer to as their sub. Not *a* sub. *Our* sub. You want to know why I hustled back from New York? I wanted to meet you."

"I don't think I'm anything special," Nic replied. "I'm the new girl in a small town, and I don't mind dating two men."

"I'm fascinated with the thought. Not that I need another man in my life. I'm surrounded by them, but I'm always intrigued by how the threesome thing works." Mia stopped, her face flushing. "I'm sorry. I wasn't talking about the sex part. I do understand that. I was more talking about the emotional parts."

"Well, we're in the honeymoon phase right now, I think. It's been great getting to know them, but I don't think those men are going to be hard to love. They're kind of like halves of a whole. They function better together," Nicole explained. "They're really brothers."

"Case has a twin, but they weren't like some I've met. They've always been very different people. I've met a couple of threesomes and they're much like you've described." Mia started walking again. "And I don't think they're into you simply because you're the new girl and they've already worked their way through everyone in town."

"Sometimes it feels like it," Nic said with a sigh. "They're not playboys, but they are healthy young men with way more experience than me."

"Josh and Grim are considered thoughtful when it comes to women. They might have played around when they were younger, but it's been obvious for the last couple of years they're ready to settle down. If they've brought you here and they're introducing you to their lifestyle family, it's because they're serious about you."

"I'm serious about them, too," she admitted. It wasn't something she would have said days before, but she'd been fooling herself. She was going to take the risk. Once she figured out how to tell them.

Hey, guys, you know that job I talked about? Doesn't exist. I've been lying to everyone. Also the name's Nora, but there's a warrant out for my arrest, and I'd like to avoid going to jail. Oh, yeah, and it's for murdering the husband I told you I divorced.

She was going to work on her confession. Delivery was important.

"I'm glad because those young men deserve some happiness." She stopped in front of an ornate door. "Here we are. This is the women's locker room. We've got pretty much anything you could need. Josh let the manager know what you required."

"I required something?"

Mia grinned as Nic walked into the gracious space. "I should have known. He's a good kid, but he's kind of a hard-ass Dom, though I would bet he's indulgent. You have what Josh wants you to have when it comes to clothes and toiletries and such. He's got excellent taste."

"That's good because I would have said get me some soap and a drug store shaving kit and I'll make it work," Nicole admitted.

"Yeah, you'll find your locker is stocked with something a little more elevated," Mia said with a chuckle.

The locker room was not like anything she'd ever seen. It was posh beyond her wildest dream, with an elegant sitting room complete with a buffet with snack foods and a tea and coffee station. Several women sat around in robes, relaxing before their nights began.

"That's my sister-in-law, Carly." Mia nodded at the pretty brunette. "She's written a bunch of cookbooks. Let me tell you her four-cheese ziti is life changing." She turned as a younger woman in bright pink leggings and a corset stepped out from behind a row of lockers. "Oh, hey, Harlow. I didn't know you were in town. How are your dads? I saw your mom a couple of weeks ago."

The lovely woman had an electric blue bob and a face that could be on the cover of a magazine. She was tall and graceful yet also managed to have some killer curves. "I heard Mom talked you into buying the whole collection for the new office. It was a good buy. The artist is very popular. The whole new Western sculpture thing is a mood right now." Harlow turned her way. "I'm Harlow Dawson, by the way. My mom runs an art gallery up in Dallas."

"Her mom is Natalie Buchanan," Mia corrected. "She's

considered one of the best painters working today. There's one hanging in the lobby."

"The one of the man in blue? It's pretty," Nic said, feeling distinctly out of place among all these wildly successful people.

"It's one of my dads, though she'll never say which," Harlow explained. "If she did then one of them would get super jealous. Dad number two can be a man baby. I come from a weird household."

"It's feeling more normal all the time," Nic admitted. "I'm Nicole Mason. It's nice to meet you."

"You're Josh and Grim's new girl." Harlow held out a hand. "I've heard a lot about you."

She felt herself flush. "You have?"

"Josh and I are practically family. We grew up together. His parents spent a lot of time at a club in Dallas my parents also belong to, so most weekends we ended up hanging out together." Harlow glanced back at Mia. "And to answer your question about my dads, they're good. They're in town, too. We're here on business, though. And luckily Mom's back in Dallas, so I get to play tonight."

"Well, tell them to call me. We can have dinner," Mia offered. "Do you mind showing Nic to her locker? I need to get changed myself."

Harlow smiled. "Of course. She's right beside me. Come this way."

She waved good-bye to the woman who looked so much like Heather and followed Josh's friend. Who he'd apparently been talking to about her. It made her gut clench. It was a good thing, right? He liked her so he talked about her.

She'd spent so long trying to hide in the shadows any kind of light felt dangerous.

"So you've known Josh a long time?" She should keep her talks as short as possible, but she couldn't help herself.

"I don't remember a time when I didn't know him. He's a couple of years older than me so he always played the big-brother role." Harlow led her down a row of beautifully crafted lockers. They were dark wood with brushed-copper hardware, and each had a name plate. "Josh is protective of the people he loves, but you've probably figured that out by now."

There was something about the other woman that put Nic on

guard. She was perfectly pleasant, but Nic had learned to trust her instincts, and every single one of them told her Harlow Dawson could be a predator if she wanted to. She wasn't sure if the feeling came from jealousy, though. She said all the right things—calling him a big brother—but it didn't mean she felt like his sister. "Yes. He's a great guy, and so is Grim. I'm lucky to know them. There I am. Thanks for showing me around. This place is huge."

"This place is tiny compared to the club I grew up in." Harlow didn't look like she was ready to leave. She leaned against the locker beside Nicole's. "Grim is great, too, though I haven't known him as long. Josh told me you're from Chicago."

Yes, she was definitely getting a bad feeling from this woman. She opened the locker door. "Born and raised. I should get ready. Is there a place I can shower?"

She hadn't intended to, but it seemed like a way to shake the curious Harlow.

"There is, and I'm pretty sure Josh gave you a robe and a shower kit." Harlow stared for a moment longer. "Well, I guess I should go. I'm actually working a little tonight. I'm waiting on a phone call, so I'll be in the lounge until I clear it up. Case is cool, but the man does not allow business calls on his dungeon floor."

"I hope it goes okay for you." Nicole pulled out the shower kit which was stocked with luxury brands. She also caught sight of her "clothes" for the evening. Well, they didn't take up much space.

Harlow stopped at the end of the lockers, looking back. Nic could have sworn her eyes went hard. "Yeah, I hope it does, too. Have a nice night, Nicole."

Nic watched the other woman stride away and wondered what kind of trouble she was going to cause.

* * * *

Grim's whole body felt alive as Nic leaned back against him, but his mind wasn't in synch. Something was going on in Nic's head. She said all the right things, but there was a tension he couldn't deny. They stood in front of the main stage, watching as Case Taggart sweetly tortured his wife with a flogger.

The good thing about Subversion was Josh hadn't grown up

with Case Taggart or the Lawless clan. There was no one here who'd helped raise him like there was at The Club or Sanctum.

Of course the same was true of The Hideout, but Josh was too fancy for that particular club. Grim kind of liked it. It was stripped down and raw. Kind of like himself.

But this was their home club, and he'd become comfortable in it. Now he had to work to make Nicole see she belonged here, too.

"How are you feeling?" He whispered the question in her ear.

Her head turned slightly. "I'm okay."

Josh was ensuring their semiprivate space was set up properly because he was a heinous control freak. It was semiprivate because there was a two-way mirror. It was sort of the best of both worlds. His sub could pretend they were alone, and his perverted exhibitionist partner could know someone was probably watching their gorgeous sub.

He took her hand and led her away from the main stage. Perhaps they should start their first official scene with some talking. "You're stiff as a board, baby. You're not okay, and you know lying to me in this space isn't cool."

She bit her bottom lip. "I'm not lying. At least I'm not trying to. I don't want to wreck this for you and Josh. I know it's important. So I'm okay, and that's all I want to say about it."

"Not how this works." He needed some backup. He did what came naturally. He leaned over and hauled her over his shoulder in a fireman's hold.

He glanced over and saw Harlow at the edge of the lounge, a martini in her hand. She sat alone with her cell phone on the table in front of her. Which was odd because Harlow was usually surrounded by friends. And she was usually in Dallas.

What was she doing here? He knew Josh had brought her in to try to figure out what was wrong with Nicole, but she could do the investigation from Dallas.

She tipped her drink his way and Grim acknowledged her with a wave before starting down the hallway leading to the semiprivate rooms. There was another floor with privacy rooms, but they wouldn't need them tonight. They would be taking Nic back up to their suite when the scene was over. That was where they intended to take her together for the first time.

"You can't pick me up and move me whenever you want, Grim," Nic complained.

He brought the flat of his hand down on her ass. Hard. "In this club I can. Unless you want to safe word out, and then I should go and get Josh because he's spent the last hour getting our rooms ready."

Josh was the planner in this case. He'd tricked out the suite with roses and champagne and the perfectly romantic plug they would use on her ass. Then he'd come down to ensure their scene space was ready.

"I'm not using my safe word," Nic protested. She was perfectly compliant as she lay over his shoulder. "I just…I just don't feel comfortable here."

So he'd been right. He passed the big Dom who was acting as a monitor for the evening. The man waved him through, holding up three fingers to let him know what room they were in.

He stopped in front of the door marked three because he was fairly certain this was a conversation Josh wouldn't understand. He set her on her feet. "Why don't you belong here?"

She steadied herself but her eyes remained on his chest. "Grim, you know why."

"I might, but you need to say it. We can't face something that you won't say out loud." He needed to make a few things plain to her. "Nicole, I'm in deep with you. I know you're planning to walk away…"

Her eyes came up and her hands found his chest, flattening against him. "You're making it hard."

"I want to make it impossible," he admitted. "But I can't do that if you're unwilling to talk to me. Look, I'll give you all the time in the world to get to know and trust me about whatever happened in your past."

Tears were suddenly in her eyes. "And if it's bad?"

"Then we'll face it. All three of us," he said. "No matter what it is. But you take your time. However, you can't lie to me in this club."

She seemed to relax. "I wasn't lying. Not exactly. I am okay."

"You're not. You're uncomfortable, and I want to know why. I want you to admit it."

Her jaw tightened. "Grim, I grew up in a rundown three-bedroom that my dad and stepmom rented. They were always late on rent and pretty much everything else. The lights would go out for weeks at a time because they couldn't pay the bill. I didn't own a car until a few years ago. I tried this. My husband's family had money, and they never let me forget it."

"I'm not your damn ex," a deep voice said.

Damn it. He'd tried to keep this between the two of them, but Josh had opened the door behind Nicole and stood there, a darkness in his eyes.

When Josh was in top space he could be a bit unreasonable. "She knows that, but this place can be overwhelming when you first walk in. I know you're used to wealthy spaces but Nicole's not, and I understand that. Let me handle her."

Nicole turned, and her hands went to her hips. "I'm allowed to have feelings, Josh."

Damn, but she was pushing him. "That's not what he said."

"You're allowed to have feelings, but you are required to talk about them." Josh stepped back, gesturing for her to enter the room. "And I can have some feelings of my own. I want to know who made you feel bad."

She sighed, and her shoulders came down as she walked into the room. "No one. You can't understand. You've never been in this position."

"She's right about that," Grim said as he followed her. He leaned in, his voice going low. "She's overwhelmed and doesn't need a bunch of jealousy thrown her way right now."

"I'm not jealous of her asshole ex," Josh replied.

"You aren't?" He knew his brother.

"Fine. Of course I am," Josh admitted with a fierce frown. "I'm insanely jealous of anyone who's ever touched her before, but she can't throw me in the same bin with him. The only thing we have in common is money. She started pulling away the minute she figured out my family was wealthy."

Nicole turned to Josh. "I adore your family, Josh. I love them. But I worry they won't love me when they figure out who I really am. And this… Everyone here is so refined. They all have these important jobs. Did you know Mia is some kind of award-winning journalist? And her sister-in-law has been on TV. Your friend Harlow said her mom is a famous artist. I don't even have an undergrad degree. I don't know why I'm here. I won't even go into the whole Andrew Tech God Lawless. Your parents are successful and they taught you how to be, too."

Josh's features softened. "Baby, success is a word we have to define for ourselves. I'm successful because my dad fought for his place. And the truth of the matter is the reason he fits in here is because he doesn't care what anyone thinks. He doesn't have a fancy degree. He and Pops grew up in foster care. My momma was a teenaged single mom who got run out of town. When you talk about me being successful, that's all because of them. My success will be appreciating what they gave me and taking care of it. It'll be in building a family with my best friend and the woman I love. I'm not successful. Not yet. If I achieve that, it might be because of you."

Tears clung to her cheeks, and Grim knew they were past the worst of this episode. "I'm the same as Josh, baby. I didn't pay for my school."

Josh turned to him, his head shaking. "No, but you survived some horrific abuse. You could have given in and become like your brothers. But you were tested, and you showed the world exactly who Jared Burch is. He's a survivor. I would bet Nic is, too. This place isn't some magical space where only the elite are accepted. There are members here who don't pay a fee. They're here because Case thinks they can get something out of this club. By the way, that man you were drooling over—not rich. All the money came from his wife. He was a soldier, and he became a soldier because he had no other place to go. This isn't about our childhoods. It's about what we do with what we were handed, and baby, from what I can tell you were not handed much. So take what I'm offering you and show me what you can make with it. I think it will be something beautiful."

Thank god his brother had a way with words. Grim was better with soothing pats and nodding along.

And he was good with the spanking she was about to get.

Nic moved into Josh's arms, wrapping herself around him. "Thank you, Sir. I didn't think about it that way. And you are so not my ex. You're a good man. You and Grim…you make me want to stay."

Josh's head lowered and he kissed their sub, their mouths mingling in a way that made Grim's cock tighten. His whole body came alive as though recognizing the hard part was over and it was time to play.

"Are you all right now?" Josh asked when he broke off the kiss.

Nic nodded. "Yes, Sir. I'm sorry. I got nervous. Everyone here is beautiful, and I met your friend Harlow and she's intimidating. I think she might like you."

Josh snorted. "She absolutely does not. Not in the way you're implying. We're only friends. Well, we're family, but she comes from paranoid stock. I swear if you ever meet her dads, you'll be able to figure out which one's sperm created her."

Grim disagreed. "Nurture is every bit as important as nature."

"And she had two completely lovely normal parents and one paranoid asshole. Using that name doesn't mean I don't love and respect Uncle Chase. He would nod and say that's a fair assessment. He's a lot to take, and Harlow got some of that drama in her. Was she rude to you?" Josh asked.

Grim would be shocked. Harlow was one of the kindest women he knew. Though she did have a habit of protecting the people she loved. In brutal ways, sometimes. Harlow was the first woman to show Grim female badasses weren't some movie myth. Women in his old world were meant to defer to men, to be godly and quiet and never complain. Abby and Olivia had taught him how amazing women could be, but Harlow…well, she scared him sometimes.

Fuck. If Harlow found out something about Nicole she didn't like, he wouldn't put it past her to take matters into her own hands, and that could go very wrong.

"She was nice, but I don't think she liked me," Nic admitted.

"Like I said, she can be eccentric," Josh explained. "We'll spend some time with her while we're here this weekend, and I promise you'll come to love her. She's a wonderful friend."

Nic nodded though she didn't look sure.

He needed a moment with Josh. "Baby, settle yourself on the spanking bench. You'll take thirty for the lying and another thirty for whatever the hell that was when you greeted Josh."

Her eyes went wide. "But…"

"Or we can try the exotic lube," he threatened.

Nic moved her ass toward that spanking bench.

"You're wearing too many clothes," Josh remarked.

Her eyes flared. "I'm barely wearing anything."

"And that's twenty more. You need to think about what shape your ass is going to be in when I fuck it tonight." Grim moved to her, his hands going to her bare shoulders. He loved how small and curvy she was. She was everything he wanted in a woman. Sweet but strong. He thought he was going to find out exactly how strong she was soon. He gently tilted her head up. "Those clothes are for the club. We're alone now."

"Mostly," Josh added, and he moved in behind their sub.

"Mostly?" Her pretty eyes had gone wide.

Josh pointed to the big mirror. "See that, baby? It's a two-way mirror. We can't see who's on the other side. Maybe no one. Maybe a whole crowd."

She stared at the mirror. "Watching us?"

"Watching how gorgeous you are. Looking at you and getting hot enough that they probably go and fuck on their own," Josh explained.

"It can get wild in that room." Grim smoothed back her hair. "We would love to show you off one day. We enjoy running scenes on the big stages so everyone can see how gorgeous our sub is. And also, Josh likes to show off his abs."

Before Josh could protest, a glorious grin covered Nicole's face. "Well, they are pretty nice."

Josh's hands ran down her torso and over her barely covered hips. "I'm glad you think I'm pretty, baby. Because I know you're gorgeous. Did you like the scenes? Did they get you hot? I got so fucking hot setting up our room and imagining what you would look like here."

"You look like my every fantasy," Grim admitted. "When I started this, I knew I wanted to end up here with one sub. I know it's not cool to say, but I only ever dreamed of having one woman."

"Well, half," Nic teased.

He wasn't going to let her think that way. "You are more than enough for both of us. You are the complete package for me and Josh."

"That's all I want. To be enough. For you and Josh. For me." There was an odd pleading in her expression, something that practically begged him to understand.

Fuck. They were almost there. She was almost ready to tell them. Patience. That was all they needed now. He took a long breath, banishing the need to ask her to talk. She would talk when she was ready. Tonight. After they took her to the suite and got her firmly in between them, she would tell them everything and they could truly start their lives together. But for now, he would show her how they could worship her body.

"Do you think anyone's behind the mirror?" Nicole asked as Josh started undoing the laces of her corset.

"I think the minute we locked that door, a light went on letting all those perverts know something's going down in here," Josh whispered.

"Baby, if you want, there's a button I can push that shields us from the two-way." He had to let her know all the options.

"Spoilsport," Josh said, never letting up on his slow undressing of their sub.

She wasn't wearing much. She looked absolutely luscious. The royal blue corset offered her breasts up and the tiny matching thong split her ass cheeks in a way that made his mouth water.

"I'm fine," Nic assured him. "I…kind of like the idea people might be watching. But only because I know they like it. They aren't judging me. They think sex is normal and natural, and as long as we're all okay with it we should have fun."

This was more than fun, but he wouldn't argue with her. She was new to this and she would find her way. "Absolutely no one will judge you here. This is a completely safe space for us to explore."

"No one's going to call me a whore here. Is that what you're saying?" Nic asked, sighing as the corset relaxed around her body.

"Arms up." Josh eased the corset up her torso and off. "No one is going to call you a whore period. Not without some punishment."

"I don't care, Josh." She frowned and turned around, but not before Grim saw a mulish expression cross her face. "I was joking, but you can't punish Alyssa. I don't care about her."

"I'll fire her if I want to," Josh replied.

Oh, things were heating up, and he was here for it. He didn't have to say a word. Just stand back and let the sparks fly.

"No, you won't because she didn't do it to you. She did it to me, so I get to say what…" Nicole gasped as Josh picked her up. "What are you doing?"

"I think you know what I'm doing, baby." Josh stalked to the spanking bench. "I'm taking care of business."

Grim grabbed his rope. It was time for him to join in. "You woke up the beast, darlin'."

"But I'm right," Nic protested. "It wasn't a big deal. It was some words."

A loud smack sounded through the room and Nicole yelped. Yeah, Grim was pretty sure Josh had meant that one. Nicole's head came up as he spanked her again.

"Josh," she began.

Grim knelt down. "Baby, you're arguing with your Doms about your protection in the middle of a club during a scene where you know the rules."

She winced as she took another smack.

"I will protect you," Josh said, punctuating each word with a smack. "I will not allow anyone to talk about you the way Alyssa did."

Tears pierced Nicole's eyes, and he wasn't sure it was all about the pain.

"He can't stop being who he is any more than you can stop being who you are," Grim said as he held up the rope. "Or I can stop being who I am, as my stepfather found out. Should I tie you down or should we talk?"

She lowered her hands. "Tie me down, and please, Grim, please kiss me. I don't want either one of you to change. I love you exactly the way you are."

Josh stopped, and for the first time in all the years they'd spent together, his best friend seemed at a loss for words.

Grim wasn't. He knew what to say. "We love you exactly the way you are, too."

He also knew the words he couldn't say yet. *Even if you have a whole life we don't know about. Even if you've got a ton of trouble coming your way.*

"Exactly the way you are, Nicole," Josh said softly.

Grim got to one knee, wrapping the length around her wrist, tying her tight enough she would feel it but not so tight it would cut off her circulation. It was an art form, and he thought he'd found his muse. He moved to her other wrist and when he was done, he stepped back. "She's not getting away from us."

"She's worked that mouth of hers tonight. I think she might need to work it in another way." Josh stepped over and selected a paddle. "Nicole, do you think you might want to make up for all that brattiness?"

Grim's cock was already hard. Now it was painful.

A sweet smile came over Nicole's face. "I can do that, Sir."

Josh gave her a quick smack. "You make it good and I'll take care of you. But first you owe me. Grim, you get ready. I'll deliver some discipline and then she can start making it up to us."

Grim reached for the ties of his leathers, ready to start their night.

* * * *

The pain wracked through her causing her to gasp right before it settled in as heat, sinking into her muscles and skin. Josh used the paddle, peppering her backside with the most delicious warmth. She would feel those smacks all tomorrow, and she would think about them.

She bit her bottom lip as Josh continued on relentlessly. He would give her ass a smack and then she would feel his fingers between her legs. She was completely open to him, her legs splayed and pussy and ass pressed up so her Doms could play with them.

Tied down and helpless to them. She knew it should scare the shit out of her, but she felt oddly free. There was no worry in this place, no fear of the future. No regrets for the past. There was the here and now, and it was perfect.

The here and now was Grim and Josh focused on nothing but bringing her pleasure.

"You dirty girl," Josh said, his voice as smooth as silk. "You like this. You like it when the big bad Dom takes a paddle to your pretty ass. Your pussy is soaking wet, baby."

She was sure it was since every inch of her body felt alive and aroused. The pain in her backside did nothing but heighten her need for sex.

She'd never needed before. Never craved physical contact the way she did with these two men. It was like breathing with Josh and Grim.

And whoever was watching them on the other side of the mirror. Yeah, that did something for her, too. She would never have thought having eyes on her would turn her on, but it was okay here. This club was a safe space for her to explore, and it turned out the first big revelation was she was kind of into exhibitionism.

And she was definitely into the big cock Grim exposed as he shoved down his leathers.

"You are so gorgeous like this," Grim said as one big hand stroked his cock. "I love it when you're all tied down and there's nothing you can do."

He was wrong. "I can think of something I can do." Another smack rocked her whole body and she winced. "When he's done, of course. I think doing it while he's spanking me might be a mistake."

Josh smacked her again. "Oh, one day you'll be so well trained and we'll figure out the perfect rhythm, and there won't be anything the three of us can't do."

"Well, until then, I'll watch until you're done," Grim said with a chuckle. His free hand came out and smoothed her hair back. He was so close she could smell his arousal, feel the heat coming off his hard as a rock cock. She could practically taste him. She would never have said she would genuinely enjoy sucking a cock, that it would make her feel powerful and loved. But here she was.

In the right place. With the right men. She was going to find out if the timing was right, too.

"How do you feel, baby?" Josh asked, and she heard the sexiest sound of his leathers moving, likely being untied and shoved down so he could get at his cock, too. "Where are we?"

"I'm green, Josh. So green." They'd talked about using the stoplight method to ensure they always knew how she was feeling. Green definitely meant go. She wasn't even close to yellow, which would slow things, and not once had she even thought about shutting things down with the word red.

"I disagree," he replied with a chuckle, and she felt his big hand stroke across her ass, making her shiver with the sensation. "This gorgeous flesh is a lovely shade of pink. I think it needs one more thing, though."

She gasped as he split her cheeks, and she felt the hard edge of an anal plug. "When did you have time to prep a plug?"

"That's the beauty of the club." Josh pressed the plug in, spreading the lube he'd used around her tight hole. "The room is always prepped and ready, so you'll never know what's coming. You won't know how we'll fuck our little toy. You'll be surprised when I slip clamps on or use a violet wand on all these pretty parts of yours."

"We'll always have rope to tie you up with, and when you're ready, we'll introduce you to suspension play," Grim promised. "All tied up and in the air so there's absolutely no part of you we can't get to."

It sounded adventurous. It sounded like heaven. "I'm ready for anything."

She meant those words. She was ready to try everything with these men.

"We'll have so much fun in this club, baby. You'll see. And we'll set up a playroom in the house. Everything we can ask for to torture our sub," Josh promised. "But you better let me in. This is my sweet ass, and I'm not going to be kept out."

Her whole body clenched and then she released a breath, relaxing and letting the plug slip inside.

She always felt so full with a plug deep inside her. Soon it wouldn't be a plug. Maybe even later tonight when they were tucked into their spectacular suite. They would make it special. She had no doubt.

"Now, let's talk about what we do and don't do in this club," Josh said, playing with the plug and making her squirm. "Who's the boss in this club, Nicole?"

They were going to make her say it before they gave her all the good stuff. Well, she supposed it was only fair since they kind of let her lead a lot of the time. For sexually domineering men, they let her pick what they watched or what games they played or what they ate for dinner. She could definitely give them what they wanted here.

"You are. You and Grim. My Masters."

"Damn straight," Grim agreed. "We're the Masters here. Here you let Josh talk all about how he's going to wreak bloody vengeance on our enemies, and all you do is smile and tell him how smart he is. Then when we leave the club you can remind him of how much lawyers cost."

"Really?" Josh asked, still slowly fucking her ass with the plug. "You know she doesn't need any encouragement in the sarcasm game. She's doing fine on her own. However, I am going to fire Alyssa for being mean to my sub."

Oh, he was not, but she knew how to play now. "Yes, Sir. You are going to protect me."

"Little brat." But she could hear the smile in Josh's tone.

She could handle being their little brat.

Grim moved closer and pressed the head of his cock to her lips. "Taste me, brat."

She swiped her tongue across his cockhead, gathering the fluid she found there. Grim's groan went straight to her pussy. She couldn't move her hands so she had to concentrate on working her mouth over him. She whirled her tongue around and around, sucking him deep.

Josh moved between her legs, and then she felt his big dick breaching her pussy. She was slick and ready, so he was free to thrust in one smooth move.

She was so full, her skin still sensitive from the spanking. Josh's hands gripped her hips, and every thrust moved the plug as well, lighting up her ass with pure sensation.

Grim filled her mouth, one hand stroking her hair. "You feel so perfect, baby."

"Damn straight she does. She feels like fucking heaven, and later on we're going to get her between us. She's ready," Josh said, never missing a beat. He fucked her hard, matching Grim's rhythm so naturally.

"We're all ready, and it's going to be special." Grim was looking down at her, watching the place where his cock disappeared behind her lips.

She'd known they were planning to take her together this weekend, to show her what they wanted.

Josh thrust in hard, bringing his hand around to rub her clit, and she went flying. The orgasm was stronger than ever, heightened by the way Grim came in her mouth, filling her with his unique essence.

Nicole's whole body pulsed with satisfaction as she drank him down and felt Josh slip from her pussy.

"Give me a second and I think we'll change places," Grim said, his lips turning up in a satisfied grin.

She could handle that. And she could handle them.

Tonight, her life began again.

Chapter Thirteen

Josh looked around the room with a deep sense of satisfaction. The whole evening was turning out even better than he'd planned. "I think that's everything. Check the wine. She likes something light and fruity."

Grim had changed into a pair of slacks and a dress shirt sans tie. They'd hurriedly gotten out of their leathers, showered and dressed, wanting to give Nicole time to pamper herself. He glanced at the clock. Twenty-five minutes more and they would go down and escort her up.

"I ordered what Liv drinks." Grim pulled the bottle out of the elegant bucket the staff had left. "This is it."

There was a well-stocked fridge with beer and soda, but he wanted Nicole's wine to be perfect.

Tonight was the beginning of the rest of their lives, after all.

"Now, we're alone so I can ask the question I've needed to ask all night." Grim turned away from the table with its charcuterie and plate of delicate cookies. Snacks to fuel an evening of vigorous exercise.

Josh sighed. He'd known this discussion was coming from the moment Nic mentioned she'd met Harlow. "Harlow wants to talk to me. To us, really. I think she's found something and wants to update us. I know she was waiting for a call. I told her we could have breakfast tomorrow. I'll find out what's going on then."

Though he rather hoped Nicole would tell them everything tonight. The words *I love you* had come out of her mouth earlier, and he believed her. It felt like they were finally on steady ground.

Grim didn't seem as sure. "I know you talked to her about looking into the situation, but I thought we were keeping it light. If Harlow came all the way to Austin, she's serious about this."

Josh's head shook. "She's found something, but I'm not worried about it. We talked about this. We need to know what's coming for her. Even if she's not ready for us to know. We can't protect her if we're in the dark."

"Just make sure Harlow knows the parameters of her assignment. It's not to fucking scare her off." Grim sighed and sank down to the big sofa where they would likely be all cuddled up and watching movies at some point. There was a big screen TV with all the streaming services they could want. "You know Harlow can get territorial about her friends," Grim pointed out. "If she finds out something about Nic she considers bad, she might take things into her own hands."

Josh shook his head. "I don't think so. At least not without talking to me. I'm pretty sure that's precisely why she's here. Do you want me to call her? We've got some time before we go down and get Nicole. We can find out what Harlow has on her."

Grim's head shook. "I would rather wait for Nic to tell us. I think she's close. It would be better if she never knows you asked someone to look into her at all. It'll be a breach of trust. I think she might tell us tonight."

"I do, too, but maybe we should talk about how to react. Our reactions to whatever secret she has will be everything. All right. Let's throw it around." Josh put a hand to his chest, his eyes lowering, and he gave his best Nicole impression. "Grim, I have a secret baby."

Grim's eyes rolled. "Take this seriously."

Josh chuckled. He was actually feeling pretty good. The sex had burned away his anxiety, but he knew Grim carried around a lot of it. "I am. I promise you. There's nothing in the world I take more seriously than our woman. But I want you to think. What could she tell us that would make us turn our backs on her?"

Grim shook his head. "I don't know. I want to say there's nothing, but the world can sometimes kick you in the ass. You don't understand that the way I do. The way Nic does."

He wasn't about to argue over his place of privilege. He knew Grim was speaking the truth. He'd had a great life and life had kicked Grim and Nic around. Precisely why he needed to protect them both. Especially from their own fears. "If she tells us she's on the run from a husband who abused her?"

In his head, it was the most obvious possibility. She cried out in her sleep asking someone to stop. That someone was likely a male partner. If she'd lied about her divorce, he would be happy to make it a truth for her.

"Then we hunt the son of a bitch down and he won't hurt her again," Grim replied as though he kind of liked the idea.

Josh did, too. But there were other scenarios churning through his head. "How about I have a couple of kids out there and I'm protecting them from someone who wants to hurt them?"

"Well, I would hope she wants more because I would like that, but I would accept whatever she is willing to give me, and I would love her kids." Grim seemed to relax.

This was how to relieve his stress. Grim needed to run through things. He needed plans. His world had been chaotic for so long. A lot like Nicole's. Josh knew how to be the calm center of things. His fathers had taught him. Even when the world seemed out of control, the key was to not panic. Panic was the enemy. Not fear, and fear was what they were facing. Fear of the unknown. Fear of losing her. "If she's done something and the law's after her?"

"We fix it." Grim sounded so much calmer now. "If we can't, then we run with her."

"Then we run with her." His decision was made. Though he was fairly certain he could deal with whatever was thrown his way without taking up the hobo life. Money could solve a world of troubles. It could buy the best lawyers. His connections afforded him the finest hackers who could build an identity to protect her. "It's not going to come to that."

"Dad…your dad is going to be a problem."

His dad was always a problem. Stubborn old man, but Grim was wrong about one thing. "Do you not want to call him Dad? It doesn't dishonor your biological father. I know Dad wouldn't mind. You slip up a lot and call Pops Pops, and you often refer to our mother as Mom."

"I don't know," Grim said quietly. "I guess I worry with my background Jack might find it distasteful."

"I'm going to beat some sense into you."

A smile broke over Grim's face. "I'd like to see you try." He sobered. "I don't know. Pops is easy. Mom is… She's the best mom in the world. It's not like I don't love the old man. I went to vet school to make him proud of me."

Josh rolled his eyes because he remembered the time well. They'd been planning on taking classes together, and Grim chucked that right out the window. "You went to vet school because he didn't like the old vet and offhandedly said you might think about it because he would love to have one in the family. You did eight years of school for him."

A wistful smile played on Grim's lips. "I ended up loving it."

"And he loves you, so drop the whole your dad thing. He's our dad. You just took your time getting to meet him. You were always meant to be part of my family. Hell, sometimes I'm sure he loves you more than me."

Grim frowned his way. "No, you're just so like him you butt heads all the time, and you need to remember that when we have to tell him what's happening with Nicole. He'll handle the secret kids real well. I should know. The man likes to take in strays. The running from the law thing could be another story."

Because Jack Barnes would try to protect his family, and Nicole wasn't part of that yet. "I'll handle it. I'll do whatever it takes."

A plan was starting to form in his head. A plan to put his ruthlessly protective father in check. It was the kind of plan his dad would have come up with if he'd found himself in this position. The key with Jack Barnes was to show him there was no moving, no maneuvering at all. The king had to be placed in check and then Josh would get what he needed—time.

Because if his father didn't come to adore Nicole and embrace her like the family she was destined to be, then he didn't know his father at all. Pops was the easy one, and his mom just wanted everyone to be happy.

Now that he thought about it secret kids would soften his dad up. It had been a while since Lexi had popped out her last, and the old man loved a kid following him around.

"If something goes down with Dad, your job is to take care of Nic and make sure she stays out of it as much as possible," Josh explained. "I'll handle the parents."

A gentle chiming went through the suite.

Josh turned for the door. "Are we missing anything?"

Grim looked around. "I don't think so."

Josh went to the door. "Well, get ready because it's almost time to go pick up Nicole. She should be done by now. It won't take her long to dress since I didn't leave her underwear."

Grim shrugged. "A sensible thing to do."

It was good they were in synch.

Josh opened the door and Harlow stood there. She'd changed into street clothes, jeans and a T-shirt and combat boots. Her uniform. Though she didn't usually look so freaked out.

"Josh, we have to talk." She charged into the room after him, her cell phone in hand. She put it to her ear. "Dad, I need you to call me. Now. Before you do anything. This is my case, and you are going to fuck everything up. I'm not joking."

Josh's gut tightened. "What's happening?"

"Should I find Nicole?" Grim put down the beer he'd been about to open.

Harlow shoved her phone into her pocket. "Guys, I'm so sorry. I didn't realize my dads were looking into Nicole, too. I gave the picture you sent to my facial recognition guy. Well, girl. Ruby is an amazing investigator, but she didn't know we were keeping this on the down-low so when Dad called her, she gave him the report first. Josh, it's bad. I'm afraid they're going to call in the police. She's wanted."

Grim started for the door. "If they take her in, I'll… I don't know what I'll do, but…"

Josh followed him. "What we'll do, but it'll be bloody, and I won't care that we're family."

He raced out the door and prayed he got to Nicole in time.

* * * *

Nic finished drying her hair and stared at herself in the mirror.

She looked like a completely different person than the woman who'd rolled into Willow Fork with two hundred dollars in her pocket and a car on its last legs.

She looked well loved.

And fancy since Josh had left her a pretty slip dress and heels to change into after she got out of her fet wear. No jeans and snarky T-shirt that had seen better days for her tonight.

Was this who she could be if she found a way to stay with them? She was still Nicole. She was still the same woman, but she was more confident, more secure. Money wouldn't change her with the singular exception of not having to worry about where her next meal was coming from. When she thought about it, she could be a truer version of herself if she wasn't simply focused on survival.

What would life be like if she didn't have to suspect every human being she met?

She would go to her grave with the memory of Josh standing in front of her telling her to take what he gave her and make something beautiful with it.

Was it that simple? Her world had been chaos for so long. The idea a life could be happy and satisfying simply because she loved her men and the family they could build seemed like a distant dream.

She heard a buzzing noise in the background. The locker room was empty. It was still early, and the club would be hopping for another couple of hours.

But her men wanted time alone with her.

Time to show her how well they could love her. Was she brave enough to take their love with both hands and trust it?

She took out the designer lipstick and brushed it over her mouth. The color was perfect, of course. Josh wouldn't screw up any details.

Would his family accept her? Even if Josh and Grim could believe her story, it didn't mean Jack Barnes would, and could she blame him?

The buzzing started again, and it was coming from the row her locker was on.

She gathered her makeup kit and moved to the locker when the buzzing noise started again. Her cell. Who would call her? She glanced at her phone's screen and it let her know she wasn't late. Josh and Grim would be waiting for her outside the locker room soon, but she still had some time.

She didn't recognize the number, but they could be using someone else's phone. She slid her finger across the screen. "Hello."

"Nic. Thank god." There was a huff that sounded like relief. "I've been trying to get you for an hour."

She thought she recognized the voice. "Heather?"

"Are you in the club?" Heather asked.

"Yes. I'm in the locker room."

"Is anyone with you?"

A knot formed in her gut. She was certain she was alone. It had been nice when she'd first entered the locker room, but now she felt a chill. "No. Uhm, what's going on? You're scaring me."

"I'm sorry but I need you to be scared right now. I found out there are private investigators looking for you, and they are in that club. I don't have a ton of time to explain but the Dawson family runs an investigative firm, and they've been looking into your background. They know, Nicole."

Her vision went slightly blurry, and she leaned against the locker for support. "They know?"

Dawson. Harlow. Harlow had been introduced as Harlow Dawson. Josh's friend knew, and she was going to tell him. She was going to tell him the woman he'd fucked was wanted for killing the last man to do that.

She was going to be sick.

"I need you to stay calm," Heather said over the line. "The Dawsons aren't people to fuck with. They won't play by anyone's rules but their own. I'm on my way in. Meet me in the lobby and I'll get you out of there."

"You're here?" It was relief in the moment. She wasn't thinking about anything but the fact that there might be a way out. Unless they'd already called the cops. "I don't want to get you in trouble."

"Don't worry about me," Heather said, and she could hear cars moving in the background. "Meet me downstairs. Grab what you can and don't stop for anything."

She was already in motion. If she had time, she would change out of the stupid silky gown that had made her feel sexy mere moments before. Now she realized how vulnerable it made her. "You need a card to get in."

"Trust me." There was a deep confidence in Heather's tone. "I can get in. Go, Nic. Go now, and leave the phone. They're probably tracking you."

Was that why Harlow had lingered? She'd read enough suspense books to know the dumbass heroine usually got her phone tagged. Tears blurred the world as she dropped her phone and stepped out of her heels. She couldn't run in them. But her sneakers would take a while to tie, and panic was stirring inside her.

With only her purse, bare feet on the hardwoods, she rushed out of the locker room. *Please don't let them be waiting. Please.*

The hallway was empty, though she saw a man coming from the lounge.

"Nicole? You okay?" Case Taggart was dressed in dark leathers as he strode down the hallway. "I can get Josh for you."

No words came out of her mouth. Nothing smart. Nothing to throw him off the fact that something was terribly wrong. Full-on, pulse-pounding panic fully took over, and she couldn't hear anything beyond her heart threatening to beat out of her chest.

It was everything she'd feared, and she couldn't face them. She couldn't look into their eyes as their love turned to disgust.

She couldn't go to jail because she knew damn well she wouldn't ever make it to trial. If she went to jail, they would come after her because they couldn't let her tell the truth. Ted wouldn't risk it.

Nic ran, feet pounding against the carpet that covered this part of the club.

She heard someone shout her name, but she had one goal in all the world right now. Get downstairs. Get to her friend. Heather would get her out of here.

How was Heather here? How did Heather know?

The questions were a distant bell ringing, lost amid the panic. The elevator was in front of her, but Case was behind her. She couldn't wait so she sprinted for the stairs.

How many stairs? Three flights? Four? She nearly stumbled but held on to the railing.

Josh and Grim had gone up to their suite. The dungeon was on two of the lower levels of the building. The rest were living spaces and guest suites. They would be at least ten flights up since she remembered the spectacular views of the city and the Colorado River. She'd stood there hours before, and the world felt like it was starting to make sense again.

Now she was back in the real world, and it was nothing but fear and chaos.

Her breath heaved in her chest as she made it to the first floor and burst through.

The lights of the lobby nearly blinded her after the low light of the stairwell. Or maybe it was the anxiety attack creeping along the edges of her consciousness. The lobby was an elegant construction, with marbled floors and a big welcome desk. The man on duty looked up from his high-tech computer, his eyes flaring.

"Ma'am?"

All she could see was the doors. She could get through the doors and run. She wouldn't stop this time. If Heather wasn't there, she would keep running.

There was nothing for her. Nothing at all.

She'd almost made it to the door when all the air fled her lungs as a big arm clotheslined her, dragging her back from what briefly felt like freedom.

"I'm afraid not," a deep voice said. "Time to face the music."

Fear choked her, and she pushed against the arm.

"Mr. Dawson." The lobby attendant approached like he was dealing with a dangerous wild animal. "Should I call the police? Does Mr. Taggart know what's going on?"

Dawson. The Dawsons knew. Heather had told her, and she hadn't been fast enough.

"I'll make that call later, Glen," the man behind her said. "And there's no need to contact Case. We're going to ask Ms…Mason a few questions. That's all. We're taking her to a place where we can talk."

And suddenly she was turned and facing another man. He was tall and built, with deep blue eyes and dark hair. He looked her over with a frown, though his words were meant for her attacker. "After all these years, you finally learn, brother." He turned Glen's way. "You do need to call Mr. Barnes-Fleetwood and Mr. Burch. We're going to all sit down and have a talk and then we'll decide what to do with our little Miss Murder."

Her stomach churned. It was her every nightmare made real. They knew. They all knew. "Please. Please let me go. I won't bother Josh or Grim anymore. I'll disappear."

How had she made this mistake again? Did she never learn?

The man shook his head. "Can't do it."

The elevator doors opened and Case Taggart strode out, a fierce look on his face. "What the hell is happening, Chase? Are you running some kind of op in my fucking club?"

"What they're doing is making a huge mistake and getting in the middle of my op," a familiar voice said. "Which I never planned to run in your club. I thought she would be safe here, Taggart. Let the girl go."

"Holy shit." Case's jaw actually dropped. "Solo?"

Heather was true to her word. She'd gotten in the building, but she looked totally different than her casual, happy friend. Her blonde hair was pulled back, and she was in all black. "I don't go by that name anymore."

"Shit," the man behind her said. His voice dropped to a whisper. "Look, Nicole, I need you to call off your friend. I didn't realize you had a bodyguard." He took a step back, dragging her with him as he spoke to Heather. "We're all going to sit down and talk this situation out. My name is Ben Dawson and that's my brother Chase. We seem to have walked into something we don't understand."

Who was Solo? Nic was so fucking confused. And scared. She was scared because she was surrounded by predators.

"Look, lady, I don't know who you are, but this is a private club and I'm going to have to ask you to leave," Chase Dawson said, turning to Heather.

"I will as soon as you let the girl go. We'll leave and you won't have to worry about the situation again. Tell Barnes his precious boy is safe." Heather flicked her hand and a baton appeared. "I'll take her back to Bliss with me and he can pretend he doesn't have a past."

"Or I can escort you out myself," Chase offered.

"I wouldn't do that if I were you," Case warned. "We should all go up to my office and discuss the situation."

"You might be out of practice, Taggart. I'm not." Chase swaggered over to the blonde. "Let's see if we can find the exit."

"Dumbass," Ben hissed. "He doesn't recognize her. Nicole, we're going to back up so when my brother gets his ass kicked, you don't get hurt."

She wasn't sure how that was possible since Chase Dawson had a hundred pounds of muscle on Heather. Heather was tall and had a slender strength about her, but Nic knew it didn't matter how strong a woman was. Physically a man could hurt her. No amount of going to the gym had ever saved her from Micah.

Chase went to grab Heather's wrist. She brought her arm up and around, breaking the hold before she kicked her knee back and up and right into the big man's balls.

Chase went to his knees. Ben groaned behind her and relaxed just enough to let her wiggle out of his hold.

"Damn it," Ben said as though he was the one who'd lost his manhood.

Heather had Chase in a chokehold, and it didn't look like the dude was getting out of it.

"Case." Chase managed to croak out a plea.

Case's head shook. "Dude, I'm smart enough to not fight the ex-CIA operative. She might not go by Solo anymore but she sure acts like her."

"Nicole, get behind me. My car is on the street," Heather who wasn't Heather ordered.

Who would she be getting in the car with? Definitely someone who'd lied to her. It was all falling into place. Ex-CIA operative? Who had Micah's family brought in? Nic took a step back.

"Nicole…Nora," Heather began. "I am here to help you. I've reviewed your case and I don't buy it for a second. Please come with me."

She couldn't trust anyone. Not a single person.

Ben got hold of her arm again. "I'm afraid I'm going to have to insist she comes with us, though I'm willing to discuss the situation once we have her secured."

"She's not going anywhere except upstairs." Case stepped in

front of her. "You've all forgotten something. This is my fucking kingdom."

Four men moved from all sides of the lobby, guns drawn.

Heather released Chase, her arms coming up to show she wasn't holding a weapon. Ben backed away, doing the same.

Chase sat up, a mulish expression on his face. "You're not going to shoot us, Taggart."

Case frowned. "I'm not going to kill you, but I think you can survive losing a couple of toes, Dawson." He turned to Nicole. "Ms. Mason, I'm so sorry this has happened to you here. We're going to go upstairs and figure this problem out."

"I want to leave," she said.

"Yes, we'll go," Heather agreed.

"Alone." She couldn't trust anyone. "I want to leave here but I'm going to do it by myself. I won't bother any of you again."

The big man's features softened. "I'm sorry. I know that you're scared, but you don't have a reason to be."

"You don't know who she is," Ben countered.

"I know she's a sub in my club and you were manhandling her," Case accused. "We've been friends for years. If you want to keep it that way, you'll get your asses up to my office and you'll start explaining."

The elevator doors opened, and her horrible night was complete. Josh stormed out, not seeming to notice there were guns pointed all around. He simply walked right into the middle of the dangerous scene while Grim rushed past him toward her.

She could see Harlow behind them. She rushed to Chase, who was just starting to get off the floor.

Before she could say a thing or take a step back, Grim hauled her up and into his arms.

"Uncle Chase, you better fucking stand down right now. I know my father put his nose right into my business, but I won't have it. You lay hands on her again and I'll forget we're family." Josh's whole body was tight.

"You don't know who she is," Ben said, joining his brother, and now Nic could see they were perfect twins.

"She's not who they think she is," Heather insisted. "Let me explain."

"In my office," Case said, obviously irritated. "Believe it or not Austin is not so weird that a standoff in a lobby that anyone from the street can see is going to be brushed off. Also, my wife is going to have my ass if she misses this. Gentlemen, please escort the Dawson brothers up to my office. Don't underestimate them. They're old and a little soft, but they used to be Navy SEALs. And don't even try to fuck with Mrs. Kent. She could kill you all and not break a nail, but I think she might behave herself."

"I want a chance to lay out what I've discovered," Heather explained, sounding reasonable now. "This situation is far more complex than it looks, and I'm worried she's in real trouble."

"It's going to be okay," Grim said, cuddling her close. "You're safe, baby."

"You should let me go." She felt hollow inside.

"Never," Grim promised.

She had to force this moment. She couldn't stand to be in this place where he was loving her and Josh was fighting for her and they would both hate her in mere moments. It was making her ache in a way she'd never before. "I'm wanted for murder."

Grim's brow rose, but it was the only sign that he was surprised. "Did you do it?"

Of all the ways he could react, she hadn't imagined that one. "No."

"Then that'll make it easier to get a lawyer." He looked up at Josh. "We're going to need to call Uncle Lucas. But for now, let's get her somewhere warm and figure out what the hell Dad's done."

"He's fucked everything up. Meddling old man," Josh said as he approached. "You okay, baby? Did they hurt you?"

"I didn't hurt her," Ben protested. "And your father is trying to protect you."

"And I'm going to protect her. Everyone needs to understand that here and now," Josh announced.

"They say I murdered my husband." It was obvious her men didn't understand what was happening. Not her men. Josh and Grim. She needed to put some distance between them. "Grim, let me down."

"You're not wearing shoes," he replied and started for the elevator.

"So the ex isn't the ex. The ex is a corpse." Josh followed right beside her. "You sure he's dead? I have to ask because it happens more than you would think."

"He was on the floor with a couple of bullets in him. Yes, he was dead." Now she was even more confused.

"Excellent," Josh announced as though pleased. "Then we don't have to worry about him. Let's get the lowdown and figure out how to proceed. And who your friend is. She looks different."

Case joined them in the elevator. "That sounds like a plan. If only the Dawsons had thought so far ahead."

"I've found the older generation is overly dramatic," Josh said as the doors closed. "Probably trauma or something. I hear a lot of crap about the eighties, man."

"Josh." Why wasn't he taking this seriously?

He reached out and took her hand. "It's going to be okay now, Nic. I'm glad this happened. We're going to drag whatever is haunting you into the light."

But they didn't understand. And when they did it would all fall down around her. The reprieve seemed cruel, but then Nic knew the whole world was.

Chapter Fourteen

Grim wrapped the robe he'd found around Nicole and wished she would relax. She was stiff, her voice a monotone when she was willing to speak at all. She'd been quiet the whole trip up, lying still in his arms.

What the hell had she been through? And who did he need to kill to ensure she never had to go through it again?

He might start with Harlow's dads. He didn't have the connection with them Josh had. He didn't call them uncle. He could easily take them out. Well, maybe not easily since they were still fit and used to be Navy SEALs, though from what he'd heard in the elevator, the blonde had taken one of them down quite easily. Heather. Except that wasn't her name, and she wasn't merely Nicole's friend. She was apparently an ex-CIA operative.

"Hey, Heather who isn't Heather, are you for hire?" Grim asked. "Because I might be looking for an assassin."

Josh frowned his way. "I think we can handle it."

"Is he talking about us?" Ben asked his twin. They were sitting across the big, luxurious space Taggart called an office, putting careful distance between them and he, Josh, and Nicole. He knew it was Ben talking because Chase had a red mark across his neck where he'd nearly been choked out by Heather not Heather and the baton she carried.

"I think so," Chase agreed. "And they should calm the fuck down because they don't know the whole story. We were only doing what Jack asked us to do which is look into the potentially dangerous situation his sons are in."

"You mean look into the woman his sons are dating. She's no threat to anyone." Heather moved across the office, clearly picking her side. She held a hand out to Grim. "And my name is Kimberly Kent. Maiden name Solomon, hence the prior nickname Solo. I went by it for years when I worked as a CIA operative. Now I work with a group that searches for missing persons. That's how I became involved in this case. And Mr. Burch, I don't assassinate people anymore, though I might be willing to come out of retirement for that one. He's obnoxious. Tell me something, Mr. Dawson, how did you figure it out so quickly? From what I understood, your daughter's only been on the case for a few days, and you for less. Did she share her intel with you?"

Harlow frowned, her arms crossed over her chest. "No. I did not. I was unaware they'd been hired. I work with a woman named Ruby Lockwood. She's an excellent hacker and has some truly good facial recognition software. She told me she would get back to me with news today. When she hadn't by this evening, I called her. She told me she didn't bother to call because my dads were going to inform me. She gave them all the information. I still don't know anything beyond the fact that there's a warrant for Nicole's arrest in Oregon. Ruby tried to explain the situation to me, but she was at a rave or something and I could barely hear her. I realized what my fathers would do and ran to warn Josh and Grim."

"We didn't want you involved," Chase said, reaching for his daughter's hand. "When we realized how bad the situation was, we made the decision to handle it for you. For all of you. Josh, Grim, I understand you're upset..."

"Oh, you have no idea." Josh strode over to his uncle, pointing a finger his way. "You could have ruined everything. Do you think I didn't know something was wrong? I sure as hell did, and I was handling it. You tell my father he'll be lucky if I talk to him in the next decade."

"He was trying to protect you," Ben insisted.

"Do I look like a child to you?" Josh asked.

"Yes," the Dawson brothers said at the same time.

Harlow's head fell back, and she growled. "You two are going to be the death of me."

They started arguing amongst themselves.

It hadn't gone unnoticed that Mia Taggart had snuck into the big office. She sat on her husband's lap, an arm draped around his shoulders. Grim was pretty sure at some point Case had called his brother and put him on speaker to listen to what he'd called "the drama." He wasn't sure which Taggart, but they definitely had an audience.

He wished they didn't, but they needed help.

Nicole was silent beside him, her eyes on the floor ahead.

He put a hand over hers. "Baby, can I get you something to drink? We can go up to the room. We don't have to stay here."

She shook her head. "You should know the truth. I have some questions, too. I'd like to know how Heather…I'm sorry…Mrs. Kent came to be hunting me."

"Call me Kim, and I wasn't hunting you." Kim sat down on the sofa as Josh was telling off Chase and threatening bloody vengeance if the police were called in. "I'm sure it feels like it, but I was searching for you. I was hired by your in-laws. They told me the police had let the case go cold, and they wanted my company to find you and bring you to justice."

"So you're a bounty hunter." Grim fought the urge to drag Nic closer. "Whatever they're paying you, I'll pay you more to walk away and tell them you couldn't find her." He had some money saved up, but it was nothing compared to Josh's trust fund. He had a sudden thought. "Or to fake her death. Tell them she's dead and give them evidence that will satisfy them."

"Grim," Nic began, and at least the blank doll look was out of her eyes. "She's not going to do that."

Kim shrugged. "It might be an excellent idea, but we would have to be careful. And I'm not a bounty hunter. This isn't the type of case I normally take. My husband, Beck, and I work with a group in Colorado that tracks missing persons. Usually children or women in danger, though we'll work with law enforcement if we feel we can help and there's a risk to the public."

"She's not dangerous." He had to convince this woman to let

Nicole go.

"I know that." Kim's voice went soft, and she leaned toward Nic. "I took this case for reasons your in-laws don't understand. My first instinct was to reject the job, but my son asked me to reconsider. He's working toward a law degree, and he spends a lot of time studying criminal cases. He found some major red flags with yours."

"Josh," Grim called out. "Josh, we can kill your uncles later. Come and listen to Kim now. She's explaining how she got involved and what she thinks about the case."

"Didn't you take a Hippocratic oath?" Chase asked, sounding grumpier than ever, but at least they'd stopped fighting.

"I'm a vet," Grim shot back. "I vowed to not harm your chihuahua. I can totally harm you."

"Grim," Nicole said between clenched teeth.

The fact that she was letting him know she wouldn't put up with his antisocial behavior gave him hope. "Sorry, baby. But I'm pissed at them. You should know I had zero to do with any of this. I was willing to wait until you were ready to talk."

"She's planning on leaving in a couple of weeks," Josh said, sounding a little like his uncle. "We couldn't be sure that she would trust us enough to tell us. She could have walked away, and we would never have seen her again. She would be all alone in the world, and I wasn't about to let that happen."

Josh stared at Kimberly Kent, who rolled her blue eyes and shifted to the end of the sofa, leaving a place for Josh to slide in beside Nicole.

"Alpha men," she muttered under her breath. "Like I was saying, my son found some major red flags when he studied the files about the murder of Micah Holloway."

"That's Nicole's husband?" Josh asked, finally seeming to get his anger under control.

"Nora." Nic was back to sounding monotone. "Nora Holloway was married to Micah. Sometimes I don't feel like I'm Nora anymore."

Josh turned her way. "Baby, you're whoever you tell me you are. You want me to call you Nicole? I love that name. Nora is a wonderful name. I don't care what I call you as long as I get to call you mine."

Nicole took a long breath and turned Kim's way. "I didn't kill my husband."

"I know that." There was a surety in Kim's tone that made Grim more comfortable with her. "Though given your hospital records, I wouldn't blame you. Guys, you should know that her husband physically abused her."

The thought made Grim's stomach churn.

Nicole nodded. "It was nothing at first. He would be rough, grab me too hard. The first time he slapped me I tried to leave. But he cried and apologized, and I started a cycle then. After a while I didn't love him, but I couldn't leave. I couldn't imagine how I would survive."

"You didn't have any money of your own." Harlow didn't make it a question. "He controlled it so he could control you."

"I saved some up," Nicole replied. "I was trying to leave when it happened. He would give me cash to buy groceries and I would clip coupons and use sales to save money. The one place he would let me go was the gym, so I had a locker there. I stashed my money and some other helpful items at the gym."

"You had a gun, didn't you?" Kim asked.

Grim's heart clenched at the thought of Nicole needing a fucking gun.

"Yes. I saved up and bought a gun from the scariest man I've ever met. I don't ever want to do that again. But he promised me it wasn't… What was the word he used? He said it wasn't a burner," Nicole explained.

Now Grim's stomach churned. "You bought a ghost gun?"

"A burner is a gun that's known to have been used in a crime," Kim explained in a calm voice. "What he was telling you is the gun you were buying was untraceable, likely made in the Philippines. They're smuggled into the US. I'm surprised you were able to find one."

"I couldn't buy one from a reputable dealer." Nicole's hands formed a ball on her lap, as though she had to keep herself from reaching out. "I would have to have it registered, and then Micah might have found out. There are some people online who help women leave their abusive husbands. One of them put me in touch with the dealer."

Ben stood, his hands on his hips, and he looked like a mad dad. "Young lady, that gun wasn't properly manufactured. It could have killed you as easily as your husband."

Josh put a hand on hers, and she didn't pull away. "I'm glad you were taking steps to protect yourself."

Nicole's head shook. "Guys, you don't know the whole story."

Kim leaned in, her expression serious. "Ted Holloway found out about your gun, didn't he?"

"Who is that?" Grim asked.

"Micah's brother." Nic stared at Kim like she might be throwing her a lifeline. "Yes. I don't know what actually happened. I know Micah either owed someone money or he'd taken money he shouldn't have. There was mention of the feds being brought in. Ted killed him so they wouldn't come after the family. Somehow he knew about the gun and he used it to murder his brother and then put it in my locker. How did you figure this out?"

"Roman did. So when he read the file, he was curious about a couple of things. It didn't make sense that you would kill your husband, put the gun back in the locker, and then go on the run," Kim explained. "Now you had it stashed in a way that kept it pretty hidden, but he didn't know about the money, did he?"

Nicole huffed. "So he left the money there? At that point I had almost a thousand dollars in cash stashed in my locker."

"Why the hell would she put the gun back but leave the cash?" Josh asked.

"My son found it confusing, and that was why he dug deeper," Kim explained. "He was the one who uncovered the rumors about mob ties to Micah Holloway and also embezzlement at the family's company. I assume the embezzlement was an attempt to pay them off. They likely wanted more. So his brother killed him?"

Nicole nodded.

"Why wouldn't he have them arrest her then?" Grim was confused.

"Because she could talk and someone might listen." Chase Dawson was obviously not. He let out a long huff. "I'm surprised he didn't kill you himself and say it was self-defense. But then he would have the problem of forensics." Chase seemed to be thinking his way through the problem. "The ballistics would match, but it's surprisingly hard to get gunpowder residue on the hands of someone who didn't actually fire a gun. He could say he wrestled the gun away, but he would have to be so careful to show Nicole had fired it first. He had a problem. If the feds came in, they could blame the whole family. They could freeze accounts. He also had to satisfy his mob contacts but keep the blood off his hands. He wouldn't want his parents to know he was going to off his brother. There would be eyes on the whole family if Micah disappears."

"I could explain this to you," Kim offered.

Ben shook his head. "It's better if you let him come to his own conclusions. He feels smarter that way."

"Asshole," Chase said under his breath.

Harlow stood as her father paced. "But if Ted Holloway could point the finger at someone, someone who had reason to kill her abusive husband, then the police wouldn't bother looking too closely at them. The mafia contacts might be willing to make a deal with the brother-in-law if he wasn't the one who owed them. Honestly, having the cops looking into a crime around the family might make the mob back off."

Chase nodded. "Yes. That was what I was thinking, daughter. It also occurs to me that having Nicole on the run would give his parents a target for their anger and grief. If their son's killer is out there in the world, they won't be bothering Ted." He turned to Nicole. "He gave you money and a car, didn't he? He wanted you to run."

"Yes. He told me he would give me a head start." She sounded more solid now, as though having people actually listen to her story gave her strength. "He did give me the option of him putting me up somewhere quiet and being his fuck toy, but I chose to run."

Grim looked at Josh and knew they were both thinking the same thing. They were going to kill Ted Holloway.

But she didn't need to hear that right now. She needed them calm, to keep her needs at the center of the discussion.

When someone is hurting, you need to put aside your own needs and focus on them, sweetie. I know it's easy to get mad, but anger causes way more problems than it solves.

He'd been angry at Olivia's college boyfriend, and Abby had

sat him down and explained his sister didn't need his rage. She needed his love and affection.

Oh, he'd still put the fear of god into the boy, but Liv didn't have to know.

His pops had taught him that.

His mom and dads. His real mom and dads.

He was going to have to do some fast talking to keep his family together because Josh was pissed and they needed Dad.

"So the parents are still looking and you took the case." Grim prompted Kim. They needed to get through the explanations so they could get to the part where he held her and made her feel safe and they made plans.

"Yes," Kim said. "I took the case because I thought she was in trouble. I've looked into the Holloways and they're a dangerous family. If I hadn't taken the case, they wouldn't have stopped."

"How did you find me?" Nicole asked. "It's because I stayed in Willow Fork too long, isn't it?"

Kim shook her head. "I actually found you in a couple of places. It's damn near impossible to disappear these days. You showed up in Seattle under the name Helen Cage. You worked odd jobs and lived in your van. When you had to dump that vehicle, you bought a bus ticket to Chicago. You lived in a homeless shelter for a while. They remembered you because you saved a man who was having a heart attack. It would have been better for you to run, you know. You had to talk to the paramedics, and the police showed up. You had to know that would happen."

"I couldn't… He was dying. I wasn't going to let someone die." She teared up.

"And then you took care of his daughter until he was on his feet again," Kim continued. "She would have gone into foster care but Nicole convinced the social worker she was the man's girlfriend and they had applied for housing. You had to fill out forms and your picture was taken. Not smart. All I had to do was follow the good deeds. They led me to Willow Fork, and I knew I was going to find a way to fix this for you."

"Not smart but incredibly kind," Ben said, his eyes on Nicole. "Ms. Holloway, I apologize for the way we met. I know you might not believe me, but we weren't going to call the police. We were taking you back to our suite to talk to you there."

"You mean interrogate her," Harlow corrected.

"And you were going to do what, daughter?" Chase asked, his brows rising in challenge.

"I was going to lay it all out to Josh and Grim and let them decide how to proceed because believe it or not they are grown-ass, competent men," Harlow replied. "They know what they want and they get to decide how to handle the situations they find themselves in. You are treating them like children who need Daddy to save them. Like you treat me."

Chase's face flushed. "Well, I recently had to save you, so you'll forgive me for not wanting you to nearly kill yourself again." His eyes closed and when he opened them there was regret stamped on his face. "Harlow, sweetheart, I'm so sorry I said that."

"No, you're not." She looked Nicole's way. "I'm sorry they got involved in this. I really did intend to do nothing more than let Josh and Grim know what was going on. I never meant for this to happen. When I gave Ruby your picture, I thought she and I would be the only ones who would ever know your real name. Outside of Josh and Grim, of course. I trust Ruby. But my dads are overprotective assholes. I'm sorry, Nicole. Look, I'm going home. If you need me, you know where to find me."

"Harlow," Ben began.

She kept walking.

Ben stared at his brother.

Chase threw his hands up in obvious defeat. "I'll go talk to her. I doubt she means she's going up to her room. She'll probably take the jet and leave us bus tickets. I taught that girl far too well."

"Nat's going to send your ass to the couch," Ben grumbled, following his brother. "Mrs. Kent, you'll take it from here? I'm afraid we've got some family issues to deal with."

"I'll take care of her," Kim promised.

"I think we'll handle it from here, but I do appreciate your help." Josh stood as the Dawsons left. He turned to Case. "I think I'm going to need to talk to your brother about security around the ranch until we can get this sorted out. I'll talk to my uncle about getting her a legal team. I hope you'll be willing to work with us, Mrs. Kent. My uncle isn't a criminal defense attorney, but he'll know what the next steps are."

Josh was taking over. It was a good thing. Grim could concentrate on taking care of Nicole, and Josh would handle the rest. He reached out, taking her hand in his. She pulled away and stood.

"What did she mean once she got the photo?" Nicole went toe to toe with Josh. "I'm careful about cameras. I always have been. Did you go through my purse? Did you take my driver's license?"

Josh's face went stony. "I had to know what was coming after you. I love you, Nicole. You can't expect me to sit back and let whatever is waiting for you to show up."

"It wouldn't have been your license," Kim said. "It's well done, and the tech on it makes it useless for facial recognition."

"So you took a picture of me without my permission and you gave it to a person who could have called the cops on me and had me hauled back to Oregon," Nicole deduced.

"I took a picture when you didn't realize I was doing it. One morning before we took you into the café to work. I was quick and you didn't notice," Josh admitted.

They were screwing this up. Grim stood by Josh, hoping to present a united front. "You can't run all your life, Nic. We want the best for you. We love you."

"Yeah, that's what Micah said, too," she whispered.

The words went straight through Grim's heart. "That's not fair."

"Life isn't fair," she shot back. "I want to go back to my room. I understand I'm basically a prisoner."

"You certainly are not," Josh argued.

"Then I can get my things and go?" Nicole asked. "Alone?"

Josh's face fell. "No. You won't be allowed out of the building alone. You take me or Grim or the bodyguard I'll have down here before morning. You're determined to make me the bad guy."

"If the shoe fits, Josh…" Nicole said. "Can Mrs. Kent walk me to my room?"

"I'll do it." Grim had to find a way to soften them both up. He was sure it was a shock for Nicole, but it wasn't easygoing for Josh, either. Or him. He was still trying to process everything Nic had been through.

Case was looking down at his phone. Mia had slipped off her husband's lap and had her own phone to her ear.

"Yeah, I'm going to need you to send extra security to the club," she was saying.

Case stepped out from behind his desk. "And I think it might be a good idea for Kim to escort Nicole to her room because you two are about to have trouble of your own."

There was a knock and then the door came open, and Grim's night was complete.

Jack Barnes stood in the doorway, a dark look in his eyes.

Things had just gotten infinitely worse.

* * * *

Josh stepped in front of Nicole because the last thing he was going to do was put her in his father's path. It was obvious his dad thought he was a child who couldn't handle his business, but the man was about to find out he was absolutely his father's son.

"Josh," his dad began.

"Move out of the way." His mother was suddenly there, and she pushed past his dad, Pops coming in behind her. Where his father looked pissed, his mother was all worry. He braced himself because his mother could be a lot when she decided her babies were in trouble. She would try to coddle him, and he had to make sure she didn't say something that would hurt Nicole.

"Mom, we should talk," he began.

His mother's eyes flashed fire. She pointed his way, and he was five years old again with his hand in the damn cookie jar before dinner. "You would do best to be quiet. I am not any happier with you than I am your father. You knew she didn't want her picture taken and you did it anyway and sent it to Harlow, who sent it to heaven knows who." She turned to Nicole, and all her anger was gone, replaced with maternal comfort. "Nicole, sweetheart, come here. Are you okay? Did they hurt you?"

He had no idea what the hell was going on.

Nicole stood stiffly for a moment as his mom wrapped her up in her arms.

"It's okay, baby. We're going to take care of you," his mom promised.

And the most magical thing happened. Nicole's arms clutched

at his mom, and she started to cry. It wasn't more than a moment before the tears became sobs.

His mom looked up. "Sam, could you escort us up to our suite? My new baby needs time and some privacy. We'll also need some tea and maybe something to eat."

"We have food up in our room." Grim didn't know his mother as well as Josh did. "We can go there."

"Were you involved in this?" His mother never stopped rubbing Nicole's back.

Grim did a perfect imitation of a deer in the headlights. "I… I…"

His mother's head shook. "Damn interfering men going behind a good woman's back." She looked over at Kim, who was watching the whole thing with obvious amusement. "Are you the PI who is trying to help my new baby out?"

Kim stood. "Yes, Mrs. Barnes-Fleetwood. Why don't I join you and we can discuss the situation? And I suggest some wine. Nic's had a rough night."

Did they think he'd been to Disney World? He'd fucking found out the woman he loved was wanted by the law and had people who would like to kill her. Was anyone offering him a beer and a shoulder to cry on? Nope. His momma was looking at him like he was a monster and Nicole… Well, Nicole definitely thought he was a monster.

"I'll escort you up myself," Case offered. "My wife is bringing in extra security. I assure you she'll be safe here while you decide what you want to do. I've already called my brother about security for the ranch."

His mom gave Case a brilliant smile. "I appreciate it so much. Tell your brother how grateful we are for accommodating us." Her smile faded when she looked back at Josh and Grim. "You should talk to your father. Maybe you can talk about trust and how bad it is when you break it."

His pops held the door open for them. "Since you've got an excellent escort, I'm going to stay here and make sure Jack doesn't say something he shouldn't to our sons."

Abby kept a protective arm around Nicole as they moved to the door, followed by the Taggarts and Kimberly Kent.

Who had done exactly what he'd done but didn't seem to be getting blasted for it.

"An excellent idea, Sam. I'll see you upstairs," Mom said with a watery smile. "Jack can take the couch."

His father's face flushed, but he merely took a long breath.

Damn. What had happened? How had they gotten here so fast? What did they know? It seemed like a lot.

The door closed and he was left alone with Grim and their dads and a whole lot of questions.

"Joshua, we need to talk," his dad began.

His pops shook his head. "Not yet we don't." He crossed over to Case's desk and picked up the handset, bringing it to his ear. "Yeah, Taggart, go to bed. Drama's over for you, old man. And try to send a woman guard, please. My sons do not need one of those playboy assholes you always hire as bodyguards. 'Night." He hung up. "Case had Big Tag listening in on speaker phone the whole time. And Big Tag's wife called Serena Dean-Miles and kept her up to date. Serena called Lexi, and naturally Lexi then called her momma. So you're going to have to explain why you paid a private investigator to ruin Nicole's life and potentially get her thrown in the slammer for a crime she didn't commit."

He felt his jaw actually drop. "That is not what happened."

Pops shrugged and found his way to the big couch, taking a seat. "Well, the story went through a bunch of people, and two of them were romance writers. As a class of women goes, they do enjoy some embellishments."

Grim shook his head, obviously as shocked as Josh was. "How are you here? It's a three-hour drive. How could you possibly know what was happening?"

Josh could answer that. "Uncle Chase called him. Or he already had plans to be here."

"And it did not take three hours." Pops was the only one in the room who looked like he was enjoying himself. "Jack got us here in two hours and fifteen minutes flat."

"I meant to come alone," his dad said between clenched teeth. "I certainly didn't mean to turn this into a circus show."

Frustration welled inside Josh. "No, you meant to quietly come in and get rid of Nicole on the down-low, didn't you? You meant for the Dawson brothers to take her out of here, and then you were going to sit in on the interrogation. Tell me something, Dad, were you going to turn her over or pay her off and send her out there all alone again?"

The thought made frustration turn to rage. She'd been through so fucking much. He wasn't about to let her face this alone, and he didn't care what his father thought.

Grim stood at his side. "We're not going to let you get rid of her. I'll leave with her if you can't stand the thought of her being around."

Pops suddenly didn't look so amused. "I don't think Jack knew what the hell he was doing, Josh. Though it sounds like you both had the same idea, different Dawsons. So let's take this down a notch and talk this out like the family we are."

Grim took a seat beside Pops. "I'm confused. So Dad called Chase and Ben and asked them to investigate. Meanwhile Josh called Harlow and asked her to do the same. Chase and Ben caught wind their daughter was looking into the situation, called her computer girl and convinced her to give them the information they found. They called you and… I'm still confused as to how you got here so fast."

It didn't get past Josh that Grim had called Dad by his proper name.

"They found out this afternoon and called me. I asked them to wait until I was close so I could be involved in talking to her," his father admitted, scrubbing a hand over his head. "And that's all I wanted to do—talk to her."

"Sure." Josh didn't buy it for a second. His father could be a ruthless bastard—a thing Josh admired him for. That side of Jack Barnes only came out when protecting the people he loved. "You find out the woman involved with your sons is wanted for murder but you weren't going to do anything."

Dad sighed. "Like I said, I was going to talk to her. I was going to figure out what the situation is. I know you don't believe it but this isn't my first rodeo. I know that all is not what it seems sometimes. I damn straight know sometimes a person can get falsely accused. I came up the hard way, son."

"He did," Pops agreed. "It made him cranky."

His father turned on Pops, frowning fiercely. "Do not forget where we are, Samuel. We can go spend some time in the dungeon if you need to."

Pops smiled, a brilliant expression. "I always need to." He stood, crossing the space between them and putting a hand on Dad's neck. Their easy affection was something Josh was not only used to but counted on. "I'm here to take the testosterone level down a bit. It's why I came along. So two alpha males don't tear each other up because they don't know how to properly communicate. I knew you weren't coming out here to meet with Chase on a bit of business. If you were going to meet Chase for business, you would be in Dallas. So much closer. I know you think this all went to hell because Lexi called Abby, but it was always going to go to hell, Jack."

His father lowered his head until it rested against Pops's, and he took a moment to breathe as though the other man gave him strength and calm.

Josh looked over and Grim was watching them with open affection. Maybe Pops was right, and it was time to bring the heat level down.

But not before he made things plain to his father.

"I'm in love with Nicole, and there's nothing you can say that's going to make me turn her away," Josh stated plainly.

His pops mouthed the words *told you* before stepping back. "Grim, do you feel the same way?"

Grim stood, joining Josh. "I do."

"Yeah, I get the feeling you'll be saying those words soon," Pops said under his breath. He returned to his seat. "I'm happy for you both. I look forward to some grandbabies. It's been too long since I was around someone on my intellectual level."

Pops winked as Dad turned, pointing his way. "That's a good twenty, Sam."

"Let's make it thirty," Pops shot back.

"Okay, I love you both, but could we dial back the sexual tension? You're my parents and it's getting to me," Josh complained.

"I know we're in a club and that's apparently a trigger for Pops to turn into an unapologetic brat, but it's gross. I say that with all love and respect." Grim groaned and sat back.

"I love freaking the younger generation out." Pops looked infinitely pleased with himself.

"I'm glad you all find this amusing, but Nicole is in trouble, and that means we're all in trouble." Dad was back to looking tense, his shoulders straight. "According to Chase there's serious evidence against her. You can't expect me to not talk about this."

"But you didn't talk about it." Josh was right back to tense, too. "You went behind my back and planned how to deal with the situation without me or Grim being involved at all. I love you, Dad. I appreciate everything you've ever done for me, but this is how you lose me. I am not a child. I am a fully grown man who you raised and trust with your business. You don't get to hand over all the things you don't want to do and then walk in and tell me how to run the place, and that damn straight includes my love life. I'm going to marry Nicole."

"We're going to marry Nicole," Grim corrected.

"You can't marry Nicole because Nicole doesn't exist," his father pointed out. "Son, you don't even know her real name."

"Her real name is Nora Holloway, but her name doesn't matter," Josh countered. "I'm going to ask you something and I want you to think about this. If you'd found out Mom was in the situation Nicole is in, would you have backed off? Or would you have trusted in the love you had for her? Would you have shrugged and moved on and hoped it all worked out for her? Or would you have fought?"

His dad went serious. "You know what I would have done."

"Don't expect me to be less of a man than you are." Josh stood in front of the man he would look like when he was older. There was no way to deny that he was Jack Barnes's biological child. It was in his hair and eye color and the build of his body. It was also in his stubborn will. But he was his mother's child, too. And beyond all biology he was Sam Fleetwood's. It was his pop's infinite patience, his quiet grace that took over. "Dad, I don't want to fight with you. Grim and I need your help. I know you see me as a kid, but I'm not. I'm ready to start my family even if that means fighting whatever demons are coming after Nicole. Even if it means fighting you."

His father took a long breath and moved into his space. "There's no fight here, son. None. I'm sorry. Grim, come here."

Grim moved in, and Dad wrapped them both up. “I’m proud of both of you. I know it was wrong and I should have talked to you, but it’s hard for me to stop trying to shield you from the world. You boys and your sisters are precious to me.”

“And Nicole is precious to us,” Josh said. “When you get to know her, you’ll love her, too.”

Dad stepped back. “I know I will.” He looked at Grim. “You all right, son?”

Grim stood there for a minute. “I don’t know. I feel weird.”

Pops was right beside him. “It’s okay, son. It’s called emotion, and it’s hard to deal with. You’ll get the hang of it in another forty years or so. Josh handles it better because he wasn’t raised entirely by religious zealots steeped in toxic masculinity. The masculinity he was raised around was open and honest, but it took us a while. Grim, you know it’s okay to cry, right? Ain’t no one here going to think less of you.”

Grim’s jaw went tight. “I love you. I don’t say it because I maybe don’t feel like I should. Or I don’t feel like I deserve it. I’ve been quiet because I don’t want to screw things up, but I’m mad, too. It’s all a fucking storm inside me.”

Dad put a hand on Grim’s shoulder, looking him straight in the eyes. “You don’t ever hold back on me because you’re worried I’ll kick you out or stop caring about you. Never going to happen. I know more than most that family doesn’t have to be blood. You are my son, Jared. I’m human and I make mistakes. I expect you to love me anyway.”

“I do,” Grim said, and there was a sheen of tears in his eyes.

“As Josh said, don’t expect me to be less,” Dad said and pulled Grim in for another hug. “I love you, son. Nothing’s going to change that.”

There was a sniffling sound, and Grim hugged him fiercely.

“Would now be a good time to tell them that we changed our wills and split the estate three ways?” Pops asked.

Grim sighed and looked more calm as he pulled back. “Of course you did. I don’t expect anything like that. Dad, Pops, having you in my life is more than enough.”

Josh rolled his eyes. Grim wasn’t very aware. “They’re talking about you. Years ago Lexi had them pull her out of the will since

Dad gave Lucas their father's estate."

"She doesn't do too poorly on her own. That was the funniest part. I was worried about how hard a ranching life is, and then her books exploded," Dad said, sounding far calmer than he'd been. "No, Lexi asked that we leave everything to her siblings. To Olivia and Josh and Jared."

Now there was no way to mistake the tears in his brother's eyes. "I don't…"

It was his turn to give Grim a hug. "You do deserve it, and before you get worried, Olivia and I were in full agreement. You're not leaving all this chaos to us. We need you."

Grim held him every bit as hard as Nic had held on to their momma.

When Grim finally let go there was resolve in his eyes. "She's mad at us. She thinks we betrayed her."

"Yeah, well, I'll be sleeping on the damn couch for a couple of weeks," his dad said, settling in next to Pops.

"Nah, she'll give in once she realizes we're all presenting a united front," Pops corrected. "You just watch. Abby's going to be our secret weapon when it comes to Nicole. Now let's call in Ben and figure out what's going on with that girl so we can kick whoever's ass we need to and move on to the baby-making part. I'm not joking. I miss having kids around."

"I'm getting him a puppy," Dad promised. "You three will take all the time you need. But he's right. We do need a plan."

Josh sat beside his brother and listened to his fathers.

Chapter Fifteen

Nicole felt oddly calm as Abby handed her the glass of white wine. She was wrapped in a blanket, feeling warmer than she had before.

Before she'd realized they'd lied to her. That they'd set their dogs on her.

Kim entered the room, slipping her cell phone into her pocket. She'd been pacing on the balcony, talking animatedly to whoever was on the other end of the line. "Okay, I'm fairly certain no one's tipped off the police. I have a friend of mine monitoring their radio and communications. Don't ask. He won't get caught. He's quite brilliant at what he does. I think the Dawson brothers were telling us the truth."

"Oh, Chase would never lie." Abby sat down beside her. "Ben might, but Chase is a terrible liar. I hope Harlow's okay. She looked so upset."

"Is she in love with Josh?" Nicole had to ask.

Abby's eyes widened. "No. They've never even hinted at that. They've always been in brother-sister mode."

"She didn't seem to like me."

"She doesn't know you, sweetie," Abby said. "And she's got reasons to be on guard. Reasons her fathers seem to have forgotten. Or rather they seem to have forgotten how to handle her with any delicacy."

"It doesn't matter," Heather said, seeming to get down to business. "What does is figuring out how to handle this case. The Holloways are getting impatient with me. I talked to my husband and business partners, and we think creating a false trail might be the best way to handle the situation for the time being."

"What do you mean?" She was in such a weird place. Abby had brought her up to this ridiculous suite and wrapped her in a blanket, fussing over her like she cared. Like she really was her kid and she loved her. Now Heath…Kim was acting like she worked for her and not her in-laws. She would have believed she was dreaming, that this was a fond fantasy, if it hadn't been for one thing.

Josh had betrayed her. Grim had gone along with it.

"I mean my team can create a false trail. You did a good job of staying off the grid. I had to do serious legwork to catch up to you," Kim admitted. "It wasn't your digital footprint I followed. I had to find people you had connected with."

"She means you were smart," Abby said, giving her a pat. "You did a good job but people remembered you because of your kind heart. I think Kim wants to trick your in-laws into thinking you went places you didn't. So when they inevitably hire someone else, they'll start looking there."

"Exactly," Kim affirmed. "I'm going to lay a false trail that has you disappearing into Mexico approximately two months ago. If I can get them to keep me on the case, I'll send you further into Central America."

"It can be dangerous for a woman to travel alone," Abby mused. "It wouldn't be surprising if you died. Do you think we could fake some records with the police down there? Money isn't an object. I'll write you a check for a retainer."

"That's not necessary." Kim waved her off. "I'm happy to screw with the Holloways. They're assholes. From what I can tell Micah married Nicole because he knew he could do whatever he wanted with her. No one wiped his socials after he died, and his DMs were full of shit I can't unsee. No one outside of his family had a good impression of the man. Or rather no one who knew him in a more than casual way. He apparently was good at pretending to not be a violent shitbag of a human for a couple of months at a time."

It was a good description of who her husband had been. "I think they only tolerated me because they wanted grandchildren. I know he messed with my birth control pills. It's why I went to Portland and got the shot instead."

"That was smart of you, baby girl," Abby praised. "You did a good job, but now you need to let us help you. Now you're not alone. You have a family around you, and everything is going to be okay."

She was going to cry again. She'd thought she was all cried out. "Mrs. Barnes-Fleetwood, you need to think about this. They're dangerous, and being associated with me could cause you problems in the community when it comes out."

Abby's auburn hair shook. "You call me Abby for now, and sweet girl, I was the whore of Willow Fork when I was seventeen years old and had only slept with one boy. I loved him but his family didn't think I was good enough. Do you honestly believe I give a damn what those people think of me? I don't. I care about what happens to you. They can go straight to hell, so put that out of your mind. And I might be mad at Jack right now, but I do believe him when he says all he was going to do was talk to you."

"He didn't call the police and he could have," Kim pointed out.

"He was never going to call the police. I'm going to admit I've been worried he would try something like this, hence me getting in the truck with him when he said he needed a surprise trip to Austin," Abby admitted. "My husband can be overly protective, and we all knew you were in some kind of trouble. He wasn't patient. I told him to wait and you would tell us when you were ready."

There was a lot of that going around. "Josh didn't wait either."

"He's a lot like his daddy. I'm afraid he's more like Jack in that way than Sam and me. Josh can be as ruthless as his father." Abby studied her for a moment. "How did he handle it? Did he get mad? I know how Jared handled it, but I'm worried Josh might let his temper flash. Jared had to learn to control himself at a young age."

"Grim asked me if I did it and when I said I didn't, he said okay." Yep. There were the tears because that moment had been so sweet, and she couldn't trust it. She wasn't sure she could trust this one. Being coddled by two older women felt too much like having moms who cared about her. It felt like something she'd never once had. "Josh yelled at the twin brothers and asked me if they hurt me and talked about lawyers."

Abby's smile was completely satisfied. "That's my boy. Jared's been an excellent influence on him. They were on each other, really. I was worried he'd screwed this up, and you haven't been with him long enough to forgive him."

"He walked in and started talking like he was taking over," Nicole complained.

Abby nodded. "Yes, they'll do that. In most cases I would tell you as long as you're not in a club or a D/s setting, you fight for your place. In this situation, I think you should hand it all over to the men who have the money and connections to fight it. There's a time and place to challenge your Dom, and sweetheart, this is not it. Let them take out their swords, and you and me and Olivia will drink mimosas and watch some trashy TV under the watchful eyes of whoever Big Tag sends to guard us. I hope he sends a couple of the young ones."

"Abby," Kim said with a grin.

Abby winked her way. "I can appreciate a work of art. From a distance. And my oldest daughter Lexi is eager to meet you, Nicole. You should know she's going to ask you a million questions. She and her friend Serena are fighting over who gets to be inspired by your story."

"I say both." Kim had kicked off her shoes and seemed to be treating this like a fun sleepover. "They are very different writers. Give them the same prompt and they'll come up with two different stories."

Nicole wished this was just a fun hang with the girls. She turned to Kim. "What kind of options do I have? I can go along with the whole Nora's dead scenario, but what kind of future can I have? Should I leave the States? There's always the possibility I could run into them someday. My brother-in-law won't be easily fooled. He'll want to see a body."

"Well, I've been thinking about this, and I talked it over with my partners," Kim began. "We actually think the best solution might be you coming back to Colorado with me."

"She's not stepping foot outside of Texas," a deep voice said. "She might not step foot outside of the ranch if she's not careful."

Josh. He was here, and he'd brought his dads and Grim along. They all looked big and tough and ready for a fight. Well, Josh and Jack did.

Grim stood next to Sam, and though they didn't have a bit of blood between them, it was clear they had a connection. They were both sighing and obviously not impressed with Josh's outburst.

Grim moved to kneel in front of her. "Baby, I know you're mad, but you have to see we can't let you leave. It's dangerous."

"She's not going anywhere, and she's going to get a hell of a spanking if she tries to run again." Josh stared down at her. "Where the hell did you think you were going? You didn't even have any shoes on. You were running out into the Austin night in lingerie?"

"Oh, they're going with a good-cop, bad-cop play," Abby whispered, though everyone could hear her. "This actually could be good for you. The bad cop is usually quite nice. At least Jack is."

"Abigail," Jack barked.

If Abby was worried, she didn't show it. She took another sip of her wine.

"I know you were scared." Grim seemed intent on playing his good-cop role to the hilt. "That's why you ran. Josh and I are going to make sure you never feel the need to run again."

"I think it might be best for me to go with Kim." If she wasn't around them, she couldn't be tempted.

Kim stood, relinquishing her place to Grim, who moved in quickly. The private investigator grabbed her purse. "I think that's for the best, too. I've got a plane waiting. We can be in Bliss in a couple of hours. I've got a spare room. My cabin is pretty isolated, so anyone who comes looking for you will be noticed."

"You know what's isolated?" Josh faced off with the blonde. "A cattle ranch. Willow Fork's not that much bigger than Bliss. She's staying with us. You think I don't know what happens in that town? I've been there a time or two, and I'm trying to figure out how I've never met you."

Kim shrugged. "I was taking a calculated risk. I knew you'd been to Bliss for business a time or two, but you tend to stay at the Circle G most of the time. I was more worried about running into Olivia, though we've never been formally introduced either. You would have recognized my son."

Josh nodded. "Yeah, I've met Roman but only because we were at a couple of parties together. I didn't ask his parents' names."

"Well, I sure as hell would have known who Kimberly Kent is," Jack argued.

Kim grinned. "Jack, I passed you in the grocery store the other day. You were buying calcium supplements. I followed you for three aisles. We've been introduced twice and never had a long conversation. You can take the girl out of the Agency, but you can never take the Agency out of the girl. I blend when I want to. Like I said, I knew I was taking a calculated risk coming myself, but I thought it was worth it. Now about getting back to Bliss."

Josh's head shook. "Absolutely not. Woman goes there to ski or look at the mountains and bam, she comes out of it with two husbands."

"Yes, Willow Fork has a lot in common with Bliss, apparently," Nicole said under her breath.

"No, because they've cornered the market on crazy in that town, and I'm not sending my future wife there," Josh announced.

Nicole felt her head threaten to spin. "Wife?"

Grim gave her a grin. "Yeah, baby, where did you think this was going?"

"I told you it was going nowhere since I was leaving as soon as my car got fixed." Now that she thought about it, she had another question. "Did you have something to do with my car repairs taking so long?"

Josh's face went blank, but Grim's told the tale.

"How could you?" Her heart ached at the betrayal.

"How could I?" Josh stood in front of her, staring down with steel in his gaze. "How could I what, Nic? How could I keep you safe? How could I ensure you didn't go out into a world of predators with no protection? With no money. How much have you saved up? Where were you going to live? In your car?"

"If I have to." She stood because this was a fight that required her to go toe to toe with the man currently attempting to control her life. "And none of it is your business."

"It's damn straight my business," he countered. "Everything about you is my business. You're not going to Bliss. The only place you're going is straight back to the ranch, and if you don't want to ride all the way there with a blistered butt, you'll go quietly."

She poked her finger right against his chest. "You won't lay a hand on me, Joshua Barnes-Fleetwood. You don't scare me. You're a big bully, and I'm not having it."

He caught her hand and his expression changed, softening as he brought it to his lips. "That's right, baby. You know I won't hurt you. You know I'm not him, and that's why you'll forgive me in the end. I love you, Nicole. I love you so much I'll fight for you. Even if the person I'm fighting is you."

Manipulative asshole. He'd put her in a corner to see if she would fight her way out.

Because she could with him. She would have shut down and gone secretive with Micah. She'd shut out everyone for years, but she'd been ready to tell them.

Did it matter? Could she trust them? Or was she putting herself in a bad position again? She pulled her hand away. "I… Josh, I think we should talk in private."

She was deeply aware of how many eyes they had on them. They'd been entertaining an audience all night long.

"I think that's the best idea you've had all night." Josh was so heartbreakingly handsome it hurt to look at him. "Let's go down the hall to our room and we'll talk this out."

"This isn't the kind of thing that can be fixed with a conversation," she argued. "You broke trust with me."

"And you told us everything was fine when you're wanted for murder," Grim said quietly.

It was nothing more than the truth. "I wasn't trying to hurt you. I thought I could have some joy for a little while."

"I want more than a little while with you." Grim moved in next to Josh. "And I don't only want your joy. I want your heartache and all your sorrows. I want a life, Nicole. But you should know that even if you don't want that life with me, I'm going to make sure you have one."

"Nicole's right. She needs time," Josh offered. He turned to Kim. "Mrs. Kent, I'd like to discuss the situation with you. I don't merely want to hide Nicole. I want to get her life back for her."

"You want me to prove she didn't kill her husband." Kim nodded, looking entirely satisfied. "I'd like to do that, too. That, though, is going to require some work. I can't do it overnight, but I think it could be a fun project for me and my son."

"Or I could run again." The words were stubborn, and she didn't mean them. She was tired, and the day had been such a roller coaster. "I'm sorry. I didn't mean it, but I also don't think I can pretend none of this happened. The truth is I was thinking about telling you, thinking about putting all of this in your hands, but…"

"No decisions tonight," Grim said. "Can we put the heavy relationship talk on the back burner for another time and place? Tonight, let's go to bed. Separately, if that's what you need. Tomorrow we'll sit down and discuss how to handle the situation you're in. We'll go back to the ranch and wait for Mrs. Kent to figure out if she can resolve the case."

"And if she can't?" Nicole asked.

"We'll cross that bridge when we come to it." His brother had the right idea. It was time to start rebuilding trust. "And I'll tell the shop to fix your car as quickly as possible so you don't feel like we're holding you hostage. I'll trust you not to run, and hopefully over time, you'll trust me again."

How could she refuse him? They were giving her everything she wanted. Time and space and maybe a way out. "All right. I'll come home with you. But I do want my car."

"About that." Jack's face had a sheen of pink.

Abby's jaw dropped. "You didn't."

"Well, I was worried she would leave," Jack said quickly. "And Al said that junker wasn't safe. She's lived in that car before. She's got pillows and blankets in it. I couldn't let her leave when she's obviously in danger. This isn't my first rodeo."

"Of course I knew that," Josh said, frowning his father's way. "Did you think I wouldn't check out her car? I wasn't going to cube it, though."

That sounded bad. "Cube?"

Abby stood up to her husband. "How could you?"

Jack shrugged. "The same way I did it to you and Sam. See, Al takes it down to the dump and there's this big machine…"

"He smushed my car?" That car was all she had.

"You can pick your new one in the morning," Josh said, sending his father a fierce stare. "We'll go shopping before we leave. Dad's paying."

"Of course I am," Jack replied like it was a forgone conclusion he would be writing a big check.

"And now Nicole's got a cube of her own." Sam wrapped an arm around his wife's shoulders. "We can show you how to style it and everything."

She wanted to argue but she was getting a new car out of it. Shouldn't she be more upset about the principle of the thing? Or should she be practical? She could find a nice, inexpensive used car.

Or she could teach all the men not to mess with her. "I like Olivia's Benz."

"An excellent choice," Kim said, settling her bag against her hip. "I'm going to get some sleep. I'll reschedule my flight back and we can discuss how this is going to work over breakfast. I'm sure Jack's paying for that, too."

"Oh, I'll be paying for a while now," Jack replied.

Abby reached for his hand. "Come to bed and I'll show you how you can pay me back, Jack."

"They have zero discretion," Grim said with a shake of his head.

She thought it was sweet they'd been married for so long and still wanted each other. Still wanted to play and hold hands and explore. Still got excited about coming to the club.

Could she have the same with these men?

Should she even want it when she knew how badly it could go?

"I'm tired." She was infinitely weary, and nothing was getting solved tonight.

"Then we'll go to bed," Grim promised. "Come on. I'll carry you down."

"I can walk."

But Grim was already lifting her up into his arms. "You still don't have shoes, baby. You know as long as you don't have them, I'll have to carry you around."

Josh's eyes lit up.

"You are not cubing my shoes," Nicole protested. Although hers were kind of ragged.

"I promise." Josh leaned over and brushed his lips across her forehead. "And I'll sleep on the couch. Grim didn't want to do any of this. He wanted to wait. He wanted to be patient. I had to push."

"I let you do it, so I was involved. I take responsibility," Grim argued.

She didn't want to go to bed alone. Josh was right. This problem wasn't getting fixed with a conversation. It would take time. "Just come to bed, Josh."

He nodded solemnly and they carried her out.

When she was finally between them, she was able to sleep.

* * * *

"You can't sleep?" A deep voice brought Josh out of his brooding.

There was no other word for it. He was brooding in the dark, looking out over the Austin night. He was high enough up he couldn't hear the people milling about on the streets below as the clubs started closing and people started finding their ways home.

His home was in a bed behind him, wrapped around Grim. It had started awkward with Nicole in the middle, but at some point she'd fallen asleep and turned into Grim's warmth.

And Josh had been jealous as fuck.

He turned to his father, who stood on the balcony beside his. Between their suite and his parents, they were taking up half the floor, and the wraparound balconies met in the middle. Which appeared to be a good thing since both he and his dad were in the doghouse.

"No. I'm afraid I can't turn my brain off tonight. I thought you would be…" How did he put this? "Making things up to Mom."

His father chuckled. "I'm not being forced to sleep on the couch. I think offering to buy Nic a car helped. It's not like your momma wants her new baby driving around in a piece of crap that's as likely to explode as it is to get her to her destination. She also understands that Nicole's destination might have been somewhere dangerous. She and Olivia have become fond of Nic."

"Yeah, she's pretty easy to love." He'd started to wonder if he could say the same of himself. "But I screwed up. I don't know she's going to forgive me. It feels like she's willing to forgive everyone else but not me."

"Well, she's not real happy with me either, though I'm hoping spending an enormous amount of money on a car will help," his father admitted. "Not that I think she's a gold digger. She's as far from it as I can imagine. Now when you were seeing Alyssa I was worried."

Josh snorted. "I was never serious about her. She wouldn't accept Grim."

His father leaned against the heavy railing. He was in pajama pants and a T-shirt that proved the old man was still built like a bull. His father was still muscular and fit. Likely because he spent so much time working on the ranch. "Yeah, I could have told you that one isn't meant for our world. She's too worried about what other people think."

"And you think Nicole is?" Josh was interested in his father's opinions.

"I know I was worried in the beginning," his father allowed.

"You seem pretty worried now."

"About her safety," Dad corrected. "Not about whether or not she's going to break your heart. That girl is pure sunshine. She reminds me so much of Sam and your mom. She's been through some terrible things and her heart is still open. See, Nicole cares about the right things. Alyssa wants people to look up to her. She's thinking about her reputation all the time, about being seen with the right people. Nicole thinks about all the people in her life."

His father didn't know Nicole yet. "She's not a saint, Dad. She can tear a strip off a man when she wants to."

"Precisely why she's perfect for you. I don't know if you've noticed but you have what I like to call a strong personality. If you don't have a woman who'll stand up to you, you'll walk all over her. You won't mean to. You'll let your dominant side take over, and you won't ever figure out it's okay to sit back and let her take control."

Josh raised his brows because there was some hypocrisy flowing from his father. "Says the man who cubed my girlfriend's car."

Dad held his hands up. "I didn't say I was perfect. I'm just saying that your momma knows how to set boundaries, and that's been good for our long-term marriage. Your pops only learned how to ask for what he needed when we got involved with your mom.

She taught him how to trust himself and value himself. Your momma taught me she can love me, Sam can love me, even when I screw up. I don't have to be in control one hundred percent of the time. The world won't fall apart if I take a day off."

"Or let your kids take over the business part so you can do the fun parts?"

His father turned his way, a smile on his face. "Exactly. I know I look over your shoulder more than you would like, but I'm getting better. I know I don't talk a lot about this. I don't talk a lot period, but I didn't have a father, Josh. I still worry I don't know how to do it. Abby had already raised Lexi by the time we met. She took the lead and showed me what to do. Sam is a natural caregiver. It comes so easy to him. It's why we worked in the beginning. I took the leader role. I hate that word because I feel like we put all the emphasis on being a leader when all the real work is done underneath. I could make all the decisions, but Sam made us a home. I got us the money for the ranch, but it was Sam who found Benita, who helped us do things like buy furniture that wasn't a Barcalounger or a TV. It was Sam who charmed everyone around us. Hell, it was Sam who found your mother. I wouldn't have touched her."

"Why?" His parents seemed so damn solid. It was odd to think there had been a time they hadn't been together.

"I didn't think she could handle what I needed from a woman, but the truth of the matter is I didn't know what I needed from a woman until I met Abigail Moore. Because I didn't need a woman. I needed her. I think that's how you feel about Nicole. Am I right?"

Josh nodded. "Yeah. I feel like Grim and I have been looking for a long time, and we thought we would find someone we could care about and settle in."

"Because in your mind the relationship with Grim was the primary relationship," his father pointed out.

"I missed him," Josh admitted. "I know it sounds dumb, but he was my first friend and then he was gone for so long. It's not fair but I was happy when we found him out on the range. I was actually happy his shit-ass stepfather had kicked him out and I got to have him back in my life."

"Son, you're being too hard on yourself. Of course you missed your friend. I know you don't remember this but when Grim was attending the school for the resort workers' kids, you actually told us you and he were going to grow up and find a wife."

Josh felt his lips kick up in a grin because he did know this story. "I've been told I was a precocious child and had an attachment fixation on the babysitter. Who ended up marrying my uncles. Ben and Chase don't let me forget it. I also was told I asked about Chloe before she was born."

"You knew what you wanted—a family. You were an intense kid, but you mellowed a lot. I think finding Nicole is bringing all those instincts to the surface," his father said. "So she made you sleep on the couch? Did you give it to Grim? You can come sleep in our suite. Your momma's not holding a grudge, it seems."

"Nic let me in bed but only to sleep. Though she seems to be fine with Grim."

"That's what happens when you play good cop, bad cop and you're the bad cop," his father pointed out. "I think it would be hard for Grim to be rough on her in any place but a dungeon. It's not his nature. You and Grim might not be perfect reflections of me and Sam, but the nature of the relationship is close. Until I met your mother, Sam was my priority, and then Abby became the center of our world and we had to find our places with her, too. It wasn't always smooth sailing."

"I'm not sure how to get out of this," Josh admitted. "I thought I was doing the right thing at the time."

"You were." His father sounded completely committed. "I should have come to you and told you I was worried. I should have worked with you. If I'd known you already talked to Harlow, I might not have brought her dads in, and then we wouldn't be in the situation we're in. Although I still would have cubed her car. It wasn't a good car. Whatever she paid for it, it was too much."

"I think she'll get over the car. Hell, I even think she'll get over me calling Harlow. It's the picture. I knew she didn't want her picture taken and I did it anyway." His gut clenched. At the time it seemed reasonable. Now it felt reckless. "I thought she had a stalker. And now that I'm saying the words, I'm rethinking everything. If she's got a stalker, pinging her information could bring him here."

"Harlow's partner is a smart young woman. She's not going to put anyone in danger. Ruby Lockwood has been trained by the best. I know she did an internship with McKay-Taggart, and Adam Miles is her mentor, so relax," his father said. "If Kimberly Kent thought Nicole was in danger, she would have found a way to get her out of here, and there would be nothing you or I could do about it. So relax about someone tipping off the police."

"How the hell can I relax?" Josh prayed his father had the answer because it seemed so far from him.

"You have to have some faith in the people around you," his father advised. "I looked up Mrs. Kent's team. They're a bunch of ex-CIA and ex-FBI agents who basically help people find missing loved ones. They're excellent at what they do and they know how to do it quietly. I think Nic caught a lucky break when the Holloways decided to hire her."

"She said she didn't want to take the case until her son pointed out he thought Nicole was innocent."

His father shrugged. "Then we're doubly lucky, and when that kind of providence falls into your lap, you trust it. I've already talked to my contacts and they say she's the best. We can trust Mrs. Kent and her team. We can trust Harlow and hers. We can trust Chase to make an ass of himself."

Josh had to chuckle. "Yeah, but he wouldn't have called the cops."

His father's head shook with surety. "Never. Chase would take care of things on his own. In this case even if Nicole had done it, he would have tried to figure out why. So when I say relax, I mean understand that part of this clusterfuck we find ourselves in is going to work out. You have to concentrate on Nicole."

"I don't know she wants me to concentrate on her." He felt a deep sorrow well inside. "I think she trusts Grim more than me. I think they understand each other in a way I can't."

"Of course they do. Josh, at the end of the day, you're the top," his father said with quiet wisdom. "You're the Dom, and you have to lead when it comes to something like this. She would have gone the rest of her life running. Grim likely would have kept quiet and she would have left. You forced the situation, and there's a cost. But it's one you've got to be willing to pay. She's coming home with us. You have something Sam and I didn't have."

He knew exactly what his father was talking about. "Mom. I have Mom. From what I can tell Nicole's never had a mother in her life. Not one who loved her. She was the outsider in her family and then she was the victim in her husband's."

"It's going to take a while to sort through this, and Nicole's a smart young woman. She's not going to run away this time. She knows she's in a good place, but she's been in a lot of bad places, and it's hard to trust good luck when you've had so much bad. Grim does understand. You, on the other hand, seem like you breezed through life, and I'm so proud to be able to give you a happy childhood. Pain and suffering don't make you a good person. A good person comes through it, but not having a painful background doesn't make you less of a man."

"It makes me lucky." He'd been lucky in so many ways.

"And wanting to share your luck with others, son, is what makes you a good man. So here is the hard part. You're feeling jealous right now and that's normal, but you need to adjust your thinking. She couldn't turn to you tonight. Do you want her to be alone?"

Josh thought for a moment. "When I think about it, I'm glad Grim's there. I'm glad she has him, too."

His father laid a hand on his shoulder. "Which is why this relationship can work. You're human. You'll feel jealous from time to time. Sit down. Think about the situation. Talk it out if you need to, but don't react. Act. Be the man you want to be."

"I want to give her what she needs. I want to give Grim what he needs, too. And I know that's me. I know it deep in my bones. We were meant to be together, but what if I can't convince her? Should I give them my blessing? I don't want to cost them their relationship."

"Their relationship doesn't work without you," his father said. "She's angry and scared and you're a safe place to put both of those emotions. Think long and hard. This is a woman who hasn't felt safe in a long time."

She'd felt fine yelling at him.

And he'd known he was on the right path. He'd known it when she didn't back down. He'd known it when she let him in their bed. It had only been the moment when she'd turned to Grim that insecurity had set in. Insecurity had no place in their relationship. It would fester and cause stress between them. He would let it go. He would continue to be her safe place even if she didn't turn to him.

Yet.

"I have to be patient." It would be the hardest thing he'd ever had to do. He wanted her more than anything, wanted to start their lives together.

She wasn't ready. She might never be, and he couldn't simply make it happen. He couldn't willpower his way through this.

"She needs some time, son," Dad agreed. "She needs to rest her soul in a place where she's safe, and we're going to give it to her. You need to be ready for her to not move into your house, not sleep in your bed for a while. This courtship of yours went fast because she thought she would leave. Now it's time to slow things down and do this right. She's been burned. Give her the time she needs to realize it's not happening all over again. Let your momma baby her. Let Olivia be her friend. Let me and your pops dad the hell out of her."

"And what am I supposed to do?" Josh asked.

His father gave him a weary smile. "Well, I was thinking she might like a job."

It wasn't a terrible idea. "She could work with me in admin. I can find her a job. Or if she wants to help out Grim, she could do that, too. She can explore and figure out what she wants while we wait for Mrs. Kent to decide how to best handle the situation. I want to get Uncle Lucas on this."

"Already called. He's coming to the ranch day after tomorrow," his father promised him. "If it's all right with you, we'll get up, have breakfast with Mrs. Kent, and make arrangements for extra security out at the ranch. Subtle security because I don't want anyone asking why there's suddenly a bunch of armed guards around."

Willow Fork wasn't a metropolis. All new people would be noticed. "It would start talk, and they would look Nicole's way."

His father nodded as though he understood and had already fixed the problem. "So we bring in a couple of new ranch hands who also happen to know how to spot security problems. She should be all right on the ranch. When she leaves, we'll make sure someone is with her, but I'm hesitant to make her feel like she's in lockdown. From what I can tell the only person looking for her right now is on our side, and she's smart as hell. Kimberly Kent used to manipulate world leaders. She can handle a couple of assholes from Oregon."

He had to be patient. He had to give her the time she needed.

And if, in the end, she chose only Grim, he would have to step back and be happy for the two most important people in his life.

Josh listened as his father spoke, but his mind was on the woman in bed.

Chapter Sixteen

"You need anything?" Nicole closed the door to the truck. "I've heard you go through a lot of beer lately."

"We're fine. And I certainly won't ask you to do our grocery shopping. The truth is neither one of us has much appetite right now." Grim hit the button to lock the truck as the new guy got out and shut his door.

The morning after the debacle at Subversion, they'd had breakfast with Kimberly Kent and it had been decided Harlow Dawson would be one of the bodyguards who watched after Nicole when she left the ranch. Harlow was known around town, and everyone would think she was simply there for a visit. She could work remotely and had told Grim she kind of needed a break from Dallas for a couple of weeks.

The other guard was a young man named Landon Vail. He was a handsome twenty-something who'd recently left the Navy and taken a job at the security firm his parents used. He knew how to ride and was quickly being brought up to speed on ranch work.

Two weeks later and he and Josh were still sleeping alone.

Harlow moved in beside Nicole—who appeared to be her new bestie. She gave Grim a grin. "Yes, you looked like you were wasting away at dinner last night. You barely ate a whole side of beef."

That got a chuckle from Nicole. He noticed her hand coming up to play with the small diamond on her new necklace. "I'm constantly shocked by how much they can eat."

He wished he'd been the one to give it to her, but Jack had. It had been part of his very generous apology. Nicole hadn't taken it off in weeks.

"Well, I have to eat with the other ranch hands." Landon was nearly as tall as Grim and looked right at home in jeans, a T-shirt, boots, and a Stetson. "You know what they like to cook? Chili. I've had chili three nights this week. And the old guy won't let me cook. My father is a chef. I literally learned how to cook in gourmet kitchens, but no, some eighty-year-old dude named Cookie won't even let me help."

He felt for Landon in this case. Cookie was stubborn and he could only make a handful of meals, but he'd been around forever. "I'll let Jack know you'd like to help."

"Well, you might not ask me to do your grocery shopping, but your mother has no such problem." Nicole pulled out the list his mom had given her. "I think she's trying to fatten me up. I've been told she usually makes everyone eat super healthy, but she's got the makings of a lasagna and enchiladas."

"We'll work out harder," Harlow promised. "You boys stay out of trouble. We'll meet you here in half an hour or so."

Harlow started for the store, but Nicole looked back. "Text me if you think of something you need."

She turned and followed Harlow in.

"That woman scares me," Landon said with a shake of his head. "She's hot. Super hot, but scary. Are you sure you want her teaching Nicole? I saw them practicing how to take out a man's balls yesterday."

In addition to acting as a bodyguard, Harlow was teaching Nicole self-defense, and she'd seemed to have taken to the subject. They sparred on the big lawn under the oak tree that had been there for years.

"I want her safe. Teaching her self-defense seems like the smartest thing we can do. Although I'm not sure I know any of those moves," Grim admitted. "I was taught to shoot, but the punching part came naturally."

Landon's lips spread in a smile sure to have every woman in the area panting after him. "Yeah, I think that's a masculine trait, but if you want to learn how to punch more effectively, I'll give you a lesson. In addition to being an excellent chef, my father was a Navy SEAL. I didn't go into Special Forces, but he made sure I learned how to fight. Of course he taught my sister, too. I understand the need, but do those two have to talk about a man's balls so much? It seems rude. There are other places to hit."

But none as effective.

Nicole didn't seem to notice Landon most of the time. Her obliviousness of the handsome bodyguard gave him some hope.

"I'm going to leave her self-defense tutoring to Harlow," he said. "Come on. I've got a date with some puppies, and then we need to grab the feed Jack ordered."

"That's the only date you're going to have if you don't stop brooding and start showing off your masculine wiles, Grim. The way I see it we know each other well enough…" Landon began.

Grim shook his head and kept walking toward the Willow Fork Animal Shelter. It was a small but well-kept building. It housed the various strays they found around the county. "We don't."

"…for me to give you some advice." Landon didn't miss a beat. "The way I heard it you and Josh were pretty hot and heavy with Nicole before the whole incident thing happened. Now she's pissed but she's also stuck, and you two are not handling this well."

"I don't need advice."

"It seems like you do. I don't think longing looks are going to work on her," Landon continued.

"I'm giving her space."

"What you should do is give the girl a show." Landon stopped and held up a hand. "Now hear me out."

He didn't want to, but he had to admit he was curious.

Landon took his silence as assent. "I work with this guy. He's in investigations but everyone knows him. Nicest man in the world, and his wife makes the best cupcakes. I mean she could give my dad's pastry chef a run for his money."

"Get to the point, Lan."

"Anyway, there's this woman who works reception part time, and I am interested in dating her. She's standoffish. Anyway, my friend told me I needed to show off," Landon explained. "Leave a couple of buttons undone. Maybe show up and need her to help me with something right after a workout. You're a vet, man. You know how this works. The male has to perform to gain a woman's interest."

"Did it work?"

Landon shrugged. "Nah, but it could work for you."

Grim rolled his eyes and started walking again.

"Nicole watches you when she thinks no one is looking." Landon rushed to keep up.

"We're giving her some room to breathe. She's been through a lot. We rushed things." Space. He was giving her space and time.

The trouble was space and time were starting to feel like separation.

In the two weeks since they'd come home, Nicole had moved into one of the guest rooms in the big house, and he saw her mostly at mealtimes. The last few weeks had been one long slog of work and worry and hope that he would see her while she was either working in the gardens with Abby or learning to ride with Jack and Sam.

She was starting a job with Barnes-Fleetwood on Monday. At least she would likely drive into work with Josh. Or maybe she would take the brand-spanking-new Volvo. It had been delivered the week before, and Nicole continued to ignore them both.

As long as she took Harlow, they'd decided she was okay, and Nicole was taking advantage of the freedom. She and Harlow and Olivia had let Abby and Sam take them all to Dallas for a weekend of shopping, and she'd come back with clothes and makeup she'd vowed to pay Abby back for.

He'd overheard her talking to Harlow about what she would do if her name was cleared.

Find a place of her own and a new job. Start over.

"She doesn't look at you like she's trying to figure you out, man. She looks at you like a kid in a candy store whose mom won't let her eat any sugar." Landon opened the door, and they were assaulted by the yelping barks of every dog in the place greeting them.

He looked out over the organized space. A few years back the only shelter had been a couple of cages in the same building that housed the city's water and sanitation departments. When he'd come back, he'd led a drive for a dedicated shelter and adoption center. Well, he'd tried, and when no one showed any interest in helping him, his parents had written a massive check, and now the Willow Fork Animal Shelter was part of the community and ran on two employees and a whole lot of volunteers. It turned out cute dogs and cats won out over prejudice most of the time.

Parents. It was natural to think of Jack and Abby and Sam as his parents now. They'd acted as his parents for a long time, but he'd always made the distinction in his head. He'd always told himself he was a charity case.

Something about learning he was in the will had changed the relationship for him.

He wasn't concerned with the money, but he damn straight wanted the place in the family.

His mom and dads. His. He had a relationship with them that went beyond Josh. He had a place even if something ever happened between he and Josh.

He had a home.

"Hey, Grim." Dakota Smart was all of twenty-two and had boundless enthusiasm when it came to furry friends. She was one of the shelter's most active volunteers and often helped him when he was working on sick animals. She would make an excellent vet, but he couldn't convince her to go to college. "We've got a litter of puppies some jerk dropped off. They're barely weaned. I think he was breeding and those dogs, well, they're definitely mutts. He didn't watch her closely enough and now he's washed his hands of the whole thing. The living things that were his responsibility. It kind of reminds me of home."

Dakota didn't have the greatest homelife. Her parents had gotten divorced when she was eight and her mom dated a lot, and not always the best men. Her father was kind but did not live up to his last name and often forgot things like birthdays. He drifted in and out of his daughters' lives. She had one sister, Cheyenne, who was frequently in trouble.

"Hi." Landon gave the pretty girl a once-over.

Dakota's eyes went wide as she took in the ex-sailor. "Hi."

Good lord. He did not have time for this. He gripped his bag and started down the row of cages. "Are they at the end?"

The end had two big cages for momma dogs and their babies. Too often they found neglected pregnant dogs who needed care.

"Yes, and I've already cleaned them all up. They're in pretty good shape, but I think they miss their mom. At least he didn't dump them. Unlike the little guy in four. I'm worried he's got a broken leg, but he won't let me touch him." Dakota stopped at a cage that held a small dog who huddled in the corner, like he could hide from the world.

Grim crouched down and reached into his bag. He always had some treats on him. "Hey, boy, you're okay now. Everything is fine."

"He's not eating," Dakota said, worry on her youthful face. Her blonde hair was back in a ponytail, and she wore a T-shirt emblazoned with the shelter's logo.

"He's scared. He's in survival mode." Grim stood and opened the cage. The dog growled but didn't look his way. Grim sat at the edge of the cage. "It's okay, buddy. No one's going to hurt you here."

He gently tossed one of the soft treats he carried so it landed close to the pup. So close he didn't need to move. The food bowl had been placed at the edge of the cage.

The dog was far more afraid than hungry, unwilling to risk his life for the temporary comfort of food.

So Grim would have to show him it was okay, that he'd landed in a safe place.

It was kind of a theme in his life now.

But then once, he'd been the stray, and the home he'd found had been worth everything.

Grim took a long breath. "I might need for you to drive the ladies home, Landon. This could take a while. I need to spend some time with this guy and see if we can get him eating. And we have some new guests. How many puppies?"

"Eight," Dakota replied. "And the momma is a pure bred golden, while I'm pretty sure daddy was what we like to call around here a junkyard dog. Those puppies are so ugly they're cute, if you know what I mean."

What she meant was they needed to get those babies adopted and fast. They would be cute as puppies and look scary as big dogs no matter how sweet they were. "Well, they'll all need their shots. Could you get them ready for me?"

"I'd like to help."

He looked up and Nicole was standing there, bags of groceries in her hands. Harlow had two big bags as well.

"Abby forgot to tell us she'd called the order in," Harlow admitted.

"Or maybe I wasn't listening. Apparently this was a list to check off." Nicole set the bags on the big reception desk. "She's worried the young man who fills the orders isn't very accurate. He was today. What are you doing?"

"Trying to get him comfortable enough to eat." He kept his voice low and gentle. The dog was sniffing around the treat, his head going up and down as he tried to find a way to get it without exposing himself. "I'm going to sit here for a while. It could be an hour or two, and then I have some puppies to vaccinate. I thought it was a quick trip, but sometimes I get pulled in. It happens a lot. I should have known and let you drive us."

Nicole gingerly opened the cage and walked in. The dog growled her way but more quietly this time.

He liked women more than men. It wasn't unusual. Dogs—especially ones who'd been abused—could have gender preferences. This dog was probably kicked by a man and so he feared them.

A little like Nicole.

"It's okay. I think I would rather stay here. I love dogs. And cats. Pretty much any animal," she said as she eased down, sitting across from him. "Maybe Harlow or Landon could run the groceries back and Josh could pick us up when he's done with work."

Landon frowned but Harlow leaned over and whispered something to him that had him looking up at the security cameras.

They should be safe here.

It had been so long since she'd been willing to be alone with him.

Landon moved to pick up the bags Nicole had left on the counter. "Call if you need anything."

Harlow held out her hand for the key to the truck. "I'll text Josh to let him know to pick you up. Are you closing soon?"

It was their short day. It was exactly why he'd decided to stop by. He fished out his keys. "In about twenty minutes, but like I said, I'll be here for a while. Josh won't mind waiting around."

He never did. He would come in and help with the chores.

They could have some quiet time with Nicole. Not to tempt her into sex. To show her she was safe with them.

"Hey, boss. I was actually needing to get home. My mom has a date, and I don't want to leave my sister by herself. She tends to get into trouble," Dakota said with a frown. "I know it's bad timing."

He shook his head. "You go and take care of business. Josh knows how to help me."

"Thank you." Dakota grabbed her bag. "I'll lock up. Josh has keys."

"And I'll show you to your car," Landon offered.

Dakota blushed. "Oh, thanks. That would be nice."

Harlow's eyes rolled, but she followed them out.

And he was left alone with Nicole.

"Do we just sit here?" she asked after a moment.

He looked over, and the dog had managed to down the treat when he'd figured no one was looking. It was a good sign.

Like Nicole willing to be locked in with him.

"The key is to get him used to people who aren't going to hurt him," Grim explained. "Dogs are a lot like people. You kick them too much and they get real scared. You have to build trust before they'll let you get close."

Her lips curled up. "Are you talking about the dog or me?"

"Maybe both."

She was quiet for a moment. "It's hard. I hate hurting you and Josh, but it's hard for me to trust. Not you. I'm kind of getting over the whole Josh sicced a PI on me thing. Harlow's been asking me all kinds of questions during our self-defense lessons, and they made me think. Josh was being Josh. The way Jack was being Jack. They're overprotective men. Good men but overprotective. He didn't mean to hurt me."

"He didn't."

"So what I'm really afraid of is everything falling apart."

He pulled another treat out of his bag, handing it to Nicole.

"Toss it about a foot away from him. Just enough so he'll have to move out of the corner to get it."

She did as he asked, and the dog's head turned slightly but it didn't move. "You're trying to show him it's safe to get closer to us."

"Yep."

"Was the car a dog treat, Grim?"

He snorted at the idea. "The car was repayment because my dad is a freak who likes to cube vehicles he finds offensive. He owed you the car, Nic. You don't have to feel bad about it. He knew he would be buying you one when he destroyed yours. He did it so Josh didn't have to. Your car was dangerous."

"My car was worth maybe three hundred bucks. I can't even comprehend how much the Volvo cost. I still have sticker shock and I've been driving it for two weeks," she said with a frown. "He didn't have to get me some luxury vehicle. I was mostly kidding when I picked it. I wanted to shock him."

Grim shrugged. "Jack knows what it means to fight to survive. The same way you and I do. I want you to think about this. If you had more money than you could ever spend, would you spoil the people you love?"

"Of course I would," Nicole agreed. "I guess it's been so long since anyone loved me that I don't recognize it. I spent a couple of days thinking he bought it as a bribe."

"A bribe?"

"So I would be nicer to you and Josh. He found out I wasn't the evil person he thought I was so he felt bad. And then I realized he does care about me. He's been teaching me how to ride. Do you know I don't ever remember a parental figure sitting down and taking the time to teach me anything? For my father I was a reminder of something he would rather forget. To my stepmother I was a bother. Being around Jack and Sam and Abby is the first time I feel like I have parents." There were tears in her eyes.

He wanted so badly to reach out and drag her into his arms.

But he was being patient. "Do you ever wonder which would be worse? Having parents who loved you and losing them or never having them at all? I do. I don't think about my mom as much as I did in the beginning. It's kind of like she died, too. I try to remember who she was before she met Ezekiel. I remember how she would drop me and my brother off at the school they had out at the resort. She teased me and Josh about how close we were. She was friendly with Abby. They sometimes took me and Josh and Olivia to the pool for lunch and we would have chicken nuggets and French fries. And then it was all gone."

She was quiet for a moment. "I think those memories are sweet, and I wish I had some. That's what your parents are giving me." A tear slipped onto her cheek. "Abby lets me help her in the garden, and Sam taught me how to play pool. And Jack's spent hours teaching me how to take care of the horses and how to ride. I'd never ridden before. I didn't know how free I would feel."

Grim couldn't remember a time he didn't ride. "I love being out alone in the early morning. I sometimes take a chore way out on the property just so I can ride. I know I could take one of the trucks or the ATVs, but I prefer to ride. I'm glad you're enjoying the lessons. How is it going with Harlow? You seem to be getting along. Are you still worried she's in love with Josh?"

She shook her head, a smile on her lips. "No. She totally sees him as a brother. I like her. She was nervous about me and I understand. She told me about how some of her friends have used her to try to get to Josh because of his money." She got solemn again. "I worry he'll wonder about that someday. I worry somewhere down the line he'll figure out I don't fit in."

"He won't because you do. Our family isn't like the Holloways. Mom and Dad and Pops worked for everything they have. They knew how to raise their kids to work hard, too, to not take their upbringing for granted. Harlow's been asking you questions. I have a few of my own. Would your husband have encouraged his father to split his inheritance in half to give it to some stray they took in?"

"Never." She obviously didn't need to think about it. "The whole family is craven about money. From what I was told money was the reason Ted killed his brother. I know you're not the same. I know it in my soul. I'm just… I need to figure out if I can be enough for you. That's about me, not you and Josh. It's my insecurity. When it's safe, Harlow wants me to come to Dallas and see this therapist friend of hers. He works with a group there, and he specializes in surviving domestic abuse."

Harlow was doing a good job with her. "I think seeing a therapist would be great. You should know Josh thinks we should talk to someone, too."

"About?" Nic seemed surprised.

"About how to support someone we care about who survived domestic abuse. We don't always talk the same language. He wants to make sure he learns yours."

Now the tears rolled from her eyes, and she didn't try to stop them. "You already know it."

"I do, but it's not the same, baby. Even though we have some similarities, it's still hard. I don't want to talk about it. Not even Josh knows everything I went through, but I've started to wonder if it's festering inside me," Grim admitted. "I thought I could bury it and it would go away, but it doesn't. It sits under the surface waiting. I realized until the moment Jack told me he'd changed his will I was waiting for him to realize I wasn't his kid. Waiting for Abby to find a reason to turn me out. Waiting for Sam to see what he saw in me."

"What who saw?" Nic asked.

This was an old ache. "My stepfather."

Her gaze softened on him. "What did he see, Grim?"

He had to tell her the truth. "Evil."

She sat there for a moment and then she moved, crawling across the floor to straddle him. She took his face in her hands, staring down at him. "There is no evil in you, Jared Burch. You are one of the best men I've ever met. I love you. I love you and Josh. Be patient with me. Please."

His heart clenched but in the best of ways. "There is no amount of time you could take that I wouldn't be waiting at the end of it."

She leaned over and kissed him. He didn't give in to the urge to take control. He let her brush her lips over his, and then she shifted her body so she was sitting next to him.

She glanced over at the dog and she gasped. "The treat's gone."

Grim reached for another. "A little closer this time."

"Hey, buddy." Her voice was gentle as she tossed the treat a full foot closer than last time. "This is for you. You're okay here."

For the first time in weeks he had some hope.

* * * *

Josh stepped into the shelter, locking the door behind him.

"It's okay, sweetie. One shot and you'll be fine," a soft, familiar voice was saying.

Nicole. He'd kind of worried Harlow had been playing a joke on him when she'd told him Nicole would be waiting on him at the shelter because she was helping out Grim with a litter of puppies and one shaky mutt.

She'd barely talked to either of them for weeks, but she didn't have the same problem with his family. She'd been getting up early to go riding with his dad and Pops. She spent her afternoons in the garden with his mom, and more than once she'd gone out to The Barn with Olivia, hauling Harlow along. On those nights Landon always followed at a distance and sent Josh texts letting him know she was okay.

The urge to follow her was almost overwhelming.

"I might give that one more than a shot. He's peed on me twice. I think he's aiming." Grim sounded irritated but only for a moment. "Baby, hold him still."

"He's a wiggler," Nicole said.

So Grim had found a way to connect with her again. Night was just around the corner, and the shelter was closed for the evening. They would make sure all the critters got their dinner, and then maybe he could convince Nicole to go out with them.

"He's so cute. Why would you have any trouble finding someone to take him?" She sounded like she was in a good mood.

There was a purring sound from his left, and Josh looked over. Bandit was an ancient tabby cat who'd wandered in one day and never left. He'd been adopted out a couple of times and the owners were all good people, but Bandit would get out of their houses and find his way back here. At some point Grim had given up and accepted Bandit was the shelter's only permanent resident.

"He's cute right now," Grim was saying, "but in a couple of months he'll weigh forty pounds, and by the end of a year he's going to be huge. The good news? I think I know who the father is. Dakota's wrong. This dog's got some Australian shepherd in him. They make excellent ranching dogs when they're trained right."

Josh knew what was coming next. He leaned down and let Bandit jump into his arms. The cat seemed to like him and enjoyed being petted for a time. He started for the back of the shelter where Grim's office was set up. "He's going to parade them by my momma, and the dads will have some new friends to help out. It's good timing. Jasper and Gordo are about ready to retire and live the lazy life."

"Hey." Grim looked up and gave him a smile Josh hadn't seen on his best friend's face for days. "Thanks for stopping by. Nic's been helping me with the newbies. They're about six weeks along, so I'm vaccinating them. Being in the shelter can be rough on a pup, but these will be ready to be adopted out in the next couple of weeks."

Nicole held a wriggling ball of fluff. "They took these babies away from their momma."

"Hey, we're honestly lucky the guy waited for them to be old enough to adopt. Sometimes they dump the puppies immediately so the mom can be bred again," Grim said, packing up his kit.

"Do you want me to find him?" Josh would beat the crap out of the dude if she wanted him to.

She frowned his way as she put the puppy in the crate with his brothers and sisters. "The fact that you are standing there petting a cat while you casually offer to beat someone up is a whole vibe with you, Josh."

He wasn't sure his vibe was a good thing in Nicole's head. "You think I should put the cat down?"

Her lips kicked up. "I think you should be less violent."

"He's mostly talk," Grim offered. "Mostly. Let's see if the little guy's down yet."

Bandit was purring against his chest. "You put a dog down in front of her?"

Nicole gasped. "He wouldn't do that unless he had to. No, he's talking about Buddy. We've spent the better part of an hour getting him used to eating treats, but he still wouldn't let Grim examine his leg so he managed to get him to take a sleepy treat."

"Nic did that." Grim started for the row of cages. "He took to her. I hope he's house trained because they're in love."

Nicole put a hand to her heart, and her whole body softened.

"He's so sweet. And scared. Someone treated him awful, and he's a baby who needs a good home."

Yep. She'd spent too much time with his momma. "Well, it's not like we can have too many dogs."

"You would let me keep a dog?" Nicole asked.

"Why would I ever stop you from… Your husband wouldn't let you have a dog," Josh surmised.

"Micah was not a pet person." She stopped in front of him, her chin tilting up as she looked him over with a sassy expression on her face. "You obviously are. I think we can take care of Buddy better at home so he doesn't get… What did you call it, babe?"

What the hell miracles had Grim been working?

"Kennel cough," Grim called back, and then he was walking toward them with a scrap of a canine in his arms. "The sedative worked fast. The good news is his leg's solid. He's got a scrape on his paw. It's why he was limping. I'm going to clean him up and we can take him home."

"Do you need help?" Nicole asked.

Grim didn't look back. "No, I'm good. I'll be ready to go in less than half an hour. Why don't you and Josh go into the storage room? We've got a couple of crates and some food and water bowls. Get this guy a nice dog bed, too."

Nicole stepped back. "All right. I can do that."

Did she only want to be alone with Grim? God, he had to stop going there. Grim and Nic had a connection he couldn't truly understand. He loved them both. If she wanted Grim and not him, then he would step back and let them be together.

Bandit let out a meow signaling the end of their session. The cat jumped out of his arms and lazily started to follow Grim, taunting the dogs in their cages with his feline freedom.

Nicole seemed to have learned the layout of the shelter quickly since she rounded the hallway leading back to the big storage room they kept stocked with everything a pet could need.

He followed her. "Are you okay? Do you want me to stay out here?"

She frowned as she turned his way. "Why? I mean I could probably use another set of hands. I know Buddy is small, but like all small things he needs a lot."

She disappeared behind the doors, and he could see the light coming on.

He walked into the storage room. "I don't want to make you uncomfortable."

She stopped in the middle of the room and turned to him, frowning as though she was trying to decide how to handle him. "You make me uncomfortable all the time, Josh."

Well, that was a kick in the gut. "I don't mean to."

"I've had a lot of time to think, and my problem is really with you. I think if it was just Grim I was dealing with I wouldn't be so scared."

His heart felt like it was twisting in his body. He took a step back. "You don't have to be scared of me. Baby…I mean, Nicole, I want you to have what you need. I don't want to be one more man who makes your life misery. If you want Grim, you should have him. I know I said we were a packaged deal, but the truth is we're not. He loves you."

She went still, staring at him. "I thought you loved me."

"I do. And I love Grim. So when I work the math in my head, I know I should step back. I want something more than my own happiness. I want yours. I want his." He was fairly certain he would never be happy without her, but it didn't matter.

Her arms crossed over her chest. "So you would let me and Grim find an apartment in town and go about our lives?"

"No. I would move into the big house and let you have the one we're in now," he replied. "Why would you… Nicole, I would never ask my brother to leave. I wouldn't ask you to leave. If you don't want either one of us, you should stay in my parents' house as long as you need to."

"Even if that's forever?"

She needed a family, and he needed to know she was happy. "Forever. We'll find a way through it. We'll find a way to be friends. I promise. This is going to be okay, Nicole. It's your decision, and you can't make a wrong move except for walking away."

"Because I found the high life and I would be stupid to leave it?" There was a challenge to her question.

He wasn't sure what she was talking about. "Because you have a home and people who love you. Because you could have a future here. It doesn't have to be with me, though I deeply hope you'll still let me be your friend."

"You mean that." She seemed to relax. "You would let me be part of your family. You would let me marry Grim and you would stand there and be my friend."

"I would still love you, Nic. I'll always love you, but I'll be satisfied if you're happy. If you're whole."

"But you wouldn't be." The words came out soft, almost sympathetic.

Was he about to lose her? "No. There will always be a part of me missing, but I'll live with it."

"I kissed Grim tonight."

His whole body felt heavy. He knew he'd said what he'd said, and he meant it, but it was going to hurt more than anything he'd ever felt. His mind was already working on the problem. He might need to go on the road more. Maybe it would be easier to not watch them settle into the house he'd hoped to share with them. Maybe a couple of months away would ease the longing to something manageable.

"So I should kiss you, too," she offered logically. "To be fair. I know it doesn't have to be one for one, but there haven't been a lot of kisses lately, and I don't want you to feel left out."

Then she was right in front of him, going up on her toes and pressing those sweet lips to his, and it was like the fucking world came back online. Like he'd spent the last few weeks in something colorless and drab and she touched him and the world was real again. Whole again.

His hands went down to grip her hips and drag her in closer, but he stopped.

He didn't want to scare her, didn't want to take something she wasn't willing to give.

Nic sank down to her feet and frowned up at him. "You're going to be like Grim, aren't you?"

"Well, if it means you kiss me and let me stay in our bed, then yes, I suspect I'll be a lot more like Grim," he admitted.

Her expression softened. "I meant you're going to treat me like I'm fragile. Like I'll run away if you make a single mistake. That isn't what I was trying to do, Josh. I'm not afraid you'll hurt me physically. I'm starting to learn you won't hurt me for anything. I'm starting to understand you are not my deceased husband, and your family is so far from the Holloways it's ridiculous."

"I can be rough," he admitted.

"And I like it when you're rough because even when you're the big bad Dom in my life, you're thinking about me. Not yourself. You're thinking about my pleasure and my comfort and what I need. I've never been afraid you would hit me. Never."

"Never," Josh promised. "Never in any way not meant to bring you pleasure. Nicole, I love you. I want to take care of you. I want to have the kind of family I had growing up."

"I know. It's what I was afraid of," Nicole admitted. "I didn't understand your family and I thought I wouldn't fit in, but I do. I thought this would all turn sour, and I know I haven't been here long, but it's not going to go bad, is it?"

Hope lit his whole soul. "No, baby. No one is going to turn on you. You have a family now. You have me and Grim and Olivia and my parents. You have our friends. Harlow adores you. The rest of our friends will, too."

"And even if I made a misstep, you wouldn't kick me out."

"No. There is nothing you can do that would make me leave you."

She frowned his way. "I can think of a few things."

She didn't understand him. "There is nothing you—Nicole Mason or Nora—could do. There is nothing your sweet soul could do that would make me run."

"You're taking a lot on faith, Joshua Barnes-Fleetwood." She stood there looking so vulnerable. "I tell you I didn't kill my husband and you believe me."

"I believe you."

"I could be lying," she said softly.

"You're not." He knew it in his bones. She wasn't lying about anything. She was exactly who she said she was. She was sweet and scared and tired of not being loved the way she should be. So he would give it to her. He and Grim would give her all the love she needed. "Stay with us. Be with us. Not physically if you're not ready, but spend time with us. We've missed you."

"I've missed you, too." She moved into his arms, and he sighed as she wrapped herself around him. "I didn't realize how much until tonight. I've been focusing on helping Kim with my case and learning from Harlow and your parents."

"You needed time. It's okay if you need more," he whispered, holding her so close. "Please spend some time with us. Let us take you out. Show you how we feel."

She sighed. "Then how about you call your mom and tell her we're eating in town. I've got a craving for Christa's chicken and dumplings."

Having dinner with her—just the three of them—would be a good start.

Even if he ended the night dropping her off at the big house and going home alone, it was enough.

It was hope.

"I think it sounds perfect." His voice was thick with emotion. "Now let's get everything that dog of yours is going to need."

Her smile was enough to warm him. Maybe for the rest of his life.

Chapter Seventeen

Grim looked across the booth at Josh. His best friend was more relaxed than he'd been in weeks, and it didn't have anything to do with the steak and fries he'd eaten. He'd also downed a salad when Nicole had pointed out vegetables were a necessary part of life. Josh had an indulgent smile on his face as Nicole told Christa all about her new friend.

Spending time with their girl had Josh looking like himself again.

"He's so cute. We think he's probably got some terrier in him," Nicole was saying.

"And chihuahua, given how he shakes," Josh joked.

Nicole wrinkled her nose his way. "He's scared. And maybe cold."

Buddy was sleeping in his crate in Christa's office. He had some excellent doggie anxiety meds which he might need for a while because that pup had seen some things.

"He looks adorable," Christa said. "I can't wait to meet Buddy when he's awake."

Christa started talking about her Labrador. The café was hopping tonight, and they'd been lucky to get a table. There was a PTA committee meeting going on in the back room and some kind of church group eating together at a bunch of tables they'd shoved together. He kept an eye on Alyssa, though. She was sitting with her mother across the way, staring over at them from time to time.

She might be a problem.

But the real problem was sitting in a booth in the back.

Ezekiel Smith.

He'd chosen the last booth and Grim couldn't see who he was with, but it was likely his brother and two stepbrothers. They never took their mom anywhere except to church and to buy groceries. He was actually surprised they would spend money on something like a meal out.

There was another man there, a taller man, though, who couldn't be one of his brothers.

Despite the peace and joy of spending the evening with Nicole, a sense of dread trickled in.

Christa stepped away to grab their desserts, and Nicole took a long drag off her iced tea.

"I talked to Kim today and she said the case is going well, though she might need to come out and interview me again," Nicole said quietly. "Jack wants to hire a PI in the area to revisit the criminal case, but I'm worried reopening it could shake some stuff up."

And she was scared. "We'll cross that bridge when we get there."

"Harlow can't stay here forever," Nicole mused. "What are we going to do when she needs to go home?"

"Harlow is fine right where she is for the time being." Josh leaned over and reached for her hand. "And we should watch what we say in public. They're always listening."

She flushed. Grim couldn't imagine how hard it was on her to have to measure her every emotion, to always try to fade into the background, though there had been times her good nature hadn't allowed it. He was grateful for those times because Kimberly Kent had turned out to be a godsend. He wasn't going to let Nicole know it, but he'd kind of listened in on the meeting she'd had with the PI. Jack and Harlow had been there, and everyone seemed confident Kim could untangle the problem.

Nicole was going to be free.

It was up to them to ensure she didn't go anywhere.

Which was why his gut tightened as he watched his father put some money on the table and stand up.

"They're watching me now," Nicole said with a sigh.

"They're watching me, darlin'." Josh gave her a wink. "No one can take their eyes off my handsome face."

Sometimes the influence of Pops showed up in his best friend. Dad's influence was always there, but when Josh smiled and winked he was all Sam. He hadn't seen that sunniness in Josh in weeks.

Nicole's nose wrinkled. "You think entirely too highly of yourself. I think they're watching Grim because of his broody good looks."

He was worried they were watching him because of something his asshole stepfather was putting out.

Josh glanced around the café. "Nope. It's definitely…" His best friend's face went blank. "Is that who I think it is?"

Grim sighed. "Yeah. He's been here the whole time. I'm pretty sure he's got at least two of my brothers with him, but I can't tell who he's talking to."

Nicole twisted her torso, trying to figure out who they were talking about.

"I can," Josh said, and his tone had gone arctic. "It's Hazelton."

A chill went up Grim's spine. Jim Hazelton ran the feed store. What was his stepfather doing with the feed store owner? He couldn't forget about the fact that his stepfather and brothers had been preaching about how sin was causing the trouble with the local cattle. And sin was the word they always associated with his new family.

Now they would associate it with Nicole.

"Maybe I should check on Buddy." If he wasn't sitting here perhaps his stepdad wouldn't cause a scene.

All the assholes in his life were right here in the café. Alyssa kept looking over like she was planning to approach them but hadn't worked up the courage yet.

He felt like all their joy was about to get slashed and burned.

Was this how it always would be? Had he brought this down on them all?

"Or you can sit here and enjoy your dessert," Josh said with a frown. "He wants to start something, I can handle him. Same with our other problem. I thought she was the only thing we had to worry about tonight."

Only because he hadn't seen the real trouble coming their way.

"What's going on? Why would Grim need to leave?" Nicole's sweet happiness was replaced with obvious anxiety.

His stepfather was talking to Jim Hazelton and reached a hand out. They shook like they'd decided on something.

He probably wouldn't like the decision.

"Maybe we should all head home," Grim said, wanting to avoid the confrontation. The public confrontation he was pretty sure was about to happen. It wouldn't bother him. Josh would actually enjoy it.

Nic was the one who would get hurt. She was the one who would see what it meant to be his woman.

His stepfather walked toward them, flanked by his stepbrothers. Peter's eyes flared when he saw him, and he slapped at John's arm to get his attention.

Sharks. They smelled blood in the water.

Grim started to slide out of the booth, but Josh stopped him.

"We're not going anywhere," Josh said. "They want to start something, we can finish it."

"That's your stepfather?" Nicole asked.

Grim nodded. "Yes, and if I walk out, he'll leave you alone. He likes to cause scenes. It makes him feel righteous."

His stepfather had a gleam in his eyes, the one he had before he started a sermon on how the world was evil and only he could protect his flock.

"Here we go," a deep voice said.

That was when Grim realized the minister of the Presbyterian church was sitting at a table to their left with his wife.

"I know I'm supposed to love everyone, but some people make it hard," his wife declared.

Pastor Mike looked over Grim's way. "You okay, son?"

Grim nodded.

"He's going to be." Josh's eyes had gone flinty.

"Is now not a good time to remind you Jesus wants us to turn the other cheek?" Pastor Mike offered with a sigh.

"What's happening?" Nicole asked again.

“Well, if it isn’t the reason we’re all in trouble.” Ezekiel stopped at the head of the booth, his sons flanking him.

“What kind of trouble are you talking about?” Josh asked, looking bored. He sat back as though he wasn’t ready to kick someone’s ass.

Which Grim knew damn straight he was. “Move along. There’s nothing you could say to me that matters.”

“We know you don’t care,” Peter sneered. “You gave in to evil long ago.”

“Evil?” Nicole asked, obviously confused. She looked his way. “Babe, I thought you were kidding or overstating things. They really use the word evil?”

“Hey, you should move along.” Christa couldn’t get to the table because his relatives were crowding her out. “They’re having their dinner.”

Ezekiel’s frown deepened. “And you’re fine with serving degenerates. If you ever wonder, woman, why no one of good reputation will patronize your establishment, it’s because you don’t have any standards.”

Christa glanced around her crowded café. “I think I’ll stick with the degenerates.”

If she thought a logical comeback would do anything to get rid of his stepfather, she didn’t know him at all. “If you want to talk to me, let’s go outside.”

Josh’s head shook. “You’re not going anywhere with him.”

Ezekiel turned, and his arms came up. “People of Willow Fork, there is a devil among you. Has anyone wondered why the good, God-fearing ranchers of this town have lost so much lately?”

They were back to this. Grim groaned.

“Is he talking about the beetles in the feed?” Pastor Mike asked. “I thought Grim was the one taking care of that.”

His stepfather had everyone’s attention now, and he preened under it. “Jared is the very saboteur who placed the bugs in the feed. He does it because he’s got Satan in him. It is a sad fact of life that some of us are born evil, and my stepson is one of them. He is here on earth to harm real men. To do Satan’s work.”

“I’m sorry. Are you fucking kidding me?”

Grim’s brows rose because it hadn’t been Josh who asked the

question. Nicole had slid out of the booth and was standing in his stepfather's space. He started to go after her. Josh held him back.

"No, you let her have her moment. She can handle this," Josh said with a surety he didn't feel.

"You think that man who spends all of his time helping animals is making them sick?" Nicole asked.

"Shut your mouth, woman," his stepfather said, his tone harsh.

"No. She doesn't have to shut her mouth at all," Christa replied. "You need to leave and don't come back." She pointed the feed store owner's way. "And if you are involved in this nonsense, you can get banned, too."

Jim Hazelton's hands came up. "Christa, I was here alone and they cornered me. I don't believe Grim snuck beetles in my feed. It happens sometimes, and I wasn't careful enough about checking it when it came in from the vendor. That's where they got in. There have been some other cases around the state. But they won't listen to me, and they're damn intimidating."

"Not as intimidating as I am," Christa declared.

"The devil lives in my stepson," his stepfather went on, his hands going up in the air.

"You say that when women wear tank tops to a gym class," Nicole pointed out.

"And when we wear leggings." The oddest supporter stepped up. Alyssa crossed her arms over her chest and stood beside Nicole. "And when we breathe in public. You know it is not my fault that your sad-sack sons can't control themselves."

Pastor Mike actually clapped. "Don't forget that he tried to get the new pizza place shut down because he doesn't understand we don't live under Leviticus. You know, Ezekiel, a good slice of pepperoni would change your world."

"Heretic," his stepfather hissed.

"We are so sick of you harassing us." Debbie Vanderburg moved in beside Alyssa. She'd gone to high school out at the resort.

"Yes, maybe it's time we take this to the city board," another voice said. "I know I'm sick of my daughter crying because those idiots call her a whore."

"You aren't listening to me." His stepfather seemed to understand this wasn't going how he'd planned. "Do you even care what's happening to our town?"

"What's happening is we have an excellent vet who managed a bad situation without losing a single bred heifer," Nicole announced. "And he didn't do it so his business got better. It can't get better. He doesn't need the money. He does it because he cares about this town and its citizens."

"Grim came out at one in the morning because my yorkie ate a chocolate bar," Shelia James announced.

"It was milk chocolate flavored," he said. "Not enough cacao to hurt her."

"But you showed up," she insisted. "I was scared as hell, and you got out of bed and came to help me. And you brought along Joshua so I had something real nice to look at."

That sent a laugh through the café.

Josh merely nodded. "I was glad to help."

"Ladies, I understand that he's a work of art, but his head is going to get so big it won't fit through the door," Nicole said with a smile.

"Well, then his daddy will buy a bigger house," Alyssa pointed out.

Another huge laugh.

His stepfather had flushed. "Does no one care that the devil is here?"

"I think you see the devil in everyone because he's inside you," Nicole said. "He sure isn't inside Grim. Grim is full of love, and he's one of the best men I know."

"Here, here." Pastor Mike raised his glass. "Best vet in Texas and a good friend to all."

John put a hand on his father's arm. "Let's go, Dad. They've all given in. They're not worth saving."

"It's because of his whore," his stepfather spat.

And then he and Josh were both on their feet.

Nicole stepped in front of them. "Nope. We're good here. I did recently get an excellent car out of this relationship, so I don't care what he calls me."

"That's because Jack Barnes is addicted to smushing cars," someone yelled.

Christa was cackling with laughter.

"We're all whores to you," Alyssa said, pointing a finger his stepdad's way. "All we have to do is exist and we're whores until we're under the thumb of some man, and you know what, then we're whores when it's convenient. I don't like Nicole. She does not dress well."

"Hey," Nicole said.

Alyssa shrugged. "Girl, you showed up in a crew neck men's shirt, mom jeans, and freaking Crocs. You were unfashionable even for this part of the world, and that is hard to do. I'm offended you dress like that and get called a whore. A whore should at least wear a damn V-neck. And some fuck-me heels."

"I'll be sure to get her some," Josh said with a chuckle.

Nicole's nose wrinkled. "I'm not really a heel girl."

"No, you like bare feet, baby," Josh whispered.

Because subs got to pick. Heels or bare feet. He liked Nic's feet. He liked to rub them and tickle them and suck on her toes.

This wasn't so bad. How had he thought for a second his Nic would wither under the pressure?

Of course he was surprised at her ally. Her mean-girl ally.

"Maybe this town ain't worth saving," his stepfather stated and then strode out of the place.

"Good riddance," Christa called out.

Pastor Mike was on his feet, hand reaching out to Grim, who shook it. "Hey, are you okay? I know we're all laughing about that drama your stepfather played out, but it also had to hurt."

It weirdly hadn't. Having Nicole stand up for him had settled his heart. "I have a dad. Two, actually, and they love me. I don't need that man in my life. I wish there had been something more for the woman who gave birth to me, but she made her choices."

"And Abigail Barnes-Fleetwood made hers," Pastor Mike said with a nod. "Good. You three, if you need anything, you let me know. I might not live your lifestyle, but I don't believe love is degenerate."

"I wish you would tell Pastor Fred at the Baptist church," Alyssa said under her breath.

"You come by any time you like, Alyssa, and we'll talk about God," the pastor said and rejoined his wife.

The patrons of the café went back to their meals, but there was a buzzing through the space that couldn't be denied.

"You three sit down and enjoy your pie," Christa ordered. "This is on the house."

"Chris…" Josh began.

She waved a finger. "Nope. I know you're a little moneybags, but I get to give gifts too, and there is no greater gift than my lemon meringue pie." She frowned at Alyssa, who was still standing there. "You going to cause trouble?"

"No, ma'am," Alyssa replied, sounding humbler than Grim could remember. "I would never endanger my momma's ability to get your Saturday morning cinnamon rolls."

Christa nodded and walked away.

Alyssa took a long breath and faced Nicole, who was tucked in beside Josh now. "Nicole, I would like to apologize to you. It has recently come to my attention that I can, on occasion, be less than fair to the people around me."

Josh's brow rose.

Alyssa frowned. "Fine. I can be a bitch. I thought I could have my cake and eat it too, and I wasn't in a relationship with Josh for the right reasons."

"It wasn't much of a relationship," Josh corrected.

"Who told you he's thinking of firing you?" Grim asked.

"He's not going to fire you," Nicole argued.

Alyssa shrugged a slender shoulder. "My mom, and she told me I would deserve it and made me go and spend time with this therapist in Tyler. I hate the whole examining my own actions stuff. It's awful. But I meant what I said to your stepdaddy. One of the things I'm working on is the fact that when I don't stand up for myself, I tend to put my anger somewhere else. Like on Nicole. But I'm not going to feel bad for saying what I did to Ezekiel Smith."

"You shouldn't," Grim replied. "You keep standing up to him. He has no right to make you or any woman feel uncomfortable."

Alyssa turned to Grim. "Also, I just got the cutest poodle and she's so sweet, and I don't want to have to drive her into Tyler for checkups."

At least he had some value. "Bring her by the shelter and I'll check her out."

"Are we okay, Nicole?" Alyssa asked. "I know I'm a bitch, but

I do feel bad about saying those things. Especially when I think about those Crocs. You don't have any other shoes, do you?"

"How about you stop at I'm sorry and I'll tell you I accept your apology and will ensure that Josh doesn't visit his vengeance upon you," Nicole replied dryly.

Alyssa's smile brightened. "Oh, that works. I like my job. There aren't a lot of places to work around here, and I didn't like the city. The people there are… Well, I didn't get along real well with them. I belong here, so I need my job until I lock down a man. Though my momma says I shouldn't trust any man to take care of me the rest of my life. Mostly because Daddy is married to a woman who's only a couple of years older than me now. I refuse to call her Mom. I remember her from high school."

"Alyssa, is there anything else you need now that we've effectively put a leash around Josh's inner beast?" Grim was getting annoyed because he wanted to be alone with Nic again.

Alyssa shrugged. "No. I'm good now. I'll bring Brit Brit by next week. See y'all at work."

"That is a woman who knows how to protect herself," Josh said with a frown. "I still think it would be better if I could fire her."

"Is she bad at her job?" Nicole asked.

Grim didn't care, but this was Nicole's choice.

"No," Josh admitted. "She's a good accountant. She catches things other people miss. But I don't like her being around you."

"Well then I won't be around her since I think I'm going to learn how to run the shelter," she announced.

That took Grim off guard. "You want to run the shelter?"

"From what I can tell right now you've got a patchwork quilt of people in charge. You're not even open at all on Tuesdays or Thursdays or Sundays. The city's animal services are terrible. I can run the shelter during daytime hours, and we have volunteers and the paid employees covering the rest. I can talk Abby into helping me fundraise. I can do this."

"I thought you were coming to work with me," Josh complained.

"Babe, I think your family has ruined me for nine to five, sit at a desk all day office work," she admitted as she picked up her fork. "Turns out I love waking up early and helping your dads with the horses. I love feeding the chickens your mom keeps and getting eggs for our breakfast. I loved working with Grim to make sure those puppies are healthy. My almost degree was in business. I can run it. I can do it."

Grim reached out a hand, covering hers. "We know you can, and I'm more than happy to turn it all over to you. Tell me when and where you need me and I'll be there. Josh is jealous because he thought he would get to have you around all day. He was thinking that once we prove you can trust us, he could haul you into his office a couple of times a week and have his way with you."

Josh leaned against her. "That's a pretty accurate representation of how I feel."

Her lips kicked up in a sexy grin. "I'm right down the block. He can walk if he wants to see me, and I'm going to have a perfectly nice office. Once I show your mom, she'll trick it out for me." Her smile went wide. "Did I mention how much I like having a mom? It's one of the world's great experiences. How did I get along without an older woman to advise and coddle me?"

Josh chuckled and turned to his pie. "You say that now. You should have been around when Grim and I were sixteen and got caught drinking beer by the back pond."

The memory was oddly sweet since it was the first time he'd realized he could screw up and Abby would forgive him. "She verbally tore a strip off our hides. And then we all sat down to dinner and Olivia kept asking us what beer we would pair with Mom's pot roast."

"Olivia was there," Josh grumbled. "Literally sitting beside us, but she took off before Pops found us so she got away with it. Our sister is a vicious brat, and I don't envy the man who has to take her on."

"Men," Nicole replied with a laugh. "Olivia promises me she's finding two men to settle down with, and she won't accept less. So I have the job?"

Grim sat back. "It's yours, baby."

She started to chat about all the things she planned to do and Grim ate his pie, perfectly happy with how the night had gone.

* * * *

Josh parked the SUV and wished the night didn't have to end.

Despite all the crap that had gone down at the café, he wouldn't change it. Yes, he'd still wanted to fire Alyssa, but Nicole seemed to be having none of it, and he knew when to back off. But that didn't mean he wouldn't watch her.

"We'll help you get Buddy up into your room," Grim offered.

"Did anyone call and tell Mom we're bringing home a very shaky… I mean, we're sure it's a dog, right? It could be a large rodent," Josh teased.

Nicole wrinkled her nose at him. "Mean, Joshua Barnes-Fleetwood. My new baby is a sweet puppy."

"I mean I wouldn't call him a puppy," Grim argued and then managed to avoid the playful slap that came his way from Nic. "Not because he's not a dog. He is. I checked and everything, but he's at least three years old. You can tell by the teeth."

"You guys have to be nice to Buddy." Nicole sat in the back seat with Buddy's crate, though the dog was still asleep and would be for hours according to Grim. In the morning they would start letting him get used to being around the family. "And no. I didn't call your mom. Do you think she's going to be mad?"

"That you brought home a sad stray?" Grim asked with a shake of his head. "Absolutely not. She loves a stray. I'm proof of that."

"And me," Nicole said, sounding happier than she had in weeks.

"Neither of you is a sad stray, and one of you is going to get in serious trouble if she continues down that line of thinking." His inner Dom knew he'd lost the war to fire Alyssa, but he was holding the line on this topic.

"So Grim gets to put himself down but I don't?" Nicole asked like that was a normal, natural question to have.

"I'm not going to spank Grim's ass if he talks bad about himself, but I might kick it," Josh replied.

"I'd like to see you try, brother. You sit in an office all day, and I wrestle large animals," Grim said confidently. "But I get your point. Why don't we pull up to the big house so Nicole doesn't have to walk."

Because he didn't want to drop her off at the big house and come home without her. He wanted her in the bed they shared, nestled in between him and Grim. He wanted to wake up next to her and leisurely make love to her before they all got ready for the day. It hadn't been long, but he'd come to love their mornings together. And afternoons. And nights. "Yeah, that's a good idea. For such a small critter he needs a lot of stuff."

"Or we could stay here and I could accept the inevitable," a soft voice said.

The words sent a shock of hope through him. "Nicole?"

Grim had turned in his seat. "Baby, I think we should talk about what happened tonight. You don't have to make any decisions. I'm fine."

She looked to Josh, confusion on her face.

"He thinks you might be willing to sleep with us because you feel bad about what happened earlier," Josh translated. He might be doing a lot of that in the future because Grim and Nicole sometimes had trouble talking about their feelings. It was something they could work on.

"I'm not asking to come home because I feel bad for you, Grim. I'm asking because I miss you both so much it makes me ache inside. I'm asking because I love you and I think you love me, too, and I'm ready to be done with letting what happened to me in the past control my future," she said quietly.

The whole world suddenly seemed warmer. Kinder. "I love you so much, Nic. Nora. What do you want to be called?"

"I like Nicole. I think I want a fresh start," she admitted. "Nora was a name given to me by two people who didn't care about me. I picked Nicole because it sounded happy. I feel like Nicole. But guys, I don't think I can handle Nicole Barnes-Fleetwood-Burch. Maybe I can keep my fake last name, too."

Josh was having none of that. He was about to do one of his patented lay-down-the-law things that might get him kicked to the couch, but Grim saved him.

"I've decided I can love my biological father without clinging to his name," Grim said with a sure nod. "He would have wanted me to be happy, and part of that is having this family. I want us to share a name. I want us to have kids someday and have all the things a family has. I'm going to change my last name to Barnes-Fleetwood. This is my family, and I'm never going to let you down."

Emotion welled inside Josh. It had been a hell of a night, and it wasn't through because he doubted Nicole wanted to sleep in the guest room. When she was in, she was all in.

There would be a wedding on the ranch, and it wasn't years away.

He put a hand on his brother's arm. "I'm glad. I know our parents will be thrilled to have you take the family name. It's your right. Dad would say it's been your right since the day we brought you home."

"Since the day I finally found my home," Grim said.

"And I found mine," Nicole agreed. "So let's get our sweet boy inside and let me show you how much I love you both."

Josh and Grim had that dog settled in no time. When Buddy's crate was set up and Nicole was satisfied the little guy was nestled down for the night, she took their hands.

"I missed this place," she said solemnly. "I missed being here with you."

Josh's whole body came alive, but he had to be sure. "Nicole, if you stay with us tonight, it's forever. I want to give you all the time you need to be sure."

"As much as I want you," Grim began, "I have to agree with Josh. I can't love you tonight and have you be unsure again tomorrow. Tonight was a lot. Baby, I know you handled my stepfather well, but he won't stop."

She shrugged as though it wasn't a problem. "He might once the women of this town start applying pressure. I think once we all start yelling back, he'll figure out he's not welcome. And if he wants to come for me, well, he's going to have to deal with my family. They're kind of intimidating."

Actually, it wasn't a bad idea. "Maybe it's time you went into town with the dads. You've been holed up on the ranch for weeks. I don't think anyone understands how fully a part of us you are now."

"But if Dad took her to dinner or she rode along with him and Pops to pick up supply shipments, they would get the message," Grim mused. "My stepfather is an asshole, but he knows not to mess with Jack and Sam."

"I'm supposed to go to some meeting with Abby next week," Nicole offered. "The historical society or something."

Josh groaned. "Then maybe you can be our inside girl. Mom is entirely unreasonable about our office building. Soften her up. We need upgrades."

Nicole got into his space, going up on her toes so she could brush her lips against his. "I'm probably going to come down on your momma's side of that fight. I think we should keep the town square as charming as it is now. One of the things I'm going to do with the shelter is upgrade the building. It's an atrocious prefab right now, and I want to offer training classes and doggie daycare. And Grim's getting an office so he can have office hours and not have to run out to everyone's house all the time."

"I am?" Grim asked.

So Nicole was taking charge. He liked it. "You are. I think what our woman is trying to say is she's going to make it clear there are boundaries. And if tonight was any indication, the townsfolk will honor them. I hope you understand how many people tonight stood up for you?"

Nicole turned to Grim. "Because they know how good you are. Because they value you for your intelligence and your kindness. They might think we're weirdos for being in a threesome, but they also understand we're still good people."

"This town is changing, and they won't put up with your stepfather's bile for much longer." Josh felt it in his bones. The younger generation had rarely had a problem with him and Grim, and it seemed they were starting to convince their parents that love was love whether they understood it or not. "It'll be different for our kids."

Because his parents had blazed a trail, and all he had to do was follow it.

"I'm afraid I'm going to have to be married before I start talking about kids," Nicole said primly.

"Oh, I can get a ring on your finger this weekend," Josh promised.

That seemed to startle her. Her mouth came open, and she bit her bottom lip. "But you can't. I mean it wouldn't be legal. I didn't think about that. Josh, it could be years before I can legally change my name. I know Kim thinks she can do it, but what if she can't clear me?"

Grim moved behind her, his arms going around her waist. "We'll find a way. I don't care if she never clears you, we'll find a way to make this work."

Those two needed some optimism. He stepped in so Nicole was surrounded by the two of them. He tilted her head up, looking into those gorgeous eyes of hers. "You will be cleared or I promise you I'll find a way to ensure the threat is taken out. I don't want you to worry about this. We have our protocols in place, and we're trusting the experts." There was something she didn't know, but now he wondered if it was wrong to keep it from her. "Kim's talking to Laura Holloway in the morning."

"My sister-in-law?" Nic asked, obviously surprised. "But she's Ted's wife."

"And he's emotionally abused her for years," Josh explained. "It's not the first time Kim's spoken to her. She talked to her at the beginning of the case, and she got the feeling there was something the woman wanted to say but couldn't. Laura wants out of her marriage, but she's scared."

"Why wouldn't you…" Realization dawned in her eyes. "You're offering her money so she can leave safely."

"Quite a bit," Josh agreed. "We're going to pay for her attorney and the costs to move her across the country back to her parents in Michigan. Laura has evidence that Ted and not you killed Micah. Kim and her son are certain it's enough to clear you and it will hold up in a court of law."

"He didn't want to tell you because he was worried you would argue with him about the money," Grim whispered in her ear, his hands on her like he could lose her if he let go.

Josh was putting all his cards on the table. "We won't miss the money, baby. But we would miss you so fucking much. My whole family agreed to this."

Nicole's eyes closed, and she wrapped her arms around him. "Thank you, Josh. And you, Grim. Thank you for loving me."

He held her and when her eyes opened, his mouth found hers. It was gentle at first, a promise the love they had would always be there. Then she turned and Grim kissed her, too. He watched as his best friend in the world kissed the woman who would be their wife. Here there was zero jealousy at all. His jealousy had been rooted in the fear he could lose them both, but now they felt settled. They felt real.

This was the start of his family.

Grim turned her toward Josh. There was a flush to his friend's face that let him know emotion was riding him hard, too. "Get her ready. I'm going to get my kit."

His kit. Because they would need lube and a plug to prepare her for what they really wanted.

Nicole's arms floated up around his neck. "You're going to make love to me together tonight."

"Is that a question, baby? Or a demand?"

"I don't know. Which one will get the big bad Dom to spank me?"

"All you ever have to do is ask." He ran his hands under her shirt, feeling soft skin beneath his palms. "Did you miss it? Did you miss the discipline?"

She nodded. "Yes, Josh. I dreamed every night about how you and Grim touch me, how you worship my body. I never thought I would crave something like this, but I do. I wouldn't if I didn't trust you, if I didn't love you and believe fully you love me, too. I've been scared I can't trust my instincts. Worried I made a mistake once so I'll make it again and again, but I've learned. I've grown. I'm not the woman who thought I could fix the man. You don't need to be fixed, Josh. Grim doesn't need to be fixed."

She'd come so far. He lowered his forehead to rest against hers. "You don't need to be fixed, Nic."

"No, I need to understand what I want and need and ask for it from the people I love. From the people who love me. I spent my whole life wondering how I would get through, how I would just survive sometimes from one moment to the next. How to please the people around me so they let me stay. Now I've started to wonder who I can be, what parts of me I can explore, because I'm not worried about pleasing people." She flushed. "It's not that…"

He knew where she was going. "Baby, you don't have to change to keep my love. You can be irritated. You can get mad as hell at me or Grim and we'll still be here. You can make mistakes and your family will still love and support you."

"Except Olivia." Grim chuckled as he walked back into the

room. "She'll throw your ass under a bus if you get caught underage drinking."

A soft smile hit her lips. "I'll try to avoid that."

"I can think of other things to do." If Grim was back then the bedroom was ready, and he hadn't done his job. He lifted Nicole up and into his arms. "Come on, baby. We want to welcome you home."

In the sweetest way possible.

Chapter Eighteen

Nicole felt light as Josh carried her through the house she'd come to think of as home. He always made her feel like she weighed next to nothing, but there was more to it tonight. She'd let go of her fears, of the worry she might not be enough for them, and it made the world feel brighter, easing her soul.

Josh set her on her feet, and his hands immediately went to the hem of her shirt, hauling it over her head.

"I thought you were supposed to have her naked and ready," Grim complained. He looked so hot. He'd taken off his shirt at some point, and his big, muscular chest was on display.

"We were having an emotional breakthrough," Josh shot back. "She's decided we're not her asshole dead ex and she loves us."

"You're slow. Nic and I had this particular breakthrough hours ago," Grim replied.

"Well, if you hadn't had to go to dinner immediately, maybe I would have had mine with her, too. Your gut always gets us in trouble." Josh's head shook as she toed out of her shoes.

Her guys. They were two halves of a whole, and she wouldn't have them any other way. "All the emotional breakthroughs are good. As soon as Jack throws enough money at the problem of my potential incarceration for a crime I didn't commit, we can get married and get super boring."

Oh, she was wrong. "We won't be boring. Trust me. I grew up around a whole lot of threesomes," Josh explained as he helped her out of her jeans. "There's never a dull moment. But the danger stuff, yeah. I'm ready for boring when it comes to real danger."

It looked like Grim had prepped the room. There was a towel on the middle nightstand, and it had lube and a prepared plug waiting for use. They would get her ready and then she wouldn't be feeling the plug at all. She would have one of her men in her pussy and one in her ass. She would be between them.

Where she belonged.

Grim moved in behind her and had her bra off with a simple twist of his hand. Cool air hit her breasts but her skin still felt hot and wanting. She watched as Josh shrugged out of his shirt. His jeans had tented with his erection, and she couldn't wait to get her hands on him.

Then she sighed and leaned back as Grim's hands came from behind to cup her breasts. She was left in nothing but her panties, and Josh went on his knees in front of her, his fingers sliding under the waistband as Grim played with her nipples. His hips moved, rubbing that big cock of his along the seam of her ass.

Josh leaned in and inhaled the scent of her arousal. "Ain't nothing boring about this, baby."

The events of the day had been overwhelming, but she couldn't remember a single one of them as Josh dragged her panties down, tossed them away, and then rubbed his nose right in her pussy like she was the best smelling flower he'd ever known. She was completely naked with the exception of the necklace she'd been given. She rather thought her men would try to replace it soon, but she loved it.

Some things had happened and it had been emotional, but what mattered now was she had a sweet dog to take care of and she was with them.

Fully and completely with them. Surrounded by them. Adored by them.

Grim kissed her neck and twisted her nipples with enough force to make her squirm. Heat flashed through her, heightening the arousal spiraling through her.

Josh rose to his feet. "I believe I owe our sub some discipline."

He wanted to spank her now. "It's okay. I'm ready. We don't have to. Take me now."

She knew it was the wrong thing to say the minute his brow rose and his eyes went the slightest bit icy. The Dom was in control. It was something she might have feared had she not gotten to know all sides of this man. Josh was the Dom and the friend and the son and brother. He was kind and open about what he felt.

But he could also spank pretty hard.

"I mean, I'm ready, Sir, and you could take me now if you want."

Grim chuckled behind her.

Josh's lips curled slightly. "Not going to save you, baby."

"I think you should go to the bed and place your hands on the mattress, ass in the air," Grim ordered against her ear. Then he gave her lobe a nip she felt in her pussy. "Now, Nic."

Josh was grinning. "Though it was a good try. I liked the use of *Sir*." His expression hardened. "Who's in charge in the bedroom, Nicole?"

An easy answer. She was. She was always in control because they would never hurt her. However, it was fun to let go. "You are, Sir. You and Grim. My Masters."

"That's right. Now do as Grim said." Josh kicked out of his shoes.

She wanted to watch him get naked, but she knew an order when she heard one. When Grim's arms came down, she marched over to the bed and placed her palms flat on the mattress. Like the rest of the primary bedroom, this bed was built for three. It was massive and comfy, and she loved sleeping in between them.

It was a good thing since she planned to do it for the rest of her life.

"Spread your legs wider, Nicole," Grim ordered. "Or I can get the spreader bar out."

She moved her feet apart, giving him the access he desired. He would do it. Grim would bring the spreader out and then spend the next hour tying her down and playing with ropes while she died of arousal. She needed to avoid the spreader because her whole body was already pulsing with need.

"Did I tell you thank you for standing up for me today?" Grim asked as his hand ran down the line of her spine. He started at the nape of her neck and brushed down her back, lighting her skin wherever he touched. "I would have told you I didn't want you to put yourself in harm's way."

"You would be wrong," Josh said. "She's part of us. She's not going to sit on the sidelines. We don't love her because she plays things safe. We love her because she's fierce."

Grim leaned over, laying kisses on the small of her back. "I did need it. You standing up for me made me feel worthy. I don't care what anyone else thinks, though it was nice to be supported. But all I need to know is I have my family."

"Always," Nicole promised.

Grim stepped back and then a hard smack against her ass had her gasping.

"But you better be careful," Josh said. "I want you to be you, but that also means being aware of the danger around you. You put Ezekiel in his place. You don't ever find yourself alone with him. Do I make myself clear?"

Another smack and the pain wracked through her followed by a crazy wave of heat. "I have no plans to be around him, and Grim, don't think I'll be messing around trying to fix your family issues. You have the best family in the world. Those others aren't family at all. They're people we avoid."

This time the smack came from her left. Grim's hand. "Keep it that way. And don't ever hold back on me. If he says something to you, I want to know. Him or those sons of his."

Sweet words. She knew at least one of those men was his brother, but he'd made his choice. Grim was leaving them all behind, and that meant leaving his fear and anxiety behind. She could do it, too. She, like Grim, had a place in this family.

"I think they'll get some pushback from now on," Josh said. "Ignoring them might have emboldened them. It might be time to look into his church. But we'll have my uncles do it. I wouldn't put a woman in that man's line of fire. Don't worry about this. She's got Harlow on her, and Landon as backup. She's safe. We're going to make sure of it."

"Or we could keep her right here in this house forever. She can stay naked and tied up and I'll never have to worry about where she is," Grim offered.

Nicole turned her head. "That is not happening, you two. I will not be locked in a…"

She'd been about to say prison when the next smack stuck the word in her throat. He'd been serious.

"You will remember where you are. We're playing and you're our sweet sub in this bedroom," Josh announced. He smacked her cheeks three more times in rapid succession, building the heat with each slap. And then a hand slid between her legs, and she felt a big finger slide over her clitoris. Josh teased her, making her bite her bottom lip to keep from calling out. "We will tie you up and spank your sweet ass and have you any way we like. Am I understood?"

Oh, she understood she was in for a hell of a night. "Yes, Sir."

His big finger slid across her clit again, and pleasure sparked through her. A bit more and she would be reeling, but she stayed the instinct to rub against his hand. It would do nothing but get her in more trouble. She didn't want discipline when she was so close to getting what she needed.

"That's what I like to hear," Grim said as his hand smoothed over her aching cheeks. "Yes. You keep saying yes to us, baby."

She would always say yes to them. Well, most of the time. "Yes, Grim. Yes, Josh."

In this she would always say yes, including when Grim wanted to tie her up and carry her around like his favorite piece of luggage.

"You need to get ready," Josh said. "So we can get her ready. She's so close she's going to go off with no trouble at all. She's so wet."

"Then I'm going to love my part of getting her ready," Grim vowed.

She heard a rustle behind her as both men seemed to take a step back. It looked like they were finally ready to move on to the next part of their adventure. She sure was, but she remained there at the end of the bed, her ass in the air because she was being a good girl for now.

Grim tossed his big body on the bed in front of her. He'd gotten out of all those clothes, and every inch of him was on display. "Come on up here with me."

Did he want her to get his cock in her mouth? A wicked sense of power always came over her when she licked and sucked and stroked their cocks. She loved it when their hands twisted in her hair and then they couldn't keep up their control a single moment longer and let loose.

Nicole climbed on the bed, crawling over Grim's muscular legs, but when she tried to lower her head, he stopped her.

"Keep going, baby. I'm sure we'll get to that sometime tonight, but for now I'm going to get you ready. Sit on my face and let me eat my fill." The words were low and sent a thrill through her.

He moved her into position, knees splayed above his shoulders as she balanced herself against the headboard. He pulled her hips down and then she felt the first stroke of his tongue. Grim groaned, the sound reverberating against her pussy. He ran his big thumbs along her labia, rubbing and stretching her so he could spear her with his tongue.

Pure sensation ran through her as she rode his tongue, and then she felt a hand on the small of her back. Josh. Josh was on the bed with them and he was…

The feel of him parting the cheeks of her ass and dripping warm lube on her threatened to knock the breath from her lungs.

"Relax, baby," Josh ordered. "You've taken a plug. You can take me. I'll make sure of it. Grim's going to eat your pussy until you can't think straight and then he's going to fuck it while I take this sweet asshole of yours. Both of us. We'll both be inside you, and we won't ever want to leave."

Desire sparked through her as Grim continued his sweet assault on her tender flesh and she felt Josh's fingers massage the lube around her hole. Her whole body tightened as he pressed in. She held her breath, trying to relax.

"Don't you keep me out," Josh whispered.

Grim slid his tongue over her clitoris as Josh thrust his finger deep inside.

"She's ready," Josh said on a low groan. "She's going to be so fucking tight. Come on, baby. Let's get Grim in position. I can't wait."

She heard the sound of a condom tearing, and Josh eased her back so Grim could wrap the condom on his rock-hard cock and settle her down on his hips.

Grim's eyes were dark with desire, his lips covered in her arousal. His tongue came out, swiping over his bottom lip. "You taste like heaven. Come here."

She could feel his cock teasing her entrance as Josh moved behind her, getting himself ready. Grim pulled her down for a long kiss, his tongue still tasting like her. It was wildly erotic to taste her own arousal on his lips, to know how much he craved her.

She kissed him, their tongues mating as he thrust his cock deep, filling her up while Josh moved in behind them.

"That is so fucking sexy." Josh's hands found her hips and then she felt something hot and hard against her ass. "Hold her still for me."

Grim's arms went around her. "Don't move, baby. Just ride the wave."

The wave was made of jangly sensation as she felt her asshole being split by a monster cock. He was way bigger than the plug, and she was already full of Grim's. Nicole forced herself to breathe as Josh worked his way in.

"You can handle him, baby," Grim promised her, his mouth hovering beneath hers. He dragged his tongue over her bottom lip. "You were born to take your men."

"You feel so good," Josh groaned, and then she felt herself relax, his big cock sliding deep. "So fucking good. Grim, I'm ready."

"I'm so ready." Grim laid his head back, grinning up at her. He looked younger in that moment, far more carefree than she'd ever seen the man. "Love you so much, baby."

"I love you, too. Love both of you." It welled up inside her, the emotion mingling with desire. It was a heady mixture that enveloped her.

Grim thrust up and then Josh guided her hips back, forcing her to take all of him.

They rocked back and forth, finding a rhythm she couldn't deny. Grim's cock would stroke the sweet spot deep inside her pussy and then Josh would light up every nerve in her asshole.

They rode her body, Nicole moving between them, the rhythm instinctual. Josh fucked her ass in long strokes. When he thrust her down, Grim ground his hips up, rubbing her clitoris.

It was all too much. She clutched at Grim as she came, pleasure overwhelming her every sense.

This was what it meant to feel free. Nicole held on as her men tightened and then released, finding their pleasure. Free to love. Free to live. Free to simply be who she was without worrying all the time if she would lose it all.

She couldn't lose them. They loved her. They would fight to stay the family they wanted to be.

Josh fell on top of her, rolling them all into a soft warm pile of arms and limbs and lips as they kissed her. She couldn't tell who was touching what, but she knew the truth.

She was finally home.

* * * *

Grim sat beside Nicole, Josh on her other side, supporting her as they stared at the big monitor connecting them to Kimberly Kent.

The night before had been everything he could have hoped for. More. Even if it had been interrupted by Buddy waking up at the crack of dawn and howling in his crate. Grim had rolled out of bed and opened the crate, easing the dog out and taking him outside to relieve himself.

Buddy was coming along nicely. He'd even forgiven them for the nap he hadn't meant to take. Sleep and not being in pain had worked wonders for the pup. Normally it was weeks before a dog like Buddy would lie in his new mom's lap, but he was curled up on Nicole's.

"Could you explain to Nicole how you came to talk to Laura Holloway and why you think this is legitimate?" Josh began.

Kimberly Kent sat next to a handsome kid who couldn't be past twenty-three or so. Roman Kent was a serious-looking young man with deep blue eyes behind his glasses and a swath of brown hair. "When I realized there was something wrong with the case, I decided it would be in the best interests of everyone involved if I did some digging."

A brow rose over Roman's eyes, and he looked up from the notes he'd been making. "You realized it?"

There was a deep snort from off camera. "Your son."

Kimberly's eyes rolled. "Sorry, guys. That's my deeply sarcastic husband, and I have to admit when our daughter is super stubborn, I blame it on him, so it's fair. When my son convinced me something was wrong, I wanted to talk to everyone in the family to get a sense of what forces might have caused the rift leading to Micah Holloway's murder. I explained I needed everyone's input on who you are as a person to help direct me to where you might flee. Ted and your in-laws were eager to speak to me."

"I bet they were," Nicole said. "I'm sure they talked about what a gold digger I was."

Kim sighed. "Yeah. They weren't exactly kind. They pretty much blamed everything on you, and in my first interview, Laura toed the line. However, she called me four days ago and told a different story. She claims she has evidence you didn't commit the murder."

"What kind of evidence?" Grim wanted it to be good. DNA. Something forensic no one could deny.

"I believe she's been putting this together for a couple of years now," Roman said. "Likely since the murder. She's shown us several files containing security logs. Micah Holloway lived on the family estate grounds."

Nicole nodded. "Yes. So did Ted. It's kind of like the ranch except without the ranch part. They own a large swath of land outside of town, and there are several homes around the property. Micah and I lived in the one closest to the main road. I had to use a clicker thing to get in the gate."

"Then the logs should show you got there after Micah's death." This could work. He wanted Nic out from under this cloud. Of course then the real danger would begin. If they couldn't prove Nicole's account of the incident, her brother-in-law would be walking around free and likely looking to silence the only witness to his crime.

"Ted is good with a computer," Nicole explained. "I assumed he could fix those records or hire someone to do it for him. The whole place was wired for security. Even inside the house there were cameras. I assumed he either turned them off or came up with some kind of deep fake to show the police."

"Can we prove he faked the logs?" Josh asked. "We know some

people who are excellent with technology."

"We have our own," Kim promised. "But I think she's going to offer us something better. I think she has the original footage. Those would show Ted killed his brother, and Nicole came on the scene long after. She's hedging on telling us exactly what it is, but I think she thinks she needs leverage. She's not what I would call a trusting soul."

"She's been in the Holloway family for almost twenty years. I can't believe she's managed to work up the will to leave," Nicole admitted. "I wasn't exactly close to her. When I got married, she told me I should keep my mouth shut and do as I was told. I probably should have listened to her."

Grim brought her hand to his lips, kissing her fingers. "That's all in the past."

"Yes, now she knows how to punch," a feminine voice said, reminding him they weren't alone. Olivia was back from her trip to Bliss and in a super sour mood, though she'd hugged Nicole when she'd come in to breakfast this morning.

"And kick a guy in the balls," Harlow said from her place on the couch beside Olivia.

"I think I should train more on that skill," Olivia said with a nod.

He had no idea what had gone so wrong in Bliss, but it had put his sister in a foul mood. She'd gotten in the night before and had been frowning ever since.

"Girls." Dad, Pops, and Mom were seated on the opposite sofa, listening in.

"The last few years have been hard on Laura," Roman chimed in. "I found some hospital records that indicate she's been physically abused. A fractured arm, a concussion. No police reports were filed."

Nicole went tense. "I didn't think Ted was physically abusive. There were times when I heard him telling Micah to stop hitting me. Not because he cared or anything. He thought Micah would get caught eventually. I knew he played a lot of mind games on her and he had total financial control of her life, but I never saw him hit her."

"I think this is relatively new," Kim agreed. "We searched

records back before their marriage and it was only six months after the murder when she started needing medical attention. It's possible the murder was a trigger that led to her husband becoming violent."

"So you think Laura Holloway is trying to protect herself?" Grim wanted to understand the situation.

"She's finally figured out nothing is going to change," Kim replied.

Nicole seemed to consider the situation for a moment. "How old are her kids now? Ted was ten years older than his brother. By the time I came on the scene, Laura had three kids and they weren't babies."

Roman nodded. "Her youngest is in college. The University of Michigan."

"Where her parents live," Nicole said as though the knowledge made a puzzle piece slide into place. "The kids are adults, and at least one of them is living close to where she would find refuge. He doesn't have the kids to hold over her anymore."

"Another reason he could have become violent. He knew he was losing control." Grim couldn't stand the thought Nicole had been caught in such a violent world. "So she's holding this evidence against her husband in an effort to get us to send her the money to safely get away."

"Are we sure this isn't complete crap and all this will do is send them straight here?" Josh asked.

Their dad nodded from his seat. Jack had been quiet most of the meeting, deferring to Josh and Grim. Grim had been grateful to have Jack in the room though. He knew there was no one he would rather have than his dad watching their backs.

"She sent us the logs," Jack explained. "I wouldn't move forward without them."

"Those security logs are proof Nicole didn't show up until several hours after the coroner reported time of death." Roman looked through his notes. "I was able to pull some security footage from a couple of businesses around town that prove Nicole's timeline. All of this is excellent news, but obviously the holy grail of this case is going to be actual video of the murder. We'll be able to clear Nicole's name entirely and quickly."

"And get Ted Holloway behind bars," Kim added.

"That's amazing," Nicole said, her hand going to pet the dog on her lap. "I could be a free woman in a matter of hours?"

Grim glanced Josh's way, exchanging a look of worry with his best friend. Josh nodded, letting him know one of them had to take the lead. "You've said the Holloway family is important to the town. How can we be sure they'll arrest Nicole's brother-in-law? It wouldn't be the first time cops let a little something like proof of murder slide for rich folks."

"Not if she leaks it to the press," Harlow offered.

"Absolutely," Kim agreed. "If they refuse to reopen the case, we'll go straight to the press, but I don't think it's going to be a problem. In the last couple of years the family's sway on the town has loosened up as the company they own downsized and moved most of the jobs overseas."

Nicole's head shook. "It won't matter to Sheriff Reynolds. He'll still be taking bribes from the family."

Roman's lips kicked up. "Yeah, he lost his last election. There's a new sheriff in town."

Kim shook her head. "You were just waiting to say that, weren't you?"

Roman nodded, looking entirely unworried he'd moved into dad-joke territory. "Yeah."

"So we think this guy will do his job." Josh sat back.

"And quickly," Kim agreed.

"But obviously he'll get out on bail." Nicole suddenly seemed nervous again.

Grim didn't want to take the smile off her face. The morning had been so lovely, and she'd been relaxed and happy. "But if the video absolves you, he has no reason to come after you. In fact, it would be bad for his case to come anywhere near you. If the tape is what she says it is, then you'll be free of the Holloway family."

"I think they'll be way more interested in your sister-in-law," Josh advised. "Which is why we'll give her some protection. I'm going to assume you think she can testify."

Kim nodded on the screen. "She'll be an excellent witness, but I'm hoping that tape leads to a plea agreement."

"I think the Holloways will do anything they can to take the death penalty off the table, which means they'll have to plead,"

Roman continued. "When we have everything, I'll send a copy to your lawyer, Nicole. Lucas O'Malley. I take it he's the family attorney."

Nicole nodded. "For the Barnes-Fleetwood family. He also handles the business."

"If we need to get her a criminal attorney, we will," Josh added. "But Lucas knows what he's doing. I want her name cleared and all warrants rescinded as soon as possible. We plan on getting married within the year."

"That's not enough time," their mom complained.

Abby had been thrilled they were back together, but she thought they needed more time. Not for the relationship but for the massive wedding she was planning.

He wanted Nicole to wear their ring, to have the name they'd all agreed on.

"So you're meeting with her this afternoon?" Grim wanted the timeline.

"Yes," Roman explained. "She's going to give us the tape, and we're handing over the cash your father wired. We bought her plane ticket. She'll be in the air before her husband knows what's happened. We originally planned this meeting for next week, but she bumped up the timetable. I think she's worried for her safety."

"She should be. Ted's already proven he can be ruthless," Nicole said.

"We're going to catch a plane and meet her early this afternoon." Kim checked her watch. "I hope to have something for you by this evening."

"We'll be waiting," Josh said with a nod, but there was a tightness to his best friend that let Grim know he was still worried.

Grim was as well, but then he would be until the minute Ted Holloway was locked away.

"Can someone go out to the motel and pick up my stuff?" Kim asked. "I paid through the end of this week, but I don't think I need to fly back out there."

Harlow held up a hand. "I can grab it when I go into town if someone has a key."

"I do," Nicole acknowledged. "And I'd like to grab my things, too. I left a lot of my stuff in Kim's room because… Well, I got a little freaked out one night."

"Yes, that motel is not known for its safety record," Dad managed to say with a frown. "A lot of criminal activity goes on there. Harlow…"

Harlow groaned. "Uncle Jack, I get enough of this crap from my dads. I assure you I can handle walking into a motel in the light of day and getting all Kim's stuff packed up."

Dad's hands came up in acknowledgment. "Sorry. I'm overly protective."

"And I was paranoid," Nicole said. "I felt like someone was watching me all the time."

Roman cleared his throat. "Uhm…"

Nicole laughed suddenly. "Of course. It was your mom."

"Hey, I'm excellent at my job," Kim assured them. "I blend into the background."

There was another masculine snort, and this time a big muscular man wearing a T-shirt and jeans walked in front of the camera. He bent over and kissed his wife's head. "You, my love, always stand out."

She winked her husband's way. "All I'm saying is I'm not the one who freaked Nic out that night. It was probably the meth dealer two doors down. Or one of the drunks. They don't always remember where their rooms are. But I think it's safe enough to send someone to pick up my stuff. This should all be done in a couple of hours. I'll contact you when I have the footage in hand."

Kim gave them a wave and a smile and then she was gone.

Nicole sat back, her hand on Buddy's fur. "I can't believe it's almost done."

Josh leaned in, brushing a kiss over her lips. "Just because we're at the end doesn't mean we skip the safety protocols. I'm going to want those in play for a while."

Grim did, too. "I want Landon to go with you guys. And before I impugn Harlow's abilities, I need someone to stop by the shelter and pick up a package for me. I would drive you myself, but I've got to check in on a couple of herds. I'll be out of pocket most of the day, but I promise I'll be back for the afternoon call with Kim."

"And I have a couple of things I need to do as well," Josh said. "I have a call into Uncle Lucas. I think I'm going to file a lawsuit against your father's church. Not sure for what, but I'll find a way. I'm going to let those assholes know I'm done with them coming after my family."

"Or we could beat the shit out of them until they leave us alone." Grim knew which way he would go.

Pops grinned broadly as he helped Mom up. "I knew one of them would take after me. Grim's the only one making sense."

Dad sighed, but it was easy to see he was amused. "Josh knows what he's doing. He'll take care of the situation with the Smiths. It's time to make things uncomfortable for them. After Nicole and Alyssa taking him on last night, I've already heard some of the other young women of the town are calling for them to be removed from the square. I think they're going to fight back now."

"They needed to know it was okay," Nicole said. "Sometimes all it takes is knowing you're not alone. Although it's weird to be on the same side as Alyssa."

Olivia stood and yawned. "Yeah. I would have told you it would be a cold day in hell, but hey, all my instincts are off lately. I'm going to up to my room. I have some calls to make. Did I mention Trev McNamara's sons are obnoxious as hell?"

"Several times," Dad acknowledged.

"Well, they are," Olivia said as she turned and walked out.

"That did not go well." Pops followed her. "I'll see if I can get her talking."

Harlow straightened her shirt, looking over at Nicole. "You ready for a session? Landon's going to be a while before he can take us into town. I saw him riding out with the hands."

"I can call him back," Dad offered.

Nicole stood with Buddy in her arms. "It's fine. We can go after lunch. I would like a training session. Can we work on ball busting?"

And it was time for him to go to work. "Love you, baby. I'm going to protect my balls though."

"I'm with you, brother." Josh shook his head Harlow's way. "I think I liked it better when Nicole was worried you were in love with us and jealous of her."

Harlow's jaw dropped. "She thought what?"

Nicole held Buddy close to her chest. "Well, I didn't know. I know now. And Joshua Barnes-Fleetwood, you are a terrible man."

Josh winked her way. "Yeah, but I'm your man. And lucky you. Grim's here and he's practically an angel."

Nicole moved to him, going on her toes to press a kiss against his lips. "You be careful out there. Those cows can kick when they want to, and despite what I said before, I like your balls intact."

"And I'll go make sure lunch is coming along," Abby said, waving her children off.

"Now you've gone and scared your momma." Jack winked Nicole's way as he followed his wife out.

"Nothing scares my momma," Josh countered then moved in to surround Nicole, pressing his chest to her back. "You be careful. I love you, baby. I'll see you this afternoon. Grim, I'll make it back here for Kim's call, too."

Grim nodded.

Then they could truly begin.

Chapter Nineteen

"Are you sure you don't want me to stay?" Landon sat in the driver's seat of the truck, looking around the parking lot of the rundown motel.

Harlow frowned his way and pointedly checked her watch. "Kim's supposed to call in an hour. If you stay with us, we'll still have to make the trip to the shelter."

Nicole didn't want to be late. "I'd like to be back in time for the call. This is my whole future on the line, and I think I should be there."

The day had kind of gotten away from her in the sweetest way. First she'd chased Buddy, who had taken off running through the front flower beds. She'd worried the dog was trying to run away, but he'd come back and run zoomie circles around her until he'd lain down and immediately fallen into a nap. Lunch without Josh and Grim was no longer any kind of awkward for her. In fact, she loved the time she got with Abby and Olivia and Harlow. They'd had a leisurely lunch and talked about how Olivia's trip to Bliss had gone.

Poorly on the romantic front since the objects of her affections turned out to have just announced their engagements. To different people. None of whom were Olivia Barnes-Fleetwood.

However, Olivia couldn't stop talking about the obnoxious

cowboys she'd had to deal with while working with their fathers. Like couldn't stop talking about them in a "they annoy me for reasons she wasn't willing to go into" way.

Nicole had found it utterly fascinating, which was precisely why they were running late.

Landon sighed. "Fine, but you two be ready to go when I get back."

Harlow waved him off. "We'll be ready. I don't think she's got a ton of stuff."

Nicole moved to the door of the motel room as Landon drove away.

It was odd to be back here now. She'd been gone for a couple of weeks, but it felt like she was a different person. She'd come to this place desperate and alone.

She wasn't alone anymore.

"You okay?" Harlow asked, tucking a strand of bright blue hair behind her ear.

Nicole took a long breath and opened the door. "Yeah."

"Hey, long time no see." Claudine walked out of the office, a stack of fresh towels in her hand. She was dressed in what she liked to call afternoon chic. A flowy housedress, her long hair in a braid. She wore no makeup, so the working girl was obviously taking a day off. "I heard you made the move to the big time. Whew. You really living with the devil?"

"He's not the devil," Nicole said with a frown.

Harlow looked at the other woman. "Are we talking about Jack or Josh?"

Claudine shook her head. "Those men are the same. I swear. And I don't say devil in a mean way, Nicole. Everyone knows Jackson Barnes is the kindest, most generous man around. But the man can also take a mean bit of revenge. I heard about Nicole's confrontation last night with that hateful old man."

"What are people saying about it?" Harlow asked. "Jack seemed to think it would get a lot of women to finally push back."

"Oh, they're pushing back. I had a date with a member of the city council, and he was complaining he's already getting calls to make laws and stuff against yelling at women," Claudine said with a wave of her beautifully manicured hands. "But don't talk about that.

A woman in my profession must practice discretion. Now I know the answer to this question already."

Nicole could guess. "I'm not coming back. I'm going to marry Josh and Grim and be happy."

Claudine smiled. "Then I'm happy for you." She started to walk toward her room. "But the asshole who took your room when you left is a pervert creepo." As she walked by the door Nicole used to call her own, she held up her middle finger. "Yeah, I'm talking about you. Creep who never leaves his room but is always watching. You're gross. Steer clear of this guy, Nic. And invite me to the wedding. I never get to go to weddings. Only bachelor parties."

Harlow's eyes had gone wide. "Is she a sex worker?"

Nicole nodded and entered the room. "Yup. And a nice lady with good instincts. Let's get out of here before the creep next door decides to stop by and say hello."

"How did you ever think this woman was some housewife from rural Colorado?" Harlow stood by the vanity in the bathroom. "Her makeup bag is Fendi. And she has not one but two pairs of Louboutin flip-flops."

Nicole shrugged. "I mean I've been wealthy adjacent, but it's not like they were interested in buying me stuff. And I didn't pay attention. I noticed her Chanel bag but she convinced me it was a knock-off."

Harlow hauled out the plain black suitcase and flopped it on the bed. "I can spot a knock-off from a mile away, and I can tell you those shoes are real and her clothes are excellent quality. This is a woman with money."

"I wonder why she does what she does." Nicole gathered up her books. They were all she wanted, though she would take her sad two pairs of jeans, three Christa's Café shirts, five pairs of underwear, one extra bra, and those crappy Crocs Alyssa had taken offense to.

"Because believe it or not, there are problems with being rich, too." Harlow started carefully folding the clothes Kim Kent had left behind. "Sometimes it can feel like the money is the only thing that matters about you. You have to find your purpose. And I know it's way easier to find your purpose when you're not worried about where your next meal comes from, but it wasn't my experience in life. I knew I always had food and a roof over my head and parents who love me, and I still had this kind of hole inside me."

She'd talked a lot to Harlow over the last week, but they hadn't touched on anything so personal as this. "Is that why you decided to become a PI? I thought it was because you were following in your dads' footsteps. By the way, you should know I forgive them. They were trying to protect you, and they didn't know me at all. I can understand why they did what they did."

Harlow's jaw tightened. "Well, I'm glad you do. Maybe I did start out because it felt familiar to me, but I'm good at my job. I don't need my dads rushing in constantly to save me. I started out working with them, and two weeks was all I could take. Of course they freaked out when I opened my own office. They thought they could indulge me for a little while and then I would end up being their notetaker or something. They don't think I can do this."

"Or they're worried." Nicole zipped up her backpack. This mission of theirs hadn't taken long at all. She already had more clothes after two shopping trips with her future mother-in-law than she'd had in years.

Of course she did have a big old closet to fill up. There was a Josh side and a Grim side, and a huge spot in the middle they'd saved for the woman they would marry.

They'd saved it for her.

"Well, their worry is making me crazy." Harlow placed the aforementioned expensive-as-hell flip-flops in the suitcase and moved to grab the makeup bag. "And when I get back I have to hire a new receptionist of my own because apparently taking phone calls from clients helps grow a business."

"Yes, I would suspect having someone to answer the phones would be helpful." It was kind of fun to see her mentor so flustered. Sometimes it was like nothing could shake the woman.

"Yeah, neither Ruby nor I are good at the office running thing. But we can crack a case," Harlow said. "Despite my dads constantly interfering. My sister had the right instincts. Greer stayed out of the investigation business. She took after our mom. She's always known she wanted to be an artist. I envied that about her."

"It's hard to not know what you want to do with your life," Nicole agreed. "I'm afraid I'm the one who did have to spend all my time surviving. But I want to run the shelter. I think it might be my calling."

Harlow softened. "Your calling is to take care of the people you love and to live this wonderful, painful, awesome, sometimes awful, magnificent life with us. I know Josh joked about me being in love with him, but you know I do love him, right?"

Like a sister. "He's your family."

"And now so are you," Harlow said. "Don't ever forget it. You're going to meet a lot of seemingly intimidating people in the next few weeks, but know every single one of them is going to love you. You walk into every room with your head held high because you should be so proud of who you are. I know I admire you."

"All I did was run," Nicole admitted quietly.

"All you did was survive, and you didn't lose your kindness. You didn't lose your ability to love. I'm worried I might have. I went through something terrible, something I haven't talked about with anyone except my business partner."

"Not even your parents?"

Harlow's head shook. "No. I…can't. But the point is I don't think I came out of it with a whole soul. Not the way you did. You were in a terrible position and you managed to still be kind, to be open when real love came your way. I don't think I can."

"But you want to." It was plain to see.

"There's a man at the club I go to." Harlow placed the makeup bag in the suitcase and started to zip it up. "He's been hanging around my world for a long time, but I don't have the feelings for him I have for Josh. That man is not my brother."

"So you do have feelings."

"Yes, but I won't act on them," Harlow admitted, pulling the suitcase off the bed and settling it on the floor. "I'll see him at the club and maybe one night I'll let him top me, but it won't go further. I'm not good for anyone."

"That is complete nonsense, Harlow Dawson." Nicole felt like Abigail Barnes-Fleetwood now took up space in her head. Her future mother-in-law was rubbing off on her. "You have been excellent to me, and I would bet all your clients adore you."

"The one who hired me to find out if his wife was cheating doesn't. She wasn't cheating, by the way, but he was, and I sent her pictures. The good news is there's no like Hippocratic oath for private investigators. We don't have to protect the assholes," Harlow explained. "Might be why I went this way when all the cool kids were going into the military or worse. The CIA."

Harlow had some intimidating friends. "I'll be happy here in Willow Fork with my fur babies and my new family."

"I know you will," Harlow said with a wistful smile. "But come to Dallas sometimes. I'm going to miss you when I go back."

"I promise." Nicole settled her backpack on her shoulder. "Now I kind of want to leave this place forever. I don't think I'm going to hang around here anymore."

"See, you're already proving to be smarter than me," Harlow admitted. "I kind of want to hang out and see what happens. Like how many drug deals happen here? Open the door and we can wait for Landon outside. We need to turn in the key."

"I'll go down and drop it at the office so you don't have to haul that suitcase around," Nicole offered as she opened the door and walked out. She would go home, see what Kim had found out, and then spend the rest of the day being coddled by her men. They would cuddle her and probably fuck her a couple of times and then cuddle her some more.

It was the perfect way to spend her first day of real freedom.

"Not on your life, sister," Harlow argued. "Look, it's got wheels. We're sticking together. I'll text Lan we're waiting."

The door to the room that used to be Nicole's swung open.

And Nicole realized her freedom might be over before it began.

* * * *

The smell of baking bread hit Josh as he walked through the door. The aroma took him right back to childhood when he and Olivia would sit in the kitchen hoping for snacks. Later, when they were teens, Grim was right there with them, telling their housekeeper about their school days while she made sure to take care of their grumbling bellies.

The memories pierced through him. Likely because he'd started to think about a family with Nicole. A vision of their kids running wild on the ranch made his heart clench.

He hung his hat up on one of the many pegs dotting the

mudroom. It looked like the mudroom might be getting some use this afternoon.

"Hey, Josh. You're home early." Benita Wells had been around long before Josh had been born. She'd run this household before his mother had come on the scene. She'd taken care of his dads when no one else wanted to work for them.

"Dad called and asked me to come back. Is that your sourdough I smell?" Josh asked with a grin.

"You know it." She no longer cleaned the house. They had a service for cleaning, but Benita still cooked most of the meals and oversaw the upkeep of the house. "Nicole likes the sourdough so she's getting the sourdough."

Like the rest of his family, Benita had taken a shine to Nicole. "Thank you for being so nice to her."

"I'm nice to her because she deserves it. She's a flower who's never had any sun, Josh. You can make her come alive by loving her," Benita said, moving to the sink. "Like your fathers did for Abby. I'm happy to see it play out all over again with you and Grim. You treat your girl right."

"I promise." The idea that he was following in his fathers' footsteps made his heart soften. "I love her very much."

"Not as much as I do," a deep voice said. Grim walked in from the mudroom. "Something smells heavenly, Benita."

"I love her way more than you do," Josh argued, a little lightness taking over. It was fun to joke with Grim about who loved their almost wife more. Of course showing her their love was even more fun.

Benita's head shook, and she was laughing as she waved them off. "You boys. That poor girl. Grim, there's a sandwich for you in the fridge. I'm sure Joshua already ate but you got too busy and forgot."

She knew them well. Josh had eaten at his desk while he was consulting his Uncle Lucas about wreaking vengeance on his enemies. Talking about vengeance always made him hungry. He could use a second lunch, but he doubted Grim would share. Their future wife, yes, but not a sandwich.

Benita offered him a cookie. "You go on now. Your father said you have some sort of meeting about Nicole."

"It's not for another hour," Grim replied. He'd already downed half the big-ass, looked-delicious sandwich. "Is Nic back yet?"

"She left about thirty minutes ago, but she was with Landon and Harlow. I swear that poor girl is never going to get to drive her own car," Benita complained. "It's a beautiful piece of machinery and it's just sitting there."

"Hopefully after today we can start to see the end of the tunnel." Josh was unwilling to pull her security right away. He knew she needed some freedom, but it would take a while. He'd already scheduled an upgrade for the security on the shelter. When it was in place, he and Grim would be able to access the cameras from their phones. "But if she wanted to drive herself around, she probably shouldn't have decided to work a block from the office."

"And directly in my office," Grim added. He'd finished the sandwich in three bites. "I'm afraid she'll have to deal with commuting in with one of us and probably having a lot of lunches at Christa's."

It was one block over. He could walk down to the shelter, and they would join him on sunny days. They would hold her hand and not give a damn about who was watching.

Or they could join him in his ridiculously big office. The one he was going to fully equip for afternoon play sessions with Nicole. Well, he would redesign some of what was already there. When he'd moved in he hadn't wanted to think about how many very sturdy hooks there were in the ceiling when his father didn't have a bunch of hanging plants.

"What did Lucas have to say?" Grim asked. "I'm worried my stepfather is going to cause trouble."

"Lucas is making a call." Josh wanted that asshole in check. "He's going to be talking to a friend at the attorney general's office about opening an investigation into the church. We all know they're not in any way following the rules of a nonprofit. In addition, the city council will be implementing a couple of new rules about public decency. It doesn't forbid street preaching, but it will shut down and fine anyone who harasses people. So more Jesus, less women are whores."

"He could still come after us. I'm worried he'll come after her," Grim admitted.

"I wouldn't be. You know your father had a long talk with Ezekiel after you came to live with us, Grim. There's a reason he didn't fight you living here," Benita said, pouring herself a cup of coffee. "I wasn't there for the conversation, but I was there when he talked to Sam and Abby about it. Ezekiel is scared of Jack. He won't physically harm anyone because he knows Jack has plans to take him out if he does."

"Dad threatened my stepfather?" Grim asked with a little surprise.

"Of course he did." Josh had no idea why Grim would be surprised. "It's why I'm not worried about Ezekiel. Between me coming after his cult and Dad and Pops very likely ensuring he understands Nicole is a Barnes-Fleetwood, the most he's going to do is run his mouth. I've heard he's already talking about selling his land and buying a spread in a less populated area."

"We're a tiny town," Grim pointed out. "How much less populated can he get?"

"I think he'll go completely off the grid at some point, and good riddance to him." Josh felt certain he would take the members of his group with him, and they would likely get weirder and closer and closer to crossing a line. But that was a Netflix documentary for another day. As long as they were out of Willow Fork, he would be content.

"Josh is right. He's put out feelers about selling his spread. He's been planning on leaving for a while now. This will push him out faster. Last night was him trying to find a way to fuck with you that wouldn't bring me down on his head. He tried to use the beetle infestation to get people to turn on you since you've become such a pillar of our society." Dad stood in the doorway.

Grim seemed to think. "Why does he hate me so much?"

Dad moved in, putting a hand on Grim's shoulder. "He's afraid of you. He always has been. He knows you're a better man than he'll ever be, and that's why he's going to leave. He's afraid at some point those boys who say they're your brothers will figure out you're not who he says you are. He's a petty man, and while I wish we could have helped your mother, she made her choice a long time ago. I'm afraid she's filled with Ezekiel's hate now."

"Bio mom. Abby's my real mom," Grim said tightly.

"Damn straight she is." Jack put an arm around him. "Son, I don't want you to worry about this. No one believes the kind and caring vet is in league with the devil. Well, unless they mean me."

Grim hugged their old man. "You're so far from that, Dad."

It was easy to see how pleased his father was to be called by his rightful title. "Now, come back to my office. Kim sent a text saying she needs to talk to us."

Josh downed his cookie in two big bites as he and Grim followed their father. "She's early."

"She must have found something." It was good to know Grim could be positive for once.

"Or something's gone wrong." Josh had a bad feeling in his gut all of the sudden. He didn't like when a person as organized as Kim Kent suddenly wanted to change up the time line. It meant she'd found something she hadn't counted on.

"Don't borrow trouble, son," his father advised. "I know it would be better to wait for Nicole, but she's still in town. I think we should find out what's happened so we can maybe have a plan by the time she gets back. If it's bad, I'd like to at least be able to give her a plan."

What could it be? "Could they have faked a video of her killing Micah?"

He wouldn't believe it. Not for a second. Nic had told him what happened, and she wouldn't lie to him.

It was right there—a solid foundation of belief in the woman he loved. It was firm ground to stand on, to build a life on.

"I don't think so." His father opened the door to the big, sunlit room he'd used as an office since he'd stopped going into the one in town. Once Josh had taken over the day-to-day operation, his father had been more than content to stay home most of the time.

Josh knew damn well not to open the door to the office without knocking. His parents could still be very…affectionate. In a naked, no-child-should-ever-see-that way.

In the way he would be with Nicole when he was old and gray and still so in love it hurt.

"Why would her sister-in-law say she can clear Nicole if she can't? Kim seemed to think she wanted the money so she could get away from her husband." Grim followed them inside.

Pops was already there, sitting behind the computer. "We're not wiring her another dime until we have what we need. Jack, Kim just sent an invitation to a meeting. We ready?"

Jack nodded. "Connect us."

They all moved behind the desk, crowding in so they could see.

Pops connected them with a few keystrokes and then Kimberly Kent's lovely face filled the screen.

Her lovely, worried face. "Jack, thanks for getting back to me so quickly. Is Nicole there?"

Josh shook his head. "She's in town with Harlow packing up your old motel room. Is something wrong?"

Kim seemed to think for a moment. "It's broad daylight. I've got to hope he's not completely insane. You said she's with a bodyguard?"

Grim nodded. "Two, in fact."

Kim released a deep breath. "All right, but maybe send Harlow a heads-up to be extra careful."

Grim already had his phone out. "I'll tell her to bring Nic back right now. I'll text Landon, too."

"Good. I would feel better if you kept her close until we can find him," Kim said.

A chill went through Josh. "Her brother-in-law's gone missing?"

"No," Kim said, every word tight. "It's worse. We've got bigger worries than her brother-in-law."

Josh cursed under his breath. He could only think of one thing worse than her brother-in-law coming after her. There was a man who'd hurt her far worse. "Damn it. She didn't make sure that fucker was dead, did she? She told me she did."

"We're going to have a long talk about ensuring the dead person is really dead," Grim said. "So they faked her husband's death and tried to pin it on her."

"According to the sister-in-law, Micah had been doing some shady shit with the bookkeeping, and it was going to bring the feds down on their heads. With Micah's death, they were able to convince the investigators it was all his and Nicole's issues and had nothing to do with the rest of the family," Kim explained. "So that got them off their backs, and it kept the parents in the dark about how much money Micah had stolen."

"Why involve Nicole?" Grim asked. "I would think a suicide would be easier to fake. I mean they had to have someone in the coroner's office on the payroll, so it wouldn't have been hard. It seems far more neat and contained than an open murder investigation."

"He needed his parents to not look too closely." Kim seemed to be in another hotel room. She sat at a small desk, the background bland but soothing behind her. "He wanted to give them something to do. Nicole being on the run is a distraction, and it's worked up until now."

"He wanted them so angry at Nicole they wouldn't ask questions of him," Josh surmised. "I take it he shared the money with his brother."

Kim nodded. "From what I can tell the parents hold the purse strings pretty tight. It was millions Micah managed to steal. Laura says Ted worked a deal with Micah's mafia contacts. Since he was technically dead, the people he owed money to were willing to settle for Ted paying them far less than what Micah owed. So they effectively bilked their parents out of millions, solved the mafia problem, and seemed to get away with it all. Ted took half of the cash left, and he's been hiding his brother in his own home. Micah is the one who's been attacking Laura. He's unhinged, and I'm worried he's going to go after Nicole."

"How would he know where she is?" Grim asked.

"Laura found out he's been paying his own PI. Roman, do you have the file?" Kim held out a hand and drew back a plain file folder. She laid it out and opened it. "He's been looking for Nicole for the last six months. I think this has a lot to do with the interviews I did with Ted and the rest of the family."

"They got worried you would find her first," Grim said. "They decided you had serious potential."

Kim nodded. "I believe that's what happened. They decided it was time to put an end to the threat, or maybe they wanted to ensure I wasn't on the right track."

"But you were," his father began, "and I assume this new PI found the same clues you did."

"From what I can tell, he caught up to her when the press did a small story on how she saved the man at the shelter," Kim explained. "She wouldn't talk, but someone had taken a picture. He tracked her from there."

Josh's stomach threatened to roll. "He knows she's here?"

"I can't be sure, but it's a distinct possibility," Kim agreed. "Up until now he hasn't had a reason to hurt her. Nicole being on the run was doing what they needed it to do. But Laura has left Ted. Roman and I took her to the airport on our way back here. They will quickly figure out what she's done."

"Should she have protection?" His father had a serious look on his face.

Pops had gotten up and unlocked the gun case.

"I've already sent someone with her. Once it becomes known the authorities have the tape, there won't be a reason to hurt her or Nicole beyond revenge. But they don't know we have the proof yet, so I worry they might try to take out Nicole to scare Laura. They should know tomorrow, but I fear the next couple of hours because we're so close. Laura also told me Micah disappeared from their basement two days ago, and she believes he left with a fake ID and cash," Kim continued. "She said Ted went looking for him, so I don't know where he is either."

Josh had his phone in hand, dialing her number. When it went to voicemail, he groaned, a frustrated sound. "Nicole, call me when you get this." He hung up and looked to his best friend. "You get anything from Harlow?"

"Nothing from her, but Landon told me he's on his way to pick them up and will be back here in twenty minutes," Grim replied.

Why wasn't Harlow answering her phone? Josh fought to remain calm, panic threatening to overwhelm him. He tried Harlow's number again. Nothing. "She wouldn't simply not answer. Nic might get distracted, but Harlow's working. She wouldn't ignore a call from us unless something's gone wrong."

A million scenarios played out in his head, all of them awful.

"How can we even be sure where Nicole is?" Grim asked, his expression mirroring what Josh felt.

"You need to find her," Kim said. "I can find Landon. He works for a firm that tracks their employees, but if he's not with them, I don't have any way of finding the ladies."

Pops cleared his throat, looking pointedly at Dad. "You going to tell them, Jack?"

His father was on his feet. "I can find her."

His father moved to the gun safe Pops had opened.

Josh followed. And prayed his father knew what he was doing and they made it on time.

Chapter Twenty

Nicole stared at the ghost in front of her. "Micah?"

He looked older, thinner. Like the years since she'd seen him last had taken any softness and left behind only the deranged predator.

Harlow had pulled a gun, a semiautomatic pistol she looked perfectly comfortable with. "Nicole, I need you to get behind me. As for you, whoever you are, don't move a muscle."

Unfortunately, Micah had a gun, too. He knew how to use it. Both he and his brother had been gun collectors and practiced regularly. He stood his ground. "I think you're the one who shouldn't move. I'm not sure what she's told you, but Nora is my wife, and we have a few things to work through."

Nicole realized she was blocking Harlow's shot, but she was terrified to move. Terrified she was about to get her friend killed. "Micah, I'll go with you if you'll let my friend go."

Harlow huffed behind her. "I'm not letting that happen."

"Oh, I think you will." Micah's smile went reptilian. "Or my brother can eliminate you."

Nicole gasped and turned, realizing while they'd been protecting their fronts, Ted had moved in behind them and had a gun to the back of Harlow's head.

"My dumb bitch wife is forcing us all into this situation," Ted said, his eyes steely. "I found out she was meeting with the blonde bimbo my parents hired. I suspect she's trying to tell her side of the story. Once I present her with your dead body, she'll know what can happen to her if she talks. It's time to clean up my brother's mess once again."

Micah's eyes rolled. "Sure. It's all me."

Nicole was sick with fear and had to shove the panic down. They were here in broad daylight, and Landon would be back soon.

Would they murder her and Harlow right here? She wasn't sure anyone would stop them.

She wanted Josh and Grim. She wanted to be safe in their arms, away from all the proof of the mistakes she'd once made. She had to be the Nicole they'd fallen in love with, not the Nora who could barely stand up for herself. "The cops will be here soon, Micah. Won't they be surprised. You can't exactly pin my own murder on me."

"Don't have to," Micah replied. "Once we get you back home, I'm going to bury you so deep in the woods no one will ever find you. Now you're going to walk out of this parking lot if you don't want me to shoot your friend there. Drop the gun, lady."

"You'll kill me anyway," Harlow replied. "Nicole, you need to run."

Then Harlow was moving, her foot going back to catch Ted in the gut. He went down, his gun going off, the shot wild. Before he could hit the concrete, Harlow was turning, ready to take out Micah.

Who fired first. The sound rang in Nicole's ears, and horror dawned as a red stain colored Harlow's white T-shirt. Chest. He'd hit her chest. Harlow dropped to her knees and fell forward.

She'd killed Harlow. The world seemed to slow down and speed up all at once, fear and regret choking her.

"Get her," Ted ordered. "We need to get out of here. Someone will have heard that and called the fucking cops. We need to get into the car and figure it out from there."

If she got in the car, she would die. They would kill her, and she would never see her men again. They would come looking for her and find Harlow's body… Harlow…she couldn't comprehend what had happened.

And then she saw it. Harlow's back moved slightly, proof she was still breathing. If she was breathing, she had a shot, and that meant Nicole needed to lead them away from her. Landon would be back soon, and he could bring the police and EMTs.

Would they kill her right here? It no longer mattered. What mattered was making sure her friend kept breathing.

Nicole made her decision. She took off across the parking lot, moving behind the big pillar at the end of the building. It was brick and gave her cover. Nicole's heart raced as she heard another shot go off. She'd been faster, but she couldn't hide here forever. She needed to put distance between them.

"Nicole? Are you all right? I called the cops," a voice whispered. Claudine. She was in her room, the door barely open as she peeked outside. "Come inside. I'll lock us in."

It wouldn't work. They would simply shoot until they got inside. They had no other choice. At this point they had to eliminate her or their whole game was over. Nicole shook her head. "Can't. When you see Josh and Grim, tell them I loved them so much."

"Nicole," Claudine said, her voice cracking.

"Tell them," Nicole said, and then made her move.

The motel was on the outer edges of town, one of the reasons it was used by the more criminal elements of the area. The woods behind the motel were thick and went on for miles. There wasn't a fence for her to get over. It was her best bet.

Those woods would lead her close to the ranch. Jack had taken her out there, showing her how to ride a horse on different types of terrain. He'd spent an afternoon teaching her how to lead her horse through the woods, stopping for a lunch by the river that eventually ran through the south field of the ranch, supplying them with water. They'd sat and talked about camping and how to forage. He'd told her about his childhood, listening to hers as well.

It had been the first time in her life she'd felt like she had a father.

She was not giving up without a fight.

Nicole took off and then a loud sound boomed behind her. Something scraped by her arm, fire lighting her up, but she kept moving. Nicole forced herself to sprint despite the fact she could feel the blood on her left arm. It didn't matter. They were following her. They were focused on her. It would give Claudine a chance to help Harlow.

The light seemed to dim as she moved from sunshine to the heavy canopy of trees that made up this part of the woods. Mighty oak trees rose high above her, blocking out the sun and heat of the day. Nicole hid behind one as she heard the men enter the woods behind her.

"Where the hell did she go?" Ted asked, his breathing heavy.

"How am I supposed to know? You think I spend a lot of time in fucking nature, brother?" Micah shot back. "You're the one who couldn't handle a single female."

They didn't try to hide the sounds of them moving through the woods. She could hear them shuffling along, trying not to miss a hiding spot.

"We should regroup," Ted said after a moment. "Someone has to have called the cops by now, and we don't know if anyone was watching out of their windows. We need to get the hell out of here."

Nicole prayed they couldn't hear how hard her heart was beating.

She took a long breath like Harlow had taught her. Panic was the enemy. She needed to be cool and assess the situation. Panic would send her running from a hiding place that was working for her. Three breaths in and four breaths out. Slow. Quiet. Calm.

"And let that bitch go to the cops? Not on your life," Micah replied. "She can't have gotten far. I'm not leaving until Nora is dead. You should have killed her the first time around."

"You know why I didn't. Our parents would have had questions." Ted didn't seem to feel the need to be quiet. His voice reverberated through the woods. "I did what I had to do to keep them off our backs."

"No, you didn't. You could have done what I told you to do," Micah argued.

Oh, she hoped they kept hashing out all their differences because time meant Landon was closer to coming for them.

"I wasn't going to kill our parents," Ted barked back. "I know you think we can get away with anything, but you're clinically insane."

She wished she hadn't left her cell phone in her purse. She'd dropped it and hadn't picked it back up. Josh could have found her if she had her cell phone. She thought he could. Her hand went up to play with the small diamond solitaire Jack had given her as an "I'm sorry I cubed your car" present. She'd thought the car was enough, but he'd insisted. When she'd realized Olivia had one exactly like it, she'd felt like part of the family.

She would miss them so fucking much. If Micah killed her, wherever she went, she would miss them all.

"You didn't mind when I managed to get us out from under their thumbs." Micah seemed to get closer.

His voice was to her left. The river was to her right. She could hear it. It was full at this time of year. If she got in, she could float to the ranch. She simply had to make it there without Micah seeing her. It would take her far faster than running, and there would be no mistaking where she was going. She couldn't get lost in the river.

"You got us all in trouble. Now I have to find a way to get us out. Maybe I should find a way to get me out instead," Ted said. "You're on your own, brother."

"Fuck you. I'm doing what I have to do," Micah growled back.

There was the sound of footsteps striding away, leaves crackling underfoot.

"Nora. Nora. I think we're alone now."

A chill coursed down her spine. Memories sparked through her, remembrances of the times he would call out her name right before he made her ache. Right before he would make her bleed. He would use that singsong voice. It haunted her dreams.

"I've missed you, baby. I've missed you so much."

He was closer. So much closer. Her fists clenched as she fought back the urge to cry. She had to stay calm. How close was he? Sometimes sounds bounced around the woods.

"You took vows, Nora. Until death do us part," Micah said. "I mean to honor our vows."

He wasn't her husband. He'd never been. He'd been the con artist who tricked her and then the monster who abused her.

Josh and Grim were her husbands. They loved her. They trusted her. They shared their family and their hearts and their futures with her.

She was not fucking giving up. She was not letting Micah Holloway take one more thing from her.

In the distance she heard a shot ring out.

"Damn," Micah said with a huff. "Guess we're not getting out of this. Well, at least I can take you with me."

Adrenaline pumped through her system and she chose. Fight.

"You can't hide from me."

She wasn't going to.

Anything can be a weapon, Nic. Look around. Get creative. But mostly remember the cardinal rule.

She could hear Harlow's voice in her head. Her friend had spent weeks training her for this moment.

And she remembered the rule.

Never fight fair.

"When I find you, I think I'll make it last. What my brother doesn't know is I've left a trail that should lead straight to him," Micah was saying as Nicole glanced around, looking for any advantage she could find. "I have the money. I stole far more than I ever let on. I'm going to take care of you and then I'll disappear. Thanks for becoming a problem again. I was getting bored. Laura doesn't cry the way you did. You were so pretty when you cried."

There was nothing around her but sticks and rocks.

Sharp rocks.

As quietly as she could she leaned over and grabbed the biggest rock she could find. It had a sharp, nasty edge to it that felt good against her palm.

"Those nights we spent together. They were the best nights of my life. Laura was a pitiful comparison to you," he said, and she felt his presence.

A step or two more and he would be on her.

Timing. They'd taught her timing was everything.

It was what a family did. They taught the other members what they knew so everyone could benefit. Abby had taught her to stay away from the patch of poison ivy a few feet away. Jack had shown her around the woods so she would know how to find her way out. Harlow had taught her how to fight.

Josh and Grim had taught her she was worth fighting for.

"Got you," Micah whispered.

She turned and brought the rock down on his face, hitting his right eye. Blood spurted and the gun went off. Nicole felt a pain in her gut, but she couldn't worry about it now.

She'd promised her men this asshole was dead. She was going to make good on her promise this time.

Micah had dropped the gun, his hand coming up to try to protect his ravaged eye.

She was supposed to go for the eyes. The throat. The balls. Vulnerable places.

She'd been the vulnerable one once, and she'd promised to never be that again. Not to him.

Micah hit his knees as she continued to strike him. He fell back.

"Nora," he groaned. "This isn't you. This isn't Nora Holloway."

"No. My name is Nicole Barnes-Fleetwood, and you don't scare me anymore." She picked up the gun he'd dropped and without giving him a chance to plead, shot him. The bullet split his forehead, and the monster who'd chased her for years was gone.

She could hear sirens in the background.

A long, slow breath heaved from her as she realized she'd done it.

Then she went light-headed. Her left side ached. She must have hit it on something. Gingerly, she touched her side and realized her fight wasn't over.

Blood covered her abdomen. She'd taken a bullet.

She had to get back to the motel. The ambulance was there. She would be fine if she could only get back.

She took three steps and then the world went wavy.

She could have sworn she heard someone calling her name, but she was falling, and the pain wasn't enough to keep her conscious.

The world blinked out as she wished she could see them one last time.

* * * *

Grim was going out of his freaking mind. "Drive faster."

Josh sped up the truck, but the truth of the matter was he was already pushing the vehicle and Grim knew it. They'd made the twenty-minute trip into town in less than ten.

"Grim, we won't help Nic if we're in a car accident." Jack was the voice of reason. He sat in the back seat beside Sam.

Dad and Pops. They were here with them. They wouldn't let their kids go into this alone.

He'd let go of any wish his childhood had gone another way the night before, but he was reminded of it now. He wouldn't want to be anywhere but here, have any family but this one.

He was wondering how Dad knew where Nicole was. The question ran through his head. They'd all followed Dad to the truck, no one even asking how or why. If Jack Barnes said he knew something, he did. He had pure trust in the man he called Dad.

Still, the question rattled through his brain as some kind of distraction from all the terrible things that could be happening to Nicole. Had he called the security company and asked them to triangulate her cell phone? She had a new one. A reliable one Dad had given her. He wouldn't put it past his old man to have a way to track her. Hell, Jack had given him his phone. And Josh's. And Olivia's.

"Call Landon again." Josh kept his eyes on the road.

Grim pulled his cell and dialed the bodyguard's number. He heaved a sigh of relief when the man picked up. "Lan, where are you?"

"I'm pulling in now. I'm sorry it took me so long, but I couldn't get the security system to unlock at the shelter. I'm glad you're upgrading because it's a piece of crap," Landon complained. "I still can't get Harlow to… Oh, god."

Grim's heart threatened to freeze at those words. "What's happening?"

Josh sped up again, taking the corner that would lead them to the motel way too fast. Grim could feel the wheels come up but Josh handled it, getting the truck stable again.

"We're going to need an ambulance out at the motel," Pops was saying into his phone. He obviously wasn't going to wait. Pops sounded calm and cool under pressure. "Yes, there's been an attack. Have the police come as fast as possible. Yes, Charlene, it's me and Jack and our boys. We've got a bodyguard who'll be on scene, too."

"Lan?" Grim asked.

"He's not going to answer. That's his truck up ahead. He's already out of it. I can't see past it, though." Josh complained tightly. "What if it's…"

"It's not. Damn it. It's not." He couldn't believe Landon had found Nicole's body. He wouldn't believe it. She was fine. She couldn't not be.

"We need to stay calm," Dad advised.

"The cops and an ambulance are on the way," Pops explained, and he shoved his cell in his pocket. "I let them know we're armed."

If this were a big city, he would worry the cops could roll in and not know who the bad guys were. But the sheriff sometimes called Jack and Sam in to help when they had missing kids or old folks. They knew the area better than anyone. They wouldn't come in shooting. Hell, the sheriff might actually defer to their dad in this situation.

Grim let a cold practicality come over him. He couldn't go into this hot. Whatever had been done to Nicole, he would fix. They would coddle her and love her back to normal. They wouldn't let her go through this alone.

"If she's hurt," Josh said as he rolled up next to Lan's truck.

"I'll take care of it until the ambulance gets here. I can stabilize her." A vet was not licensed to work on humans, but this would be an emergency. He could stabilize her until they got to the hospital.

Please let her be alive. Please. Let her be alive. He could handle anything as long as she was alive.

Then he saw what had caused Landon to hang up and run. There was a body on the sidewalk.

"Harlow," Dad said. "Fuck. That's Harlow."

She lay on the sidewalk outside the room Kim had occupied. He knew it was her from the shock of blue hair. Landon was on his knees next to her.

Grim was out of the truck before Josh put it in park. He grabbed his emergency kit and ran. It was smaller than his normal working kit. This was the one he used when someone needed first aid. A ranch could be a maze of minor injuries, and he was always ready to help.

What had happened to Harlow was anything but minor.

The light-colored shirt she was wearing was stained in blood. Her skin was a stark white, her eyes closed.

"I turned her over." Landon had gone pale. "I shouldn't have done that, but I panicked. Damn it. I know not to turn her over. Did I hurt her?"

Pops was back on his phone. "Yes, ma'am. We've got at least one gunshot victim. Let them know. We're looking for the second woman. She might have been kidnapped."

Or they might find her body somewhere else.

From what Kim had said, there was no reason to kidnap Nicole. They'd come here to silence her.

Harlow was pale but she was breathing. Her eyes opened, and she looked up at him. "It's hard to breathe, Grim."

Okay. He could do this. "Pops, I need your help."

Sam Fleetwood was by his side in a heartbeat. "Jack and Josh are doing a sweep. They will find her, Grim. I promise. Hey, Harlow, sweetie. Looks like you got into some trouble."

"She ran," Harlow managed, pain obvious on her face. "I think Nicole ran toward the woods. I'm not sure. I couldn't see."

"She did." A tall brunette in a caftan was beside Harlow. "Nicole ran into the woods, and those two men who were coming after her followed. I was in my room. I saw the whole thing. I came out and held this woman's hand. I called the police."

"They're on their way," Pops replied. "And I thank you for staying with her."

"Is she okay?" Landon asked.

Harlow tried to take a breath but a rattling sound came out. He knew exactly what was happening.

"The bullet nicked her lung. Or maybe it's lodged there," Grim explained, finding a latex glove. "We need to be careful when we move anything."

"We need to seal the wound. That glove should work," Pops said. "Hand it to me and I'll hold it until the paramedics get here."

It was exactly what he'd been about to do. The prettiest of his fathers was calm and cool under pressure. And knew way more about sucking chest wounds than Grim would have imagined.

"The ambulance is a few minutes out." Landon was on his feet again, and there was a gun in his hand. "I'll make sure no one comes near her until then."

Pops took the glove out of his hand and lifted her shirt, easing it over the wound he found there with a competence that shocked Grim. He sealed the wound, holding his hand over the glove, and immediately Harlow was breathing more easily. "Hey, I've learned a thing or two over the years. I'm more than pretty, son. Now go with Josh and find your girl. Lan and I can handle this."

"Her husband is alive," Harlow said with a grimace, but she sounded far more solid. "I don't know how but he's here, and he's going to kill her. The brother-in-law is here, too. Both armed. She ran into the woods."

Where Dad had been taking her and teaching her to ride and navigate. Where she could hide. Smart girl. She'd lured them away from Harlow, and he prayed it didn't cost her.

He heard sirens in the distance.

"Hey!" Josh shouted.

Grim stood and saw what Josh had seen. A tall man dressed in black pants and a black sweater walked out of the woods, his path about to take him to the parking lot. The man stopped, obviously caught by surprise. Nicole's brother-in-law. He'd seen pictures of the man. For a moment he seemed stuck, utterly unmoving. Then he raised his gun and pointed straight at Josh.

A loud blast cracked through the air as Dad shot the shit out of Ted Holloway. No hesitation. He'd watched the man take aim, and he'd done what he had to do. Unlike whoever had shot Harlow, Jack Barnes's aim was true. That had been a heart shot, and the man wouldn't need an ambulance.

The man in all black slumped to the ground.

"Damn it, Dad. We needed him alive," Josh shouted.

"Am I supposed to let him kill you?" Dad had his cell phone out. He pointed to the left. "And we do not need that asshole. She's this way. I told you I know where she is."

Grim joined them, his heart threatening to thud out of his chest. What did it mean that Ted Holloway had been coming out of the woods? Nicole wasn't with him. Were they going to find a body?

"I was handling it," Josh insisted, but then followed their father. "Is Harlow okay?"

"Yes, she's stable. Pops has her. Says he knows a lot about gunshot wounds or something. We might need to delve into parental history when we get out of this, brother. Also, she says there were two men. I'm pretty sure the one Dad shot is her brother-in-law. Harlow said her husband is here, too."

"We'll have a lot of questions since Dad seems to have LoJacked our woman," Josh said, his voice tense.

"I personally am happy about that, sir." Grim moved through the woods, trying to be as quiet as possible.

"I know how damn dangerous the world can be, and I'm not about to let it take one of my kids without a fight," Dad said, his eyes on the screen again. "Damn it. It's hard to read. I think we're going the right way. She's not moving. She hasn't for a couple of minutes."

"Then they might have..." Josh began, and then his jaw tightened. "Then she's hiding and we need to get this guy away from her."

"She's close," Dad whispered. "I think I can hear something."

"Those nights we spent together. They were the best nights of my life." A deep voice came from somewhere in the woods to the east. The fucker sounded like he was talking to a lover. "Laura was a pitiful comparison to you."

It turned his gut because he was absolutely certain Micah Holloway wasn't talking about sex. At least not the consensual kind. He was talking about torturing the woman he'd promised to protect and love and how much he'd enjoyed her pain.

"I'm going to kill him," Josh vowed quietly.

"If he's talking, she's alive," Grim pointed out. "She is our priority. Dad can kill him. He seems to be good at it. You have to shove your anger aside and think only of her safety."

Josh frowned, but he nodded. He looked to their dad. "Where is she? Sound bounces through the woods. I can't tell where it's coming from."

"She's close," Jack said, putting his phone back in his pocket. "I think that's as close as we're going to get using technology. It can't pinpoint her. But I can. Look. Someone ran through here and recently."

He looked down, and the ground showed signs of sneaker prints. Two large, one small. One backtracked. Ted. He'd walked back this way to get to the parking lot. So Micah and Nicole had gone further into the woods.

Dad led the way, moving across the soft earth, making far less sound than a man his size should.

She was alive. Grim gripped the handle of his kit with one hand, the gun in the other. It was strictly for emergencies. He would drop that sucker the minute they got to Nicole. He would protect her, hold her together if need be. In this case, his medical kit would do more good than the gun.

They moved quietly, and then they heard it. A loud shot cracked through the woods, and Grim simply ran. He and Josh ran toward the river where the shot seemed to have come from.

His heart threatened to stop as he saw Nicole on the ground. She wasn't the only body, but she was the only one who mattered.

Josh got to her first, falling to his knees beside her. Tears tracked down his brother's face.

He'd never seen his brother cry. Not once in all the years they'd lived together.

Grim felt stuck. Like the world stopped, and as long as he didn't move, it wouldn't go further than this. He could be stuck in this moment, pretending she might still be alive, that she wasn't still on the ground. Facedown in the mud where her abuser had put her.

"Josh, Grim, I'm so sorry," Dad managed to get out.

"I am, too," the sweetest voice said. "This hurts. I'd like some drugs now."

Nicole. The world sped up again and he rushed to her, dropping his kit beside her. "Don't move, baby. Where are you hit? I don't see an exit wound."

But there was blood staining the ground. It soaked into his jeans.

"Uhm, it's my stomach. Or somewhere close to it." Her eyes opened. "It hurts when I try to move."

"Don't," Josh said, holding her hand. "You let Grim take care of you."

"I'm going to get the EMTs up here." Their dad took off.

"Is he dead? I think I killed him this time, but I should make sure. He came back. Like a bad movie. I don't like this part of the movie," she said, sounding a bit loopy.

Blood loss. "Nic, he's dead, and I don't want you to talk."

"Harlow," she began.

"Is alive and being taken care of," Josh promised.

"We have to turn her over." He didn't want to, but he had to minimize the bleed.

"I think I should stay here," Nicole said.

"I'm so sorry." He nodded Josh's way. "We're going to move her gently, and then we're going to put pressure on the wound. Nic, baby, this is going to hurt."

She groaned as they turned her over, and Josh gasped at the amount of blood on her clothes.

Her eyes rolled to the back of her head, and she passed out. Grim applied pressure and prayed the EMTs got there in time.

Chapter Twenty-One

Josh held up the pudding cup as Nicole groaned.

"I would rather have a cheeseburger," she said with a frown. "Christa will totally bring me one."

"Says the woman who recently had abdominal surgery," Grim replied with a shake of his head. "You're on a soft foods diet for the next two weeks, and don't think you can get our momma on your side. She used to be a nurse, and she will watch you like a hawk."

He wasn't wrong about that. Mom had been up here every day since Nicole had been admitted. She went over her charts with the nurses and discussed the physical therapy Nicole would need. Their mom was taking care of her newest baby bird, and Nicole was about to find out how fierce Abby Barnes-Fleetwood could be when protecting someone she loved.

Oddly, he thought Nicole wouldn't mind, her cheeseburger cravings aside. "I got you chocolate and butterscotch."

"No vanilla?" Nicole asked.

He leaned in and brushed his lips over hers. "Baby, you left vanilla a long while back. You're never getting vanilla again."

She blushed but winked at him. "Yeah, I guess I did. It's a good thing I've got a taste for butterscotch. Has anyone checked in on Harlow? Did she make it back to Dallas?"

That had been fun. "Oh, yes, but I think she should have hidden out here for a while. Uncle Chase was a paranoid bastard before. He's vowing to get her out of the PI business."

"And Harlow is basically not speaking to him. She might have just had surgery, but she knows how to use her middle finger." Grim sat up, stretching.

The cots they'd been sleeping on were hell on a man's back, but they weren't about to leave her. Luckily there was an actual Barnes-Fleetwood wing to this small rural hospital, so no one tried to keep them out. "It didn't help they brought Greer along. Greer is the perfect child. Or at least that's how Harlow sees her. Greer is perfect, and she's the wild child everyone worries about. She loves her sister, but it's an interesting dynamic. Kind of like ours. Grim is the perfect one in our case."

His brother merely grinned. "I can't help it."

Nicole picked up her spoon and the butterscotch pudding. "Well, you weren't perfect a couple of days ago. You could have been a little faster finding me. I think I'm going to avoid getting shot again. All my girlfriends used to say it. Go to a small town. Get shot. It's so much fun. They were wrong."

His stomach took a dive even at the thought. "You are never leaving the ranch again."

"That'll be hard to do since I start work soon." Nicole looked so much better after a couple of days of healing. "Also, Kim told us everything is cleared up now. The Holloways don't care about me at all anymore. They blame Laura for everything."

"Kim is helping her." They were all worried about Nicole's sister-in-law. She'd risked a lot. "She's safe, and they've hired a lawyer to ensure they can't get to her. There's nothing they can do."

"And there's nothing they can do to me, either, so I'm going to enjoy my new car when I drive Buddy and me to work in a couple of weeks. He's going to be my work friend," Nicole announced.

"I thought we would drive in together," Josh pointed out.

"I'm sure we will sometimes, but I'm going to have meetings to attend. Abby wants me to join the historical society and a couple of her charity boards. I'm also thinking about going back to college. Either online, or I can drive into Tyler a couple of times a week. I'd like to finish my degree."

"I think that's great." She wouldn't have to worry about money for the rest of her life. She wouldn't have to work. But he wanted her to pursue all of her dreams. He would happily support her in everything she did.

He loved this woman, and the fact that she was alive and whole was everything.

There was a knock on the door and then his parents were invading. If Olivia hadn't had a meeting in South Texas she would have been here, too. His sister seemed to have shoved all her problems aside in favor of keeping her almost sister-in-law company. And Harlow, before her paranoid dads had come with a private helicopter to take her home.

He would have to watch those situations. Just because he was happy and starting his own family didn't mean he would leave the old one behind. It was a lesson he'd learned from his dad.

Who was walking in and had some things to answer for.

"You want to tell me what I'm wearing that has a locator device in it? At first I thought it was probably my phone, but then I remembered you're a ruthless bastard and I can leave my phone behind." Josh wasn't at all pissed at his dad. Merely curious. The truth was they might have been screwed without Jack Barnes's determination to keep an eye on his loved ones. Also, Josh was thinking of the future. He could use some pointers.

His dad had stopped, at a loss for words for once.

Not so his pops. "I think you'll find it's in your watch. You remember. He gave it to you for your sixteenth birthday. And when you switched to a smart watch, he got you a new wrist band. Yeah. It's there. Grim's is in his watch as well. He put two on Olivia. The first one was a necklace, but when she decided to get a belly button ring, Jack saw opportunity."

His mom laughed. "Yes, he used that bit of rebellion against her."

"Not against her." Dad sat down next to Grim and looked a bit defeated. "It's a hard world, and you kids can be made targets."

"I'm so glad you did it, Jack," Nicole said, all her humor pushed to the side. "I don't know I would be here if you hadn't. Is it in the necklace?"

His father nodded.

"I like to change my jewelry. I might need a locator where I know what it is so I don't accidently not wear it one day. I was married to a man who would do something like that in order to control me. You wouldn't, but you have to let me know." It was obvious Nicole was going to put up some logical boundaries. "I'll be happy to share my location. I don't want you to worry."

"Dad, I'm not mad. Grim's not mad," Josh said.

Grim leaned against their dad. Damn but he'd come a long way. He used to be stiff and formal, and now he leaned against the old man like he had the right to comfort him. Because he did. "I like my watch, too. Don't worry about it, Dad. My main question is where did you put the one for Pops? He loses everything."

Pops chuckled. "He had Big Tag…well, tag me a long time ago. It's in my right butt cheek. If it helps, he's got one in his butt, too."

"Well, mine is in my everyday collar," his mother announced.

Josh shook his head. "Necklace. Can we call it a necklace?"

"Prude," his mother admonished. "Now we can share the app he uses and all keep track of one another."

"I only use it in emergencies." His father had put an arm around Grim. "I promise. I know I call Chase paranoid, but I've seen some things in my time I can't forget."

"And apparently Pops has too," Grim said with a whistle. "He knew exactly what to do when we needed to close Harlow's wound."

His mom shook her head. "Yes, we all remember how to do that. It's burned in my brain forever. But let's talk about more pleasant things. I know you guys are happy with the guest house, but we thought you might need more room."

"We're fine." Grim looked horrified at the thought. "The guest house is perfect. It's great."

"They're not kicking us out." Josh knew exactly what scared his brother. "And those three bedrooms with no office and no…space for other things is going to feel tight after a while. We might take some time before we talk about having kids, but we'll want more room when it happens. I was going to suggest finding some land close by."

They'd sat by her bedside the night before and talked about the family they wanted to build. Nicole had told him she wanted at least two kids, and maybe three, and she wanted them close together so they wouldn't feel alone. Like she had.

"We bought the ranch next door, and it's our wedding present to you," Dad announced.

Grim's eyes went wide. "You bought Ezekiel's land?"

Dad nodded. "I told you he would leave when he realized the town is changing. The sheriff had a long talk with him about the fact that he's going to start ticketing him and the boys when they harass the citizens. I made him a good offer, and he'll be out in three weeks. Grim, I hope you're not upset about your brothers leaving."

"My brother is here," Grim said quietly. "My brother would never leave me."

From here on out, he thought Grim wouldn't worry about his family. The universe had made a mistake, and he'd been born to the wrong people. It was corrected now. Or maybe there was no fate at all, merely a wide-open willingness to let more love in. Like his parents always did.

"So you bought us a ranch for a wedding present? You know when you go over the top, you go way over the top," Josh said with a grin since he knew exactly what his dad was doing.

"We're so grateful," Nicole began.

"Yes, and Olivia will be, too, when she moves into the guest house and our parents can go back to their pre-children naked time," Josh said with a shake of his head. "You better change the locks because we'll still walk in at all times of the day."

"Oh, I'll keep a robe in every room," his mom said, her arm around Pop's waist. She cuddled against him. "I remember how to do it. And it's going to be a while because you're going to need to build. That ramshackle old house needs to come down, and I would prefer you built a wee bit closer to the big house. I don't want my grandbabies having to walk miles to see their mimi. Who will be dressed for the grandbabies. But I have to admit, I'm looking forward to some privacy. Just a little."

He might joke about his parents' sex life, but he was happy for them. They were still so in love. It was everything he and Grim wanted with Nicole.

"I get to build a whole house?" Nicole asked.

His mother nodded. "Yes. It's going to be so much fun. We'll bring in a designer and get it perfect. But we also have to start talking about the wedding. I assume there is going to be a wedding."

"Not that anyone has asked me properly," Nicole replied with a grin.

"I think you should be patient, baby. We might have plans," Grim offered. "We're going to do this right. How about you get better and we go back to Austin for a weekend? I bet you come home with a ring on your finger."

Because they'd already found the perfect one. It was being resized for Nicole, and they intended to slip it on her finger when she was healed. They had sat in the waiting room while Nicole had been in surgery, and they wouldn't even think about something going wrong. They'd planned the future because there wasn't much of one without her. They had a whole game plan on how they were going to make it an engagement night to remember.

"I have some magazines with wedding ideas," his mother was saying.

"We're going to have to up our prices," Pops said with a shake of his head. "She's going to turn this into a royal wedding."

His mom and future wife were off, planning and laughing.

"I think we can handle it," his dad said with a satisfied smile. His smile suddenly turned upside down and super serious. "Now we only have to worry about Olivia."

Pops groaned. "Yeah, that's a whole different story. That girl's going to give me a heart attack."

His sister finding her partners was likely to be an adventure. She'd picked out the boys she'd wanted when she was very young. She barely knew those boys and knew even less about them as men, but she was stubborn.

He had to hope she could adapt because his sister deserved every bit of happiness she could find.

She deserved all the happiness he'd found with Grim and Nicole.

"Well, at least we're in the right place for it," his dad said, giving his pops a wink.

Flirtatious parents. He was surrounded by them.

He was going to be one. Someday.

But for now he was going to focus on her. On their amazing future.

"What do you say we head down to the cafeteria and grab some coffee?" Dad stood up, stretching. "We can bring back some more snacks for the ladies. Planning is hard work."

Work he was willing to do, or to leave in Nicole's hands since he wanted this to be her perfect day. He wanted her to have a fabulous wedding. All he wanted was a fabulous marriage.

"Sounds good, Dad."

He walked out, joking with Grim, who looked, well, Josh was pretty sure his nickname was only that because Grim looked happy all the time now.

"She's going to make Buddy our ring bearer, you know," Grim said with a shake of his head. "We're going to have to get that dog trained and fast."

Somehow Josh thought it would all work out. After all, he and Grim had met in preschool, became best friends, and decided one day they would find a wife together. Then they were apart for years and years, and yet here they were.

The universe worked in mysterious ways, but Josh was finally where he wanted to be.

Author's Note

I'm often asked by generous readers how they can help get the word out about a book they enjoyed. There are so many ways to help an author you like. Leave a review. If your e-reader allows you to lend a book to a friend, please share it. Go to Goodreads and connect with others. Recommend the books you love because stories are meant to be shared. Thank you so much for reading this book and for supporting all the authors you love!

Sweet Little Spies

Masters and Mercenaries: New Recruits, Book 3
By Lexi Blake
Coming September 17, 2024

Since he was a kid, Aidan O'Donnell has known two things about the world. Tristan is his best friend, and Carys is the love of his life. Sharing her with Tristan was oddly easy. They both loved her deeply, and they never cared what anyone else thought. They were a team and everything was wonderful. Until the day it ended.

Carys Taggart has spent the last year and a half of her life living a lie. A lie Tristan forced on them all. She understands that it was meant to protect her and Aidan, but lately when Tristan says he doesn't love her, it feels more like the truth. The wedding she's dreamed of has been put off far longer than he promised. When he asks her and Aidan for another delay, she's ready to move on without him.

Tristan Dean-Miles has a good plan and the best of intentions. Go undercover as a ruthless arms dealer so he can find a deadly bombmaker at the top of the agency's wanted list. It might be taking longer than expected, but he's so close he can taste it. Unfortunately, getting this close meant getting in way too deep. He knows he will succeed, but if he can't convince the love of his life and his best friend that he's worth the wait, his victory will cost him everything.

About Lexi Blake

New York Times bestselling author Lexi Blake lives in North Texas with her husband and three kids. Since starting her publishing journey in 2010, she's sold over three million copies of her books. She began writing at a young age, concentrating on plays and journalism. It wasn't until she started writing romance that she found success. She likes to find humor in the strangest places and believes in happy endings.

Connect with Lexi online:

Facebook: Lexi Blake
Twitter: authorlexiblake
Website: www.LexiBlake.net
Instagram: AuthorLexiBlake